continued . . .

The Dragon DelaSangre

Named by *Booklist* as One of the Top Ten Horror Novels
of Recent Years

"Comparisons with *Interview with the Vampire* are almost inevitable . . . however, *DelaSangre* ultimately carves out its own territory . . . unabashed fun, with just enough moral ambiguity to raise it above the level of a pure popcorn book. A promising debut."
—*Locus*

"Any book that has us cheering for a human eating dragon is definitely well-written."
—*Chicago Sun-Times*

"As equally fascinating as the man who wrote it."
—*The Miami Herald*

"A very thoughtful and rewarding read."
—*New Mobility Magazine*

"*The Dragon DelaSangre* is the most original fantasy I've read in years, its strength coming in no small part from Alan Troop's remarkable ability to deliver a sympathetic but distinctly non-human protagonist. Just when I thought there was nothing new in contemporary fantasy, along comes Alan Troop's terrific *The Dragon DelaSangre* to prove me wrong! I loved this book!"
—Tanya Huff, author of *Summon the Keeper*

The Seadragon's Daughter

Alan F. Troop

A ROC BOOK

ROC
Published by New American Library, a division of
Penguin Group (USA) Inc., 375 Hudson Street,
New York, New York 10014, USA
Penguin Group (Canada), 10 Alcorn Avenue, Toronto,
Ontario M4V 3B2, Canada (a division of Pearson Penguin Canada Inc.)
Penguin Books Ltd., 80 Strand, London WC2R 0RL, England
Penguin Ireland, 25 St. Stephen's Green, Dublin 2,
Ireland (a division of Penguin Books Ltd.)
Penguin Group (Australia), 250 Camberwell Road, Camberwell, Victoria 3124,
Australia (a division of Pearson Australia Group Pty. Ltd.)
Penguin Books India Pvt. Ltd., 11 Community Centre, Panchsheel Park,
New Delhi - 110 017, India
Penguin Group (NZ), Cnr Airborne and Rosedale Roads, Albany,
Auckland 1310, New Zealand (a division of Pearson New Zealand Ltd.)
Penguin Books (South Africa) (Pty.) Ltd., 24 Sturdee Avenue,
Rosebank, Johannesburg 2196, South Africa

Penguin Books Ltd., Registered Offices:
80 Strand, London WC2R 0RL, England

First published by Roc, an imprint of New American Library,
a division of Penguin Group (USA) Inc.

First Printing, December 2004
10 9 8 7 6 5 4 3 2 1

Copyright © Alan F. Troop, 2004

All rights reserved

Cover art by Kovec

 REGISTERED TRADEMARK—MARCA REGISTRADA

Printed in the United States of America

For my mother, Bernice M. Troop,
the first woman in my life and a bright star in the
universe that now unfortunately burns no longer.
She will always be missed and she will always be
remembered with much love.

Acknowledgments

To Susan, my wife and my love, who has shown remarkable forbearance in sharing this writer's life for the past sixteen years. To Rocky Marcus, a great friend, a good critic and the best creative writing teacher in North Florida. To fellow writer, Jim Hesketh, for your support and candid opinions. To Dave Kupferman for your computer expertise and to the Cuban contingent, Miriam Duque and Madeline Rosales for the Spanish help. To Jen Heddle, many thanks for believing in me and much luck in all you attempt. And to Levi Daniel Foster—welcome to the family.

1

My stomach growls as I circle over the Zapata Swamp. My flight has taken longer than I anticipated and been less productive. Ordinarily when I choose to hunt over Cuba, I have to range no further than the rural farm areas not too far inland of Varadero. But tonight I've spotted no prey—even with the aid of a full moon and a clear late-night sky.

If a sudden flash of light hadn't drawn my attention, I never would have flown so deep into the island. Now I see only blackness beneath me. I glide in wide circles, peering into the dark, sniffing the air for any scent of man, my wings extended to their full thirty-two-foot span, my tail stretched out behind me.

Light slices through the dark again, a narrow beam far below me. I spiral down toward it, swallowing saliva, ignoring the ache of my empty stomach.

The man crouches by the edge of the water, a flashlight in one hand and a small trident-shaped spear—a frogging gig—in the other. As I pass over him he strikes with the gig and lifts a struggling bullfrog from the water. Its belly glistens bleached white in the flashlight's glare for a moment before the light winks off.

I let out a low, satisfied growl. The man looks to be large and beefy and—most importantly—alone. Inhaling a deep breath of cool night air, I flap my wings and gain altitude before circling back.

Just as I reach attack position, the flashlight winks on again. I fold my wings and plummet, letting gravity rush me on, my eyes focused on the frog hunter, his gig in position to strike again. How fitting, I think, the hunter about to be taken by a superior hunter—one who doesn't need to use a light to freeze his prey.

I flex my jaw in anticipation of the attack, hard enough so my fangs grind against each other and my jaw muscles ache from the effort. Near the ground I unfurl my wings, catch the air with them and level off, rocketing forward, the air buffeting my scaled skin, my mouth open, my claws ready.

I expect the man to look up, to discover just moments before his death what manner of beast will take his life. I wonder if he'll scream, or try to run, or if he'll hurl his gig at me in one last, futile gesture. I can almost taste the rich, thick flavor of his blood, the sweetness of his flesh.

Something nudges my right side. I take my eyes from the man, stare to the side and see nothing. A sigh follows and I whirl around to find only empty, dark sky. My attack momentarily forgotten, I become aware of deep, regular breaths and listen until I realize they come from me.

Consciousness comes slowly. First I sense the hard mattress beneath me, then my sleeping wife's warmth at my right side. Chloe sighs again and shifts her body beside me. This time I recognize the movement and the sound for what they are and open my eyes.

Staring into the darkness, almost gasping to find myself in my human form, my heart still throbbing from the dream, I wait for another movement, for a break in her breathing, for any sign of wakefulness. But my young bride stays deep in her dreams.

I lie still and listen to the slow, steady rhythm of her breaths. How I envy her ability to sleep through the night. I stifle a sigh. Once sleep came easy for me too. Now even the slightest disturbance seems to wake me.

If my father, Don Henri DelaSangre, were alive he'd laugh at my restlessness. When I was growing up he often said to me, *"Life can be harsh, Peter—even for beings as powerful as us. Expect nothing in your life to be constant but change."*

In my youth I doubted those words. But over the years, both murder and betrayal have taught me their truth. I frown into the dark. All the more reason I shouldn't have allowed myself to become so accustomed these past few years to a life of happiness and ease.

I let out a breath, try to clear my mind of thought. Closing my eyes, I match my breathing with Chloe's, will each muscle in my body to relax. However, instead of letting sleep overtake me, I become more and more awake and more and more aware of the warmth of her naked flesh pressed against mine.

Finally I turn my head and glance at the clock. It reads 4:48. I wonder whether to go back to sleep or to make love to her or to simply get up and go outside to wait for the dawn.

My bride's body twitches. She grasps and ungrasps her hands, a low growl breaking from her lips. Another growl follows and a third before she sighs and begins again to draw in one deep breath and then another. A hunting dream. I smile. It's only fair that they overtake her too. After all, they roil my sleep any time too many days pass between hunts.

I sigh. This time too many months have passed.

Chloe's movements have pushed down her covers and exposed her right breast. I stare at her dark skin, the darker circle of her nipple and consider cupping my hand over it. Sleep, after all, seems to be no longer a possibility for me this night.

However, I know if I wake Chloe, I'll also miss an opportunity to go outside, to spend a few precious moments alone. I shake my head. To think that once I feared loneliness more than anything.

But more than three years have passed since Chloe became my bride and joined my son, Henri, and me on our small island, Caya DelaSangre. Over two years have gone by since our daughter, Elizabeth, came into the world, biting and clawing and mewling her resistance. Our three-story, coral stone house—once a large, empty building that I wandered through alone and lonely—now seems at times almost too full.

As usual, Chloe's draped one of her naked legs across mine and one of her arms over my chest. I lift her leg, sidle out from under both limbs and ease out of bed. After throwing on a pair of briefs and a pair of cutoff jeans, I open the bedroom's large oak exterior door and step out onto the veranda.

With dawn still almost an hour away, the dark still rules. I breathe deep, smell the salt-tinged freshness of the cool early-morning air, smile and close the door behind me.

Dew has already soaked the veranda's oak deck, leaving it cold and treacherously slick for my bare feet. To avoid slipping, I walk slowly as I make my way to the ocean side of the veranda, finally stopping by a rectangular cutout in the waist-high coral parapet that encircles the veranda—one of the many cannon ports Father placed long ago for our defense.

The cannons have long since been stored away, along with Father's other ancient armament, in four arms rooms, each located on a different side of the house. Leaning against the rough, ancient stone, I stare past the dark shadows of the grass and sea oat-topped dunes, over the pale contrast of the beach's flat white sand, to the black surface of the ocean. Only thin white ribbons of foam show in the dark as the waves break and roll to shore. A gentle breeze blows over them, carrying with it the soft, wet thuds of the breakers surging against the beach.

A mile off shore, the Fowey Rocks lighthouse blinks through the gloom. I smile at its bright warning light and turn my face into the wind, letting it push against me. It reminds me of flying and I sigh.

The matching growls of twin diesel motors break the quiet of the early morning—their sounds loud enough to signal their closeness. Staring past the waves, I search until I spot the moving lights and the dark shape of a patrol boat cruising just a few hundred feet past the surf line. I curl my lip at it.

I understand the special circumstances that have brought them so close. They have every legal right to patrol here. Still, I am a DelaSangre. Like my father before me, I consider the waters near my island to be my property—every bit as much as the sand and stone of the island itself. I think of calling the office later to get my man, Arturo Gomez, or his associate, Ian Tindall, to arrange that no patrol dares to come so close again. But then I shake my head. *"Only the wise,"* Father always said, *"understand the limits of their powers."*

After the sun breaks free of the ocean and rises over the horizon, I come back inside, undress and slide into bed. I've barely warmed myself against Chloe before the alarm buzzes to life. She reaches for it with a bare brown arm, slaps it quiet, turns on her bedside lamp, yawns and nestles against me.

"I dreamed again," she says.

I hug her and say, "Of hunting?"

Chloe shrugs. "What else?"

"I couldn't sleep before," I say. "I went outside. Those damn idiots had a patrol boat out at that hour—just yards from our island. They need to look someplace else. No one here has done any of the things that have driven them all so crazy. . . ."

"And no one has accused us of anything," Chloe laughs. "They're patrolling everywhere."

"You can laugh all you want to. Yesterday when I was dropping Henri off at school, some guy snapped a picture of us. By the time I tied up the boat and got off he was gone. I asked the school about it. No one had any idea who it was."

"It was probably just another parent. No one's investigating us, Peter. Not that we wouldn't deserve it. You know, you're like the criminal who protests—way too loud—when he thinks people suspect him of the one crime he actually didn't commit." She pulls free of me, stands and waits, hands on hips, for me to get up too.

The lamplight makes my young wife's milk-chocolate skin look like soft brown velvet. I make a show of staring at her, her brilliant emerald-green eyes and full lips, the roundness of her breasts, the dark triangle of tightly curled pubic hair nestled between her long brown legs. Pushing the covers aside, I motion for her to return to bed.

"Oh no," she laughs. "Save it for the weekend. This is a school day. You don't want your son to be late, do you?"

"I think you and I care far more about his being on time than he does," I say.

Walking to Henri's room, I watch where I place my feet. No matter how often Chloe and I go into a cleaning frenzy, toys, games, dolls and action figures seem to end up scattered almost everywhere. Both of us have stepped on, kicked, broken or tripped over more of the children's things than we care to remember—even on the steps of the spiral, wooden staircase that runs up the center of the house to all three levels.

Only the bottom floor of the house manages to escape the children's litter. It's Chloe's doing really. "I don't want any children playing down there. It's too dark and gloomy for my taste," she said shortly after she came to live with us. "I know Henri's been down there God knows how many times with you. But you've been lucky he hasn't asked yet about your father's holding cells. He's too young. He doesn't need to hear what they were used for."

Just before I open Henri's door, Elizabeth's laugh signals that Chloe's with her, teasing her awake. I smile at the sounds. When I grew up, barely any noise broke the quiet of the house. Now during waking hours the children's laughs, screams, shouts, giggles and occasional wails fill the air. And Henri's pet dog, Max, adopted from the pack of guard dogs I keep on the island, often adds to the ruckus with his loud barks and growls.

While neither the children's mess nor their noise usually bother me, it does make me smile when I think how my father would have growled if he'd been subjected to any of it. But I grew up in a far different household than the one Chloe and I have decided to build for our children.

I often marvel at how ordinary my small family's life now seems, how much our routines mirror the daily activities of those who live on the mainland. Still, I have no doubt how horrified any mainlander would be if they learned of our true nature.

2

"Peter, it happened again," Chloe says, standing in the kitchen area, busy sawing with a serrated knife on a large slab of frozen beef when Henri and I finally come up to the great room for breakfast. Elizabeth, playing with a Raggedy Ann doll on the floor near her, smiles at me and gives her half-brother an even wider grin.

Rubbing his eyes with the back of his hands, Henri stands next to me, looking as if he were almost still asleep.

I shake my head. "That makes how many boats?"

"Fifteen boats found floating without anyone on board—all in the last twelve weeks. The *Herald* says that makes it twenty-six people either missing or dead—that they know of." Chloe pauses cutting, points with her knife at the open wireless laptop sitting on the large oak table where we take our regular meals. "I left it on the article if you want to read it. They had it on the news too."

"No thanks," I say, glancing at the computer, Chloe's latest and currently favorite toy. "I still don't like reading for very long on those things."

Chloe flashes me a superior smile. I may be older, larger and stronger and I may be the master of all things mechanical in our household, but we both know she's the one to turn to when a computer screen freezes or a new program needs to be installed.

"At least this time it was just one fisherman that disappeared," she says. "Channel Seven's saying it's a terrorist plot. The rest of the news shows are calling whoever's doing it the Nautical Killer. They think it's some sort of serial murderer."

"Same pattern?" I say, turning to the windows that look east over Biscayne Bay toward the skylines of Coconut Grove and Miami. Barely a ripple shows on the calm blue water. Ordinarily this early on a March morning I wouldn't expect to see more than one or two boats. Today I count five—two clearly marked with the orange angular slash of the Coast Guard, the others, I think, most probably Marine Patrol or news media.

"The same. They found the boat floating. No one on board. No blood this time though."

"Damn! I'm tired of this," I say, turning back. "Whoever's doing it should move on. They're just going to panic everybody more. The authorities already have more boats out patrolling today."

"I know," Chloe says. "I looked before. They have a helicopter out there too. It passed by when you were downstairs helping Henri."

"Didn't need any help," Henri says. "I can get ready by myself."

I tousle his hair with my right hand and say, "If only you'd do it."

Henri grimaces and smooths his hair with his hand. "I was tired," he says. He brushes past me, sits at the large oak table in the center of the room. The boy—almost eight now and finally large enough to sit without his feet dangling—stares at the TV. Elizabeth shouts, "Enee!" and toddles over to play on the floor near him. He continues to gape at the TV as if she didn't exist.

I look at my recalcitrant son and wonder why he's recently chosen to rise late each school morning. Elizabeth babbles something incomprehensible and I turn my attention to her.

Both children possess the emerald-green eyes and tendency toward muscularity and wide shoulders that all of our kind have. I say, "Well, there's no denying these two are related."

Chloe nods. "They'd look even more alike if Henri had known his mother."

I can't resist turning my head toward the north windows, which overlook the grave of my poor murdered first wife, Elizabeth—my daughter's namesake and my wife's older sister. "True," I say.

Henri shows no trace of his mother in his appearance. He's chosen to mimic my blond hair, cleft chin and Scandinavian features. Our daughter Elizabeth, however, can't be denied by either of us. On her, Chloe's Jamaican features, full lips, wider nose and wiry hair combine with my chin and hair color. Even Elizabeth's complexion is a mix—mocha only a shade darker than her half-brother's well-tanned white skin rather than the rich milk-chocolate brown of her mother.

"You have to admit they're both beautiful children," I say.

Chloe sniffs. "Like beauty is hard for creatures like us?"

I grimace at the remark. It reminds me all too well of my father's disapproval when, in my youth, I chose to reshape my features using popular movie actors as my models. *"We change our shapes for our survival, not to feed our vanities,"* Father said.

Not that my father or my mother or any of Chloe's family ever chose to appear in their human forms as anything less than attractive.

Joining Chloe in the kitchen, I take down plates and utensils for our breakfast and set the table while she warms the steaks in the microwave. The aroma of blood and near-raw meat fills the air, and Henri's dog Max pads into the room and lies down near the boy. With black fur and a massive head and jaws, he, like his pack, looks more like a hyena than any domestic breed of dog.

Chloe brings a full platter of meat to the table, puts a thick steak on each of our plates and puts another plate of meat on the floor for Max. Elizabeth grabs her steak with both hands and bites off a chunk just as quickly as the dog bites his. She barely chews before she swallows and rips off another chunk.

"No Lizzie, wait, let me cut it for you," Chloe says.

Elizabeth nods, swallows saliva as she watches her mother cut the near-raw meat into bite-size pieces. As soon as Chloe finishes, our daughter grabs a piece, devours it and then does the same to another. My wife laughs. "So much for using our fork today."

Chloe begins to eat her steak, and I cut off a piece of mine and put it in my mouth. I close my eyes at the rich taste of raw flesh and blood. When I open my eyes I see that Henri has yet to eat a bite of his breakfast.

Henri glowers at his meat, the blood puddled around it. "We always have meat," he says. "I want Froot Loops. Brian Edelstein told me his parents always give him Froot Loops for breakfast!"

I sigh, glance at Chloe. She stifles a grin, busies herself with her food. {*Not really fair,*} I mindspeak, masked so the children can't hear me. {*You're the one who insisted we send him to school on the mainland. I told you how difficult it was for me when my mother sent me there.*}

{*And you're the one who can relate to how it feels. I never went to school with them. Don't you think you're the one who should handle it?*}

Henri, who's noted our silence and watched our expressions says, "I hate when you guys do that!"

"Don't you mindspeak to Lizzie sometimes so we can't hear you?" Chloe says.

The boy shrugs, pushes his plate away.

I frown at him. "You're not going to get Froot Loops. Eat your breakfast."

"But Brian . . ."

"Forget what Brian eats or doesn't eat," I say. "He isn't of the blood and you are." I pause, shocked to hear how much I sound like my father.

"I wish I wasn't!" Henri says.

"Put out your hand!" I mindspeak, glaring at my son.

The boy's lower lip trembles but he holds out his right hand. I hold mine out too, so our fingertips almost touch. *"Watch!"*

Willing the bones of my hand to lengthen, I smile at the small thrill of pain that shoots up my arm as they grow, my hand's flesh turning to scales and my nails lengthening and hardening into sharp talons. Henri stares at my hand, pulls his back as mine grows to its natural shape and length.

"Now you," I mindspeak.

We both watch his hand as the skin contorts and hardens, as the fingers grow, as the nails thicken and extend. I make a clawed fist and then open it, and he mimics the movement. *"It feels good doesn't it?"* I say.

Henri nods.

"We are what we are boy. Don't ever forget it. We eat meat. We hunt. We kill," I mindspeak. *"We are People of the Blood. Our kind once ruled this earth. Men called us dragons and were right to fear us. Any one of us can kill any one of them with a flick of a claw. Your grandfather built this house that we live in. He built the company that keeps us rich.*

"What did your friend Brian's grandfather build, a law office? Brian can't mindspeak. He can't change shape. He can't fly. He can't hunt. . . ."

"We don't do any of that anymore either!" Henri says, his arm still extended, his hand still in its natural shape. "You promised I could go with you when I'm eight but we don't practice anything anymore. We never eat fresh prey . . . not ever."

I draw in a breath and look at my son. It hadn't occurred to me that our self-imposed abstinence from hunting would weigh as heavily on Henri as it does on Chloe and me. Other than saying, "It isn't safe right now," I haven't explained why we haven't flown or hunted in the last few months. Nor did I think it important to share how much surveillance the authorities have placed in the waters near our island or what danger that would bring to us should any of them discover any of us flying overhead.

Willing my hand to return to its human shape, watching as Henri does the same, I wonder if I've been too cautious. When I was little my father always repeated, *"Peter, no one ever died from taking too much care."* But I doubt Don Henri would have chosen to go so long without fresh meat just because some humans were in an uproar.

I mull over all my favorite hunting areas and the time it usually takes for me to fly to them. Of course, I think, some could be reached by other means.

"What if I promised you that this weekend we'll do all the things—change into our natural shapes, fly and hunt and eat fresh prey—just like we used to?" I say.

"Really?"

I nod, and for the first time this morning, Henri smiles. He pulls his plate back and begins to wolf down his food.

After the boy leaves to ready himself for school, Chloe looks at me and says, "Okay, you're the one who's been telling me how careful we have to be. So just how do you plan to keep your promise?"

"The boy's right. It's been too long," I say, a grin growing on my face. "They can put all the patrols around here that they want. There's no rule that we have to stay here while they do."

3

On Saturday morning Henri wakes before any of us. I find him outside, on the dock, taking the canvas cover off my twenty-seven-foot Grady White motorboat. I watch, nod my approval as he carefully unsnaps each fastener and folds and stows the canvas as he's been taught.

"We're taking this one, aren't we Papa?" he says.

I smile, say, "Yes." Once it would have been the only choice. But now, thanks to Chloe, boats of all types crowd our little round harbor, take up the entire length of the dock. Her sixteen-foot red Donzi, a sleek, low-riding speedboat she loves to race around in on calm days, sits tied up behind the Grady White. Behind that, ever since Chloe saw one speeding by our island, we now keep a twenty-four-foot Corsair trimaran. Two Polaris personal watercraft sit on the harbor shore near the dock next to a pair of Mistral windsurfers, matching pairs of one- and two-man kayaks and a sixteen-foot Hobie catamaran sailboat.

All the boats and Chloe's frequent use of them, as well as her insistence that I upgrade the motors on my Grady White from twin two hundreds to twin two-twenty-fives—for more speed—have caused me to install two fifty-five gallon fuel drums with electric fuel pumps. I supervise Henri's topping off of the Grady White's fuel tanks before we go upstairs for breakfast.

We leave shortly before ten, all of us in bathing suits and bringing with us beach blankets, towels, some extra clothes, water and a quantity of plain, rare roast beef sandwiches no different than the ones Chloe makes each day for Henri's school lunch.

Chloe insists on taking the wheel, and I grin when she shoves the throttles forward as soon as we exit the harbor. "The day couldn't be more perfect!" I say over the roar of the boat's two Yamaha outboards. "I checked the weather reports and they say the ocean should be like glass for the next few days."

Nodding, Chloe concentrates on guiding the boat through the winding curves of our unmarked channel. She knows, as well as I, that rocks lurk beneath the surface on either side of us. Sitting between us, Elizabeth laughs at every movement of the boat, smiles at the wind rushing through her hair. Henri goes back, opens the stern bench and sits sideways, his head turned to the rear so he can watch our wake spread out behind us.

As soon as we emerge from the channel, Chloe takes a long, looping turn to the north and then shoots through the narrow channel between our island and Wayward Key, an uninhabited bird sanctuary. Henri points to our wake smashing against both islands and laughs, "Look, Papa!"

I nod. I can't count the number of times I've railed against boaters who've done the same thing. But that was before I married a speed demon. We barely make it into the ocean before two Marine Patrol boats approach us, rotator lights flashing.

Chloe slows the Grady White, then drops the motors to idle as the patrol boats come closer. One boat hangs back while the other pulls alongside us. An older policeman, dressed in full dark blue uniform, gun strapped on his hip, comes over to the side of his boat and holds onto the railing for balance as he says, "Sorry folks. With all the fuss going on we have to stop everyone." He looks around at the deserted waters, grins a wry smile. "At least the few who are still willing to venture out."

The other cop on the patrol boat, younger, dressed the same as his companion, glances at Chloe, studies her skimpy red bikini and then looks away, only to look back a few moments longer. While my bride has let herself age in tandem with her years, at twenty-one she still looks far too young to be Henri's mother. The young officer, who can't be much older than Chloe, seems puzzled that she'd be with someone who appears almost ten years older, like me.

I frown at him, think how much more confused he'd be if I told him how long my kind live and my true age—more than three times hers. The other policeman clears his throat, begins to ask me questions. "We live on that island, Caya DelaSangre," I say. "You'll find it called Blood Key on the charts. My name's Peter DelaSangre and this is my wife, Chloe, and our children, Henri and Elizabeth."

The policeman smiles at Lizzie. "She's an adorable little girl."

I nod, look at my daughter too, glad she can control her shape and behavior at such a young age. I credit Chloe's patient teaching for that. Under my tutelage, Henri at the same age was incapable of holding his human form for very long. I doubt he'd have been able to resist attacking any human who came too close.

"With all the disappearances recently, aren't you concerned for your family's safety out on the water, sir?"

"Papa!" Henri says.

I motion him to be quiet, shake my head, say to the officer, "No, not at all. We're going to Bimini. As far as I know no one's reported any difficulties over there."

The policeman nods, asks for my ID. I hand it to him and Henri says, "Papa, Mama, a dolphin!"

"Your father's busy, Henri. We've seen dolphins before," Chloe says.

"But . . ."

"Later, Henri!"

After the patrol boats leave, I turn to my son. "So where are the dolphins?"

"It left," he says.

"Just one? You sure it wasn't with a pod, some others?"

Henri nods. "It was alone and it came right up to the stern and poked its head out of the water. I tried to pet it but when I did, it dropped back into the water."

"Maybe it didn't want to be touched," Chloe says, pushing the throttles forward. "They are wild after all."

"But it came back . . . a couple of times. It's funny. It wouldn't look at me but it finally let me touch it. It did," Henri says. "I swear."

My bride looks at me, raises an eyebrow, and I shrug.

4

It only takes only a little more than an hour and a half for us to cross the dark waters of the Gulf Stream and arrive in the clear, light blue shallows near Bimini. While I know the island I want lies near Victory Reef, I can't find it on any of the charts we have.

"What's its name?" Chloe says.

I shrug, take the wheel from her and guide us from one small spit of sand to the next. "I could find it from the air in a second," I say. "It doesn't look like much, just a glorified sandbar with a few trees and bushes—maybe three quarters of a mile long and a quarter wide. The whole thing barely sticks out of the water except for one sand dune on its north end . . . I don't think that's more than twelve feet high."

Chloe searches the waters around us, points to a pine tree-crowded island a few hundred yards away. "How about that one?"

"No." I shake my head. "This is a specific island. My mother died there. My father buried her there, and when he died, I buried him next to her. As long as we're near I want to visit it."

As more time passes, we make a game of it, looking for a flat island with a hump at one end. After dozens of false sightings by each of us, Henri shouts, "I see it Papa!" He points to an island no more than a half mile away, one I'd glanced at and rejected. "See! There's the hump!"

I study the solitary dune on its north end, partially obscured from view by some pine trees, and nod. "That's it," I say, turning the boat in its direction.

Bright white sand covers a small, gently sloping beach shielded from the wind by the dune at the north end of the is-

land. I run the Grady White in toward the beach, slowing the
motors, trimming them up as we approach and the water be-
comes more shallow. Finally, a few yards from shore the boat's
bow digs into the sandy bottom and we stop.

"Can I, Papa?" Henri says.

I nod and he jumps off the boat into the clear, shallow water.
Chloe laughs, says, "Watch Lizzie for a minute," and jumps off
the boat too, splashing Henri as she lands. He splashes her back
and a water fight erupts between them, both of them slapping at
the knee-high water and drenching each other.

Smiling at the mayhem going on in the water, I busy myself
gathering up the blankets, towels, food and drink we've
brought and preparing to bring them to shore. Once Henri
throws up his hands and surrenders, a very wet Chloe comes
over to the boat. I hand her a towel, wait for her to dry herself,
then pass Lizzie to her.

After I dig an anchor into the sand and we set up camp in a
pine tree-shaded area just inland of the beach, I take my family
to visit my parents' graves. We climb the dune together, Lizzie
in Chloe's arms, and stand next to the small rock piles that mark
each of their graves. "This is where my father and mother are
buried," I say.

Henri nods, stands by my side for a few moments, then wanders off to explore the area while Chloe and I remain staring at
the piles. "I know you told me your mum was killed, but you
never told me how," my bride says.

I smile at the British accent that suddenly appears in her
speech. She spoke that way when I first met her. Born in Jamaica, raised by parents who spoke English like they were at
tea in London and servants who spoke as if they were from the
streets of Kingston, Chloe can flip from an English accent to a
Jamaican one in the same sentence. Now, after a few years' exposure to our TV, she most often sounds like an American.

"My mother was careless," I say.

Chloe cocks an eyebrow.

"It was toward the end of World War Two. I wasn't much
older than Henri. She and Father put me to bed before she went
hunting—just like you and I do with the kids." I sigh, remembering the night. "She called out for us. *'Henri! Peter! Come*

quickly! Please!' It woke me, and then my father was in my room—already in his natural form.

"I changed too and we flew to this island." I look around until I spot a small circular area of sand at the base of the dune. I point to it. "We found her there. She was lying there bleeding, gasping, with terrible holes ripped through her body." I shake my head.

"It was too late. Father said too much damage had been done. She died a few minutes after we arrived. We buried her up here and piled stones to mark her resting place. Afterwards, on the way home, Father told me she'd tried to swoop down and snatch a sailor off the deck of a surfaced U-boat patrolling in the Florida Straits. He said, *'I told her not to attack any armed ships. I told her it was too risky. But she did it anyway—at least eight times without a problem. This time a German machine-gunner managed to fire a burst in her direction and hit her. It's our curse. Our women are too reckless.'* He was right you know," I say.

"I prefer to think we're just braver than you males," Chloe says.

"Could be," I say, staring at the graves. "Either way, I wish my mom had been a little more careful. She died too young. At least my father lived as long as he wanted."

"How old was he when he died?"

I say, "Over four hundred," and Chloe widens her eyes. I smile at her surprise. Our kind expects long lives. Why shouldn't we? We can change our shapes at will, heal most of our own injuries and illnesses. But still few manage to maintain themselves past three hundred.

Father always said that most didn't care to live much longer. *"If it wasn't for your mother and you, I'd never have stayed so long in this life,"* he said.

We spend the rest of the day swimming, exploring the island and collecting driftwood. By the time the sun begins to set, Henri and I have already dug a depression in the sand and stacked driftwood in it. As the night turns cool, I light the wood afire.

With nothing to do but sit on our blankets, gorge ourselves

on roast beef sandwiches and watch the flames as they leap and dance, Elizabeth and Henri soon fall asleep. Chloe and I sit side by side, our bodies touching, both of us watching the sleeping children and the fire. Neither of us speaks.

Finally Chloe stands and motions for me to do the same. Both of us have put on sweatshirts. She pulls hers off, throws it on our blanket, then does the same with mine. Chloe glances at the children, to make sure they're still asleep and then gives me a half leer, half smile and yanks my bathing suit down.

I step out of it and reach for hers. She shakes her head, backs up a step and removes her top, then the bottoms, by herself. Tossing them on the blanket she takes my hand and leads me away from the fire, my body instantly chilled as soon as we leave the protective circle of its warmth.

Chloe tugs me along, away from the campsite, up the dune. At the top, I pull her close, hold her until her naked warmth and mine start to warm us. When I begin to grow hard, she pushes me away. *"We didn't need to come here for that!"* she mindspeaks, grinning at me as her skin tightens and ripples, her face lengthens and her shoulders swell. *"Look at the sky, the moon, the stars. What a fine night to hunt!"*

I turn my eyes from my bride's transformation and look up to the three-quarter moon overhead, the bright pattern of stars filling the clear, dark sky everywhere I choose to stare. I grin. Creatures like Chloe and I need only a few stars or a sliver of the moon to see in the dark. Tonight it's as if we're bathed in starlight.

Chloe's wings rustle as they emerge from between her shoulder blades. She spreads them so quickly that they snap when they reach their full extension. I turn my attention back to her. *"Well?"* she mindspeaks. *"Do I hunt alone tonight?"*

"Hardly," I say, studying this clawed creature standing beside me, the wings held at the ready, the long tail stretched behind her, the light green scales covering her body everywhere except her cream colored underbody. I suck in a breath, remembering how it feels to make love to her in this form and will my body to change too.

"It's about time," Chloe mindspeaks. I ignore her and concentrate on the thrill, the pleasure and the pain of stretching

bones and flesh, growing fangs and claws, hardening skin into armored scales. When my wings finally burst from my back, I groan and spread them to their full extension—yards fuller than Chloe's.

She backs up in mock fear and mindspeaks, *"Eeek! I think it's a dragon!"* I swat her with my tail and she slaps back with hers, so hard that it stings.

I grapple with her, both of us struggling until I finally enfold her in my wings so she can't move.

"Okay tough guy, you're bigger than me. I admit it," she mindspeaks. *"Now can we get on with it? I'm starved."*

I release Chloe, flex my wings, my stomach growling, saliva flooding my mouth at the thought of fresh prey. The full stomach I had before I changed is only a memory now. It's one of our limitations. Shifting shapes burns energy, sometimes far too much.

The wind gusts against me and I block it with my wings. I take a few practice flaps, then rush forward, my wings scooping air, shoving it behind me. *"Now!"* I mindspeak. The sound of Chloe's wings beating air just behind me follows me as I leap into the air.

No creature should be denied the joy of flight. I bank in a wide spiral over the island, my eyes fixing the shape of it in the dark in my memory. Chloe, flying by my side, does the same.

We circle a dozen more times, building altitude, before Chloe folds her wings and dives toward the sea. I follow, plummeting through the cool, dark air, spreading my wings only a few yards over the surface of the ocean, skimming over the wave crests, chasing Chloe, who somehow manages to stay just feet in front of me.

Far from the island, we climb again and I roar into the night. Chloe's giggle fills my mind. *"What are you roaring at?"* she mindspeaks. *"Trying to scare somebody?"*

I ignore her and roar again. *"It feels good,"* I mindspeak. *"We've gone too long without this."*

Chloe spots a fishing boat cruising not too many miles away, banks and begins flying in its direction.

I bank too, chasing her, finally flying in front of her. *"No *boats. If a crew goes missing here, the Bahamians might con-nect it to what's going on in Miami."*

"Then where? I don't want to go too far. Lizzie or Henri might need us."

Banking, turning southeast, I mindspeak, *"The kids will be fine. If either wakes they can call out to us. Henri's old enough anyway to take care of most things."*

"But, Peter . . ."

"It's okay. I'm taking us to Andros. It's not too far. I've hunted there before. The island's huge and mostly unpopulated. But they do have some small communities scattered along the coasts—enough to make for good hunting."

We approach Andros from its northwest corner, the land a vast black mass sprinkled with few lights.

"Are we really going to find anybody here?" Chloe mind-speaks. *"Couldn't we have just gone to Bimini?"*

"Bimini's too developed, too civilized these days. Parts of Andros don't have roads, power or even running water. We can hunt here without worrying about attracting any attention."

Chloe follows as I descend to a hundred feet. We glide over the water together, passing over a long, deep white beach, then trees and flat tilled fields. Everything remains dark beneath us until finally we come to a dimly lighted area, an open-air patio outside a white concrete building. Men crowd its six wooden tables, hunched over games of dominoes, drinking from bottles.

We circle over the patio, listening to their voices, to the island music blaring from outdoor speakers, smelling the aromas of beer and cooked food and the scents of the humans below us. Our stomachs grumble and we circle, swallowing saliva, watching, waiting.

Four men finally get up from a table and walk away from the lights. Chloe flies off after them. *"It's too many!"* I mindspeak. *"Why not wait until one leaves by himself?"*

"I'm tired of waiting. I'll follow until they break up and then take one of them."

I stay over the patio, wondering if I should have followed my bride. But fifteen minutes later a single tall, muscular male rewards my patience by leaving his table and walking off into the dark alone.

He crosses a nearby field, singing, drinking from a beer bottle. I follow overhead and wait for him to leave the bar and the others far behind. After the field, the man turns onto a dirt path, drains the last of his beer and throws the bottle into the bushes. He walks forward in the direction of the sea, muttering to himself, occasionally laughing.

No homes lie in sight, no other humans. I wonder if he's a fisherman or a farmer, whether he's returning home to a wife and family or an empty house. No matter. My stomach aches.

I dive, rush at him from the front. He opens his mouth, his eyes wide, clearly about to scream. Slashing out with a foreclaw, I slice his throat, the rich aroma of fresh blood filling the air as I seize his thick, warm body with my rear claws, yank it into the air and fly toward the sea. *"Chloe come! Fresh meat!"* I mindspeak.

"I have some too, Peter," she says. *"Don't be mad. It seemed like they never were going to break up. I took all four."*

I find her on a deserted beach, four bodies laid on the sand near her. I land, lay my kill next to hers. *"Chloe? Four? It's such a waste. . . ."*

"I know Peter, I know." She sniffs at my kill, inspects each of hers. *"I shouldn't have . . . but it's done now."* She chooses the smallest of her victims, drags it over to me.

As is the custom for our females, she selects a tender morsel of meat and serves me first before she feeds. I take it and swallow it and then we feed together side by side until we're satiated. Langour overtakes us then and we allow ourselves to lay together on the sand and doze for a short while.

Chloe stirs first. She nudges me. *"We should get back to the children and let them feed too."*

I stretch, rest my tail over her tail, press my body close to hers. *"There's something else we could do first,"* I mindspeak. *"We haven't done it in our natural forms in a long time."*

"And we won't for a while longer," Chloe says, pulling away from me. *"We have children, Peter. We have to give them the*

chance to change into their natural forms and feed while there's still enough night left."

I know she's right. Still I refuse to move until she's chosen which kills she wants to bring back with us and until she's disposed of the extra bodies in the waters far off the shore.

5

No newspapers or television stations report any new disappearances in the waters off of Miami that weekend or the week that follows or the week after that. The local stations stop broadcasting their endless conjectures over who or what has been causing the disappearances. The Marine Patrol and the Coast Guard cut back on their patrols and for the first time in months, Chloe says, "Maybe we could think of going hunting together sometime soon."

I nod. As much as we and the children enjoyed our foray to the Bahamanian Out Islands, I much prefer flying from and returning to our own island. "We'll give it another week," I say. "If things are still calm, I think we'll be able to start getting back to normal."

But the next morning, when I come up to the great room for breakfast, Chloe greets me with a frown and says, "It happened again."

Looking out the window I see the patrol boats cruising on the bay—just as many as before. I shake my head. "You know nothing says we have to stay here while this is going on. We could go to Jamaica, stay at Bartlet House, visit with your parents and your brothers at Morgan's Hole."

Chloe looks at me and grins. "You want to visit with my family?"

I shrug. "Everyone has their in-law problems."

"Everyone's in-laws haven't tried to kill them," Chloe says.

"But that's over now," I say. "Anyway, your brother Philip was never part of it, and your Dad pretty much made up for it before he left here for Jamaica." I think of Chloe's older brother, Derek, and the frown he wore for weeks after I defeated him and his father. "I could live without ever seeing Derek again. But as long as he's polite he won't bother me."

"Pa would never let him be anything but pleasant to you."

"Then there will be no reason to avoid Jamaica. I know Henri would love to start riding horses again. Lizzie's never been there. We could get a little pony for her. We could fly when we want. Hunt when we want."

"But school won't let out until June," Chloe says.

I shrug. "So? Henri's already far ahead of most of his class. He won't have any trouble catching up next year. I can call Tindall. Tell him to arrange with Granny and Velda to open Bartlet House, get it ready for us."

"Maybe you're right," Chloe says.

"You should call your parents and let them know to expect us."

Chloe laughs. "Why don't I call Tindall and tell him to arrange things—and you try to call my parents? I told you the satellite phone we got them would be a waste of money. They've never once picked it up to call us. They don't think that way. In my family, when someone leaves home, they consider them gone for good. Remember how it was when I called them after Lizzie was born? It took forever before Mum picked up and then she scolded me for making her talk on the damned thing. She hates it."

"Still you should give them a call," I say.

"Maybe," Chloe says, then sticks out her tongue at me.

The more I think of Jamaica and our vacation home, Bartlet House, far inland of Montego Bay, close to the wilds of Cockpit Country, the more I like the idea of going there. I've little doubt it will take much time for our groundskeeper, Granville Morrison and his wife, Velda, to get the house in order, the stables filled with gentle horses and the swimming pool crystal clean.

The thought of visiting Cockpit Country again—a wild and overgrown area with an irregular terrain so full of closely bunched, almost pyramid-shaped mountains and plunging sinkholes that few people dare to visit it—makes me yearn to go. It still is the only place I've ever been able to fly over in my natural form during daylight.

I'm so preoccupied with my thoughts of Jamaica that I barely pay attention to Henri as we get in the Grady White, cast off from the dock and head toward his school. We're already across the bay and near the channel to his school, before he tugs on my arm. "Papa! I said slow down. Please!"

I push the throttles up, look around for any possible danger as the hull lowers into the water, the boat slowing, coasting forward, beginning to wallow. But the only other boats I see moving on the bay are far away, heading in other directions. I scan the sky for any signs of bad weather, study the few clouds scattered overhead, puffy white things that can't even threaten to provide a sun shower. I look at Henri. "What?" I say. "What's wrong?"

"Nothing, Papa. Look!" He points to the water about twenty yards behind our boat. I see nothing for a few moments and then a gray fin breaks the surface, the dolphin arching its back for a moment, then disappearing.

"So it's a dolphin," I say.

"It's been following us, Papa. Ever since we left home. I think it's the same one as before."

"Maybe," I say, watching for the fin, spotting it when it breaks water again, only ten feet from our boat. I push the throttles forward again. "We still have to get you to school on time."

Henri's school, Coral Bluff, my alma mater, sits on land that would make any developer cry with envy. Occupying fifteen acres of prime bayfront land just a few hundred yards south of downtown Coconut Grove, the school boasts some of the finest tropical landscaping and some of the oldest coral stone buildings in the county—as well as the best academic reputation. All of which enables it to collect tuitions worthy of an Ivy League college.

It is also the only local school I know of that has its own boat channel, docks and fleet of boats.

We enter the narrow channel, motors slowed down to a purr, the Grady White just ghosting along, and pass the boathouse where the school keeps a half dozen rowing sculls and fifteen

Optimist sailing prams, sitting one after another in a neat line along the south bank of the channel. The rest of the school's fleet—twelve glistening, white Precision Sixteen sailboats—float tied up at the dock nearby. I smile at the array of boats and wonder if the children who attend this school realize how privileged they are.

As per usual no boats are tied up at the visitors' dock. As far I know, I'm the only parent who brings his child to school each day by water. Henri goes to the bow as I approach the visitors' dock, and jumps off when I push the throttles to neutral and let the boat brush to a stop against the dock's rub rail. "Look, Papa!" Henri points to the canal behind us. "It's still with us."

I turn, see the dolphin's gray fin, the outline of its gray body just below the water's surface. From the size of it I assume it's either a female or an immature male. I shake my head. I'm used to the small pods of bottlenose dolphins that frequent the waters near my island. I rarely have seen any of them swimming by themselves and certainly have never seen any dolphin follow a boat into any narrow channel.

The dolphin swims by the boat slowly, as if it's examining it, then flips around under the water, and with a kick of its tail shoots back out the channel. "See that?" Henri says, a wide smile on his face.

I nod, watch the water for any sign that it might be returning. Its behavior's so peculiar, I'm tempted to turn the boat around and chase it just to see what it will do.

"Excuse me. Mr. DelaSangre?"

Turning toward the voice, I find the school's head administrator, Sam Maxwell, standing a few yards from the dock. Short and round, wearing a glossy black suit with a white shirt and a narrow deep green tie, his bald scalp glistening with sweat, he hardly looks like the type to be comfortable outdoors, certainly not under a bright and hot morning sun. "May we talk for a minute, Mr. DelaSangre?"

I nod, motion him forward, wondering what mischief Henri's done. Henri, I see, has the same thought. When I cock an eyebrow and look at him, he just shrugs and stares at the ground.

As soon as Maxwell steps on the dock, he turns to my son. "Class is about to start, Henri. It wouldn't do to be late."

Henri nods, says, "Bye, Papa," and scampers off to class smiling, obviously happy to be dismissed.

Maxwell watches the boy go, then turns to me. "Mr. De-laSangre, I'm so sorry," he says, his hands out, fluttering as he speaks. "We believe in honoring the privacy of our students' families. You know how many high-profile people, politicians and performers, attorneys and doctors, successful businessmen like you send their children here. You know how we try to control access to our grounds. I'm sick to my stomach that it occurred here. Absolutely disheartened. You must believe me."

My forehead wrinkles as I try to understand what he means. "I'm absolutely willing to believe you," I say. "But I have no idea what you're talking about."

His eyes go wide, his face flushes a bright red. "You haven't seen it yet? No one's called you about it?"

"About what?"

"The picture. The article," Maxwell says. He unclips a walkie-talkie from his belt, barks into it. "Miss Simon! I'm down on the dock with Mr. DelaSangre. Please bring me the paper that's on my desk." He pauses a moment, listens, then says. "Yes, that one. Now!"

"What picture and what article?" I say.

Maxwell takes a breath, sighs, flutters his hands. "I'd rather you see it yourself. I assure you I don't believe a word of it. It's not like it was in a legitimate paper. I want you to know we have a professional security force. They've been trained to keep the paparazzi out. We've already investigated and found the one who let him in." The administrator huffs out an indignant breath. "For a hundred dollar bill, no less! Believe me, Mr. De-laSangre, we've already sent him on his way."

Miss Simon, a tall, thin woman in a light green dress that on her looks as shapeless as a cylinder, runs down from the administration building. Her high heels clack on the dock's wood deck as she rushes up and hands Maxwell a thin newspaper. He hands the paper to me.

I recognize it as one of the trashy weeklies that masquerade as underground newspapers and make their income mostly from restaurant and entertainment ads. This one's masthead proudly proclaims itself as *The Weekly Dish*. A single color picture of me dropping Henri off at the school's dock takes up most of the front page. The headline below the picture says, CAN THIS MAN BE A KILLER?

Shaking my head, clenching my jaws, I open the paper, glance at the article long enough to see my name and those of Maria and Jorge Santos. Another name, Pepe Santos, also appears in the first paragraph. I read just enough to see he's my accuser and then shut the paper.

Glaring at the administrator, I spit out my words, "Can I keep this?"

He takes an involuntary step back, caused no doubt by either my expression or the tone of my voice or both. "Yes, of course, Mr. DelaSangre. We have plenty of copies in the office."

My lips compress against my teeth. It takes all my self-control not to strike this fat, simpering, pompous little man.

Maxwell realizes what he's said and blanches. "Not that anyone's going to keep any of the copies. I've already ordered that all of them be thrown out. There's no place for trash like that in an institution like ours."

I nod, fold the paper, stuff it in the open compartment below the boat's wheel. Without another word to Maxwell, I yank the wheel all the way over and throw the boat in gear, the motors roaring as I accelerate into a turn just tight enough to miss scraping the seawall on the other side of the channel.

As soon as I straighten out, I gun the motors and race out the channel throwing a vicious wake behind me that crashes water over the seawalls, dislodging a few of the school's prams, washing them into the channel. Ordinarily such rude seamanship would draw an angry rebuke from the school. But I doubt that Maxwell feels anything but relief to see me gone.

As soon as I clear the channel, I jam the throttles to full speed and mindspeak to Chloe, masked so Henri can't hear us, {*I'm going to the office before I come home. Remember the photographer I told you about? A couple of weeks ago? Some damn paper has the picture—Henri and me—plastered all over its front page.*}

{*It's just a picture, Henri. There are worse things than that.*}

{*It's not just the picture,*} I mindspeak.

Chloe says, {*Peter, I rung up Mum—like you suggested. She*}

*was furious. She can't stand to hear it ring. Mum swears she's
throwing out the phone. Anyway, I just got off the phone with
her*—}

I interrupt her. {*They have an article too! About me and
Maria Santos and her brother, Jorge.*}

{*Now? After all these years? Why?*}

{*It's all the disappearances. They've interviewed the Santos's cousin, Pepe, and now they're questioning whether I might
have something to do with all the missing boaters.*} I turn the
boat left, head for the old seaplane channel just north of Dinner
Key Marina.

{*Peter, that's terrible. How can they do that? Couldn't your
people stop them?*}

I pass the main channel marker, slam the wheel over so violently that the Grady White skitters sideways as it turns toward
Monty's docks. {*Maybe they could have stopped them. If they
knew about it. We don't own any stock in that paper. It's too
damned small. We own enough to control all the majors. Who'd
have thought that a piece of crap like the* Dish *would ever
bother us?*}

{The Weekly Dish?} Chloe mindspeaks.

{*That's the one.*} I cut back on the throttles as soon as I speed
past the NO WAKE sign at the entrance to Monty's marina. It's
one thing to rock a few little sailboats, quite another to send a
few millions of dollars worth of motor boats crashing into their
docks and each other.

{*I'll look it up online. But I fear there's worse, Peter.*}

I groan, mindspeak, {*What now?*}

{*Mum says Derek's gone. She says he disappeared more than
three months ago.*}

6

Ordinarily I enjoy the leisurely pace of the final approach to the docks, cruising the last few hundred yards to my slip at Monty's, the Yamahas rumbling gently, everything slowing down after a fast dash across the bay. But now I grit my teeth, tap my hand against the boat's wheel as the Grady White glides through the water, leaving only ripples in its wake.

Today I wish I could ignore the NO WAKE signs. I just want to dock the boat and get to the office.

I can't stop thinking about my brother-in-law, Derek Blood. I shake my head as I maneuver into my slip. I go from wondering if he's somewhere in Miami to doubting that he could be so stupid. After all, he is Chloe's older brother. He shares the same genetic background with her. But I have to admit he's never exhibited any of the cleverness I've seen in the rest of her family.

The very clumsiness of all the disappearances. The very greed of taking so many, in such a small area, in so short a time all point to someone as limited in scope and judgment as my brother-in-law. I tie the boat off, roll up my copy of *The Weekly Dish* and jump onto the dock.

Fortunately, it's a weekday and the dock's clear of other boaters. I have no patience to tolerate idle chat now, no willingness to suffer any fools. Should someone interfere with me today, I'll gladly lash out at them.

I huff out a loud sigh. The creature would be dead now if it weren't for his sister's intercession. Had I killed Derek three years ago, when he and his father tried to take over my company and my holdings, he would be no worry today. But this time, if Derek has been stupid enough to return to Miami, I doubt Chloe will intervene on his behalf again.

Rushing down the dock, I ignore the few workers readying the tables under the thatch-top cheekee huts at Monty's outdoor dining patio nearby. I realize only after I first place foot on the asphalt surface of the restaurant's parking lot that I'm barefoot. Unless I plan to go ashore, I rarely wear more than cutoffs and a tank top when I take Henri to school.

No matter. I smile. Few people pay notice to any of the many boaters who walk around near the Grove's waterfront. The guards at the Monroe building are used to seeing me come in dressed for boating. Surely my bare feet will hardly register with them.

Striding across South Bayshore Drive, I pay no attention to the stoplight or to the cars that screech to a halt or zoom around me. I barely glance up at the Monroe building on the southwest corner of the intersection. I know full well the height of it, the green-and-beige design of its exterior. It, like the company it houses on its topmost floors, belongs to me.

Men in dark suits and women in equally stuffy business dress come and go from the six brass-door elevators that service most of the building. The two guards who oversee this constant bustle spot me as soon as I enter the marble-floored foyer. They ignore everyone else, rush to keep up with me as I walk to the private elevator on the other side of the lobby—the only one that goes to LaMar Associates' executive offices.

"Mr. DelaSangre, how you doing today?" says the heavier of the guards, a pock-faced man who I remember goes by the name of Harry.

I nod, force a smile and walk on. At the elevator door, I put my hand in my pocket and find it empty. "Damn!" I say. "Look, Harry, would you use your key? Mine's at home."

The man's rough face flushes pink. His right hand reaches for the ring of keys hanging from his belt, then drops away from it. "Mr. DelaSangre, you know I'm not supposed to use my key without Mr. Tindall's permission. You know how he is."

I nod. I know exactly how Ian Tindall is and I understand the guard's fear of him. Unlike Arturo Gomez, who likes to warn people before he acts, Ian never tolerates any violation of his rules. To him any offense, no matter how trivial, merits at least immediate dismissal. I've seen him do worse to the few employees who've been stupid enough as to openly oppose him.

Still, the security guard should know better than to refuse me. "Did you forget who Ian works for, Harry?" I spit out. "Open the damn door!" I also tell him to call ahead, tell Ian, Arturo and his daughter, Claudia, to meet me in my office.

The elevator door opens opposite LaMar Associates' reception desk. Sarah, the receptionist, already standing, says, "Good morning, Mr. DelaSangre. Mr. Gomez and Mr. Tindall have been notified that you need to see them in your office. Ms. Gomez won't be in for a few more minutes. She called to say she'd been delayed."

I nod and say, "Thank you, Sarah," and grin at her rigid posture, the forced smile on her face. Whenever I'm near her, the woman gives off an aroma tinged with just the slightest acrid scent of fear. Understandable, I suppose. With a word I could have her gone.

Still, I wonder. Other than Sarah's timidity in my presence and her constant battle with her weight, I know little about her. Father told me a few humans, very few, can sense our difference. *"They don't understand it. They just know we make them uneasy. You have to watch for them, Peter. Fear always makes humans unpredictable."*

I'm tempted to stay near her for a while—just see how she'll cope with it. "It's beautiful out there today," I say.

Sarah's eyes widen. She looks around the room, down the mahogany-paneled corridor, then lets out a sigh. "Oh, there's Mr. Tindall," she says.

Turning, I see the tall, skeletal frame of LaMar Associates' legal counsel and co-manager. "Peter!" he says, his black suit obviously well tailored but still hanging loose on his too-thin body, his pale, thin lips pressed into an insincere smile as he reaches out to take my hand. "This is an unexpected pleasure."

I take his bony hand in mine, squeeze it just hard enough to make him wince. Father never tired of warning me. *"Never trust any of them. I've never seen an honest Tindall. They're nothing but scoundrels. But useful,"* he said. *"After all, what*

*need would we have for an honest lawyer—if we could find
such a thing?"*

Ian talks about sports, the Miami Heat basketball team, as he
follows me down the hall to my office. "You should let me get
tickets to the games for you and Chloe next year," he says.
"Everyone goes to them, the mayor, the archbishop, everyone
important."

I enter my office, barely glance out the large window overlooking the marina and Biscayne Bay beyond it and sit down
behind my desk, putting *The Weekly Dish* face down on the
desktop, motioning for Ian to take one of the leather seats facing me. "Just what I need," I say. "Chloe's already talked me
into season tickets at the Coconut Grove Theater, the Philhar-
monic and the Theater of the Performing Arts on Miami
Beach."

The thin man waves his hand as if to dismiss my objections.
"Don't forget, Peter. I'm the one you called to arrange your
seats. You may complain a lot, but I know you love doing it for
her," Tindall says.

"True," I say, nodding, thinking about my wife and her desire to expose herself to all the things she missed growing up in
her secluded valley. Because of her, I've seen more theater,
more music and more art in the last few years than in all the rest
of my life.

A waft of Aramis cologne enters the room. I shake my head.
Wishing that sometimes my sense of smell could be dulled, I
look toward the doorway. The scent of Arturo Gomez's amply
applied cologne always precedes him. "Hi, Arturo," I say, just
before the man steps into my office.

Wearing a perfectly tailored Armani suit, his dark complexion made even darker by hours of boating in the sun, the man
flashes me a smile full of bright white, capped teeth. "Peter! I
didn't expect to see you so soon."

I nod. I own LaMar Associates, but Arturo's the president.
He and Ian Tindall and Claudia make all the day-to-day business decisions. Except for the rare occasions when I'm called
in to sign papers, I come and go as I please. Since Chloe's arrival, I've been pleased to come very little.

Motioning for Arturo to take the other seat in front of my

desk, I wait until he sits before I push my copy of *The Weekly Dish* toward him. "Turn it over. Look at the cover page," I say.

Arturo picks it up and lets out a soft whistle as he studies it. When he finishes, he shakes his head and passes it to Tindall. "This sucks, Peter," he says.

Tindall mutters, "Shit, shit, shit," as he reads. When he finishes and looks up, I say, "I don't want to see any more of this."

"That's easy to say, Peter, but it's a news story. They only quoted what Pepe Santos said. They had every legal right to do it," Tindall says, putting the paper back on the desk.

I turn toward Arturo. Of all humans, I trust him and his daughter most. His family has served mine since Don Henri first came to America. Unlike the Tindalls, who've served us almost as long and who've been responsible for all of our legal work and our political connections, not one Gomez has ever betrayed us. "I said I want it stopped," I say.

Arturo nods. Besides being responsible for overseeing all aspects of LaMar Associates, he is also the person I turn to when what I want can't be accomplished by legal means. He runs his hand over his hair, going mostly gray now, but still almost as thick as when he was young. "I understand what you want. I just have to figure out how to do it. There's more than one problem here. . . ."

Claudia Gomez rushes through the doorway, a rolled paper clutched in one hand and says, "Wow. I guess you guys saw this week's *Dish,* huh?"

"We did," I say.

"Bet you're pissed," Claudia says. "Does Chloe know?"

I nod, watch the girl as she breezes into the room, kissing her father on the cheek and doing the same to me. She acknowledges Tindall with a curt, "Hi, Ian," and grabs a chair from by the wall, pulling it over by her father, then sitting, rearranging her short brown skirt, tugging on it to cover a bit more of her long, tanned legs before her father glares at her.

Claudia notices me watching her and shrugs, flashing me a quick, wide-mouthed smile. We both know that if she had any choice, she'd be coming to the office in shorts or jeans. Arturo's the one who insists on more formal dress. A head shorter than her father, she looks like his female version—younger, thinner and more attractive to be sure, but just as square-jawed and strong-willed, and rebellious enough to always choose skirts almost too short for her father's comfort.

"Sorry I'm late," Claudia says. "I had to stop at the Brickell Emporium."

"For breakfast?" Arturo turns toward his daughter, raises an eyebrow, his face otherwise devoid of expression. Besides her dress, her penchant for tardiness has led to many run-ins between them.

The girl laughs. "Relax. I wasn't goofing off. I had to meet Toba."

Arturo nods, tilts his head toward me. "Toba Mathais, one of our operatives," he says. "Sharp little girl, tough, blonde, pretty, great shot . . ."

"And good," Claudia says. "She called me last night and asked me to meet her for breakfast so she could turn in her report on the new county manager." She looks at me. "You know how Pops is about the operatives. He never lets them come to the office."

"Anyway when I got to the Emporium . . ." She swivels in her seat to face her father and says, "Okay, so I was a little late for that," then turns back and holds up her copy of *The Weekly Dish*. "So Toba was already sitting at the table reading this when I came in. As soon as I sat down she showed me the cover. I couldn't believe any local paper would dare do that!"

Ian smiles, his lips too close together to show his teeth. "You don't know Jordan Davidson. I've met him at parties. He's an arrogant little *fag* who wears nothing but linen pants, boat shoes and Tommy Bahama shirts. He struts around acting like owning that piss-ant gossip sheet has made him the next William Randolph Hearst. I've heard him brag that he actually does his own editing—even writes every headline himself. I think there's nothing he'd rather do than be in the middle of a great big fuss."

"Can he be reasoned with?" I say.

"Not if you mean, can he be bought off." Ian's grin widens as he shakes his head. "From what I hear, his mother bought the paper for him after he flunked out of journalism school. It's lost circulation and money every year since. The word is, he has no problem covering the losses out of the allowance his mommy gives him."

"Is he really gay?" Claudia says. "Maybe we can find something there?"

Ian says, "I doubt it. Everyone knows he's homosexual. He's open about it. He's going to be a tough one. He's too rich to be bought and too stupid to be threatened."

"But he can be eliminated," Arturo says.

Ian glares at him. "I didn't need to hear that!"

I sigh. Don Henri, my father, would have given his approval to a plan like that with a wave of his hand. But Chloe and I have discussed living our lives differently than our parents, teaching our children a gentler way. We've agreed it's one thing to kill because one must—both to serve hunger and instinct. Neither of us wants to turn to killing as a knee-jerk reflex to every problem. "We don't need to consider that yet," I say.

Claudia nods, smooths out her copy of *The Weekly Dish*. "There might be other ways we can approach this." She points to the byline on the cover story on the first page. "Andy Malcondado. He's a freelancer. Toba volunteered to see what she can find out about him and Pepe Santos."

"Then in the meantime we should notify Davidson to tread lightly where Peter's concerned." Arturo looks at Ian and then at me. "Libel law may apply you know. He should understand he could lose all of his mommy's money."

Ian shakes his head again. "It's not a good idea. I've watched this guy get in fights before. He always takes them right to the front page."

Arturo says, "It's up to you, Peter. You're the one whose name is going to be out there."

All three look at me. I stare at my copy of the *Dish*, take my time answering. When I was young Father made me learn chess, insisting we play each evening. *"Every move is a lesson,"* he said. *"It's easy to move quickly. But a rash move without studying all the possible consequences can lead to just as quick a defeat."*

"Can we make sure the rest of the media will ignore the story?" I say.

Arturo nods. So does Ian.

"I already planned to take Chloe and the kids to Jamaica until this settles down. That's one of the things I came here today to discuss."

Ian cocks an eyebrow.

"Yes, Ian," I say. "I was going to ask you to contact Granny and tell him to open up Bartlet House. I want the stable stocked with horses for us and ponies for Henri and Lizzie. I'd like the same household staff, if he can put it together. And I want you to arrange air tickets as soon as we decide on a date."

"That's easy enough, Peter," Ian says. "But are you sure you should leave town while this is going on? It could look like you're running away."

I shrug. "So be it. My son's old enough to be affected by this. He doesn't need to hear the other kids talking about it at school. I see no reason why he should suffer. Anyway, if none of the other media pile on, then Jordan Davidson can piss in the wind for all I care. But I do think Arturo's right. We should threaten suit. It can't make matters much worse."

Ian frowns, but says, "You're the boss."

"And Claudia," I say. "Get your Toba Mathais busy on that writer and Pepe Santos. It wouldn't hurt to look into Jordan Davidson too. Maybe we'll have some luck, find something we can use."

Claudia smiles. "Toba's great. I'm sure she'll come up with something. But I think I'll have a different operative concentrate on Davidson."

"Fine," I say.

Ian stands and says, "Well, if that's it, I'll be getting back to work. It appears I have a threatening letter to write."

I nod and say, "But Arturo and Claudia need to stay a few more minutes. And Ian—please close the door on your way out."

The thin man frowns, but still does as he's told. After he leaves Arturo says, "Poor Ian never does like being left out of the loop."

"He doesn't have to hear any of this," I say. I explain about Derek's disappearance.

"You think he's here?" Claudia says.

"I don't know. But if he is, he could be involved with all the people that have gone missing."

Arturo sighs. "Just great," he says. "Just great."

"Last time he made himself look like you. How are we going to find him if he can change his appearance like that?" Claudia says.

"If he's here," I say. "And no one's saying that he is. But if he is, I'd bet that he's staying with his own appearance. Otherwise, he'd have to have someone make up new papers for him. He's not that smart or that resourceful."

"Ian would be," Claudia says.

I nod. So far, Ian is the only Tindall who's never done anything to betray my family. I'm sure only the lack of a good opportunity and the fear of my response have prevented him from trying. "A good reason why you should have some of your people watching him now," I say. "But he was smart enough not to ally with Derek the last time. I can't see why he would now."

"Well, we should still have Derek's picture from when we made up his papers for his return to Jamaica. I can distribute it to some of our operatives," Arturo says.

"Good," I nod. "Have them check the better hotels. Derek likes to live well. And check with the police for missing women on land too. Derek can never stay away from them for long."

"And what do we do if we find him?" Claudia says.

My brother-in-law has already made my life difficult once. My stomach tightens at the thought he could be doing it again. "My father taught me that anyone can make a mistake once. He said that to make the same mistake a second time is unforgivable," I say. "I let Derek go last time. This time, if you find him, just notify me." I grin. "I'll enjoy taking care of it myself."

7

To my surprise, Henri objects when we first withdraw him from Coral Bluff. "All my friends are there!" he says. "It's boring at home. At least at school we sometimes get to play games."

He sulks the better part of a day before he finally begins to follow me about as I go from room to room in the house, readying things for our prolonged absence. By the next morning he volunteers to help as I shut down a generator and begin to take it apart—to lubricate it and see what else might need repair.

Unwilling to be left out, Lizzie joins us, picking up one greasy part after another from Henri's pile, placing them where he directs. By lunchtime, when Chloe comes to inspect our progress, she breaks out laughing when she finds her husband, her son and her daughter all equally smeared with grease.

In the afternoon, I reward Henri for his help by taking him out in Chloe's Donzi. While it's too fast for him to take out unsupervised, at sixteen feet it's far more manageable for him than my Grady White. Once outside our channel, in the bay, I let him take the wheel and start to teach him how to handle the boat.

We race down the bay as far south as Boca Chita Key. Because Henri's never seen the small gray-stoned lighthouse on the island from close up, and because on weekdays the island's small harbor provides a quiet place to practice docking, I say, "Let's slow down and go explore the island."

Henri grins. He cuts back on the motors and I guide him into the island's channel. It's a pretty island, so flat and so small and so sparsely treed that in places you can see from the bay to the ocean. On the weekends campers and boaters crowd both the land and the harbor, but today we find only two boats tied to the concrete seawall.

"How come no one lives here?" Henri says.

"When I was young someone did," I say. "A millionaire. He had a big house here. The story is, he built the lighthouse so at night, after card games on the mainland, he could still find his way home—even if he'd had too many drinks. When the park service took over the island they tore down his house. But fortunately, they left the lighthouse."

"Are they going to tear down our house too?" Henri says, his lip pouting out like when he was younger.

I resist smiling at his obvious distress and put my hand on his head and ruffle his hair. "No way. Of course, they'd like to. They've tried to take over our island a number of times, but your grandfather and I and our people at LaMar have always been able to stop them."

Henri says, "But what if you can't?"

I think of all the money that Tindall and Arturo dole out to politicians, of all the favors we've done for the top bureaucrats in the park service and smile. "There's little likelihood of that," I say.

It isn't until we've tied up against the concrete seawall in the harbor that Henri points to the water and says, "Look Papa!"

I frown at the protruding fin, the small, sleek gray shape of the dolphin as it lazily coasts toward us. Usually I like dolphins nearby. I admire the creatures' apparent joy as they go about their activities. But this one, if it's the same one that's followed us before, makes me uneasy. In a land-going wild animal like a raccoon or a fox, odd behavior like this would prompt suspicions of rabies. "You think it's the same one?" I say.

Henri nods. "Sure, Papa. I recognize her."

"Her?"

"I don't know for sure, Papa, but I think it's too small to be a 'he'. Anyway, when she visits she always seems too nice to be a guy. She never splashes me or anything."

"When she visits?" I say.

My son nods. "She's come into our harbor a few times before."

As the dolphin glides past our Donzi, Henri leans over and strokes its exposed fin. He smiles at me. "See. She likes me."

The beast turns and comes back. I study it. It looks like any other bottlenose dolphin, maybe a little smaller than usual, but its presence puts me on edge. When it comes alongside the boat, I reach over to stroke its fin. With a flick of its tail, it shoots away.

"You scared it," Henri says.

I watch the dolphin hump and disappear from sight, then a few moments later resurface near the harbor entrance. "How do you know it's always the same dolphin?" I say.

Henri looks at me like I'm hopelessly dense. "Duhh. Because she's smooth everywhere," he says. "Didn't you notice?"

Frowning at the scorn in his voice, I think how my father would have reacted had I dared to use such a tone with him. But I decide to let it pass without comment. He's had other pre-teen moments before, and Chloe's warned me there will be more. "He still loves you. It's just a natural part of growing up," she said.

The dolphin swims back toward us, but this time when it passes it stays out of reach. Still, in the clear water, it comes close enough for me to see that Henri's right. Unlike most other dolphins I've seen, this beast has no markings, no scars, no little nicks on its fins or tail. I wonder what charmed life this creature's led to avoid the accidents and fights that seem to mark most of its kind.

"Can I jump in and swim with it?" Henri says.

"I don't know," I say, watching as the dolphin swims toward the harbor entrance and hoping it will decide to go.

"Please, Papa."

I can't think of a reason to say no. We've jumped into the water with pods of dolphins dozens of times before and never once had any problems. I sigh and say, "Go ahead."

Henri gives me a wide grin, yanks off his T-shirt and shoes and jumps from the boat.

As soon as he splashes into the water the dolphin alters course, turning, swimming straight for us. "Come here, girl," Henri says, treading water by the side of the boat, patting the water's surface in between strokes. "Come here, girl."

I doubt that the dolphin either hears or understands his words, but its speed increases so quickly that the water boils behind it. Watching its rapid approach, my heartbeat speeds up too. Just moments before the beast reaches my son, I lean over the side of the boat and grab the boy.

"Hey!" Henri shouts as I yank him from the water.

The dolphin shoots by only an instant later, then dives from sight. "Why'd you do that?" Henri says, staring at the water, trying to spot the dolphin. "She just wanted to swim with me."

"She was coming too fast," I say, concentrating on slowing my heartbeat.

"She would have stopped."

"Maybe. Maybe not."

"You shouldn't have done that," Henri says.

"My father taught me to never ignore my instincts. It's something you should learn too. It just didn't look right," I say. "Even more important, it didn't feel right."

Henri glowers at me. "You watch. Now she won't come back."

"Go below and dry off," I say. "I think we should go check out the lighthouse. Then we'll see if she comes back or not."

To Henri's disappointment, we see no sign of the dolphin when we return from the lighthouse, nor does it reappear to follow us home from Boca Chita. He goes to our island's harbor each day after that and watches for it. But each evening he informs us that she hasn't visited again.

After a week passes, he declares, "I don't think she's ever coming back!"

"You never know. They're wild creatures, Henri," I say. "She could have gone anywhere. She could come back tomorrow or in three months or never." I don't share with him that my choice, if it were up to me, would be never.

8

Chloe and I have finished most of the maintenance needed on our machines and equipment and we've selected almost all the clothing we plan to pack before Ian Tindall finally calls. I expect him to give me our travel plans. Instead he says, "Is it okay if everything's delayed a few weeks more? I'm afraid Bartlet House can't be opened just yet—unless you want me to hire a new crew for you."

I say nothing.

"Peter, I called down there just like you asked. But it seems that your man, Granville Morrison, can't make himself available for at least two weeks more."

"Why?" I say. "He's still our caretaker, isn't he?"

Tindall clears his throat.

"Ian, damn it! What's going on?"

The man sighs. "I was just trying to save you money. It's been years since you've gone down there and we've been carrying both him and his wife on the payroll—for doing almost nothing. So I made a different arrangement with them."

I think of the big Jamaican and his wife, Velda. I'd hate to have to replace either one of them. "You didn't fire them, did you?"

"No, Peter, nothing like that. I just cut them back to part-time status. They agreed to watch over the property on weekends. That's more than it needs. Believe me, they were still well paid for the little bit of work they had to do. When we worked it out I told them they could get other jobs but they had to promise they'd be available whenever you needed them. Granny swore it would be no problem. But now his wife tells me he has a job in Montego Bay. The man insists on giving them two weeks' notice."

Shaking my head, I say, "Damn it, Ian, you should know better than to cut costs at my expense."

"I know. I'm sorry. I was just looking out for you. It'll just be a few more weeks, okay?"

I turn to Chloe and explain the situation to her. "If you want, we can get someone else for the first few weeks," I say. "Or stay somewhere else until the house is opened."

She thinks a moment, then shakes her head. "No. You told me how much Henri likes Granny. It won't be any big deal if we wait here, Peter."

"Okay," I say into the phone.

He lets out a relieved breath. "By the way," he says. "I sent your letter out four days ago. The one to Jordan Davidson. We haven't heard anything back yet."

"It's early," I say. "Was there anything more in this week's *Dish?*"

"No. Claudia's been watching for us. She said this week's was DelaSangre-free."

"They should all be," I say.

In truth, neither Chloe nor I find staying on our island for a few extra weeks to be any hardship. With all the extra time we have, the few remaining chores we have to perform to ready our house for our absence become easy tasks. Without any need to take Henri to and from school on the mainland each day, five days a week, it begins to feel like a mini-vacation.

Chloe, who has never loved rising early, stops setting the clock's alarm. We get up when the children wake. In the evenings, after both Henri and Lizzie go to sleep, Chloe and I turn to each other and make love in our human forms, exploring each others' bodies, taking time for each other, like we did when we first met.

Other than the usual daily cleaning the house needs and tending the garden and Elizabeth's grave, we have little we must do but wait for notification that our home's ready in Jamaica. The weather conspires to lull us into relaxation. The blustery winds of early March give way to calm spring breezes. The regular visits of cold fronts and the showers they bring stop, each new day of mild weather and sunny skies becoming a monotonous repeat of the last. If it weren't for the disappearances still being reported every few days and the increase of the boats patrolling near our island, I'd just as soon not bother going anywhere else.

I count it as a gift to have my son home from school each day. We set aside the afternoons for each other, fishing some days, boating or sailing on the others, Henri growing good enough that I readily give the helm to him. In the evenings, with no safe possibility of either flight or hunting, I begin to teach him chess, as my father taught me.

On nights when his interest flags, I turn to telling stories of our family's past, Henri usually saying at some point, "Tell me about Don Henri's pirate fleet!" I smile and point out Don Henri's old cutlass on the wall, the boy's eyes growing large as I pull out the old log books and nautical maps that still remain stored in the same wooden chest that Don Henri had placed in the great room long before I was born.

Henri peers at the old maps and leafs through the log books. He touches the raised ink of my father's script—the words written in Spanish and equally incomprehensible to both of us.

My father may have been Spanish-born, but he never spoke the language at home, speaking French with my Hungarian-born mother whenever they felt the need to converse in a foreign language. Other than a few phrases and a few curse words, I've long forgotten whatever Spanish I learned in school. Like far too many English speakers in Miami, I've just been too lazy to truly learn the language.

They'd terrorized the Carribean for over a hundred years, each ship commanded by a person of the blood—Captain Jack Blood from Jamaica, Captain Giscard Sang from Haiti and, of course, Don Henri, their leader. Still, the boy frowns when I point to Jamaica and Haiti on the maps and then show him the tiny ink spot that signifies our island. "We should have as big an island as they do," he says.

I smile and say, "We have all we need."

Each day blends into the next so that after only another week passes, I could swear we'd been living like this for months. We're outside, under the gumbo limbo tree, Lizzie sitting between my legs, leaning back against my stomach,

Henri sitting cross-legged at my side, Max's huge head in his lap. Both children listen, open-mouthed, as Chloe retells the ancient story of the great war between the four castrylls—the giant, flame-breathing Zal, the seagoing Pelk, the airborne Thryll and our castryll, the Undrae—that once made up the People of the Blood.

Unlike my mother, who spent most of her youth being raised among humans, Chloe has been taught all the history of our people and the necessity to pass it along. I know when my daughter's older she'll be taught even more of it—as well as the uses of every herb and plant in our garden and how to prepare them.

Since I've heard the story before and know the fighting was over dwindling food sources after a cataclysmic explosion ripped through the earth—a battle the Undrae eventually won—I pay only partial attention to Chloe's words. My eyes wander down to our harbor and out to the bay.

I smile when I spot the dark blue speedboat racing toward our island. If it stays on course it will soon arrive at the entrance to our unmarked channel. I've taught only two humans how to negotiate the channel's treacherous twists and turns, and I know which one of them owns a speedboat of this color. I wonder if Arturo Gomez knows his daughter's out on the water on a workday.

Two patrol boats speed toward her boat and intercept it before it reaches the channel. I frown, wishing that boats could come and go on the water as they did before. By now I've been stopped so often that I know many of the people on the patrol boats by name.

Fortunately, such stops are usually brief. It takes only a few minutes before Claudia's on her way again.

She's still wending her way through our channel when Chloe finishes her story. "Are all the others gone?" Henri asks. "Aren't there any Zal or Pelk or Thryll anywhere anymore?"

"All the others were defeated," Chloe says. "Most either were killed or married Undrae. My mother told me some small groups from other castrylls still exist. But not one of our kind has ever reported seeing any of them."

The breeze brings with it the low rumble of Claudia's outboards, and Max's ears perk up. He lets out a loud woof, scrambles to his feet and runs toward the dock.

Henri looks toward the harbor, sees the dark blue speedboat and shouts, "Claudy!" He jumps up, turns to me and says, "Can I, Papa?" I nod and he runs off after his dog.

A few moments later a dog barks from the other side of the island. Another follows, and soon the whole pack fills the air with barks and yelps. One beast after another scrambles over the sand dunes and through the brush, until the whole pack crowds the shore near the dock.

They number over twenty now—more than enough to guard our small island. Standing, picking up Lizzie, I look at Chloe. "We really shouldn't let the pack get much bigger," I say.

"It's not time yet," she says, her emerald-green eyes staring into mine. "We can afford to let them have a few more litters. You know how much the kids love the puppies."

"I know how much you love them," I say and begin walking toward the dock, Chloe walking at my side. "But we already have enough."

She brushes against me. "Just a few more litters and then we take care of the older ones, okay?" she says.

I stop, look at her. She's always made a face every time I talked about how Father and I used to cull the pack.

"No." Chloe shakes her head. "There's no need for that. You can take them to a vet. Get them fixed."

"I'm sure that would go over well," I say, grinning, picturing the commotion that would ensue if I ever tried to bring one of our half-wild beasts to an animal hospital. Even if we could control the dog in such an unfamiliar setting, I doubt any other pet owners would feel comfortable in its presence.

"So," I say. "Weren't you the one who recently killed four humans on Andros because you were too hungry to wait until you could take just one?"

"Peter, I said I was sorry about that. . . ."

"And yet you're worried about doing away with some guard dogs? Don't you find this a little inconsistent?"

"And don't you love that about me?" she says, bumping her hip against mine.

I nod, put two fingers to my mouth and whistle a sharp, loud burst. The dogs look in my direction, their ears flattened, their tails tucked in. Slowly, one by one, they slink into the underbrush. "At least you haven't spoiled them completely yet," I say.

With all of our dock space taken up by our boats, Claudia pulls her boat alongside my Grady White. Henri places fenders for her and has her tied off by the time we arrive. Killing her outboard engines, Claudia grabs a briefcase and makes her way from her boat to mine and then to the dock.

I wait while she hugs and kisses Henri, saying, "Thanks for the help," then hugs and kisses Lizzie, finally embracing Chloe before she turns toward me.

Staring at her powder blue spaghetti-strap T-shirt and matching shorts and bare feet, I say, "Did your Dad give you the day off?"

"Hardly," Claudia says. "He sent me." She opens the briefcase and takes out a small tabloid newspaper. "Pops thought you might want to see this week's *Dish*. I told him there was no way I was going to ride out here in a dress and heels."

Chloe takes the paper first, studies it and then passes it to me. "Nice picture," she says. "You think we could get the original?"

Frowning at her, I say, "Funny." This time, instead of the picture taking up most of the front page, it covers only the middle third. Instead of Henri and me, the photo's a closeup of my face, taken, I guess, with a telephoto lens as I guided my boat into Monty's marina.

Above the picture a headline blares,

WE WILL NOT BE INTIMIDATED!

Below the picture another headline asks,

WHAT IS THIS MAN TRYING TO HIDE?

"There's an editorial inside, on page two," Claudia says. "It tells all about them being threatened by Ian's letter." She takes the paper back, opens it and points to the section of the editorial. "Read how he ends it."

One would think, if Mr. DelaSangre is as innocent as his attorney claims, he would be demanding to speak to us and to anyone else who would listen rather than threatening those who ask legitimate questions. If he would like to visit with us and tell us his side of the story, we'd be perfectly glad to hear him out.

No one at this newspaper has any interest in any of our stories mistakenly blackening anyone's reputation. But if Mr. DelaSangre insists on siccing his legal attack dogs on us, he'll find our appetite for legal battles to be every bit as keen as his and our pockets every bit as deep.

I shake my head and pass the paper to Chloe. "Ian said this might happen," I say.

Claudia says, "Surprisingly, Ian's not gloating. He really doesn't like the guy. He wants to know if you want him to send Pepe Santos a letter threatening suit too."

"Have you located him?"

"That and more," Claudia says. "I really love working with Toba Mathias. The woman had both men's contact numbers, cellphones, addresses, even E-mail addresses, by the day after our meeting."

Chloe says, "That doesn't sound very hard to do."

Claudia nods. "No, but then Toba started E-mailing the free-lancer, Andy Malcandado, telling him she admired his investigative report, that she always wanted to be a writer. Asking him questions about writing?"

"And that worked?" I say.

"Not until she E-mailed him one of her pictures. She called me a couple of days ago to tell me they finally made a date to meet—a breakfast date for seven-thirty at the Brickell Emporium."

"I couldn't resist." Claudia smiles. "By the time I got there, about seven-fifteen, Toba was already waiting by the restaurant's door, decked out in a tight pair of red shorts and a skimpy halter top." She laughs. "I went inside and took a table by the front window—where I could watch. You should have seen the look on that poor guy's face when he pulled up in this old battered Pinto and saw her waiting by the door. He went beet-red. I swear!

"When they came inside, they sat fairly near to me. Toba didn't miss a trick, all wide-eyed, asking questions, batting her eyelashes, flashing her cleavage, touching his arm, his shoulder as they talked, barely giving him any chance to ask questions of his own, finally looking at her watch, telling him she had to go and then rushing out of the restaurant.

"After he drove away, she came back in and joined me at the counter and told me what he said. I have her written report in the briefcase if you want."

"Just tell me," I say.

"Toba said, 'It's easy with a writer. Just ask them about their writing and let them talk.' She said he's thrilled with the play *The Dish* has given him . . . and the money. He's been trying to make it as a freelancer for years. Now he thinks he's finally broken through. Andy said his luckiest break was running into Pepe Santos at John Martin's during happy hour. He told her he almost went broke buying the guy drinks. But it was all worth it. His editor's asked him for at least two more follow-up stories. Toba said the guy couldn't stop bragging about the money."

Claudia shakes her head. "She said Andy insisted his old beat-up Pinto and the crummy one-room efficiency he rents on the outskirts of Overtown were sacrifices he made to be able to pursue the truth. But now that he's found it, he swears it's time for him to cash in. When the story's all done he wants to find an agent and try for a book deal."

I shake my head and say, "Not that *that* will ever happen."

"When's the next story coming out?" Chloe says.

Claudia grins. "We have some time. He told Toba he has most of it written but he's been having a little trouble tracking down any of the witnesses from when Maria Santos disappeared. He finally got a line on a wino named Sam Pratt, said the man was washing dishes at the Half Moon Raw Bar in Key West. He's planning to go down and interview him this coming weekend."

I start to say something but Claudia continues, "Pop has already been on the phone to someone in Key West. He told me to assure you that Mr. Pratt will be moving on again. This time maybe to California or Hawaii."

"What are we going to do about the rest of it?" I say.

"Malcandado's the easiest part of the problem," Claudia says. "We can probably buy him off with an out-of-town job offer. There's an ex-Herald editor working at a paper up in Washington who owes Pop some favors. And we can turn Toba loose on that Pepe Santos character. Her plan is to start going to John Martin's on Fridays for happy hour. See if she can meet up with him and find out what he's about. . . ."

"And Jordan Davidson?" I say.

Claudia sighs. "Ian was right. He's tough. He doesn't hang out with anybody. He lives alone, on the water in Gables on the Bay. He's a fishing nut. He keeps a fishing boat at the house and goes out at least a couple of nights every week by himself."

"What about what Ian said, about his being gay?"

"We had to go outside for that. None of our guys are gay. We hired a real honey by the name of Prescott Boyd. The guy knows everyone in town and at all the clubs. But it turns out Davidson doesn't frequent any of the gay hangouts. The man may be openly gay, but he's real private about whatever relationships he might have. Prescott said he mostly uses male prostitutes. He met one that told him about some pretty kinky sex. It seems Mr. Davidson likes to make believe he's a killer. He actually insists on using a loaded gun as part of his sex play. Prescott assures us the prostitute can be counted on to talk with anyone we want—as long as the money's good. We're trying to confirm his story but haven't found any other male prostitutes yet willing to give us anything we can use."

"What about the other problem?" I say.

Claudia looks at me. "Derek?"

"Derek?" Chloe says, staring at me.

I nod. "I asked Claudia and Arturo to keep an eye out for your brother—in case he's here."

Chloe waves a hand toward the bay and the nearby patrol boats. "You don't think he's responsible for all that?"

"I think we don't know where he is, and I wouldn't put it past him," I say.

"Well, whatever you guys think, we haven't seen any sign of anyone like him," Claudia says. "In the meantime you need to tell me whether or not you want Tindall to write that letter to Santos."

I shrug. "Sure, tell him to go ahead. Worse comes to worse that jerk Davidson will just write another editorial."

9

Chloe spots the girl just before sunset, just after Henri and I have set up a pre-dinner game of chess on the dining table in the great room of the third floor of our house. "Peter, come look at this," she says, squinting out the window, one hand up to block the glare of the setting sun. "I think there's a young girl down in the water."

I groan at the thought. "The last thing we need is more attention," I say, Henri and I both getting up, joining her.

My mate points toward a shallow place near the end of the channel where a sandbar always appears at low tide. The late-afternoon sun's rays, joined by the reflected brilliance from the water, burn through the window and obscure my view. Even squinting I can only make out the shape of a female sitting cross-legged on the sand, staring out across the water.

"I don't think it's a girl," I say. "It looks more like a small woman."

"Don't you think we should take the boat out? See if she needs help?"

I squint out at the woman again. "She doesn't look like she's in any distress."

"She could be dazed. She could be from one of those boats where everybody disappeared," Chloe says.

I sigh. "I'll take the Donzi. It'll be quicker. There's no need for all of us to go."

Chloe nods.

Looking at Henri, I say, "Want to come? You can steer."

"Sure, but she won't be there when we get there," Henri says.

Chloe and I both stare at him. "How do you know that?" she says.

The boy studies his feet, always a sure sign he expects to be in trouble. "I've seen her before," he mumbles.

"Where? When?" I say.

Henri points to the end of the channel. "Not out there," he says. He moves his hand to point at the windows on the side of the room, the ones that face north, toward the Wayward Island Channel. "Over there, on the rock."

I nod. I know the rock well. It juts out into the channel, a perfect spot for a young boy to stand and throw things into the current without getting wet. When Henri was smaller he would spend hours throwing leaves and twigs into the water and watching them float away. I did the same when I was little. "You saw her there?" I say.

The boy nods.

"When?"

"Different times," he says. "Usually for a few seconds. Then she wouldn't be there anymore."

"Did you see her go? Did she dive into the water or hide?" Chloe says.

Henri shrugs. "If I batted my eyes or looked away, she wasn't there when I looked again."

My wife looks at him. "Why didn't you tell us?"

Eyes down, the boy shrugs, says nothing.

I squint through the glare again. The girl or woman turns, seems to face in my direction. Her image shimmers in the late afternoon's light and I realize I can't make out any sign of clothes on her body, not even the lines of a skimpy bathing suit. "Was she naked, Henri? Is that why you didn't tell us about her?"

My son nods.

"What did she look like?" I say.

"She had long, black shiny hair," he says. "I thought she was pretty."

By the time we reach the end of the channel, only the last tip of the sun shows above the mainland, and the sky has turned gray, almost dark. We find the sandbar empty, the water lapping around it, and we sit with the Donzi's motors in neutral, the boat bobbing with each passing ripple.

"See. I told you she'd be gone," Henri says.

I nod, search the water around us. *"She's gone,"* I mindspeak to Chloe.

"I know," she mindspeaks. *"I was watching her while you were going out the channel. She was there one moment and gone the next. She must have slipped into the water."*

"It doesn't make any sense," I say, frowning. I motion for Henri to throw the motors in gear and turn for home. As soon as he does so, something large splashes behind us. I whirl around, find only a few rings of ripples expanding in the darkening water.

10

Boaters disappear the next three nights in a row. So many Coast Guard boats and Marine Patrol boats crowd the bay that Chloe and I find we can't take our boats out without being stopped at least two or three times.

One of the evening patrols starts to take special interest in circling our island and shining his searchlights directly at our windows as he passes. "There's no call for that," I say to Chloe.

"Just ignore him," she says. "He's only on duty until midnight. None of the other boats bother us."

I nod. Still I venture out the channel a few times in the next few nights, just to be stopped so I can see who's on board the boat and note the numbers on the bow.

Ian Tindall calls at the end of the week. "Everything's ready in Jamaica," he says, his voice low, almost unsure.

"What's wrong, Ian?" I say.

The man sighs and I can picture the gloom on his face. "Well, I have to tell you sooner or later."

"Tell me what?"

"Those lawsuit threats you had me write look like they've really pissed off Jordan Davidson. And I'm sure Andy Malcandado telling him he was leaving for a new job in D.C.—for Arturo's editor friend—didn't help either."

"So?" I say. "Sounds like we're starting to pull his teeth like Arturo and you planned. Now if Toba Mathais can find a way to get Pepe Santos off my back."

"Yeah," Tindall says. "Good old Toba. Seems she's already gotten very close to Mr. Santos. She called Claudia and told her he really believes you had something to do with both of his cousins' disappearances. More importantly, Toba said that Davidson's hired a lawyer to work with Santos. They're planning to serve papers here for you on Monday. They're naming you in a wrongful death lawsuit."

"*What*? How can they do that?"

"Come on Peter, you know you can always find some lawyer willing to sue for anything. Look at the jerks who are suing the fast food restaurants for making people fat," Tindall sighs again. "It's going to be in this week's *Dish* too. You're going to be sued for the wrongful death of Maria Santos by her mother, Hortensia Santos, and her cousin, Pepe Santos."

"It's ridiculous," I say.

"No, it's all bullshit. I'm sure we'll get it thrown out in a few months. . . ."

"A few months?"

"Yeah," Tindall says. "But in the meantime it's too big a story to keep out of the rest of the media. Arturo's already making sure they play it down as a crank lawsuit."

"Good," I say. "You, Claudia and Arturo can take care of it. Now that the house is ready, I'm going to take my family to Jamaica."

Tindall sighs yet again. I take a deep breath. I find I'm growing tired of his nonverbal sounds. "What?" I say.

"There are going to be depositions, Peter. You shouldn't go. It will look better if you stay. Send Chloe and the children. You need to stay here. You really do."

11

At first Chloe says, "No. We'll stay here with you."

But soon Arturo Gomez calls. "Sorry, Peter," he says. "All of our guys at the newspapers and the TV stations have been calling. They say they can't keep ignoring the story. It's getting too big. They've all promised to try to keep the heat off of you as much as they can, but they have to cover the story."

News helicopters show up only a few hours later, followed by boats crowded with reporters. They return each day, the helicopters hovering over our island, the press boats joining the other craft patrolling the waters off our island, and Chloe soon decides that leaving would be the best for the children.

It takes only a day for Tindall to finalize all their travel plans. Our last dinner together is a quiet thing, Henri morose and toying with his meat, Chloe touching me every time she passes close, even Lizzie too silent, barely babbling.

"Everyone's not leaving until morning," I say. "And anyway we're only going to be apart for a few months."

"I don't care about the 'copters and stuff," Henri says. "I don't want to go."

I study my son's face, realize how much I'm going to miss him and my daughter and my wife. A searchlight from the evening patrol boat shines through our window, and a flash of anger burns through me. I think of my father's words, "Only a fool acts because of anger alone," and will them away. I don't need to be mad to decide it's time to make sure that no more searchlights shine into my home.

"Sometimes we have to do things we don't want to do," I say. "But it will all be over faster than you think. And anyway, if everything works out maybe we'll all have a treat together before morning."

Henri looks at me, eyes wide. Chloe gapes at me too. In our house a late-night treat means just one thing. "Can I come?" Henri says.

"No, it's too dangerous," I say, smiling.

{*What about me?*} Chloe mindspeaks, masked.

{*Of course,*} I mindspeak. {*You're part of the plan.*}

{*And what part is that?*}

{*After the kids are asleep, you'll see.*}

Ordinarily Henri would resist going to sleep before ten, but with a treat promised for later, he goes to bed without protest. By ten-fifteen Chloe comes up to the great room, "Okay. They're both asleep. Now what?" she says.

I look at her, sigh at the thought of being away from her for months. "Now you and I are going downstairs to prepare to hunt." I pull her close to me, kiss her, marvel at how I love the feel of her lips against mine, the way she presses against me.

Chloe pushes away. "But you've been saying it's too dangerous all this time."

"Yes, I have, and yes, it is," I say. "But I think I've figured out how to do it."

"Where do you plan to hunt?"

"Not far from here," I say. The patrol boat's searchlight plays through the windows again and I curl my lip at it.

Chloe lifts an eyebrow and stares at me.

I shrug. "You had to know, sooner or later we'd have to do something about that."

Chloe follows me down the circular staircase from the great room. She pauses at the second landing, where the bedrooms and the doors to the outside are, but follows me as I continue down the stairs. At the bottom, I head for the smallest holding cell.

"We're going out that way?" Chloe says. "Isn't that a little much?"

"No," I say, entering the cell. "I don't want any chance of us being seen." I yank up on the foot of the prison cot in the cell and grin as it moves upward, a system of hidden counterweights and levers below groaning into life, lifting the bed and the slab of stone floor beneath it into the air.

While my father designed most of the cells to hold human prisoners so he could fatten them up for later meals, he built the smallest cell strictly to use as a hidden passageway. I've shown it to Chloe before, taken her down to the treasure room below and to the passageway that leads to a hidden doorway in the bushes near the dock.

I step into the dark hole beneath the cot, motion for her to pass me and go down the steep stairs first. Once she does so, I follow, pulling the cot down over us, the floor clunking into place, everything turning dark around us, so black that even we can't see.

"This is way too melodramatic for me," Chloe says, giggling as she feels her way down the stairs.

It takes only a few minutes for us to negotiate the passageway to the door, and only a moment more to stand in the night air. "Okay, Mr. All Wise Dragon," Chloe says, "Now what?"

I reach for her blouse's top button, undo it and the next. "We're going swimming," I say, undressing her, taking my time, pulling off her blouse, cupping her breasts in my hands.

"After that," I say, kissing her. "I plan for us to hunt, maybe make love in our natural forms . . . You think that's a good plan?"

"A fine one," Chloe breathes, reaching for my clothes, pulling them off as I do the same to hers.

We remain in the bushes, pressing against each other, touching, kissing, until we hear the patrol boat approach, see its searchlight wash against our house. Once it cruises by our channel we cross the dock and slip into the water.

Chloe shivers at the coldness of it, says, "You just wanted to get me to go skinny dipping with you, didn't you?"

"You found me out," I say, concentrating on my body, willing it to change. Next to me Chloe does the same, both of us treading water as our skin ripples into scales, our wings and tails emerge.

"Now I'm going to be starving," Chloe mindspeaks.

My stomach growls and I nod in agreement. Those of my kind may be blessed with an ability to change shapes, but it comes with a cost. Even the slightest shift burns enough energy to bring on hunger. Changing form completely always leaves me famished.

Chloe swims at my side, sculling the water with her tail, both of us gliding through the light chop, our bodies mostly submerged, only the tops of our heads out of the water. To my delight, dark clouds crowd the evening sky, blocking almost all sight of the moon and stars.

We reach the end of our channel before the next circuit of the patrol boat and I mindspeak, *"I gave Claudia the evening patrol boat's numbers. She found it's based out of the Park Service's docks next to Homestead Bayfront Marina. If we fly low, I think we can follow and take them without anyone discovering us. Sound okay?"*

"Believe me," Chloe mindspeaks, *"even if I thought you were wrong, I'm too hungry now to argue about it."*

The patrol boat circles the island two more times before another patrol boat pulls alongside it. After a few minutes the first boat pulls away and angles off, speeding up, heading southwest toward Homestead.

As soon as both boats move away, Chloe and I break from the water, our wings almost slapping the wave tops as we strain to build speed without circling and gaining altitude. *"Why do we have to do it this way?"* Chloe mindspeaks, her breaths coming hard, her wings scooping air.

I breathe hard too, finding it tougher than I imagined. Watching the patrol boat's lights move away from us, I wonder if I, if we, have the strength to pursue it. I breathe deep, concentrate on flapping my wings, a little bit harder each time. *"We don't know what radar they're using or what airborne surveillance,"* I mindspeak. *"Just concentrate on building speed."*

Somehow we manage to find enough strength to start gaining on the patrol boat. Its lights no longer seem to be running away from us. By the time it reaches the Featherbed Channel that leads to the south end of the bay, we've drawn close enough to make out the silhouette of its dark form.

The boat slows to negotiate the channel and we slow down too, before we shoot past them. By the time the boat emerges from the channel and picks up speed, we're close enough to smell the gas stink of its exhaust and make out the forms of the two men aboard it.

"They're young and in good shape," I mindspeak. *"They've both been really nasty when they've stopped me, especially the jerk at the wheel. I think he's the one that keeps shining the light."*

"So he's the one you want to take, dear?"

I look around us, see no other lights anywhere near. Picking up speed, I say, *"If you'll take the other one at the same time."* Saliva floods my mouth. It's been far too long since we've hunted.

Pumping my wings and taking deep breaths, I surge forward, the wind buffeting me, the wet salt spray behind the boat stinging my eyes and coating my scales. For the first time in weeks I feel completely alive. How I wish I'd done this the first time the patrol boat glared its searchlight through our windows. I've tolerated too much, controlled my behavior for too long.

Chloe flies alongside me, matching my speed, racing ahead too, both of us rocketing toward the stern of the boat. Neither man glances back or shows any awareness of our approach.

We almost scrape our undersides on the stern of the boat as we shoot over it, Chloe taking her prey an instant before I take mine. My talons dig into my prey's shoulders, and I roar into the night and yank him from the boat. Both men scream into the dark for only a few moments before Chloe's and my sharp claws silence them forever.

The rich smell of fresh blood fills my nostrils and I find it hard to think of anything but my hunger. Rather than wait to land and let Chloe ritually select my first morsel, I tear a hunk of meat from the man's carcass as I fly and gulp it down. Chloe does the same.

The patrol boat, now unmanned, continues to race ahead. With no one to guide it, it curves away from its course, speeding so far away from us that we can follow it only by watching the movement of its lights. They stop near land an instant before the loud, wet crunch of the boat's impact with a sandbar carries across the bay.

"There's going to be an uproar about this tomorrow," Chloe mindspeaks.

"Tomorrow you and the children will be gone. That's all I care about." I mindspeak.

I turn and fly toward Sand Key, the island just to the south of Boca Chita. Chloe follows. *"The island we're going to has a lagoon in its middle—a little like ours but with its own beach,"* I mindspeak. *"The waterway leading to it is very shallow and almost completely hidden by the mangroves. Few humans ever try to go there."*

"Or we could take our prey home to the kids," Chloe mindspeaks. *"While it's still warm."*

"We have plenty of time for that," I mindspeak, skimming above the water, correcting course once I spot Sand Cut Channel in the night's gloom. Too shallow and treacherous for most boaters, the channel barely separates Boca Chita and Sand Key by more than fifty feet. I shoot into it only a foot above the water, a black shadow racing through the dark night, Chloe just inches behind my tail.

Halfway through the channel I bank hard to the right, flying between two large mangrove trees, barely managing to avoid clipping my wings on the tree branches that crowd the sides of the narrow channel that leads to Sand Key's lagoon.

Chloe, who almost loses me in the turn, grumbles, *"It would have been easier to head home."* But in a few moments the trees fall away, the water widens and we find ourselves flying over our own private lagoon.

I bank toward the wide beach at its eastern end. Slowing my approach, I flare my wings as soon as I reach the exposed sand, settle to the ground and lay my prey out beside me.

Coming in faster, my wife shoots past me. She banks in a tight turn before the beach ends, flaring her wings so sharply when she comes up beside me that she stalls and settles at the same time, spraying sand as she lands.

"Whoa!" I mindspeak.

"You're not the only one who can fly fancy," she mindspeaks. *"That felt good."*

I nod, look at my prey, nudge it with my snout.

"Oh no," Chloe mindspeaks. *"This time we do it right."* She makes a show of examining both carcasses, finally selecting a morsel she knows I'll like. I take it and eat it slowly. Then we both feed together, her left flank pressed against my right, my tail laid over hers, our mouths only inches apart.

Afterwards we doze together long enough for our feeding languor to abate. Chloe stirs first. *"Peter,"* she mindspeaks. *"Shouldn't we get going?"*

"Aren't you forgetting something?" I mindspeak.

"Do we have time?"

I frown. Motherhood has made Chloe much more cautious. Once, she wouldn't have asked such a question. Looking up I find the cloud-obscured, dull glow of the moon still high in the sky. *"We have plenty of time,"* I mindspeak, stroking her tail with mine.

"Here?" she mindspeaks.

In answer, I rise, flex my wings and mindspeak, *"Follow me."*

This time I lead her out the channel to the ocean, flying far from shore before I veer south. When we pass the Carrysfort Reef light, south of Elliott Key, I begin to spiral skyward. *"The attention is all back by Miami. No one's patrolling near the Keys,"* I mindspeak.

Chloe spirals past me and I'm sure she's just as relieved as I am to breathe the cold, clear air far above earth, to feel its bite as it passes through her nostrils. I chase after her.

But she dives and loops, dropping like a stone one moment, shooting toward the stars the next, turning over on her back, displaying herself to me. *"I thought you wanted me, Peter?"* she mindspeaks, dropping away. *"Did you forget how it feels inside me? Have you changed your mind?"*

I remember all too well how it feels to plunge into her warmth. I fold my wings and dive after her. Her laughter rings in my mind when she spirals away from me.

"I like it best in the air. Don't you?" Chloe mindspeaks, flying toward me, brushing against me as she passes, dropping away before I can hold her.

It's an old game, one we've played many times, yet it still makes my heart race. Roaring my frustration into the darkness, I chase her even though I know I won't catch her until she tires of teasing me.

Tonight the chase takes us skyward, far from any eyes on land, far above the clouds, into thin, cold air that barely holds up our wings. Chloe lets me catch up to her there and I drive myself into her, gasping at her moist heat, ignoring her claws as she digs them into me and her teeth as she seizes my throat in her jaws, driving claws and teeth deep enough to draw blood.

I roar at the pain, but rather than disengage, I fold my wings over hers, dig my claws into her scales and draw her close against me. Chloe roars too, bucking against each thrust.

Locked into our embrace, our bodies tight against each other, we fall through the night, out of the thin, cold air and down through the moist clouds. We only separate when the ground looms too close, breaking free and spiraling skyward again until we're high enough to engage again. We repeat this three more times until, finally, Chloe bellows and writhes against me in mid-fall, my orgasm coming just seconds after hers.

We fly close together, our wings almost grazing as we return to Sand Key. Feeding again, we rest just long enough to heal the wounds we've inflicted on each other, and then we take the remains of our prey and head back to our island.

Neither Chloe nor I say anything. We know what the next day will bring. Words won't lessen the pain of separating. For the time being we content ourselves with each others' presence and the delight Henri and Lizzie show when we wake them to feast with us.

12

The drum of helicopter rotors far too close to our house wakes us shortly after dawn. Chloe stretches in bed next to me, yawns out her words, "I told you they'd be upset."

I breathe deep, stretch too, wishing the helicopter gone, wishing we could loll in bed. Moving closer to Chloe, I lay my head on her bare breast, smell the sweet aroma of her skin. I marvel at how soft she is in her human form, and how much effort it took to drive my claws into her scales during our love-making in the night.

The helicopter passes overhead again.

"We might as well get up," Chloe says. "They'll be searching all day."

"Screw them," I say. "I'm sick of all their searches and patrols. I hate that you and the kids are going and I have to stay."

Chloe places a finger over my lips. "This time we did cause this, you know. They're just doing what they think they have to do. It'll all settle down once they find what's causing all the other disappearances. I'm sure Arturo and Ian will find a way for you to come join us in Jamaica soon."

"I hope so," I grumble.

By eleven I have all of Chloe's and the children's luggage secured on the Grady White. Chloe boards with Elizabeth and sits next to me. Ordinarily she'd ask to take the wheel, but today she voices no objection to my having the helm. I turn the ignition key, fire up both outboards and wait for Henri to cast off our lines and jump onboard.

As usual my son goes to the stern seat. I glance back at him as we motor out of our harbor. The boy's eyes are fastened on the retreating view of our island.

The disappearance of the two marine patrolmen has brought out a new swarm of patrol boats. By the time I reach the end of our channel, I've counted at least a dozen in view on the bay alone. Two planes and three helicopters patrol overhead.

We're stopped just yards from our channel entrance and stopped again on the other side of the bay near the approach to Dinner Key. I let out a breath as we finally glide toward our dock at Monty's. "At least they won't be bothering us here," I say.

Chloe nods.

"Papa, she's back!" Henri says. "Look!"

Chloe and I both turn, watch the dolphin as it swims toward our stern and then angles away from the outboards, passing the boat on my side, then diving out of sight. "Strange," Chloe says.

"Very," I say, turning my attention from the water, concentrating on pulling into our slip.

The dolphin reappears once I've docked and killed the engines. It swims past us and returns as I unload the baggage and help Chloe and Lizzie up onto the dock. It swims past again when Henri and I get off, then dives out of sight.

"Maybe she came to say good-bye to you," Chloe says to Henri as we walk to the car. The boy shrugs.

Because Ian chartered a private jet, a Lear, to take Chloe and the kids to Jamaica we don't have to brave the congestion and confusion of Miami International Airport. We drive instead to Tamiami, an executive airport on the southwest side of the county.

As soon as Henri sees the plane, and the pilot invites him to ride in the cockpit, he's ready to go. But Chloe and I linger, repeat our good-byes. We haven't spent more than a few hours apart since we've settled onto our island.

It takes all my self-control not to ask her to stay. I know going is best for the children, but I dread the thought of returning to empty rooms and empty halls. After Father died, before I left in search of my first wife, Elizabeth, I had more than my fill of loneliness, learned all I could bear of the emptiness of an unshared life.

I sit by the runway for a long time after the plane takes off, then drive to Dadeland Mall. Wandering its walkways, I can at least listen to snippets of conversation, feel the press of bodies, the closeness of other living, sentient beings.

"But we're too different, Peter," my father explained to me long ago. *"Humans can never provide the companionship we need. At best they can be favored pets. It's a pity there are so few of our kind. But somehow we manage to find each other."*

The sun already rides low in the sky by the time I return to the docks. I search the water, see no sign of the dolphin as I motor out of the marina. But just as I pass the NO WAKE sign, the creature breaks through the surface a dozen yards to my side. It reminds me too much of my son, and I jam my throttles forward and race away from it.

This time the patrol boats ignore me. I shoot across the bay at full speed. Letting the wind tear at me, the boat carom from wave to wave, I ignore the wet salt spray that coats me at each impact, try to think of nothing but steering the boat. When I reach my island's channel, I race through it too, seeing how close I can get to the jagged chunks of coral and stone that I know lurk beneath the water.

Max sits waiting on the dock. He neither barks nor wags his tail as I approach and dock. But he comes over to me when I get off the boat and stands close to my side. Though I've rarely ever touched him before, I stroke his massive head now. I understand how the beast feels.

Unwilling to venture yet into my empty house, I walk up to the garden and to Elizabeth's resting place. Max follows me and together we stand on the grass under the gumbo limbo tree and watch the sun begin to settle over the mainland.

After a few minutes, Max stiffens and looks away, toward the north end of the island. I follow his gaze, try to make out what has captured his attention. The dog gives out an almost inaudible *woof* and takes off running. I run after him, both of us scrambling through bushes, clambering up and down dunes.

When we break free of the brush, on the flat sand near the

Wayward Channel, I finally see what interests the dog. She's sitting on the flat rock jutting into the water, only her dark silhouette visible in the dying light of the sun. Max bays out in triumph as he draws near to her, and before he can reach her she slips away into the water.

The dog is busy sniffing where she sat on the stone by the time I arrive. I study the water, look for bubbles and see nothing. "It makes no sense," I say aloud, looking further out for any signs of a swimmer. But the water reveals nothing.

Max sniffs his way back to the shore, stops by the sand, his snuffling coming louder, his tail lashing from side to side. I go over and kneel beside him. Pushing his snout away, I search around in the sand with my hand, touching something metallic and round. I pick it up, brush it off and examine it. Even in the waning light, I can see it's a thin gold ring.

Running my finger over the surface I feel the faint resistance of something scratched or etched in the gold. But as much as I stare at the ring, I can't make out anything in the gloom. I head for the house, Max following behind me.

I throw on the lights as soon as I enter my room. Holding the ring up to the light I try to fit it on my small finger and smile when I find it too small even for that. I move closer to the light, study the ring again and gasp when I see the letters etched in the gold—*Delasangre*.

Holding the ring in the palm of my hand, I stare at it. I know the lettering all too well. I saw it every day until my mother died—on the ring she wore on her wedding finger whenever she was in her human form.

I make a fist around the ring and rush from the room. Dashing down the spiral staircase, taking stairs two at a time, I try to think why such a ring would be lying in the sand on that part of the island. I make my way to the small cell, yank up on the cot and rush down the steps without bothering to pull the cot back down.

At the bottom, I feel for the light switch, throw it on and walk over to the steel-plated treasure-room door. Thick chains fastened by a modern, stainless steel combination padlock secure the door. I transfer the ring to my pocket, grasp the padlock in one hand and dial the combination with the other. But I miss the combination on my first two tries, only getting it right the third time, after I stand still a few moments, thinking only of my breathing and the combination.

After the padlock snaps open I rip the chains out of the way, throw the door open, click on the light and rush to the jewelry box my father stored in the far corner of the room, near the stacks of silver and gold bullion. After we buried my mother, he'd brought me to this room so I could see where he placed her jewelry. *"I don't want to bury it with her, Henri,"* he'd said. *"I want it where I can look at it when I want. After I die, save it for your daughter or your son's daughter. That's what would please your mother best."*

I breathe deep as I undo the box's hasp. I can't open the jewelry box without thinking of my mother's touch, feeling her presence. Inside are compartments holding gold and silver chains, and diamond, ruby and emerald earrings, but the ring sits alone in one velvet compartment at the top.

Taking the other ring out of my pocket, I pick up my mother's. Hers is larger and less delicate, but the lettering of *Delasangre* looks as though it were etched by the same hand.

I sigh and put both rings in my mother's jewelry box. Max pads up behind me, shakes his head and lets out a snort. I turn, laugh and grab his head, scratch him behind his ears. "I don't know, boy," I say. "Your guess is as good as mine."

In the evening, when Chloe calls, I listen as she tells me about the flight and their drive into the interior to Bartlet House. "Oh, and I tried to call Mum but there was no answer," she says and giggles. "I think she made good on her promise to throw out the satellite phone."

Toward the end of the conversation, I say, "I saw the girl again. This time on the side of the island, on the rock at the Wayward Channel. But she was gone before I could get to her or really see what she looked like." Then I tell her about the ring.

"How strange," Chloe says. "Do you think your mother or father lost it there?"

"I have absolutely no idea," I say.

·

13

Chloe and I talk by phone every evening and every morning. While we discuss most things, I say nothing about my new habit of wandering from room to room, touching her things and the kids', sleeping sometimes in Henri's bed and sometimes in Lizzie's. I do tell her that Max has become my constant companion.

Not surprisingly, Henri and Lizzie seem to be adjusting to life in Jamaica with hardly any problems. "They miss you, dear," Chloe says. "But between horseback riding and fishing with Granny and visiting Cockpit Country, their days are pretty full."

With my first deposition still a month away, I've little desire to visit the mainland. I busy myself tending Chloe's garden and doing the routine maintenance the house and its machines can always use. Another boater disappears, but no more after that. Soon the number of patrol boats lessens again.

I look in the harbor every day to see if Henri's dolphin has chosen to make an appearance. But it never does. I always make sure to check the rock jutting into Wayward Channel and the sandbar at the end of our channel for any sign of the girl. But I never see her either.

Ian calls me three weeks after Chloe's departure. "We need you to come in for a practice deposition, Peter," he says.

I sigh and say, "Weren't you supposed to have the damn suit quashed?"

"We're working on it. And Arturo and Claudia are working on Pepe Santos too," he says before I can ask. "Toba's dating the guy now, for Christ's sake. We couldn't get any closer to him unless you adopted him."

"So what good is it doing?" I say.

"He's a stubborn guy. Relax. We just need to find the right leverage."

Frowning, I say, "Well, find it already."

But I smile when it's time to leave the island for the practice deposition. I've lived alone too long already and done too little with my time. Besides, Chloe's informed me that she and the kids are leaving to spend the next week with her parents at their home in Morgan's Hole in Cockpit Country. Knowing I won't be able to talk on the phone with her magnifies my loneliness.

Just kicking the motors alive on my Grady White makes my grin widen. Max barks as I pull away from the dock, and for a moment I consider going back and bringing him along. I shake my head, thinking what Ian Tindall's reaction would be if I brought the beast to our office.

Besides, I know the poor dog would be miserable in the boat on a day like this. While the sky is mostly clear and a brilliant blue, a brisk north wind blows over the bay, churning up waves and white froth.

A blast of wind hits the Grady White as soon as I motor out of the harbor. I welcome the challenge after my weeks of inactivity, steer the boat through the chop as it tries to throw me out of the channel and crash me into the rocks.

I'm so intent on helming the boat I don't notice the dolphin until I'm almost on top of it. It shoots a breath out of its blowhole and kicks away from me. I laugh when it returns, cresting a wave just a few yards to the side of the boat. Like it or not, I know it will be my companion as long as it wants. As rough as the water is, I've little chance of outrunning it.

The dolphin stays with me all the way across the bay, disappearing from sight one moment, reappearing dozens of yards away the next. But when I get to Monty's marina, it dives out of sight. As much as I search the water, I can't find any sign of it.

If anything can make someone hate lawyers a deposition can. Ian starts as soon as I sit in his office. "Remember. Just answer the questions. Never volunteer anything."

"Okay."

He looks at a notepad and says, "Did you know Maria Santos?"

"Not really. She waited on my table once. She gave me her phone number."

"No, Peter, you don't have to volunteer about the phone number. Just answer the questions." He clears his throat. "Are you in the habit of dining alone."

"I was when I was single."

"Maria told friends she gave you her phone number."

"She did."

"Did you call her?"

"No. I threw her number away."

"Wasn't she attractive enough for you?"

"She was very attractive, but I wasn't interested."

"Did waitresses often give you their numbers?"

"Some did, but I didn't call them either. I'm a rich man. It's hard to trust strangers' motives."

"Good," Ian says. "What did you do that evening?"

"I went home, read and went to bed."

"Can anyone verify that?"

"No."

"Did you own a Chris-Craft speedboat or one that looked like it?"

"Never. I owned a Grady White, the same as I do now."

"And you never met Maria Santos anywhere at any time other than at dinner that night?"

"Never."

"You do realize she disappeared only a few weeks after the night she waited on you?"

"Yes," I say.

"Did you have anything to do with that disappearance?"

"No."

The questions churn up memories of her unfortunate death. It takes all my self-control not to sigh. When Tindall insists we review the questions again and again I begin to glare at him.

Finally, just before I'm about to lash out at him, he says, "We're doing this for practice. So you can be prepared. I'm on your side, Peter. Remember, I really am."

But still we go over the same ground for hours more. By the

time I get back to the boat the late-afternoon sky has turned gloomy, dark clouds scudding by overhead. I no longer have any great desire to spend time fighting the wind and waves. Ian's practice deposition has battered me enough.

I toy with the thought of staying on land for the night, taking a room at the Grand Bay or the Ritz. But then I remember Max. The last thing I want is to leave the poor dog waiting all night on the dock.

This time the dolphin shows itself just after I reach the last marker in the channel. I smile at it and then turn my attention to steering through the waves. When I look for it again, I see no sign of it.

The sky darkens even more as I cross the bay. Drawing near my island, I glance behind me, see the few final rays of light slowly sinking away and put on my running lights. While I can see perfectly well in light like this, I certainly don't want some dim-eyed fool to run into me.

A girl or small woman jumps up on the sandbar by the entrance to the channel and begins to wave, her left hand open, something, maybe a thin stick, clasped in her right fist. I squint but I'm still too far away to make out just what it is or to see her features or expression. While I hear no shouting, from the way she waves her arms, I assume she needs help.

I look around. Seeing no sign of any other boats, I slow my motors and steer toward her. She keeps waving, beckoning me forward until I'm near to running aground. At that close distance, even in the dusk, I can make out some of her features, her long hair and small breasts—the fact that she's naked.

Before I can shout out to her, she dives into the water, cutting it so cleanly that she leaves barely a ripple, and starts swimming toward the boat. Yanking the wheel so the Grady White turns sideways to the wind, I throw the Yamahas into neutral.

Waves immediately begin to batter the boat's windward side and push it southward. I shrug. If the girl swims as well as it appears she can, I calculate that it will take her only a few moments to reach me.

Making my way to the windward hull, I hope she knows

enough to approach from this direction. If she swims up on the leeward side, the waves will drive the boat over her.

A large breaker slaps the Grady White, pours water into the cockpit. A second wave follows, spraying salt foam everywhere, stinging my eyes, blinding me for an instant. And then a small hand, still holding a stick, reaches above the coaming of the boat.

Somehow the girl manages to take hold of the boat's side without losing the stick. She raises her thin left arm and reaches up for help. I rush forward, putting out my right hand, close enough now to see the flat shape of her stick, how it tapers to a sharp point on one end. "Why don't you just drop that damned thing?" I say. "It's only in the way."

Saying nothing, she grabs my right hand with her left. I gasp at her viselike grip and shift my stance, my weight on my rear leg in anticipation of lifting most of her weight. But when I yank her up it's like lifting air. The lack of resistance throws my balance off and I gasp and stumble backward as the small woman flies out of the water, her shape beginning to shift, her face contorting, her jaws opening, showing off her growing fangs.

She falls with me, reaching for my throat with her teeth. I try to shove her away but she growls and thrusts her stick forward, burying its pointed end in my midriff. A hot pain burns into me and I howl. Adrenaline jolts through me. Shifting my shape too, I open my mouth, my jaws expanding, my teeth still growing as I lock my mouth on hers.

I land on my back on the cockpit floor, the girl on top of me, her jaws opening and trying to close, my teeth blocking hers, both of us bleeding, the smell of our blood mixing with the damp ocean air around us. Unsure what type of creature has attacked me, I continue to change shape, my clothes ripping apart as I grow, the other creature writhing, pushing her stick deeper into me, trying to find any advantage.

When I reach my full size, the creature suddenly stops struggling, opens its jaws and goes limp. Standing, I shove it away and watch it fall to the deck in front of me. My eyes locked on it, I extend my right claw, ready to rip into it should it even twitch. Grasping her stick with my left claw, I yank it out of my body and throw it forward, out of the her reach.

Blood gushes from the wound. Stifling a groan, I concentrate on stopping its flow. Once it diminishes, I turn my mind to healing that wound before I begin to heal all the puncture wounds the creature's bites have inflicted on me, my claw still ready, my eyes still focused on the creature lying before me.

Far smaller than I, its scales a dull black-gray, it gazes back with emerald-green eyes and mindspeaks, *"Hello, cousin."*

14

Another wave slams into the side of the boat, forcing it still further southward. I look up, drop my mouth open when I see how far we've been driven from my island. Glaring at the small creature now lying on the cockpit floor in front of me, my heart still pounding from the attack, I flex my sore jaws and consider tearing it to pieces.

Surely it wouldn't take any great effort. It looks something like one of my kind, but the pitiful thing barely measures half my size. Its wings look so small that I wonder if they're deformed. Even its scales appear deficient—too smooth and too close to the body to provide proper armament.

"Why shouldn't I kill you?" I mindspeak.

"I am no threat to you," she mindspeaks.

"No threat? You attacked me!"

She dismisses my words with a slight motion of her right claw. *"Only to confirm what you were."*

"What about all the other boats? Did you attack them too?"

The creature nods.

"Are there others of you?"

"Not here."

The boat shudders as yet another wave collides with it. If I don't do something soon I know it will be driven onto rocks or pushed aground or, even worse, noticed by a patrol boat. After all the centuries of my family protecting its identity, I'm not about to let some puny creature cause us to be discovered.

"We have to get underway again," I mindspeak. *"I need to change into my human form. You too. But stay where you are. If you attack me again, you'll die. Quickly. Understand?"*

The creature nods and I turn away from it, shifting to my

human form as I rush to the boat's wheel. Throwing the throttles forward, I grab the wheel and yank it over, steering away
from the waves. The boat wallows for a few seconds, then ac-
celerates into a sharp turn, going up on its side for a moment,
straightening and shooting south.

We strike something underneath us, a shudder running
through the boat, the port Yamaha, pitching forward, its motor
howling. Yelling, "Shit! Shit! Shit!" I kill its throttle, hoping
we've just sheared a prop, that the drive shaft isn't bent.

The boat slows but continues forward, the starboard Yamaha
still howling at full speed. I cut back on its throttle a little, so as
not to put too much strain on the one remaining motor, and try
to turn the wheel to the right, to circle back to the north. With
one motor now deadweight, I find I have to tug on it, hard, to
have any effect.

Still the Grady White turns, slower than I'd like, starting a
long loop that will take us northward, back to my island's channel. The boat slices through a wave, and a blast of salt spray
showers me, coating my naked flesh. Instantly chilled by the
wind, I shiver and turn, glancing at the tattered remnants of my
clothes on the cockpit floor and the girl in her human form,
naked, sitting cross-legged near them, smiling as she returns
my stare.

"You said cousin?" I say.

She shrugs as if she doesn't understand. *"Can't you hear
me?"* I mindspeak.

*"I can hear but I don't understand very well. At home, we
only mindspeak."*

"But you said you were my cousin?" I mindspeak.

"Yes," she mindspeaks. *"I am."*

I doubt I've ever seen a paler woman. Her ghost-white body
glistens from the salt spray, seems almost luminescent in the
gloom. Wet, long black hair hugs her scalp, hangs halfway
down her back, a few stray wisps plastered to her front, tracing
dark lines from her long, thin neck over the gentle curves of
breasts too small and too firm to sag. One strand curls around a
crinkled, light pink nub of a nipple made tight by the cold.

I shake my head. She may be of my people, but even in her
natural form I could hardly see any resemblance to my family.

Her human form seems even more distant. While her round face and almond-shaped emerald-green eyes give her an exotic, strangely oriental look—one that would attract me if I were single—almost everything about her seems streamlined.

Her ears lie flat against her skull. Her nose barely protrudes, her nostrils showing as hardly more than fleshy slits. When she opens her mouth or smiles, her pale lips grow full and inviting. But they flatten into raised lines when her mouth closes. Except for the hair on her head, her body's hairless—no eyebrows, no eyelashes, no pubic hair. Only the mature curves of her body assure me she's not a prepubescent girl.

That such a thin, little thing, a few inches less than five feet tall, would dare attack someone my size amazes me. But then I need only remember the strong grasp of her hand and the pain she inflicted on me. She may look young and delicate, but I've already seen her true nature.

"We both need clothes," I mindspeak. *"We can't have a patrol boat find us like this. There are sweatshirts and sweatpants stowed with the foul weather gear in the locker below."* I point to the hatch leading into the boat's cabin. *"My wife's will be large on you, but it's better than nothing."*

She returns, Chloe's sweatshirt hanging on her, the neck large enough to show part of her collarbone, the sleeves rolled up so many times they look like large rings of cloth wrapped around her arms. Chloe's sweatpants fit even worse, and the girl has to keep tugging them up with one hand as she hands me my clothes with the other.

"I do not see how you can stand wearing these," she mindspeaks as I step into my sweatpants and pull them up. I throw on the sweatshirt and sigh at the warmth that envelops me.

"Weren't you cold?" I mindspeak.

She shrugs. *"Nothing that diving under the water would not have fixed."*

Another wave tries to knock the Grady White off course, and I tug the wheel over a few inches, push the throttle forward just a touch until I hear the Yamaha's pitch increase. *"Under the water?"* I mindspeak. *"Don't you think it's time to tell me what's going on here? What makes you think you're my cousin?"*

"Not a first cousin." The girls smiles, sits on the seat by my side, where Chloe usually sits. *"My father named me Lorrel. You are Peter DelaSangre, the son of Don Henri, are you not?"*

I look ahead toward the dark shadow of Caya DelaSangre, the island Don Henri bequeathed to me. *"What do you know about my father?"* I mindspeak.

"Apparently more than you do." Lorrel lets out a trill of laughter.

Frowning, I glare at her. *"If you know about the DelaSangres, then you know we're not a family to be toyed with,"* I mindspeak. *"Don Henri would have killed you for that attack."*

"Obviously his son would not," she mindspeaks. *"Do not be so sure you cannot be defeated. We both come from strong stock."*

"But not the same stock," I mindspeak. We come up to the entrance to my channel and I tug the wheel over, steer toward the island. The waves fight me, and it takes all my concentration to keep the boat in the channel, away from the rocks. With only one engine left, I'm keenly aware of the need to keep it running. I've little desire to leave the boat unmanned and adrift.

"The same stock," Lorrel mindspeaks. *"Did you not find my great grandmother's ring?"*

"Your great grandmother's?" I stare at her for a long moment, then finally nod.

Lorrel grins at my reaction. *"My father, Mowdar, your half-brother's son, gave it to me and told me to bring it to you."*

I shake my head, shake it a second time. *"My mother is dead. I was her only child. My father is dead too. Before he died he told me all his other children had died long before him. I never had a half-brother. . . ."*

"Not one he told you about," Lorrel mindspeaks, *"Mowdar says you Undrae like to pretend—just because you won the Great War—that none of us exist anymore. But he says he has seen and killed Thryll himself, and he thinks if you search long enough and far enough you can find still find even a few Zal. . . ."*

Something splashes in the water near us and Lorrel turns her head toward the sound, studies the dark water for a moment and then turns back toward me. *"All of Don Henri's other Undrae children and all of his Undrae wives died just as he said. But he had another wife too, one of a different kind."*

"What kind was that?"

"Have you not guessed?" The girl mindspeaks. She holds up her right hand and spreads her fingers wide.

I gape at the thin membrane that forms a web between each of her spread fingers.

Lorrel trills another laugh and mindspeaks one word, *"Pelk."*

15

That the people of another castryll still survive doesn't amaze me. Chloe's said it was possible. Even humans seem to keep finding Stone Age tribes of their kind in jungles all over the world. But my father, Don Henri DelaSangre, had few enough good words for any of the others of our own kind. I shake my head, trying to picture him taking a mate from another castryll, especially a seagoing one like the Pelk.

"The ring proves nothing," I mindspeak. *"Anybody can make a ring."*

"But is it not inscribed in the same script as your father's other wives' rings were? Who would know how to inscribe it but your father?"

A large fish jumps, flashing silver in the night before it splashes back into the water just a few yards from the boat.

Again Lorrel's head swivels in the direction of the noise. This time she gulps and mindspeaks, *"Would you like to eat? I can gather some fish—in only a few minutes—and meet you at the dock."*

I shake my head.

"Has changing not made you hungry?"

All of our activity, the shapechanging, the fighting and the healing has left my stomach so empty it aches. But I've little desire for fish, and less for the girl to leave my sight. *"I have food at the house,"* I mindspeak, saliva flooding my mouth at the mention of it. *"We can eat after we dock."*

Yet another fish jumps. Lorrel gazes at the water, and for a moment I think she's going to dive off the boat. Instead she crosses her arms and huffs out a sigh.

*   *   *

How I wish Chloe and the children were home waiting to greet me. But at the dock only Max awaits me. He begins to bark even before the Grady White enters the harbor, setting off a cacophony of barks, yelps and howls among the rest of the island's dog pack.

Lorrel stiffens at the sounds, stares toward the dark shore and moves a little closer to me. She relaxes only after I let out a sharp, shrill whistle and the dogs fall silent. *"They're only dogs,"* I mindspeak.

The girl nods, mindspeaks, *"I do not know dogs."*

Max barks, wags his tail at her when I pull up to the dock, but she looks away from him and stays seated until I've docked and tied off the boat. After I beckon for her to come off the Grady White, she stops to pick up her stick and then steps onto the dock, making sure I'm between her and the dog.

I look at the stick and hold my hand out.

"I told you I no longer have any reason to attack you," she mindspeaks.

But I keep my hand out until she hands it to me.

The last of the sun has gone and I stop by a switch box at the bottom of the steps and throw on the outside lights. Lorrel's large eyes widen even more as she looks around. She runs one hand over the rough coral wall of the house but says nothing as we go up the wide stone steps to the veranda.

I stop by one of the oversize oak doors that open onto the veranda, point to it. *"We can go in this way through my bedroom."*

The girl nods, follows me as I open the door, enter and throw on the lights. Humming to herself, barely loud enough for me to hear, she surveys the room, then walks over to the bed and tests it with one hand while she pulls up on her loose sweatpants with the other. *"You sleep here?"* she mindspeaks.

"Yes," I mindspeak, going to the closet while Lorrel waits, humming random notes that somehow weave into a song unlike any I've heard before. I find myself straining to listen as I rummage through Chloe's belts, finally finding one I think can be cinched tight enough to hold up Lorrel's pants.

She tests the bed again. *"And you like lying on this?"*

I nod, sit on the bed, put the stick down next to me and beckon for her to come over, stand facing me. When she approaches, her hum intensifies slightly in pitch and I notice her salt-laced scent for the first time. I breath it in and smile. It reminds me of the smell of the ocean on a clear, sunny day.

Lorrel stands still, turns quiet while I put the belt around her waist and tighten it. After I finish, she plucks at her clothes and mindspeaks, *"Would it not be easier if I took all this off?"*

Again I wish my wife hadn't left. If Chloe were here I could hand the girl off to her, let her contend with all of Lorrel's questions, let her deal with Lorrel's obvious preference for nudity. I shake my head. *"Not right now,"* I mindspeak. *"Let's go upstairs and get something to eat. You're the hungry one, aren't you?"*

Lorrel swallows and nods.

I pick up the stick, turn it over in my hands. A little more than a foot long, dark gray, mostly flat but curved on each side to a sharp edge, it has neither the feel, nor the look, nor the heft of wood. I grin when I realize what it is. *"You made this from a swordfish sword, didn't you?"*

"Not me," Lorrel mindspeaks. *"I am not permitted yet. Only the old ones can."*

Something that looks like a translucent, deflated balloon is tied to the thick end of the sword with monofilament fishing line. I touch it with a finger. *"And this is?"* I mindspeak.

Lorrel looks at it and sighs. *"Please let us eat first and then I will tell you what I can."*

In the great room, I put the sword down on the kitchen counter and take three steaks from the freezer. Lorrel stays close, stares as I put each in the microwave, one by one, to cook the chill from the meat. She crinkles her forehead when I leave all three in plates on the counter while I get silverware and napkins and set the table.

But the girl sits where I indicate and waits for me to bring her food to her. I put her plate in front of her and place another on the floor for Max. As he attacks and devours his meat, I go back to the kitchen for mine. By the time I return with it and sit down across from the girl, he's already licking his now empty plate.

Picking up my knife and fork I begin to cut a piece of near-raw meat. Lorrel stares at the blood on her plate and makes no move toward her meat. Spearing my piece with the fork, I mindspeak, *"Go ahead. Eat."*

The girl ignores her silverware and picks up her steak. Blood drips from it, splattering on her plate as she takes a huge bite from the meat. Barely chewing, she gulps it down, takes a second bite and gulps it too. I chew mine more slowly, savoring the richness of the meat, breathing in the blood smell that blossoms around us.

Lorrel stops eating, holds the meat up in one hand and mindspeaks, *"What is this?"*

I take another piece. *"It's beef."* She makes no expression, so I mindspeak, *"You know, cow?"*

She shakes her head. *"I know seacow. This does not taste like seacow."*

"Not manatee," I mindspeak. *"Cow, like in bulls and cows."* I put one finger up on each side of my head, like horns, and moo.

Lorrel looks at me as if I've lost my mind. *"Show me where you find them. I have never seen a beef,"* she mindspeaks.

"Never mind that for now," I mindspeak. *"Is it good?"*

She nods.

"Then just eat."

After dinner, after I've cleaned up, I go to one of the two leather reclining chairs that Chloe's bought and placed near the fireplace facing the television. Leaning back, my feet swinging up as the bottom of the chair raises into a footstool, I motion for Lorrel to do the same.

Lorrel approaches her chair slowly, as if it were a living thing. Finally she sits, shimmying back, looking almost as small and lost in the chair as Henri does when he sits in it. She looks at me and smiles. *"My people live very differently than you."*

I grin, look from her face, to her small hands, her equally small bare feet and her tiny webbed toes, and mindspeak, *"We've eaten. It's time now for you to tell me what's going on."*

"My father, Mowdar, sent me to find you. . . ." Lorrel stops, grimaces, hacks out a cough and then another. *"Sorry,"* she

mindspeaks, wiping her mouth with her sweatshirt sleeve, leaving a red smear of fresh blood on it.

Sitting up, I point to her sleeve. *"Is that from dinner?"*

She looks at me. *"No. This is not from beef. Eating opened one of the wounds you gave me. It is nothing. . . ."*

"Can't you heal?"

"Of course I can!" Lorrel mindspeaks, daubing her mouth with her sleeve again, showing me a new, smaller smear. *"But I, we, are not Undrae. We heal differently than you. And I have been gone from my srrynn for too long."*

"Srrynn?" I mindspeak.

"Yes," she mindspeaks. *"We are all together, many of us—like a family. Everyone in a srrynn protects each other, like the dolphins do, the way they gather in pods. If we were there now I would already be healed."*

"How?" I mindspeak.

Lorrel shrugs. *"We draw strength from each other."*

"Are there many srrynns?"

"Not since Atalan." Lorrel gazes across the room toward the windows and the dark night outside. *"Another day is gone,"* she mindspeaks almost to herself. She turns to me. *"I am to find you and bring you back. Mowdar will explain everything when you meet him. We must go very soon."*

I glare at her. *"What makes you think I'd just leave with you? First you attack me, and then you barely explain anything other than claiming to be my cousin. And then you tell me we have to leave, soon. To where? How?"*

The girl looks down, the way that Henri does when I scold him. In Chloe's far too large clothes, she looks a bit like a child caught playing grown-up. I find it hard to keep a frown on my face. Leaning back in my chair again, I mindspeak, *"No one's leaving for anywhere. Not until I know what's going on."*

"Everyone in our srrynn must do as Mowdar instructs. You can ask me what you want, but I may not tell you certain things."

"Didn't you say Mowdar is your father?" I mindspeak.

She nods. *"Many of us are his children."*

"Where is your srrynn?"

"In the islands across the Gulf Stream. I can take you there, but I am not allowed to disclose any more."

"Can you say why you aren't allowed?"

Lorrel shakes her head.

I sigh. *"What can you tell me?"*

"I left my srrynn months ago. It took me days to reach here."

"Days?" I mindspeak. Assuming Lorrel meant her srrynn lived in the Bahamas, I can't imagine why it took her so long to travel. I've often ranged over the islands during my hunts. Not even flying to and from the furthest has ever taken me a full evening.

"Unlike you Undrae, we can only fly short distances," she mindspeaks. *"I swam. And then I looked for you on this island. But you and your family only showed yourselves in human form. I watched you and followed you for months. I could not be sure what we had been told was true. . . . Not until a few weeks ago when I saw two adult Undrae flying from the island in the night."*

The girl shakes her head. *"Even then I worried whether I would ever find the opportunity to reveal myself to you. Mowdar insisted only you could be approached. He gave me the ring so I could prove our relationship."*

"You said you were told about me?"

Lorrel nods. *"We were told you lived on your father's island."*

"Who told you?"

The girl shrugs. *"Only Mowdar can say. You will learn that when we are with the srrynn."*

"And if I refuse to go with you?" I mindspeak.

"I am afraid you cannot." She smiles. *"You cannot even afford much delay. Believe me, I would not mind staying here a little longer. Ordinarily we eat mostly fish and dolphin. I have never had so much human meat as I've had in the last few months. I have come to like it very much."*

Sitting up, I turn toward her. Her foray into my territory has brought only tumult and trouble. Had she never come and never killed so many humans, my wife and children would be with me now. I ball my fists, growl my words. *"I could just kill you, you know."*

Lorrel shrugs. *"That would be unfortunate for you."* She looks toward the kitchen counter, points at the swordfish sword. *"You asked me about that before. Why don't you get it?"*

Anger flushes through me. *"You're hardly in the position to either threaten me or suggest what I should do,"* I mindspeak, stifling the impulse to jump from my chair and rip her to little pieces, but getting up nonetheless, standing over her, glowering at her.

The girl looks up, shows no sign of any distress. *"This brings me no pleasure,"* she mindspeaks. *"I am only a messenger. Save your anger for Mowdar—don't waste it on me. If you want to confront him, come with me now."*

She stands, stares into my eyes. *"If you will not get the sword, let me. I want you to understand what you face before you decide to refuse my father."*

I nod and she walks to the counter. As she picks up the sword, she mindspeaks, *"Your women mix potions, do they not?"*

"Yes."

"We mix potions too, and other things," Lorrel mindspeaks. She points to the limp, translucent balloon at the sword's thick end. *"This is the air bladder of a fish."* Unwrapping the line that holds it to the sword, she smiles. *"And this is fishing line. Once we wove our own line from strands of seagrass, but fishermen lose so much of this. . . ."*

The line finishes unraveling and Lorrel deposits it and the bladder on the counter, holds the sword point up to the light and stares with one eye through the thick end. She nods and brings it to me. *"Take it. Look through the thick end. Point it at the light,"* she mindspeaks.

Doing as she says, I see the thin pinprick of light that travels through a small shaft in the center of the sword and runs from its point to its thick end. *"It's hollow,"* I mindspeak.

"Yes, it is," Lorrel mindspeaks, taking the sword back from me. *"There is a blowfish that our people know how to find. In its head it has a tiny sac of poison, dangerous for other fish but not too much so for beings like us. But if you grind up red coral and mix the two . . ."* She looks into my eyes. *"You end up with a slow-acting poison that can kill even the biggest Undrae.*

That is what I had in the fish bladder. That is what is now in you."

I suck in a breath. Running my right hand over the now-healed spot on my midriff where her sword had pierced, I shake my head. How could this insignificant creature have the power to kill me? How could I die without seeing or talking to my wife and children again?

"Undrae, you are not dead yet," Lorrel mindspeaks. *"I told you it is slow-acting. You will not feel it until the third day. Then it will be as if a fire erupted where I stabbed you. The pain will grow outward from there until every part of your body is on fire. Without the antidote, no one lives to see the fourth day."*

Walking over to the windows facing the ocean, I sigh and stare at the few scattered boat lights traveling on the dark water. *"May I assume you have the antidote?"* I mindspeak.

"Yes, but not here." Lorrel walks over to me, stands next to me, staring out too. She points in the direction of Bimini. *"I left it near Bimini. But only one dose. It is temporary. It only lasts three days."*

Turning, I glare at her.

She shrugs. *"Mowdar wanted to make sure you would come with me. We have all the antidote you may ever need at my sr-rynn."*

Far out at sea, a cruise ship passes by heading south, its many rows of lights cheerfully glimmering in the dark. I watch it pass and envy its passengers and their carefree vacations.

The ship could easily be traveling to Jamaica. If so they'll come closer to my family than I can. I wish I could talk to Chloe, discuss all this with her. But she's unavailable by phone and more than a thousand miles out of mindthought range. Not that I see any options anyway. If all is as Lorrel says, I have no choice but to accompany her to her srrynn.

I turn, go to the phone and dial the number for my home in Jamaica, just in case Chloe hasn't left yet. But the phone rings until the answering machine comes on. I listen to Chloe's taped voice and then say, "It's me. If you can't get me when you return, call Claudia. Love you."

Hanging up, turning toward Lorrel, I mindspeak, *"When did you want to leave?"*

"Now. If we swim without resting we can be well past Bimini by morning."

I look at her, shake my head. *"I'm the one with poison in my veins. I understand how little time I have. But it makes no sense to swim when we can travel so much quicker in my Grady White. I can repair the motor tomorrow morning, straighten out a few things and still get us to Bimini by mid-afternoon."*

"We do not need your boat. It cannot take us to my srrynn. We should leave now. You need to drink your antidote as soon as possible. . . ."

"Not really," I mindspeak. *"You said it would take three days until I felt it, didn't you?"*

She nods.

I grin. *"Then we have plenty of time—at least two and a half days until I feel the poison. We can go over to Bimini tomorrow, get the antidote and wait until I feel the first pains. I certainly won't swallow anything you give me until I'm sure I have to."*

"But," Lorrel mindspeaks, arguing with me until I tire of it and turn my back on her.

I snap my fingers at Max and walk toward the door. The dog gets up and pads after me. *"I'm going to bed,"* I mindspeak to the girl. *"If you want, you can sleep here or in one of my kid's rooms."*

Lorrel says nothing more, follows us down the spiral staircase to the second landing. I take her to Henri's bedroom and open the door. She looks at the bed inside and mindspeaks, *"In our srrynn we sleep on beds of seagrass."*

I frown at the difficult creature, wonder why she can't just take what's offered. *"In my family we sleep on regular beds. But others of our kind prefer beds of hay. We keep our infants on such beds. Fortunately for you, my daughter, Lizzie, still has hers."*

Leading the girl to my daughter's room, I open the door and point at the hay piled neatly in the corner. *"Will that do?"* I mindspeak.

Lorrel nods, walks into the room, humming again, the tune loud enough now that I can hear the harmonics of it. It makes me think of the throat singing they practice in the far east or the drone of an Australian diggery-doo. *"What are you humming?"* I mindspeak.

"An old one taught me this song. Do you like it?" she mindspeaks, humming even louder.

I listen and nod, a smile growing on my face.

In the middle of the room she turns, pulling off her sweatshirt and undoing her belt. Her loose sweatpants fall, crumpling at her feet. She steps out of them and examines her ghost-white body for a long moment, humming, the tune softer now, the notes undulating as she touches herself with both hands, her nipples blushing pink as she passes her palms over them.

Turning her attention to me, she smiles as if I had just walked in on her, her grin almost a leer. *"I like my human form,"* she mindspeaks. She saunters back to the doorway and, still humming, she stands in front of me—as close as she can without touching.

The fresh, saltwater smell of her envelopes me as she mindspeaks, *"I wouldn't mind sleeping in your bed with you. It might be fun."*

In my single days I might have chanced it, if she hadn't attacked me and if she hadn't filled me with poison. But as tempting as she is, nothing could make me betray Chloe now. Forcing myself to step back, I mindspeak, *"I have a wife."*

"I know," Lorrel mindspeaks starting to step forward.

I put my hands on her bare shoulders and stop her from coming closer. *"We mate for life."*

Lorrel trills out a laugh. *"We Pelk don't."*

16

In the morning, I smile when I go to the dock and find the Yamaha needs only minor repair. By the time Lorrel appears, coming down the coral steps from the veranda, just as naked as she'd been the night before, I've already replaced the propeller's shear pin and stocked the boat with a cooler full of food.

Max jumps to his feet and barks once, his tail slashing from side to side, and Lorrel stops at the bottom step and points at the dog. *"Do I need to worry about him?"*

I look at Max, his wagging tail and laugh. *"Only if you're afraid of being licked."*

"I was hungry, so I woke up," the girl mindspeaks, walking toward me. Her black hair, dry now, flows down her neck, some billowing down her front, reaching her mid-stomach, the rest cascading down her back. Her emerald eyes blaze in contrast to her pale face and trim white body.

Turning away, I busy myself undoing the boat's starboard gas cap, just as glad not to look at her, more conscious than ever of the three weeks that have already passed since Chloe's departure. *"After I gas up the tanks, I'll go upstairs and warm up some steaks,"* I mindspeak.

"No. No more beef," she mindspeaks. She walks past me, brushing one hand against my shoulder—the way Chloe sometimes does—and then dives, cutting the water with only the slightest splash as it parts to accept her.

I watch the small ring of ripples she leaves expanding on the surface, the pale image of her body shimmering in the clear water as she swims away. When she's no longer in sight I turn my attention to fueling the Grady White, going to the drums of gas, switching on the pump and dragging the fuel line back to the boat.

Something splashes in the harbor and I look out at the water expecting to see Lorrel. But I find the small gray dolphin instead. It swims toward me, scooting between the Grady White and the Donzi, shooting half out of the water so its belly rests on the dock. I look at its emerald-green eyes, the large fish clenched in its mouth and shake my head. *"I wondered if you had something to do with the dolphin too,"* I mindspeak.

The dolphin opens its mouth, leaves the fish flopping on the deck as it shimmies back into the water. *"What other form would have worked?"* she mindspeaks. *"Neither humans nor you Undrae ever worry about the dolphins around them. The fish is one of my favorites—a yellowtail. Try it."*

I look at the flopping fish and curl my lip. *"I think I'll have a steak upstairs instead."*

"Suit yourself," Lorrel mindspeaks, swimming toward the center of the harbor and diving from sight. The dolphin's gray form swims toward the dock underwater, thinning and lengthening, turning pale, Lorrel's long hair flowing in a black stream as she swims. The girl breaks out of the water, grabs the dock with both hands and pulls herself up and out in one fluid motion.

She reaches for the yellowtail, holds it in both hands and sits crosslegged on the deck, seawater dripping from her body and hair and puddling around her. *"You should try this,"* she mindspeaks. *"In my srrynn we will have no beef to feed to you."* She takes a bite from the fish's midsection, scales and all, and holds the fish out to me, oblivious to its last dying spasm, the blood and other fluids dripping from it.

I shake my head. *"I don't plan to stay with your srrynn long enough for that to matter."*

Lorrel laughs and returns to devouring her fish. It takes her only a few bites. Standing, she tosses the fish's remains into the water and then looks down at her bare skin, the streaks of fish fluid and the red splotches of fish blood now staining it.

"I will be back in a moment," she mindspeaks, diving from the dock, swimming out of sight.

Putting the gas nozzle into the fuel tank, depressing its lever,

I smile at the mechanical flutter of the fuel pump going into action. Without it, I'd have to venture to the mainland or Key Biscayne for fuel. I doubt Lorrel would like me to do so this morning.

The Pelk breaks from the water again and joins me on the dock. Her body rinsed clean, she stands next to me dripping, sniffs the air and grimaces. *"It smells bad,"* she mindspeaks.

Tilting my head toward the fuel nozzle, I mindspeak, *"It'll go away as soon as I finish fueling."*

Lorrel nods, reaches behind her neck, gathering her wet hair, wringing it out. *"I don't understand why you bother with all this,"* she mindspeaks. *"That stink, all the boats, all the machines, the clothes, as if you were humans. Mowdar says the Undrae lost their way a long time ago. He says you have forgotten how to live the old way."*

Her words make me think of how my father objected when I first installed generators on the island, and how Chloe's parents complained when we installed both power and a satellite phone in their home. Yet Don Henri soon came to like the convenience of having frozen beef whenever he wished, and while Charles and Samantha Blood rejected their phone, they've been perfectly pleased to have electric lights and running water.

"The old ways aren't necessarily the best," I mindspeak.

Lorrel shrugs, turns toward the sun, closing her eyes, spreading her arms and legs as if to catch every last warm ray. A quiet hum breaks from her lips.

I look away from her pale, trim body, the tight, round curve of her buttocks, and busy myself topping off the tanks and stowing the fuel line. By the time I've finished the sun has baked her dry, yet she still stands spread out to its heat. *"You like that don't you?"* I mindspeak.

Lowering her arms, turning toward me, she nods. *"All Pelk like to bask. I think it is because of all the time we spend below."*

She looks at the boat and then back to me. *"Do we leave now?"*

I shake my head. *"No. There are some other things I have to do first. Besides, I want to eat and find something for you to wear while we're on the boat. . . ."*

She trills out a laugh and moves closer to me, her ocean smell filling my nostrils. *"You want to make me wear clothes so you do not have to see me? I have seen how you look at my body,"* she mindspeaks. *"You say you are mated for life, yet you still stare at me that way."*

Once again I wish Chloe hadn't gone. She remains the only female I desire. But Lorrel is far too correct in her assumptions for my comfort. I certainly never would admit such a thing to this irritating creature. I turn away from her and walk toward the house, mindspeaking, *"You Pelk have a high opinion of yourselves. I'm not about to risk being stopped by a patrol boat with a naked girl onboard who looks hardly more than thirteen."*

"I am no girl! I have twenty-nine years," Lorrel mindspeaks.

"And no mate?"

"Never."

I turn and stare at her, amazed how much older than my wife she is. *"Has no male come for you?"* I mindspeak.

Lorrel glares at me. *"Until now Mowdar has forbidden it. Pelk females are not slaves to their bodies like the Undrae. We do not spray our scent into the air as soon as we reach our maturity. We do not come into heat and have to accept the first male who comes close enough to poke his thing into us."*

"Yet you wanted to come to my bed last night?"

"Because Mowdar willed it," she mindspeaks. *"He will be disappointed that you refused me."*

"It had nothing to do with who or what you are. I told you that I'm mated for life."

"And I told you that Mowdar would be disappointed." Lorrel gives me a huge smile. *"I was perfectly pleased to sleep alone."*

Upstairs, Lorrel once again mindspeaks, *"No beef,"* when I offer to maker her a steak. Still naked, she lounges in Chloe's recliner, staring open-mouthed at the morning shows on TV, reclining and righting her chair over and over again, ignoring me as I eat and then call the office and ask for Claudia Gomez.

"Hey, Peter, what's up?" she says.

"Quite a bit," I say. "I'm going to have to leave for a little while. . . ."

"Ian isn't going to like that. You have a deposition coming up."

"I know. I know. But I'm not really concerned with what Ian likes or not. This thing has come up and I have to deal with it."

"Whatever you say, Peter. Just tell me what you need."

I smile, glad once again that Arturo had insisted that his daughter come to work at LaMar. In all the centuries that the Gomez family has worked for mine, not one of them has ever disappointed my father or me. "Chloe's out of reach right now and I didn't want to say too much on her answering machine. I told her to call you if she couldn't get me when she came back. If I'm not back by then, tell her I've run into a problem with the Pelk—probably somewhere in the Bahamas."

"P-E-L-K?" Claudia says.

"Right. Tell her I need for her to come back but she should leave the children with her parents until everything's resolved."

"And she's going to understand all this?"

I sigh, not entirely sure whether I understand completely why a naked little seadragon would want to disrupt my life. "I don't know, but she'll understand enough to know I need help."

"You sure I can't help more on this?" Claudia says. "Whatever this is."

"No, just pass on the message," I say, arranging for her to also visit the island each day—to feed the dogs and make sure all remains as it should.

Before I get off she says, "Oh, Peter, get this, Toba says that guy, Pepe Santos, is for real. She absolutely adores the guy. They're both freaks about fishing. She says he has his own boat—a Mako eighteen-foot open fisherman—they even take it out night fishing a couple of times a week. She has a great time with him."

If he's like his dead cousin, Jorge, I've no doubt how likeable he is. I still occasionally think of the man, regret that our lives had to play out the way they did. "So we're paying her to date him, and she's falling for him?"

"Sort of," Claudia says. "Ian's pissed about it, but Toba's still a pro. She'll come through for us. I promise, boss."

I shrug my shoulders. Don Henri always said no problem ever existed that couldn't be dwarfed by a greater problem. I look over toward Lorrel, my greater problem. "Hopefully I'll be back within the week," I say.

17

When I ask Lorrel to come downstairs with me to see whether anything of Chloe's might fit her, she shakes her head. *"I will not wear clothes just because my human form makes you uncomfortable,"* she mindspeaks.

"It's patrol boats that make me uncomfortable," I explain again.

It takes more than half an hour to coax her downstairs. We take an equally long time going through the closet and drawers, Lorrel rejecting every piece of clothing my wife owns, except for a tiny blue bikini that Chloe bought and then wore only once because "it was just too tight."

At the dock, after the Grady White's Yamahas have been lowered and kicked to life, just before I'm about to cast off the last line, Lorrel mindspeaks, *"My grandmother's ring! I must bring it back to Mowdar."*

I groan and look at my watch—11:12 A.M. As much as I know Bimini's only thirty-five miles away and that we have plenty of time to cross the Gulf Stream and cruise to any of the islands near it before dark falls, I'm ready to get underway. *"I've put it away. It will take a little while for me to get it,"* I mindspeak.

She trills out a laugh. *"Now you want to leave? Do we no longer have time? Or is the ring already in your treasure room? Mowdar told me how much you Undrae love your treasure."*

"Okay already," I mindspeak, *"I'll be back as soon as I can."*

Leaving the motors growling in neutral, I step off the boat. Lorrel gets up to join me and I hold up one hand, open palm toward her, mindspeak, *"Just wait here,"* and walk toward the stairs to the veranda. For all her avowed disinterest in treasure, I'm still not about to let this Pelk see the DelaSangre treasure room or how to access it.

"Oh, the Undrae wants to keep his treasure secret," Lorrel mindspeaks. *"He wants to make sure no one steals one of his coins."* Her laughter follows me all the way into the house.

To my chagrin, no patrol boats stop us as we shoot out the Wayward Channel into the ocean—though I'm sure the skimpy blue bikini and Lorrel's trim, small body would have made any patrolman stare at me as if I were a dirty old man out with an underage girl. I wait for Lorrel to say something about our not needing to be so concerned about being stopped, but the girl sits beside me, silent, slipping her grandmother's gold ring on and off her ring finger.

The ocean, so sleepy and calm in the early morning has woken up, and I guide the Grady White through swells that grow higher the further we venture from shore. By the time we reach the Gulf Stream, the swells have grown to the size of small hills.

I grin as I work the wheel and the throttles, the Grady White responding exactly as I wish, the deep blue waters of the Gulf Stream rising and falling around us, the air rich with the wet, clean smell of the open ocean.

"You like this?" Lorrel mindspeaks.

"Sure." I nod.

"It would have been so much simpler to swim."

I gesture toward the side. *"Be my guest. You'll find me anchored in Bimini Harbor."*

Shaking her head, Lorrel mindspeaks, *"We are going near Bimini—not to it."*

The swells diminish as soon as we leave the Gulf Stream and enter the clear, light blue shallows of the Bahamas. I throw the throttles forward and race the rest of the way toward Bimini. For the first time Lorrel stands, searching the sea, the horizon for something.

She sees Bimini rising into sight first and points toward it. *"That way,"* she mindspeaks.

The closer we get to the island the more boats we see, sailors, fishermen, large yachts cruising over for a few days' relaxation. Some come close enough to wave, and when Lorrel waves back, I mindspeak, *"Aren't you glad you're wearing that suit?"*

Lorrel shrugs. *"I am sure they have seen naked boaters before. Have not you?"*

She guides me closer to the island, sniffing the air, peering at the water, making me circle until we face the narrow strip of pine tree-studded sand and mangrove swamp that make up North Bimini.

"Do you know where you're going?" I mindspeak.

Lorrel nods. *"It is easier to find underwater. But I know."* She points to an area a little less than a mile off from the island. *"Over there."*

"Bimini Road?" I mindspeak, turning the boat toward it. I know the area. I've taken Chloe and the kids to it a number of times, to swim and dive and sightsee.

"I do not know it by that name."

"There are rock formations there. Because they're pretty uniform and placed all together like giant stone pavers, some people think they were cut and put in place. . . ."

"They were *cut and put in place,"* Lorrel mindspeaks.

The certainty with which she says it makes me turn to her. I've heard the conjectures for years and treated it as a fun tale to tell Henri when we dove over the rocks. *"So you think it's Atlantis too?"* I mindspeak.

She shakes her head. *"Atlantis is a myth for humans. Once they called my people mermaids too."*

At the rocks, Lorrel motions for me to slow down. My depthfinder reads fifteen feet, but in the clear water the wide, flat, rectangular stones look as if I could reach down and touch them. I shake my head at the mammoth size of it all, wide as a major expressway, sixteen hundred feet long. *"Why would anyone want to put this here?"* I mindspeak.

Lorrel grins at me. *"Ask Mowdar."* Walking to the bow, she points for me to cruise up the middle of the stone formation.

We anchor where the stones flow into a wide J at the end of the formation. I look around, study the other boats anchored nearby, a sailboat, two tour boats and a rubber inflatable, none within shouting distance. *"Do not worry. I will not draw attention. I will keep the bathing suit on,"* Lorrel mindspeaks, smiling. She inclines her head toward the water. *"You can come if you want."*

By the time I pull off my T-shirt, she's already sliced into the water. I watch her reach bottom, skimming just over the stones faster than I can ever hope to swim. Taking a deep breath, I dive after her. After the Pelk girl's near silent dive, mine sounds more like a buffalo doing a cannonball. I swim toward Lorrel, but as fast as I go her pale body and blue bikini keep drawing further away.

She stops near the far end of the J, swimming from stone to stone, examining each one, feeling around its exposed edge. One particular rock, a slightly elevated one, seems to draw her special interest and she settles beside it, digging beneath it with one arm, sand billowing around her, forming a sand cloud that obscures any view of her and the rock.

I slow, then stop as the sand cloud starts to swirl, the water above the rock turning turbulent. The disturbance expands outward until a final belch of sand shrouds everything within a dozen yards of the stone.

"Lorrel!" I mindspeak, *"Lorrel!"* swimming forward as fast as I can again. The water turns still but no answer comes. Trying to stare through the murky water, I rush toward the rock and find only the stone and the sand slowly settling on it.

Calling out to Lorrel again, I reach under the bottom edge of the rock as she did. But my lungs start to feel tight. Knowing they'll soon begin to ache for air. I stop my search, shoot to the surface and tread water, taking deep breaths, building up my lungs so I can spend a few more precious moments below.

I consider changing into my natural form. I know it would allow me to spend much more time between breaths, but I can't risk it with so many humans nearby. I call for Lorrel again, receive no reply, take one last deep gulp of air and dive.

This time I let my body settle beside the stone just as Lorrel did. I find a shallow depression in the sand under the rock, deep enough for me to extend my arm into it. My fingers encounter sand and the top of something hard, possibly metallic.

Like Lorrel, I begin shoveling sand away from the object, the water around me growing cloudy as I remove enough sand to allow me to work my hand around what feels like a metal rod. I tug on it. Nothing happens and I tug on it again. It budges just the slightest bit, and wedging my shoulder against the rock for leverage, I yank as hard as I can.

Sand boils around me, the stone swiveling up as if on a hinge, and the sandy bottom beneath it dropping away. I kick my legs and flail my arms, trying to swim away, to reach the surface, but the water rushes under the rock, sucking me along, carrying me down a tunnel that turns dark, in an instant, as the rock swings back into place above me.

Stone walls scrape my skin as the current pulls me downward. I stop fighting it. With no room to shift shape, I concentrate only on relaxing my body, saving as much air as possible, preparing myself to react to whatever may come.

All downward motion ceases. A weaker current draws me along another tunnel, or corridor, even narrower than the first, carrying me forward for a few long moments until I come to rest against what feels like a huge, woven net, slick with algae.

Ignoring the tightness building again in my chest, I feel around it, fingering the knots, noting the regularity of the large square holes. Wondering whether I've been caught in some peculiar monster's trap or if this is some device of the Pelk, I use each knot hole to pull myself up, hoping it will lead me to something before my air runs out.

The climb takes only a minute, but each second of it drags as my lungs constrict and my chest begins to ache. When my head finally breaks free of the water, I gasp into the air, almost gagging at the dank, stale smell of it. Still I gulp one deep breath after another. Lorrel laughs somewhere near me. *"Were you really worried about me?"* she mindspeaks. *"Or were you just concerned about the antidote?"*

Turning in the water, I find her sitting crosslegged on a wide stone ledge not more than ten feet from me. A small round depression full of water on the floor near her gives off a dull green glow that lights the area, showing the stone walls of what I assume is a cavern. I swim toward her, pull myself out of the water and instantly shiver in the cool air. "That was a nasty thing to do," I growl. When she doesn't react I mindspeak the words.

"Mowdar believes in tests," she mindspeaks, getting up, walking toward the inside of the ledge, returning with what looks like a blanket. She hands it to me. *"A Pelk wove this from seaweed. It is rough but it will warm you."*

I wrap the stiff, scratchy thing around me. *"So at least did I pass your test?"* I mindspeak.

She smiles. *"You are here and you are alive, are you not?"*

"No thanks to you or Mowdar."

Lorrel shrugs and walks away, back toward the inside of the ledge. Ancient wooden chests, the same sort as Father used in our treasure room, line the floor in front of the rear wall. Three rows of rough stone shelves full of bottles, wood boxes, clay urns and cloth bags run the length of the wall above them.

"Whatever this place is, it looks well supplied," I mindspeak.

"It has to be," she mindspeaks, taking a small bag from the shelf. She returns with it, kneeling by the depression and pouring powder from the bag into its water. Once the bag empties, she swirls the water with one hand and the green glow brightens, chasing any remaining shadows into the furthest recesses of the cavern.

The Pelk turns toward me and grins. *"Phosphorescence. We make it from dried plankton. We call this a glowpool. You think you are so advanced. You with your generators and electric lights. Our srrynns have been using glowpools, making their own light, since long before the Great War."*

She motions to the shelves and chests, the stone walls and the whole cavern with a large sweep of her arm. *"Pelk built this safehold before any Undrae first thought to name himself DelaSangre."*

I wander over to the shelves, open a chest and wrinkle my nose at the rancid smell of the slabs of dried fish it holds.

"Make all the faces you want," Lorrel mindspeaks. *"We have enough food and supplies for the two of us to live here for over a year. If necessary a small srrynn could live a month without leaving this safehold. How do you think we hid from you Undrae in the old days?"*

"Actually, I never thought about it," I mindspeak, thinking how little my father ever taught me about the history of my people. *"Until Chloe told me about the four castrylls and the Great War, I didn't even know the Pelk had ever existed."*

"We exist." Lorrel joins me by the shelf, reaches for a small antique glass bottle and hands it to me. *"This is your antidote. Drink it."*

Turning the bottle over in my hands I examine it and the cork stopper that seals it. *"Did the Pelk make this too?"* I mindspeak.

"Why would we bother?" Lorrel mindspeaks. *"Thanks to the humans' ineptitude, there are shipwrecks everywhere. We take what we need from them."* She looks at the bottle in my hands. *"You should drink your antidote, Peter."*

I shake my head. *"Not until I know you're telling the truth. I'll drink it once I feel the poison, not a moment before."*

She hisses at me. *"Undrae, you are a fool! That is the only dose of antidote we have. You will die if you lose it."*

Tucking the small bottle in one of the front pockets of my damp cutoffs, I mindspeak, *"I don't intend to lose it."*

Lorrel turns silent, takes a slab of dried fish and sits by the edge of the stone ledge, dunking the fish into the water and munching on it. When I mention wanting to go back to the boat, she shrugs her shoulders and mindspeaks, *"Not until the tide changes."*

"How will we know when that is?"

The girl smiles. *"When the time comes, Atala will breathe."*

I sigh, sit down beside her and say nothing more. If Lorrel can pass the time in silence, then so can I.

The slab of fish has long been eaten and the green phosphorescence has lost half its brilliance by the time the water beside the ledge ripples ever so slightly. *"Atala,"* Lorrel mindspeaks, standing up.

I stand up too, staring at the disturbed water, wondering what comes next.

The Pelk girl takes one of my hands and tugs me back from the edge. *"It is coming now,"* she mindspeaks.

Water leaps before us, spraying wet as a giant belch of fresh air erupts into the cavern. *"Atala's breath!"* Lorrel mindspeaks. *"Come! We have little time!"* Still holding my hand she rushes forward, tugging me along, mindspeaking, *"Take a breath!"* just before she lets go and dives on the far side of the net.

I gasp air in twice and follow her, the current grabbing me as soon as I submerge. Its strength surprises me, and I find I need only to keep my body straight and let the water do the rest. Lorrel's hand suddenly touches me on top of my head, and I realize she's slowed herself to allow me to catch up with her.

"The passage will only take a few minutes," she mindspeaks. *"But I know your lungs are not yet developed."* She pulls up on my hair and I let my head get guided upward, gasp as I find my nostrils clear of water.

"As long as Atala's breath holds we will have air to breathe," Lorrel mindspeaks, floating beside me, letting the current take her just as it carries me.

"What is Atala's breath?" I mindspeak. *"Where is the current taking us? And don't tell me to ask Mowdar."*

Lorrel trills out a laugh, and as much as she can irritate me, I find the sound of it makes me smile. *"Atala's breath is a tale the old ones tell to the children. You know there are caves everywhere around these islands, don't you?"*

I nod.

"And you know about the blue holes too?"

"They're lagoons that are connected to cave systems," I mindspeak.

"And sometimes round holes in the ocean bottom too," Lorrel mindspeaks. *"Some of the ocean blue holes suck and blow water when the tide changes. I'm not sure how any of it works, but I think that when an ocean blue hole connects by caves to an inland blue hole, the sucking or blowing action draws air from any connected dry caves. We call it Atala's breath."*

Our forward momentum slows and the girl mindspeaks, *"Breathe!"*

I have barely time to gulp in air before water floods the top of the tunnel. Lorrel tugs on my hand and I follow her, swimming forward in the dark, aware of her presence only because of the turbulence her kicks make in front of me.

After a few minutes the water begins to turn light, and I

begin to make out the shape of the Pelk girl swimming in front of me. She doesn't pull away from me until the water has turned light blue all around us. Then she shoots away, upward toward the bright surface.

I follow, breaking water beside her, breathing deep, laughing. Looking around, blinking at the bright, late-afternoon sun, breathing in the fishy smell of brackish swampland, I swivel my head, stare at the mangroves ringing the blue hole. *"Where are we?"* I mindspeak.

"North Bimini," Lorrel mindspeaks. She points to a gap between two trees. *"There is a saltwater creek over there. It will take us to the ocean. Your boat is not far from there."*

We anchor for the night in a small deserted cove I find in North Bimini. Protected from the waves by a sandbar that runs almost fully across the mouth of the cove, shielded from the night wind by rows of tall pine trees, the Grady White barely moves beneath us.

Between the gold glow of the quarter moon riding low above us and the brilliance of all the stars scattered across the clear black sky, I find no need to turn on any of the boat's lights. Pulling on a light sweatshirt to ward off the night's chill I offer one of Chloe's to Lorrel.

The girl shakes her head. She sits on the boat's stern bench, staring at the dark, still water, humming a new song, one that has no discernible melody or rhythm. But still it affects me, and I find myself listening to it, anticipating after a bit when her tone will rise or dip, when the song's momentum will rush forward or slow or stop.

The air smells of the sea as it does on my island, and I sigh thinking of the warm lights at home, the sounds of the boats bobbing in the harbor, the voices and giggles of my wife and children. The tempo of Lorrel's tune picks up and I look skyward.

I consider shifting shape and flying off in search of prey, but all is so calm around me and Lorrel's song so soothing that I can't summon the energy. Going to the cooler, I take out a roast beef sandwich and hold it out to the Pelk girl. Her nose wrinkles as she shakes her head. *"No more beef,"* she mindspeaks.

"Tomorrow I will take you hunting the Pelk way—if you still insist on waiting for the poison to attack you."

Humming, the Pelk girl motions for me to come sit on the stern bench beside her. I bring my sandwich, sit a foot away from her, leaning back in the seat, staring at the sky, eating, my mind blank except for Lorrel's tune. She sidles over, close enough to me that her body warms my side where it touches, and my nostrils fill with her salt-laced scent.

The warmth of her touch builds and I think of Chloe and move away a few inches, finishing my sandwich, turning my head, breathing in air clear of the Pelk girl's aroma. Lorrel's tune turns plaintive and slow, somehow magnifying the languor that always overtakes me after meals. I fight to keep my eyes open but find myself sinking into that twilight place just before sleep.

The girl sidles close again and, as much as I wish it were Chloe instead, I welcome the warmth of her touch. *"Relax, Peter,"* she mindspeaks. *"I know you are mated. I accept that we cannot do such things with each other."*

As close as she is, her humming almost vibrates through me as her tune softens even more. I force myself to point forward, toward the Grady White's small cabin and mindspeak, *"I should go below and turn in."*

Lorrel's song intensifies, filling my mind, and I nod when she stands and takes my hand, tugging me upright. *"I should sleep too,"* she mindspeaks.

Below I stretch out on one of the two vee berths and sigh, my muscles relaxing, my body ready to give itself to sleep. Lorrel, still humming, sits down beside me. I point to the other berth and try to form the words to tell her to lie down there, but no words come.

She takes my hand and guides it down to the side of my body. *"Really, Peter,"* she mindspeaks, her saltwater scent overtaking me, her humming vibrating through my body. *"I told you that I understood your commitment to your mate. But we Pelk women are taught certain things. It would be silly for you to not let me soothe you to sleep."*

Placing my head in her small lap, she strokes my temples with her small fingers, her song slowing, growing quieter, the fresh saltwater scent of her blanketing me, the warmth of her skin almost burning me where mine touches hers.

Her bikini still holds just the slightest trace of dampness. I smile at the contrast between its coolness and the warmth of Lorrel's skin as her touch and her strange song take me deep to sleep.

18

Heat wakes me. I open my eyes to find Lorrel stretched out at my side, pressed against me, both of us sticky with sweat. Holding up my arm, I check my watch and find we've slept past ten, long enough for the sun to bake the cabin. Sitting up, I nudge Lorrel.

The Pelk girl sits up too, grimacing. *"It's too hot!"* she mind-speaks. She stands and rushes out of the cabin. In a moment the quiet, wet sound of her body slipping into the water follows. Pulling off my sweatshirt, following her outside, I put up the boat's blue canvas bimini top and sit by the wheel under its shade. The clear, cool water in the cove tempts me, but I shake my head at the thought of joining the girl.

I shift my body in the seat and something hard in my pocket pokes me. Remembering the small bottle of antidote in my pocket, I pull it out and examine it in the morning light. Its amber glass prevents me from seeing the color of the liquid inside.

I pull the cork out and sniff, prepared to pull my head back if it's vile.

To my surprise, except for a hint of something citric, it gives off no odor. I consider for a moment drinking the damn thing, getting on with the trip to Lorrel's srrynn, but instead I push the cork back in place and put the bottle in the map compartment below the wheel. By the afternoon after this I'll know for sure if she truly poisoned me.

Something splashes near the boat's starboard side and I turn and look. A large Carribean lobster flies into the cockpit, followed by another and then two more. Lorrel appears next, pulling herself up, over the side, standing, dripping, a smile spread across her face.

Picking a lobster up, twisting off its tail and slicing it open with one finger transformed into a sharp claw, she offers its near-translucent meat to me. Because of Chloe I've eaten lobster—but cooked white and firm, not raw and quivering like this. I shake my head.

"It is time you learned to eat like a Pelk," she mindspeaks, still holding the lobster tail out to me. *"Try it. It will not harm you."*

I take the tail and bite into it, the meat firmer than I thought it would be, its lack of smell and its sweetness surprising me. Gulping it down, I watch Lorrel separate and cut open the others.

After we've consumed all the lobster tails, we both dive into the water to rinse off. Lorrel swims close to me and I back away, treading water, shaking my head. *"You need to stay further away from me,"* I mindspeak.

"Why?" she mindspeaks, treading water too. *"What have I done that is so wrong?"*

"I have a wife and children. . . ."

Lorrel nods. *"I know. I have seen them."*

"I can't have you sleeping in my bed. I don't want you humming any more tunes around me."

"We only slept, Peter. I only soothed you. It is what Pelk females are taught to do."

"And I was taught that Undrae mated for life."

The Pelk girl turns away from me. *"We did not mate! If a simple song can turn your heart, if sleeping next to someone like me tempts you so much, maybe you should question what you were taught. I am not responsible for your weaknesses."* She dives out of sight.

The sun rides high in the sky and my cutoffs have long dried by the time Lorrel decides to come back to the Grady White. She pulls herself onboard and stands dripping, wringing out her long black hair with both hands as she mindspeaks, *"We should leave now. We have many miles to go."*

She says nothing else as I pull up the anchors, start the motors and guide the boat out of the cove into the open water. Then she points southeast, waiting until I round Bimini and set course in the general direction of Andros Island before she sits down next to me, making sure to leave over a foot between us.

"Are we going to Andros?" I mindspeak.

Lorrel shakes her head. *"We are going to Waylach's Rock. We will leave your boat there."*

"And then where will we go?"

The Pelk girl hisses. *"You will learn then, Undrae. I would not have come back at all if I had not promised Mowdar I would bring you. Now drive your boat and leave me be."*

By the time we reach Waylach's Rock most of the afternoon has passed. The tiny island seems to consist of nothing but rocks and stones jutting out of the water, far from any other island, Andros just a low shadow rising on the horizon. I circle the island three times without finding either a sandy beach or a protected anchorage. *"We can't leave the boat here,"* I mindspeak. *"The first storm that comes up will either set it adrift or drive it into the rocks."*

Lorrel shrugs. *"You wanted to bring it."* But on our next circuit of the island she points to an indentation in the rocks. When I pull the Grady White close to it, I find a narrow channel running between two huge boulders and leading to a small protected cove.

After guiding the boat in, I go up to the bow and drop the anchor. Then I turn to Lorrel. *"And now what?"* I mindspeak.

The Pelk girl stands up, pulls off her bikini top and drops it. Pulling down her bikini bottoms, she steps out of them. Kicking them to the side, she mindspeaks, *"You said you do not want to go to my srrynn until you know I have spoken the truth to you."* She pirouettes so I can see every bit of her, the flush of her pink nipples, the tight curve of her buttocks.

Lorrel grins at me. *"I know my body makes you uncomfortable, Peter, but I have no more need for human clothes now. We are near my srrynn. If you were not so stubborn, we could be there tonight. I see no reason to sit with you and hold your hand while you wait for the poison's pain to come."*

Standing by the wheel, she takes off her grandmother's gold ring and tucks it in her mouth, between her teeth and her right cheek, her body growing and stretching, her pale skin turning dark and forming shallow, smooth scales. *"I do not understand why you like your human form so much,"* she mindspeaks, purring out a groan. *"This feels so good."*

I stare at the Pelk female. Far smaller than an Undrae woman, her form reminds me more of a sea otter's body—thinner, more elongated, more obviously adapted to the water than an Undrae female. She turns her back to me, showing off her tail, the flared tip at its end. *"We are not like your women, are we, Peter?"*

"No," I mindspeak, shaking my head.

"I will not force my presence on you any longer. I will return tomorrow after the poison makes itself known." She walks to the side of the boat and slips into the water with barely a sound.

Alone, with nothing to do but wait, I find it impossible to stay in one place on my small boat. I sit at the stern for a few minutes, then move to the seat at the helm. I wander to the bow to check the anchor line and then rush to the stern to check the motors. I eat the last of the roast beef sandwiches, standing, throwing crumbs from the stale bread into the water, hoping at least to attract a fish.

Nothing comes. No fish. No birds. No signs of boaters on the waters outside the channel. The day drags to an end and I embrace sleep as soon as dark takes over the sky.

I wake late in the morning to a cloudy day full of blustery winds. The water in the island's small cove moves more than I care for, and I dive below to make sure that my anchor has set properly. I find it resting on the rocky bottom, hardly dug in enough to hold the boat fast.

It takes six dives for me to dig enough into the rocks to make the anchor fast. If anything, I wish it would have taken longer. I return to pacing and waiting. I help matters little by constantly glancing at my watch. Finally, when it reads five, I let out a sigh and begin staring at the water, waiting for Lorrel to arrive.

The day finally darkens. The wind shifts directions, turning my boat on its anchor, and yet Lorrel doesn't appear. A slight tinge of heat starts to burn in my midriff. I rub the place with my right hand and wonder if it's my imagination. But the burning increases until I wince. It feels like a lit cigarette being pushed into my skin.

"*Lorrel!*" I mindspeak. "*Okay. You were right. I'm going to take my antidote. Come back so we can get on with the rest of it.*"

The pain diminishes and returns minutes later, more intense, burrowing deeper into me. I groan. "*Lorrel!*" I mindspeak, and still receive no answer.

Getting up from the stern bench, holding my hand to my midriff, I rush forward to the helm, the burning intensifying with each step I take. I reach into the map compartment for the small bottle and gasp when I find it gone.

19

"Lorrel!" I mindspeak.

A rush of pain hits me and I double over, crumpling to my knees. *"Lorrel, god damn it come back!"* I mindspeak. *"Lorrel!"*

Fire burns through every centimeter, every cell where the Pelk girl stabbed me. I writhe on the deck, try to heal it away, but nothing I do relieves the pain. I call out to Lorrel again and damn her when she doesn't reply.

By nightfall the pain has blossomed into a fireball burning in the middle of my body. I alternate from curling in a fetal position to lying stomach-down on the deck. Nothing helps. I think of the pain growing until it burns from my fingertips to my toes, as Lorrel warned, and I groan.

Later—how long I'm not really sure—a large splash erupts from the water on the starboard side of the boat. Something wet thuds down on the deck not far from my feet. Lorrel follows, barely making a sound as she comes over the coaming in her natural form. In the murky moonlight of a cloud-crowded sky, she looks like a black shadow flowing toward me.

"Where's the damn antidote?" I mindspeak.

"Quiet, Peter." She stands over me, studies me with her emerald-green eyes as I writhe before her. *"Do you believe me now, or would you rather wait until it gets worse?"*

"I want the antidote!"

"I could leave and come back in the morning. You would still be alive then."

If I could I would lash out at her, rip her, leave her bleeding and dying on the boat's deck, but I can do little more than shift my body in a hopeless search for relief. I draw in a breath, wince and mindspeak, *"I believe you. You were right. Now would you please give me the antidote?"*

"Much better," Lorrel mindspeaks. She opens her mouth, reaches one claw into it and pulls out the small amber bottle. *"You are a doubter. If I left the bottle where you placed it, you would have taken the antidote before you felt the full force of the poison. I did not want you to underestimate its power later."*

Lorrel crouches next to me, pauses, mindspeaks, *"It will be easier in my human form,"* and shifts to her human shape. She sits beside me on the deck, her legs splayed out and turns me on my back, guiding my head onto her naked lap.

Moving sends new bolts of pain shooting through me. I moan and Lorrel starts to hum, the notes low, vibrating through my body. *"I know. I know how much it hurts."* She strokes my head with her right hand while she lifts the bottle to her mouth with her left. Pulling the cork with her teeth, she spits it aside.

Cradling my head tight against her flesh just under her small, firm breasts, the Pelk girl puts the bottle to my lips. *"Not too fast, Peter. But remember, you must drink all of it,"* she mindspeaks, pulling the bottle away after I take just a sip.

Greasy, warm liquid, bitter like tea brewed too strong, glides down my throat, heating everything it touches, but somehow cooling the fire inside me by a few degrees—though not enough—and leaving a bitter, lemony aftertaste. I reach for the bottle with my mouth, and Lorrel allows me another sip, her hum lightening, the tune washing over me, soothing me as each subsequent sip quenches the heat just a little more.

A quarter of the bottle still remains when the last vestige of fire disappears. I become aware of the wet touch of Lorrel's bare skin and the fresh saltwater scent of her aroma. I try to lift my head and sidle away from her. But she holds me down, her hum growing louder, the notes washing over me.

"Be calm," she mindspeaks, placing the bottle to my lips. *"You must finish everything in the bottle. Otherwise the pain will come back too soon."*

Her tune reverberates in my head. I find it hard to think or resist, and continue to lie still, drinking from the bottle as long as she places it to my lips. By the time I finish the last drop, the antidote's warmth and the gentle notes of Lorrel's song have brought me to the edge of sleep.

"Remember this will only hold off the poison for a few days. You will need more then," she mindspeaks. *"Now, rest. I brought something special. I'll wake you in a little while to share it with me."*

Sleep comes and I allow it to take me. But I remain aware of Lorrel's humming, the tune keeping me on the edge of consciousness, my subconscious flitting from dream to dream.

I wake to the sound of Lorrel dragging something large across the cockpit floor. It lets out a weak, high-pitched whistle, clicking a few times as she pulls on it, and I sit up and stare at it.

The creature reaches hardly a few inches more than three feet, an infant dolphin. I look at the poor thing, blood still seeping from claw gouges beneath its jaw and from a bite taken from the middle of its underside. *"It's a miracle that it's still alive,"* I mindspeak.

The Pelk girl grins. *"I was lucky. Its mother and most of its pod were busy feeding on a huge school of fish. I saw it swimming on the edge of the school and took it before any of them noticed. Old Notch Fin and the rest of the males must be furious."*

"Notch Fin?" I mindspeak.

Shapeshifting one finger into a claw, Lorrel nods, grabs the infant dolphin, holding its mouth closed with one hand as she cuts the beast open from front to rear with the other. It bleats out a shrill, brief whistle, shudders once and goes still.

She leans over the dead beast, mindspeaks, *"Notch Fin is the lead male. You should see him. I do not think I have ever seen a larger dolphin. Mowdar says he leads the gathering of the pods. He has killed his share of Pelk. I have no doubt had he caught me, he would have killed me too."* Cutting a large chunk from the dead infant's flank, Lorrel holds it out to me.

I eye the raw meat, saliva flooding my mouth, my empty stomach rumbling. *"I don't like to eat the young of any kind,"* I mindspeak.

Lorrel laughs. *"Undrae, how many humans have you killed*

and eaten? Were you so queasy with each of them? You try to take an adult dolphin by yourself! Even two of us sometimes fail at such a task. Now, eat it. We might not have a chance to feed again before we reach my srrynn."

"My father always said he liked dolphins too much to feed on them. I always agreed with that," I mindspeak. Still, the meat tempts me. It smells not much different than dog, which I've fed upon, mostly when culling the island's dog pack. My empty stomach growls, but I still hesitate. *"I've never eaten one before."*

"And I had never eaten a beef until you gave it to me." Lorrel pushes the meat against my closed lips, and the smell of its fresh blood overwhelms any resistance I have left. Licking my lips, I take the meat from her and swallow a bite.

The taste reminds me of dog or pork, not as lean and slightly fishy, but sweeter too. Lorrel cuts two more pieces, hands me one and takes a bite from the other. We eat in silence, devouring chunks of meat, stopping only when the carcass has been devoured.

Lorrel points at me and laughs. *"Look at yourself!"* she mindspeaks.

I glance down at my blood-streaked chest and shorts, touch my face and feel the grease and other residue from my meal. Looking at Lorrel, I point back at the streaks coating her skin. *"It looks worse on your white skin,"* I mindspeak, laughing as she stares at herself and laughs too.

Shaking my head at the mess our meal has left on the boat's deck, I stand, pick up the remnants of the poor little dolphin and carry it to the starboard side. Lorrel looks up just as I throw the remains overboard. *"No, Peter! Do not throw that!"*

What remains of the dolphin makes a pitiful splash as it hits the water. *"You should have said something earlier. I didn't think you wanted any of what was left."*

The Pelk girl shakes her head. *"We are not the only creatures with a good sense of smell,"* she mindspeaks.

I want to dive into the water, to wash myself clean, but Lorrel insists we wait. She sits and studies the water on the starboard side of the boat, insists on my doing the same on the port side.

A half hour passes without a strange ruffle or ripple in the water anywhere in our sight. Still, Lorrel insists we wait a half hour more before either of us dives into the water.

When the hour passes, she mindspeaks, *"Do you think you could be more quiet this time? I cannot believe how clumsy you Undrae are in the water."*

"And I take it you want to show me how gracefully you Pelk fly?" I mindspeak.

Lorrel grins. *"My apologies. The old ones teach us that each one of us carries his own gifts. Sometimes I forget that. But you still must try to be quiet tonight."*

I go to the stern of the boat. *"I won't dive. I'll just lower myself into the water."*

Lorrel follows me, stands closer than I prefer. *"Thank you. That should help."* She reaches for the snap on my cuttoffs. I step back.

"Your shorts are too soiled to be cleaned by a simple swim," she mindspeaks. *"Besides you will soon be in my srrynn. We wear no clothes there. It is time you forgot such foolishness."*

I can't think of any retort. Ordinarily nudity, mine or anyone else's, matters not a whit to me. I wonder at the unease that overtakes me around this Pelk female, wish I could be indifferent to her or at least find her less attractive. She reaches for my shorts again, and this time I let her take them.

"Good," she mindspeaks, brushing past me, slipping into the water without a sound. *"Do not stay in the water any longer than it takes to rinse yourself off."*

Nodding, I follow her. Lowering myself from the boat. I barely disturb the water as I slip into it.

Lorrel swims by me, the water hardly rippling as she does so. *"Better, but I can still hear you!"* she mindspeaks.

I ignore her, take a breath and sink below the water, swimming away from the boat with a slow breaststroke. Surfacing fifteen yards away, I tread water, looking back toward the Grady White, searching to see where Lorrel is while I rub my body clean with my hands as best I can.

Something erupts from under the boat, shooting toward me. *"Change, Peter, change!"* Laurell mindspeaks. I start to will my body to shift shape, but something hard and large rams into my right side before I can, cracking my ribs, forcing me to expel a loud huff of air.

Gasping for breath, I try to put my mind away from the pain and concentrate on changing shape. Something crashes into my left side, lower this time, and I bellow. Gulping breaths, my chest heaving, I slash through the water around me as soon as my claws emerge.

Lorrel shoots by, just out of my reach, already in her natural form. *"Do not waste energy,"* she mindspeaks. *"Finish changing. They are circling. They always do. They will return as soon as they choose a good point—one that will let them pick up more speed."*

I sigh as my wings break free of my back and my tail stretches back behind me. Flexing my jaws, gnashing my newly grown fangs, I let out a low growl. *"Just who are they?"* I mindspeak.

Both beasts ram into my chest at full speed. I yowl, rake one of them down its side as it swims away, its blood spreading out in the water.

"They are dolphin males—from Notch Fin's pod, I think," Lorrel mindspeaks.

My ribs ache. Even worse, I taste my own blood rising up my throat. *"Not Notch Fin himself?"* I mindspeak.

"If he was one of your attackers, you would already be dead."

"Why are they leaving you alone?"

"You are the bigger threat. They will turn on me when you are finished or whenever I attack one of them."

"You might try that."

"They are coming again!" Lorrel mindspeaks.

"Let them." I flex my wings, scooping water with my first beat, shooting upward, grabbing air with the second beat of my wings, my attackers passing below me as I take to the air. From above, even in the cloudy night, I have no problem seeing their fins, the roiled water they leave behind them.

I fly upward just another few wing beats and then dive, striking the water and one of the males at the same time. The beast gives off a shrill whistle and tries to bolt away. But I dig all my claws, front and rear, into it. Frantically clicking, it dives to the bottom, twisting underwater, rubbing me against the stony bottom.

The beast has to measure over ten feet—larger than any of the dolphins I'm used to seeing near home. I drive my claws further into its body, bite down just behind its blowhole, blood streaming all around us. Still, it batters me again against the bottom.

The other dolphin, too close to gain much ramming speed, clamps its teeth on the meaty section of my tail. Stifling a yowl, conscious of the tightness building in my chest, I strengthen my hold on the first dolphin, rip at it, tearing chunks from it. Yet the beast continues to struggle, slamming me against the bottom again and again.

Lorrel darts past me, raking the second dolphin with her claws. Blood billows around it. It releases my tail and chases after her.

I continue to rip at my dolphin, chew at it until my teeth scrape against the bone of its skull. The creature manages to batter me against the bottom one last time before one of my fangs breaks through. Its once mighty tail twitches, then goes still. I know only one more bite or one more slash will end it, but I need air.

Releasing the dolphin, I shoot to the surface, gulping huge breaths as soon as my head breaks clear. Splashes sound near the boat, the water swirling as two creatures circle and collide. *"Peter! I need your help!"* Lorrel mindspeaks.

"Can it wait?" I tread water, draw in another breath.

The water erupts closer to me. Lorrel and the dolphin rise partially out of the water, the dolphin's teeth sunk into the Pelk's neck, holding on no matter how hard she gouges it with her claws. They stay that way for just a moment, then sink from view.

I gasp in a final breath and swim after them, the dark water so bloody that I have to rely on sound and touch to find them. Bumping into Lorrel's haunch first, I feel my way to the dolphin male, rip my claws into him as I work my way to the underside of his jaw. I bite into his throat there, tearing at it until he releases Lorrel.

The Pelk girl goes into a frenzy, gouging thick furrows in the dolphin's hide, biting, ripping, long after it ceases to move. I disengage and search the cove for the other male. I finally find him floating near the surface, his blowhole out of the water, wheezing as he takes short, shallow breaths.

My ribs and chest ache. Grimacing at the taste of my own blood still rising up my throat, I shake my head. Father would have been impressed with how these two fought. I can't imagine having to fight more of them.

I dispatch the brave beast with a final swipe of my claw. *"Lorrel,"* I mindspeak. *"Are you okay?"*

"You saw what it was doing to me."

Swimming back down, I find her still clinging to the dead, mangled dolphin. *"It didn't do anything that you can't heal,"* I mindspeak, tugging her away from her kill, towing her toward the boat.

She reaches back toward the carcass. *"But we will need it for nourishment. How can we heal if we have nothing to eat?"*

I look at the ragged condition of the dead dolphin's body and shake my head. *"You aren't the only one who just killed a grown dolphin. There's more flesh left on my kill. It will provide more than enough to eat."*

Leaving Lorrel lying on the deck of the Grady White, I swim back and search for my kill. Just getting its carcass into the boat takes both of us struggling together. We push and tug the dead beast for almost half an hour until we finally slide it into place on the deck. By then Lorrel hardly has the strength left to rip its mid-section open.

We both fall on it as soon as she does so, our stomachs empty from the energy spent shapeshifting and fighting. Lorrel feeds by my side, both of us burying our snouts in the fresh raw meat, ripping chunks, gulping almost without chewing. The Pelk girl's cheek presses against mine as we feed, her flank warming my flank, her tail draped over my tail.

Afterwards, Lorrel continues to lie beside me. She begins to hum. *"I have to. It is part of how we heal,"* she mindspeaks. *"It soothes me."*

I know I should object or at least move away, but the tune weaves itself into my thoughts, soothing me too. I smile as my muscles relax and I concentrate on healing my own wounds. If anything, the warmth of Lorrel's body pressed against mine and the irregular notes she hums seem to help.

As my healing comes to an end and languor begins to overtake me, I mindspeak, *"So, you've already poisoned me, shanghaied me and led me into a fight with dolphins. Any special activities planned for tomorrow?"*

Lorrel presses slightly closer, stroking my tail with hers. *"Sleep, Peter. Save your questions for Mowdar. If all goes well, we will be with him by tomorrow night."*

20

In the morning, Lorrel wakes me by slapping her tail lightly on mine. *"Get up, Peter. We have much to do."* I sit up, look at the gore our kills have left on the Grady White's deck and groan. Then I wonder if any new dolphins have come and whether we'll have to fight again.

I get to my feet. Peering into the water, now calm and clear enough that I can see bottom in all directions, I study the entire cove. *"I already looked. There are no dolphins here,"* Lorrel mindspeaks. *"But I am afraid of what we might face on the outside."*

Staring out at the open water, I mindspeak, *"Just how many dolphins are in Notch Fin's pod?"*

"Not very many. But there are times when he leads a joining of the pods—a gathering—sometimes a hundred dolphins swimming together, sometimes more—males, females and children."

I turn back to her. *"So many? The pods around us rarely have much more than a dozen."*

Lorrel nods. *"Ocean-going pods are bigger. I have seen a few of Notch Fin's gatherings number over two or three hundred."*

"And you took one of their young?"

"I was hungry. You ate it too!"

Shaking my head, I notice the rows of angry red wounds, closed but still not completely healed, on Lorrel's neck. Reaching out, I touch my claw to the side of one wound and mindspeak, *"Are you healed enough to travel?"*

She pulls back. *"I told you we heal differently than you Undrae. My injuries will not interfere with what I need to do. All I need is to rejoin my srrynn. Then all will be made well. We have not even a half day's swim to go. . . ."*

I groan. *"We could take the boat."*

The Pelk girl shakes her head. *"It might bring attention too close to my srrynn. If you are willing, I can teach you a way we can most probably pass Notch Fin's pod safely. But you will have to trust me."*

After one last check of the anchor, Lorrel and I swallow down the last of the dolphin meat and slip into the water. *"Now what?"* I mindspeak.

The Pelk girl's form begins to shrink and smooth out, turning gray, growing fins and then flukes. *"We swim,"* she mindspeaks.

I look at the gray bottle-nosed dolphin now in front of me. Only its emerald-green eyes and the puncture wounds give any sign as to her true identity. *"You swim,"* I mindspeak. *"I have no idea how to change into a dolphin."*

"But I do," the Pelk girl mindspeaks. *"I can show you, if you let me."*

She swims close to me, both of our heads out of water. Pressing her head against mine, she begins to hum a strange, low tune. Its notes vibrate into my skull and tingle my teeth. I jerk my head back.

"Peter! You must allow this!" Lorrel presses her head against mine again. *"Listen,"* she mindspeaks, resuming her tune. *"Do not fight it. Empty your mind of thought. Allow the music to overtake you."*

The notes bore into me. I stare across the cove at a large boulder and focus my eyes on it. An image of Chloe comes to mind and fades away as the tune intensifies, vibrating through me. I concentrate on each note, on the rise and fall of the strange melody, the irregular rhythm of the song—all of it rushing into me, receding and rushing in again.

"Are you floating with it now? Does the tune have you?" The words seem to ebb and flow somewhere inside me. I think about nodding, and sometime later I do.

"Good." Lorrel's humming grows louder. *"I am going to*

join you now. Do not be alarmed. I will leave as soon as I show you the way. Do not fight me. If you do, we both could be lost."

The tune washes through me, and a slight pressure begins to build within my mind. I twist my head, stretch my neck, wishing it gone. *"No, Peter!"* the words say. *"Let me be with you."*

I relax and the tune quiets. Warmth flows into me, the words saying, *"Does it not feel good now?"*

Yes, I think, and the words say, *"You will be ready soon."*

Warmth courses through me, traveling down my veins and arteries, expanding into each cell of my body. *"I like it here,"* the words say. *"I will miss it after I leave."*

I float along with Lorrel's notes, cocooned in the warmth her tune brings. Time means nothing. I think of nothing but the susurration of Lorrel's notes and her warmth pulsing through me.

"It is time for you to change," the words say.

To what? I think.

"Whatever you choose. I will be with you and guide you to your new form."

Can't we stay as we are?

"I would like to, but we would die. I can only linger so long before your subconscious revolts and forces me to lose my way. Without me, you would never find your way back. Neither of us wants that. Please change now."

I don't know if I can, I think.

The tune changes, turning faster, the melody brighter. *"Try,"* the words say.

I start to shift myself to human form, but something blocks my thought and nudges it in a new, strange direction. I stop and try to pull back.

"Peter," the words say, *"Do not fight me."*

It feels bad, I think.

The nudge turns into a push. I shove against it. *"Give in to it. The bad feelings will pass,"* the words say, the humming turning louder. *"Please let me help you."*

I sigh and surrender, my body shrinking, turning unfamiliar as my wings pull in and join together to form a dorsal fin. My claws and arms follow, compressing, smoothing into flippers. My tail shortens and thickens, my rear legs folding in and broadening into a powerful pair of flukes.

Lorrel's tune suddenly seems too loud to bear, and I pull my head back, aware of the sound of every breeze no matter how slight, every ripple on the surface of the water no matter how small. Her humming ceases, a cool rush running through my body as she withdraws from me. *"Now,"* she mindspeaks, *"We can be on our way."*

21

What joy it is to be a dolphin. It takes me only three timid circuits of the cove before I submerge and start to pick up speed. *"Stay in the cove,"* Lorrel mindspeaks. *"We don't know what waits for us beyond the channel."*

I circle the cove as fast as I can, each switch of my tail shooting me forward, the water parting as if glad to welcome me. Circling again, fast enough to churn the water, I turn upward just before I reach Lorrel, breaking out of the water, shooting skyward with a mighty kick of my tail that sends my entire body airborne. Stalling at the apex of my jump, I fall back, splashing down, a white plume of water rising as I hit and sink from sight.

"Feels good, does it not?" Lorrel mindspeaks.

I surface, clear my blowhole with one strong blast and suck in air. *"Feels great! It's almost as good as flying."*

The Pelk girl sinks into the water, moves away with a flick of her tail. *"I prefer it,"* she mindspeaks. *"Wait here. I need to see whether any dolphins wait ahead."*

"But we look like them now. Why do we have to be concerned?"

"Look at me!" she mindspeaks, staring at me with her emerald-green eyes. *"Your humans may have forgotten what these green eyes mean, but the dolphins understand full well. We have hunted them and fought them too many times for them to think of us as anything but their enemy. No Pelk has ever been able to learn their language or conceal his eyes. Traveling in their form only protects us from them at a distance."* She swims to the narrow channel that leads to the open water and disappears from sight.

Submerging again, I take a few lazy loops of the cove. Lorrel returns just as I surface and clear my blowhole again.

"There were no dolphins in sight. We can go," she mindspeaks, passing my flukes as she swims up to me, her body brushing against my right flipper.

I take in a breath. *"I can't believe how sensitive they are. I sensed your body's warmth as soon as you were near my tail,"* I mindspeak. *"When I move, I feel the water streaming across my skin everywhere. Just your brushing against my flipper was almost too intense."*

Lorrel nods. *"Some of the others have had sex in their dolphin forms. They say it is quite incredible. You will find you have other senses too. Try closing your eyes and swimming around the cove."*

Taking a breath, closing my eyes, I submerge. *"Okay. I don't see anything."*

"Click," Lorrel mindspeaks. *"Like this."* She emits a series of clicks, the sounds traveling away from us, rebounding, almost tickling my lower jaw as they return and their sounds register in my middle ears.

It takes me six attempts before I manage to imitate her clicks, the sounds somehow magnified through my bulbous forehead. The speed and the intensity of the clicks' return form a sort of image inside my head, and I swim forward clicking, certain of my location and of everything around me.

"They can see in the most murky water that way," Lorrel mindspeaks, swimming past me.

I follow her out the channel, into the open sea.

We swim near the surface, breaking the water every few minutes to clear our blowholes and take fresh breaths. Lorrel leads. I follow her course and match my pace to her comfortable cruising speed. *"Why aren't we going any faster?"* I mindspeak.

"Dolphins usually do not race from here to there. We travel at their normal speed. To do otherwise would invite attention. We only have forty miles to travel. We will be there in less than four hours. That is soon enough."

It could take longer for all I care. We pass over reefs and

miles of sandy bottom, the bottom slowly dropping away, the water turning deep and dark blue. When the dark blue lightens, signifying slightly shallower water, Lorrel stops. *"I am hungry,"* she mindspeaks.

I let out a burst of clicks and wait for their return to reveal what might be nearby. They show only my traveling companion. *"We're in the middle of nowhere,"* I mindspeak.

"We are not nowhere. We are over a shipwreck. It is a deep dive, but there are always fish there."

"Why don't we wait until we reach the next reef? There are always fish on those too."

"There are bigger fish below," Lorrel mindspeaks, clearing her blowhole, inhaling and diving.

I follow her, the light dimming as we descend, the water growing colder, its pressure bearing down on us, squeezing us.

On the bottom an ancient cargo ship lies on its side, its rusted hull split open in three places, cases of cargo scattered on the sand, fish flitting in and out of the ragged openings.

A large grouper pokes its head out of one of them, spies us and tucks back in. Lorrel shoots toward it and I follow. By the time I make it into the deep recesses of the ship, the Pelk girl has already found and killed the fish. Blood fills the water around us, attracting smaller fish who feed off the grouper's remnants as Lorrel and I take turns ripping pieces from it and gulping them down.

A dolphin's shrill whistle sounds from outside the ship and Lorrel and I freeze, let the last remnants of the grouper float away from us. *"Do you know what that's about?"* I mindspeak.

Lorrel shakes her head.

We stay still, listen to the dolphin's clicks and its occasional whistles. After a minute all goes silent. *"Do you think it's left?"* I mindspeak.

"I have no idea," Lorrel mindspeaks. *"But we will need to breathe soon."*

I nod. We swim side by side to the gash in the metal that had allowed us entry to the ship. When neither of us notices anything threatening in the water nearby, we venture out and swim toward the surface.

Five large dolphins swim up from the other side of the ship. Four of them angle away, but one swims in our direction.

"Just keep swimming toward the surface," Lorrel mindspeaks, shifting position so that my body blocks the other dolphin's view of her. He shifts position too, rising on her side of me, accelerating toward us.

The Pelk girl shifts again to my other side. *"Do not look at him! If he notices our eyes he will call the others."*

"What do you think he wants?" I mindspeak.

"We are strangers to him. He may be curious. He may be on guard or . . . he may be interested in me."

We reach the surface, blasting our blowholes clear, taking in fresh breaths. *"Keep your head up!"* Lorrel mindspeaks. *"It will make it harder for him to see your eyes."*

The dolphin breaks the surface a few yards from us, blasts air from its blowhole and coasts toward Lorrel. As he passes her he rubs one of his fins over hers.

Lorrel looks away from him and shifts to my other side again. The dolphin shifts too. *"Doesn't he see you're with me?"* I mindspeak.

"Unfortunately, dolphins are not monogamous. I don't think he cares who I am with."

This time the dolphin approaches on his side, one fin pointing skyward, his pale underbelly showing flushed pink. Lorrel shifts sides once again and the dolphin whistles and clicks at her. When she doesn't reply he turns back onto his belly, circling both of us, whistling and clicking.

"In a minute he'll dive and call for his friends," Lorrel mindspeaks. *"Move away. When he comes close to me—rush back."*

I drift away from Lorrel until over six yards separate us. She turns on her side and somehow manages to flush her belly a dull pink. As soon as the dolphin sees it he races toward her.

Lorrel waits until the beast comes close enough to brush his body against hers. Shifting one of her flippers into a clawed arm, she rakes him as he rubs by her, slitting him open from chest to tail.

His shrill whistles fill the air and water. He thrashes, the water churning, turning red with his blood. I speed toward them, shifting my mouth and jaws, my fangs growing, my flippers changing into deadly clawed arms.

By the time I reach the flailing creature, Lorrel has ripped him open a second time. I clamp my fangs on his throat just under his jaw, crunching down, breaking bone and cartilage, digging into him, robbing him of whatever remains of his life.

The dolphin's body goes limp and Lorrel tears a chunk from him and gulps it down. *"Feed quickly!"* she mindspeaks. *"We have little time until his companions realize what has happened and come after us. We must shift back to our dolphin forms and get to Dryndl's Tomb before they catch up to us."*

I swallow down dolphin meat, gorge on as much of it as I can. *"Why don't we change the rest of the way to our natural forms and fight them here? There are just four of them."*

"It is a fight we might win. But we could lose it too. We saw only four others, but have no way of knowing how many others swim within calling distance. If need be, I can outswim them in my natural form. You have not learned how to do that yet. It is better for you if we stay in our dolphin forms," she mindspeaks. *"We must leave now!"*

Lorrel shoots away and I race after her. I've watched dolphins many times as they kept pace with all but my Grady White's highest speeds, so it comes as no surprise to me that we can slice through the water so quickly. Still, I worry how long we can keep up the pace. *"How much further do we have to go?"* I mindspeak.

"No more than ten miles. Can you not swim faster?" The Pelk girl speeds up, pulling away from me. *"They will be coming soon."*

I would rather turn and face them, but somehow I manage to find the strength to kick harder and speed up to her. The ten miles pass in a blur of water and white foam.

Dryndl's Tomb turns out to be a tiny, sand-covered island rising barely three feet out of the water, sporting only a half dozen crooked and dwarfed pine trees. It lies just past the south tip of Andros Island—so close that I can make out the green outline of its mangrove and pine swamps.

We circle the small island once, the waters clear and shallow on three sides, dark blue and deep on the eastern side. After repeating our circuit a second time, we stop, floating just off shore, both of us sucking air into our blowholes, our sides heaving from our long sprint.

I search the waters around us, looking for the first sign of a dorsal fin approaching, listening for the first telltale whistle or click. *"Where to now?"* I mindspeak.

"Mowdar said to look for two large rocks sticking up from the sand by the edge of the island. We have to go through them to find the entrance to Dryndl's Tomb. Look around. Do you see any large rocks sticking up?"

Raising partway out of the water, balancing on my tail, I study the island and find nothing. *"Are you sure you have the right island?"* I mindspeak.

"Undrae! I am a Pelk. We do not lose our way!"

Water breaks fifteen yards ahead of me. A blast of air follows as a dolphin clears its blowhole. Three more blasts follow—all four beasts positioned between us and the island. Lorrel and I both dive, racing toward the bottom, trying to pass under them.

"We don't have to stay in the water," I mindspeak. *"We can change shape and go up on the island. After dark, I could fly us to your srrynn."*

"Only if everything else fails," Lorrel mindspeaks. *"Mowdar wants me to bring something from the tomb. It would be best to find the rocks."*

We manage to pass under the four beasts before they react and dive. I follow Lorrel as she speeds ahead, the Pelk girl rising to the surface to circle the island and search. But instead of swimming on the surface I stay below, watching in case one of the dolphins threatens to catch up to her.

By the time we reach the dark blue waters of the deep side, two dolphins race into sight from the other direction, and two appear behind us. Rather than speeding after Lorrel all four dive toward me.

Flipping over, diving, I mindspeak, *"Lorrel! They're after me! Go ashore before they can turn on you next."*

I plummet downward, the water turning cold, rushing past me, pressure building around me. The four dolphins click and whistle behind me, their sounds still far away but drawing a little bit closer every few seconds.

"I'm coming," Lorrel mindspeaks. *"Swim toward the island! We may find a hiding place there."*

"So we can run out of air and suffocate while we hide?" I mindspeak. But I angle toward the island, staring at the sheer drop its stone side makes, from the surface to the sandy bottom somewhere below.

The light dims the further I dive, until all goes dark around me. Without using my clicks and hearing to see, I would be blind. I swim on, the clicks and whistles of the beasts behind me continuing to draw near.

Finally, my clicks rebound almost instantly, showing me I've neared bottom. I level off, scraping my underbelly on the sand as I shoot toward the island's stone wall. I hear/see two large rocks jutting from the sand toward my right and gasp. Altering course toward them, I mindspeak, *"I found your rocks!"*

"Swim through them!"

I race between the two rocks, a hole in the sheer stone wall suddenly looming before me. Shooting into the hole, I find myself in a large, circular, stone chamber. As I circle it without finding an exit anywhere on its walls, one dolphin after another slips into the chamber and begins circling me.

Each one seems larger than the next, none of them less than ten feet long. I consider shifting to my natural form—my deadliest. But I realize if I do so, I'll lose all ability to see in this dark water. Just shifting my mouth would prevent my jaw from receiving the reflected clicks that now make up my sight.

The four dolphins continue to circle, spreading themselves out until they have me surrounded on all sides. The largest of them lets out a whistle and they rush toward me.

With no choice but to stay and fight or to swim upward, I shoot up with a kick of my tail. But I find the stone dome of the cavern after only thirty yards. With four angry dolphins hot behind me, I scrape along the ceiling, looking, searching for any possible advantage.

The lead dolphin bites down on my left fluke. I rip it away from him and kick away, my blood seeping into the cold water.

Kicking frantically, trying to leave him behind, I almost shoot past the crevice.

It's barely six feet wide. I have no idea where it leads, but I slip into it and follow it upward. The lead dolphin trails just behind me, closing in and biting my poor fluke once again. But this time, in a closed place, with no danger of more than one creature attacking, I shift my good fluke into a leg and lash back at him with my rear talons.

Bleeting shrill whistles, the creature falls back. I ignore its pain and continue to rise. *"Lorrel? Where are you?"* I mind-speak.

"Just past the rocks. Where are you . . . and they?"

"I found a crevice in the chamber ceiling. It seems to go up. I think the dolphins are still in the chamber—though one of them's probably pretty unhappy right now."

"You should come to Dryndl's Tomb any moment."

With no dolphins in pursuit I become aware of the tightness building in my lungs. *"I hope so,"* I mindspeak. *"How much longer can the dolphins hold their breath?"*

"They cannot go more than about fifteen minutes between breaths. You should be able to go longer."

"I think I did," I mindspeak.

"Just go a little further. I am sure all will be well for you. But I am not sure how to join you. . . ."

My head breaks clear of the water and I let out a blast of air, clearing my blowhole, sucking dank cave air in. *"I just made it up to the tomb. I'm going to swim back down. I'll call for you to join me in the chamber when I do. You have a while until you run out of air, don't you?"*

"I was the last to dive."

"Good," I mindspeak. *"They have to start feeling a need for air pretty soon."*

Taking one last breath, I dive down the crevice, racing for the bottom as quickly as my flippers and flukes can carry me. Calling out to Lorrel, *"Now!"* I burst into the chamber, ramming the largest dolphin in his side, biting his flukes as he writhes in agony.

Another dolphin shoots toward me, and Lorrel slams into it, leaving the stunned creature and biting another. The fourth dolphin turns and streaks out of the chamber, toward the open ocean. I wheel and ram the Pelk girl's first target, the beast shuddering from the impact and swimming away slowly toward the chamber entrance.

With only one healthy dolphin left, I mindspeak, *"Go find the crevice!"* and turn, rushing at the creature. But, either low on air or unsure it can win, it turns and flees too.

Just the large dolphin remains, its body twitching on the chamber floor. I consider finishing it, but my lungs have already begun to ache for fresh air. Leaving it to die, I speed upward to the crevice and climb until I burst from the water. My sides heaving, my heart still racing, I clear my blowhole and suck in deeps breaths of cave air.

"Do you still find dolphins so lovable?" Lorrel mindspeaks.

I look up from the water. Already in her natural form, the Pelk girl has begun pouring phosphorescent powder into a glowpool, a green glow growing, chasing the dark from the small cavern.

"I find I like fighting them even less than I like eating them," I mindspeak.

Lorrel trills out a laugh. *"It appears to me you do both equally well. Mowdar will be pleased."*

"Mowdar's opinion means nothing to me."

"Undrae, take care. It will go better for you if he respects you."

"What will go better?" I mindspeak.

She shakes her head. *"Come join me. This is another safehold. We have dried fish stored here. Change form, eat and rest. We are not far from home. You will have all your questions answered soon."*

My wounds ache, as do my lungs and my empty stomach. I yearn to be done with this, to be home, to rest in my bed, not on a pile of seaweed in a cold, dank cave. *"Not soon enough,"* I mindspeak.

22

This time I accept when Lorrel offers me a dried slab of fish. This time I offer no objection when she sits next to me, so close that her haunch warms mine. After all, I've allowed the Pelk girl to penetrate my consciousness. How can I object to such a small, innocent physical thing as our sides touching after such intimacy?

Besides, Caya DeLaSangre and Miami, Chloe and my children, seem so far away, so long ago. I count the days and shake my head. Only three have passed, and the fourth still has many hours until it ends. Chloe won't even be back from Morgan's Hole for days more.

I frown, wonder how I've come to feel so distant from my family in such a short time. Focusing my mind on my wife, I picture her and our children until I finally ache for their company again.

Lorrel nudges closer, pressing against me. *"You fight as well as any Pelk. I think I would have died before without your help,"* she mindspeaks.

"I think you would have escaped to the island and waited for the dolphins to leave."

She strokes her tail over mine, the underside of hers smooth and pleasant as it massages me. *"I gave you a compliment, Undrae. Accept it."*

"Sure," I mindspeak, my stomach full of dried fish, my body relaxing after our hours of tension and effort, the Pelk girl's warmth joining with the rest to make me drowsy. I lean toward Lorrel, press slightly against her before I catch myself and pull back. Chloe, I think, Chloe. How I wish she were with me now.

Lorrel nuzzles her snout against my shoulder. *"We cannot*

sleep now, Peter. We must go. Mowdar will be impatient if we stay here too long," she mindspeaks. *"I will make a nest for you tonight. You will be able to sleep long into morning."*

I shake my head. *"In the morning I will want to leave as soon as possible."*

"Of course," she mindspeaks. *"Whatever you and Mowdar decide."*

Lorrel leads me away from the water to a dark passageway at the far side of the small cavern. *"Dryndl and his srrynn carved this passageway during the Great War. They cut an entire staircase out of the rock. This was the first Pelk safehold. Dryndl died defending it from the Undrae, and his srrynn entombed him somewhere in its walls. Mowdar says the staircase will lead us to another cavern where we will find our way out."*

"Mowdar told you about the two rocks too, right?"

She looks at me and shakes her head. *"I have nothing to carry glowlight in, so follow me as best you can."*

After a few steps, we leave the green glow of the cavern behind us. I feel my way up each wide stone step, aware of Lorrel scuffling in front of me.

We reach another cavern after only a few minutes of climbing. Lorrel feels around until she finds supplies stacked on stone shelves. Once again she sprinkles phosphorescent powder into a small glowpool. She returns to the shelves, searches until she picks up a small package, wrapped in what looks like leather, about the size of a hardbound book. *"Good, this is what Mowdar wanted."*

"And it is?"

"I only know that I was to find something wrapped in dolphin hide. We use that to make things waterproof. I am sure Mowdar will explain what is inside."

I laugh. *"He's going to need a list to explain all the things you've promised."*

The Pelk girl ignores me. *"We can leave now,"* she mindspeaks, pointing to the far corner of the cavern, where water laps against the stone. *"That underwater passageway will take us to the outside. It will not be too much farther before we reach*

*my srrynn's hunting waters. Few dolphins venture there any-
more. We will have no need to change from our natural forms."*

Heaving a long sigh, I frown at the dark water. I want no
more dampness, no more swimming underwater until my chest
threatens to burst. *"Can't we go another way?"* I mindspeak.

The Pelk girl shakes her head. *"There is no other way."*

After the dark of the deep water and the caverns, I emerge
from the passageway expecting night. Instead, we swim into
water made warm and light by a late-afternoon sun. Lorrel
swims toward the surface and I follow her, both of us skimming
just under the surface, taking breaths when we please. She sets
the pace, holding the package in her front claws, using her
broad tail to propel her forward, swimming in a straight line toward the southern tip of Andros Island.

"So we are going to Andros after all, aren't we?" I mindspeak.

"My srrynn has made a safehold there," Lorrel mindspeaks.
*"We will soon reach a blue hole. We can wait until it sighs, the
way it did in the safehold in Bimini, and dive into it and let its
current carry us underground to my srrynn. Or we can swim to
the south tip of the island and follow Lusca Creek until it disappears into the mangroves."*

"All things being equal," I mindspeak. *"I could do without
being sucked down a hole again. As long as we don't have to
worry about humans. . . ."*

*"Where we are going is wilderness. No humans live near it.
No fishing boats or kayaks can penetrate the mangroves. Few
natives would care to go there anyway. They have a legend
about a sea monster they call a Lusca. It is supposed to lurk in
blue holes and kill humans. Mowdar said the Indians gave our
kind that name hundreds of years ago."*

Close up, the south end of Andros Island looks like nothing
but a jungle of mangrove trees slashed open occasionally by a
narrow creek or indented by a small bay. No landmark differ-
entiates Lusca Creek from all the others, still Lorrel leads me
into it without hesitation.

Within minutes we've lost all sight of the open water. We

take so many turns and pass so many false passages that I doubt I could ever swim my way out. The waterway narrows and soon we find ourselves swimming under a canopy of mangrove branches.

"In a few minutes we will reach a small lagoon. It is another blue hole. I am afraid you will have to dive with me again," Lorrel mindspeaks, slowing, waiting for me to swim by her side. *"I will be glad to rejoin my srrynn, but sorry for this to end. I hope you do not think me too terrible. I have only done what I must."*

She presses a little more against me and then shoots forward, toward a solid wall of mangroves, diving under the largest one. I follow, passing under its roots, emerging into a small, circular lagoon.

Lorrel dives and I follow again, shooting down, descending forty or fifty feet until a dark hole shows in the far wall of the lagoon. The Pelk girl races toward it and I speed after her.

We swim through the black darkness of the underwater passageway and then up, emerging into another lagoon, this one larger, surrounded on all sides by a huge cavern, green lights glowing from dozens of glowpools scattered on the ground beyond the sandy shore.

The Pelk girl swims to a sloping, sandy beach and walks up onto dry land. She waits there for me, other Pelk emerging from the shadows, dozens of them, male, female, young, old—all in their natural forms, most as dark and sleek as Lorrel, a few lighter and tending toward gray, none anywhere as large as me. I walk up to her. *"This is my srrynn, Peter,"* she mindspeaks.

I nod, mindspeak. *"And Mowdar?"*

"He does not come to others. We must go to him."

We push through the crowd, Lorrel mindspeaking to each one as they greet her, telling each one's name to me. After the first few, I give up trying to remember any of their names or appearances.

Some of the Pelk follow us as we make our way through their safehold. Others fall away, wandering off to nests of seaweed—some tented tepee-style with woven seaweed supported by irregular branches of driftwood, and some open to view. Other Pelk gather together in small groups around the dull

green light of their small glowpools. We pass them and piles of
what look like, at best, the flotsam and jetsam one would find
on the beach. We pass other stacks too, made of nautical and
fishing gear obviously salvaged from the sea.

Mowdar sits on one haunch on a nest of seaweed, his back
against the wall of an alcove cut out of the cave's stone wall.
Drapes woven from seaweed hang on either side of the alcove's
opening, like curtains at a theater. Piles of seaweed form seat-
ing areas in a semicircle facing the alcove with a large, bright
glowpool between the seats and Mowdar.

A few Pelk have already seated themselves, waiting along
with the Pelk leader for our arrival. I stare at their backs, frowning at that of a large one, the creature shaped and colored far
more like one of my own kind than a Pelk.

Mowdar stands on his rear legs. At most he may be a few
inches taller than Lorrel. His scales have turned irregular with
age, and his color lightened to an ashen gray. Picking up a trident, a three-pointed spear, with his right claw, he motions with
it for Lorrel and me to take the center seats facing him.

"You have taken a long time to arrive," he mindspeaks.

Lorrel bows her head ever so slightly. *"It was unavoidable,
Father. The Undrae did not come willingly."*

The creature coughs out a laugh. *"He is his father's son."*

*"And he wants to know why you sent your daughter to poi-
son him,"* I mindspeak. *"If you truly knew anything about my
father, then you should know better than to make an enemy of a
DelaSangre."*

*"Well said, old man. Well said. Does the old bugger good to
have someone put him in his place."*

I turn and stare at the large creature seated just a few feet
from me, and my jaw drops open.

My brother-in-law, Derek Blood, returns my stare. *"Sorry
about all this, old man. I didn't mean to get you involved."*

23

Mowdar hisses, slashes his trident in a short arc in front of him. *"Enough!"* he mindspeaks.

He stares at me, making a show of examining every inch of my body. *"Undrae,"* he mindspeaks. *"You are not the only one here who has DelaSangre blood running in his veins. I am Mowdar, son of Gedalia, the only child from the union of my grandmother, Dalhanna, and my grandfather, Don Henri DelaSangre."*

I shake my head. *"My father made no secret of his history. He told me about the wives he had before my mother and about his other sons and daughters. He never once mentioned the Pelk or a Pelk mate."*

The Pelk leader turns his gaze on Lorrel. *"Daughter, did you bring it?"*

She nods, gets up and walks to Mowdar, the small package she brought from Dryndl's Tomb held in her outstretched claws. He takes it from her and then stares at her throat. Touching near the partially healed puncture wounds with his trident, he mindspeaks, *"You have been much injured?"*

"Not terribly so. It is just a dolphin bite. . . ."

"Just?" The Pelk shakes his head. *"We have lost others to such wounds. I will have a healing circle come to you later. They will help you become whole again."*

"Thank you, Father." Lorrel nods and backs away.

Mowdar looks at me again. *"Your father, my grandfather, did much harm to my people. I cannot say just why he kept you in ignorance, but I would think he did not want you to know you had relatives among the Pelk. I doubt he wanted you to go searching for us."*

I frown. *"At least I'd think he'd want me to know that your srrynn was living so close to our island—in case I needed to defend myself."*

"He would have been sure there were no such need. By the time you were born we had been gone for centuries. Your father attacked us with his ships and cannons, at night when we were asleep in this safehold. He killed most of us in the attack, sparing Dalhanna and my father, and allowing the twelve others who survived to leave with them—as long as they swore to go far south and to never return.

"Our people have long mourned that exile. We had lived in these waters since before the rule of Atala. You cannot imagine the joy that went through our srrynn when that one"—Mowdar points his trident toward Derek—*"told us that Don Henri no longer lived."*

I turn and glare at my brother-in-law.

Derek shrugs and mindspeaks, *"Look, old man, I told you it was unintentional. I was in the same fix as you are now and just making conversation . . ."*

"You," Mowdar mindspeaks, pointing his trident at Derek, glaring. *"You will have much time to talk later—if he cares to listen."* The Pelk leader looks at me again. *"Because of that wonderful news, Gedalia decided to send part of his srrynn to reestablish our home here. He also instructed me to find you and bring you into our family."*

Mowdar turns his attention to the package, slitting it open with a pass of his claw. He lets the dolphin skin drop to the ground and holds up the slim, ancient book that had been inside. *"We do share a common blood. You already saw my grandmother's ring. This was your father's,"* he mindspeaks, holding it out to me.

Taking the old manuscript from him, I examine its cracked leather binding, find no sign of words ever having been printed on either the front or rear cover. *"It's not one of his log books,"* I mindspeak, opening it, small flakes of brittle paper crumbling and falling as I leaf through the pages. Squinting at the hand-written words, I struggle to make out what they say, wish I had more to read by than the green light of the nearby glowpool. Still, it takes only a moment for me to realize that the words have been written in my father's hand, and to regret that he chose to write each one *in Spanish*.

"*My father wrote this,*" I mindspeak.

"*I know. My grandmother said he wrote in it every day he was among us. She hid this in Dryndl's Tomb when she left. It was a safehold your father had never been shown.*"

"*I don't understand. If he married your grandmother, why would he turn on her?*"

The Pelk sighs. "*Like you, Undrae, we are not a numerous people. But we also suffer having mostly female offspring. Without occasionally adding outside male blood we would become too ingrown and wither away in only a few generations. It is our tradition to get that blood by luring others in—the way Lorrel has done with you and the way Dalhanna did with your father.*"

"*But I'm already mated,*" I mindspeak.

"*True,*" Mowdar mindspeaks. "*Your father was not. Gedalia said that Dalhanna told him Don Henri's first wife had died and he was lonely. He came here willingly with her and laid with her without protest. It was only after he was told that he could not leave that his anger grew.*"

"*My father was very powerful. How did they think they could hold him?*"

Mowdar looks to his daughter. "*Lorrel, has he felt the poison?*"

Lorrel nods.

He stares directly into my eyes. "*Then you know how we were certain we could hold him.*"

A chill goes through me. I look around the semicircle. More Pelk have drifted over, some taking up all the remaining sitting space, and the rest standing behind. Glancing back, I see that two males have taken positions behind me. Both hold tridents like Mowdar's.

"*But either you neutralized the poison and let him leave or my father found a way to do it himself,*" I mindspeak.

"*No one knows how Don Henri overcame the poison. Certainly no Pelk helped him.*"

I attempt to stand up, but tridents are pushed against my sides, just hard enough to let me know how sharp they are.

"Relax, Peter. You are our guest. Life can be very pleasant among the Pelk. Can it not, Derek?" Mowdar mindspeaks.

Derek nods. *"I've no complaints. Really, Peter . . . except for having to eat all the bloody fish. I'd do almost anything for a bite of fresh meat again. . . . But besides that, things couldn't be much better. No one expects me to do anything but boff their women. I've three mates now, each one sweeter and more willing than the next. They might not be Undrae, but so what? It beats mucking about with human females and searching all over hell and gone for a mate."*

Shaking my head, I mindspeak, *"If that's all you want, then good for you, Derek. But don't forget I'm married to your sister. We have two kids."* I look at Mowdar. *"My wife will be in Miami in a few days. I need to be there."*

"We all have needs," Mowdar mindspeaks. *"I need to eat soon. Lorrel needs to heal. You will be needing another sip of antidote soon, won't you?"*

I turn to Lorrel and she mindspeaks, *"Tomorrow night."*

Looking back to Mowdar, I mindspeak, *"Not until then."*

"Good," Mowdar mindspeaks. *"So for tonight, let us tend to our immediate needs. We can all worry about our futures later."*

"I have a wife and children!" I jump up and remain standing, ignoring the two Pelk males, their tridents pressed against my scales.

Mowdar walks forward, until he stands within a trident's distance from me. He thrusts his at me, stopping just centimeters from my chest. *"My people found during the Great War that we could not prevail against Undrae without weapons. We learned to make these from ironwood. We found tiger shark's teeth to be especially hard. We inset them at each point. They are most sharp."*

He presses the trident against me, pushing it forward. I gasp as the trident's three points each penetrate my armored scales as easily as if they were piercing cardboard. Mowdar mindspeaks, *"You are our guest now. It would be a shame if you insisted on being our prisoner instead."*

Pulling back his spear, each tip now red with my blood, he motions with it, and other Pelk come forward with gold and sil-

ver platters stacked with fish and lobster. Two Pelk males drag
a large dolphin up to Mowdar and leave it at his feet. A female
cuts a slice of meat from it and offers it to the Pelk leader. He
shakes his head and motions for her to go to me.

"Please share our feast with us," he mindspeaks as she
brings the meat to me.

After the meal, Mowdar retires to his nest, and most of the
Pelk drift off to theirs. Lorrel mindspeaks, *"I promised to make
a nest for you,"* and wanders off too, leaving just Derek and me
sitting on the seaweed seats.

"You really like it here?" I mindspeak.

The creature thinks for a few moments before answering.
*"You know me, old man. A full belly, a warm and willing female
and no chores gets as close to paradise as I can imagine. At
home Pa and Mum were always going on about my responsi-
bilities and what I had to do to help them maintain Morgan's
Hole. Here I only have to worry about which wife I want to take
to bed."*

"So you joined them willingly?"

*"Don't be daft, man. I knew Pelk existed, but I didn't know
any lived anywhere near Jamaica. I was just out prowling late
at night, on the beach in my human form. You'd be surprised
how many tourists, single women, go off wandering down the
sand in the dark by themselves.*

*"All I wanted was a bit of a roll with one, and of course a
meal. But I ran into this most extraordinary girl, tiny really, not
a lick of hair on her body, white as ocean foam. She didn't say
a word, just laid down for me and spread her arms and legs and
let me do whatever."*

Derek stretches and sighs. *"It was magnificent. I wish I could
go back and experience it for the first time again."* He pauses
and looks at me. *"But you know what I mean, don't you, old
man?"*

I shake my head. *"Chloe and I are mated. I refused Lorrel."*

"So you haven't had her yet?"

"Nor will I," I mindspeak.

Derek guffaws. *"You have much to learn about Pelk females,"* he mindspeaks.

I think about saying that I don't want to learn any more about any Pelk. I just want to go home. But instead I just shrug. *"What I'd like to know,"* I mindspeak, *"is how you ended up joining their srrynn and how they learned enough to come after me?"*

"I didn't join anything. It was awkward after I finished with Sybyli—that's her name. I mean, she had been extraordinary, and I wasn't sure I wanted to lose out on any more of that by eating her. I still thought she was human then. No, I didn't notice her eyes, old man. There were better things than that to stare at. But she knew what I was. And while I was lying there mulling over what to do, she stabbed me with this thing. You know all about how it works, don't you?"

I nod.

"Anyway, after I calmed down, Sybyli explained that she'd seen me shift shape at the beach months before and had been waiting to meet me. She said I could choose either to have a painful death or to return to her srrynn with her." Derek huffs out a laugh. *"Not much of a choice for a creature like me. I went right to her syyrrn with her that night. I couldn't believe it! They had a safehold in this huge cavern underneath one of the islands off Port Royale. They've been living just next to Jamaica for over two hundred years, and none of us have ever known."*

"And why did you mention me?"

"Don't flatter yourself, old man. You are not on my mind all that much. I was lying with Sybyli a few nights after I came to their srrynn. It was after sex and we were just having a sleepy conversation before we both drifted off. I asked if any of the Pelk had a problem with my being different, and she told me that she wasn't the first Pelk to take an Undrae lover—that their leader Gedalia was half Undrae himself.'

"She said Gedalia's father was a monster who had killed many of the Pelk, that Gedalia cursed the day his mother met Don Henri DelaSangre and wished each night for his death. All I said was that Don Henri had been dead for years. The next morning, I was called before a council of the srrynn's leaders, including Mowdar and Gedalia himself. They demanded to hear everything I knew about your family."

Derek stretches and rises. *"And that was that, old man. Now I think I'll go back to my nest to rest a bit. It's Tantra's turn to be with me tonight. I'll need all the energy I can muster for that."*

I rise too and look at the creature. He stands a good half foot taller than I, and he measures at least that much wider—all in muscle. We've fought before and I've beaten him, but I respect his strength if not his character and intellect. I wonder if I could find any way to enlist him as an ally if the need arises. And I wonder if it would be worth the bother.

"I'm sorry my words got you into this fix. Believe me, I had no idea what their plan was," Derek mindspeaks. *"If you decide to leave I wish you luck. But take care with how you go about it. These Pelk are more than they appear to be."*

I watch him walk away, weaving his way through the scattered nests and piles, the dull green glow of each pond growing and shrinking his shadow on the stone floor as he passes. Wondering about my brother-in-law's words, his cryptic warning, I look around the safehold.

The seaweed drapes over Mowdar's nest have been closed and now block any view of any activities within it. Most of the other Pelk have erected tents over their nests, ensuring their privacy too. Four females bustle in an alcove to the right of Mowdar's, raising drapes that look like his. One turns and looks at me and I realize it's Lorrel.

"Hi," I mindspeak, walking toward her.

She turns her back, busies herself helping one of the other females. *"We're almost ready,"* she mindspeaks. *"The nest is finished. You can lie down if you wish."*

The other females look away as I pass. I enter the nest, circling a few times to work out a comfortable place and then settling onto the bed of seaweed. It gives a little beneath me, surprising me with its silky, soft texture. I stretch out and then curl my body, my tail curling to the outside of that, my head resting on top of my front claws.

I sigh and let my eyes partly close. The day has been a long one, and my body aches for me to let it drop off into sleep. But I'm unwilling to yield to slumber just yet. Eyeing each female as they bustle around me—one adding phosphorescence to the

small glowpool next to my nest, another bringing yet more seaweed to plump up the far corner of my nest, Lorrel and the
other one finishing hanging the seaweed drapes and drawing
them closed—I find myself feeling like the turkey who was in-
vited for Thanksgiving dinner.

The other females withdraw and Lorrel joins me in the nest,
lying down beside me, snuggling close. I shift away a few
inches. *"Why must you be like that?"* Lorrel mindspeaks.

"Why don't we have separate nests?"

*"I have just now finished this one. I am weary and my
wounds ache. Are you going to force me to leave and spend
hours more building another nest?"*

I sit up. *"I can go."*

She reaches up and pulls me back. *"You cannot. Mowdar will
lose respect for me. I will not bother you for anything you do
not care to give. We have slept side by side before, Peter. Please
do not make me go."*

"I want no one but Chloe," I mindspeak.

"Yes, Peter, I know that well." Lorrel sidles closer. *"Your
warmth comforts me. That is all. Did you not find it comfortable to sleep beside me last night?"*

I nod and the Pelk girl snuggles against me. In truth, I like
the feel of her body pressing against mine. Her warmth relaxes
me. If it stirs nothing in my loins, if it brings no thoughts of desire to my mind, what harm can it bring? Closing my eyes, I listen to her breathing and start to drift away.

Something rustles outside the drapes and I open one eye.
Soon more rustling sounds come and I open my other eye and
raise my head. *"Calm yourself, Peter. It is just the healing circle gathering. Remember? Father promised to send them to
me?"*

"Am I in the way? Is there something I should do?" I mindspeak.

*"Just stay where you are. Let me lie with you like this. As
soon as they have a li-srrynn, a gathering of fifteen Pelk females, they will start."*

"What are they going to do?"

"Shhh, just sleep," she mindspeaks.

I close my eyes again, sleep creeping over my body, making

my limbs heavy and my breathing slow. Outside the drapes one of the Pelk begins to sing a single note. Unlike Lorrel's humming, this note rings high and clear, a delicate, slight sound that somehow seems to penetrate every molecule around and inside me.

Another Pelk joins in, singing a lower note in such perfect harmony that I sigh. Then another starts singing and another, their notes rising and falling, slowly weaving over and under each other, more Pelk singing, their song forming a blanket of sound that settles over Lorrel and me.

Opening my eyes, I glance at the Pelk girl. Her eyes closed, her breathing slow, she looks as if sleep has taken her. The angry red puncture wounds on her neck have already shrunk to mere pinpricks. The last of the Pelk outside joins in and the song wells up around us. Lorrel sighs and presses against me, her tail wrapping over mine.

The rhythm of the tune speeds and slows and Lorrel sighs again and begins to undulate her body against me in time to the tune. I try to pull back, try to concentrate on Chloe, but the notes invade my mind and pulse through my body, vibrating through each cell.

I sigh too, my body beginning to move in rhythm with the tune, in counterpoint to Lorrel's. Congestion grows in my loins and I feel the first stirrings of desire. *"I do not want this!"* I mindspeak, as the music swells and Lorrel thrusts herself hard against me again. I press back and moan, as much with grief as with desire.

Lorrel opens her eyes and pulls away for a moment, her breathing ragged now, her motion smooth, almost snakelike as she moves her body. She makes no display of herself the way an Undrae female would, nor does she offer herself to me. Rather she pushes her snout under my jaw and begins to hum the same tune as the Pelk outside the drapes.

Their tune grows quieter, one voice after another dropping out, a few Pelk at a time rustling off until only Lorrel's humming fills the air. If anything it penetrates me even more. I have no will to push her away. I want whatever she plans, my body throbbing, pulsing with her rhythm, my heart pounding.

"I have wanted you since I first saw you," Lorrel mind-speaks.

I mindpeak, *"No! Please stop!"* but she touches her tail between my legs and my body betrays me. Stroking down the inside of my legs and back up, she guides her tail over mine, running it up and down a little further each time until she arrives back at the space between my legs and touches there too. I gasp as her feather-light strokes bring me to full rigidity, quivering at each stroke, my chest heaving as I gasp my breaths.

Still humming, her notes still coursing through me, Lorrel pushes against me and guides me onto my back. I concentrate on Chloe. I want only her. I try to picture her in my mind, but find I can't summon her image. When Lorrel lies on top of me I manage to repeat, *"I do not want this,"* but can offer no resistance.

She slides her body down mine until I feel the wet warmth of her resting at the tip of my cock. Digging her claws into my chest, Lorrel changes her tune, low notes vibrating through me as she lowers herself onto me ever so slowly.

The tune and the hot, tight pleasure of her contact drive all thoughts of Chloe out of my mind. I try to writhe, try to press up against her, but even the slightest tightening of my muscles brings a warning, *"No!"* and the sharp pain of her claws digging into me.

When the Pelk girl has taken all of me inside her, she trills out a laugh and quickens her song, the notes coming between ragged breaths, the tune rising and falling in ever quickening cycles. I lie still beneath her, gasping, dying to grab her, mount her and ram into her, but amazed at the tight hold her body has on me, as if the Pelk girl has fingers inside of her.

I lose all sense of time, pay attention only to the sounds and sensations of our coupling, Lorrel's song becoming just a succession of high and low notes, her tail slapping on top of mine, her body beginning to move, her claws digging into me as she bites down on my throat with her teeth, piercing my scales, drawing blood.

"Now!" she mindspeaks and I thrust against her, her grip inside almost unbearably tight, her body thrusting back, her song turning to a single note droning on and on until it suddenly

turns into a high-pitched growl. Lorrel's body freezes and goes rigid, pulsing from tight to loose inside, shuddering as she orgasms, shrieking out an almost inaudible note as I orgasm too.

Lorrel's song slows but doesn't stop, her body still spasming inside, her contractions slower now, less powerful. I find the tune still impossible to resist, glad to let it lull me toward sleep, glad to let it keep my mind away from Chloe and from anger and my shame.

When the last of Lorrel's spasms comes and goes and I shrink away from her, she rolls to my side and presses herself against me. As we both drift into sleep she mindspeaks, *"Now we shall have a son. His name will be Dela, and one day he will rule this srrynn."*

24

A distant splash wakes me. Opening my eyes, I stare into darkness and wonder whether morning's come, or late afternoon, or if I've only slept a few hours. I curl my lip. I am no stranger to caves. I've spent time underground before. I dislike most the lack of the natural pattern of darkness and light.

The bed of seaweed beside me smells of Lorrel, but she no longer lies beside me. Sitting up, I listen for her breathing and hear only the slight rustle of the drapes as they move with the sighing of the cave air. I'm just as glad to find myself alone. The Pelk girl has brought little good into my life.

Stretching, I wince at the wounds Lorrel inflicted upon me the night before, the tightness of my sex-sore muscles. I frown at the memories the pain brings, wish I could wipe them from my mind. But I can forget them no more than I can ignore the hard-used ache in my loins.

I think of Chloe and smile when I find I can picture her again. Whatever Lorrel and the Pelk have done to me, however they've overwhelmed my will, they have not conquered my thoughts. Still, I moan when I think how lost I was in Lorrel's embrace.

Curling my claws into fists, I strike my head once, then again and again. How could I have allowed such a thing to occur? I rake a claw across my chest and welcome the aroma of my fresh blood flowing. How can I expect Chloe to forgive me? I rip myself again. What right do I have to ask for her help? I dig furrows down my right thigh. Letting my blood flow and the pain throb, I stare into the dark and moan.

But after a while, my blood clots on its own and my pain lessens and I tire of my self-pity. Whether or not Chloe will ever be able to accept what I've done, I know I owe it to her and to my children to find my way out of this place. I owe it to Henri to make sure no Pelk female ever can overtake his life the way Lorrel has mine.

I suck in a breath and stretch my body and concentrate on healing my injuries. I am Don Henri's son, I think. If he could find his way out of this place, then so can I.

It takes me only a few minutes to heal my wounds and soreness. Standing up, I feel my way forward, shaking my head at the blackness around me. As well as my kind can see in the dark, we do require some light, if only just a flicker of it. When I stumble into the seaweed drapes, I fumble with them until I finally find the center.

Parting them, I step out from my alcove and find the srrynn's safehold virtually deserted. Only a few glowholes still give off their feeble green light. The seaweed tents of the night before have all come down, and only a few Pelk still seem to be sleeping in their now open nests.

I smile at a thin shaft of bright daylight that burns through the gloom near the cavern's far right side. Weaving my way around nests and the piles of nautical junk the srrynn has collected, I make my way toward the light.

Halfway there I come across the bulk of a large creature sleeping in an open nest under a seaweed blanket. Since I have seen no other Undrae among us, I kick its rear haunch and mindspeak, *"Derek! Wake up, you lazy creature!"*

He moans, digs further under his blanket, and I kick him again.

"Damn it! Have some bloody mercy," he mindspeaks, throwing off the blanket, sitting up, holding his head with both front claws.

"You got me into this. The least you can do is help," I mindspeak.

He looks at me with one bloodshot green eye, motions at a large gourd by the side of the nest. *"Look, old man. Why don't you pass that to me?"*

Liquid sloshes inside it as I pick it up and hand it to my brother-in-law. He upends it and takes a long swallow before he lowers it. *"There now. That's a bit better."* He holds out the gourd to me. *"Care to take a draw of it?"* he mindspeaks.

I shake my head and he shrugs and takes another swallow before he puts it down. *"Remarkable stuff you know. Different from ours."*

"Our what?"

He snorts a laugh. *"Dragon's Tear wine, old man. What else do you think would make time more bearable in a dark hole like this?"*

"I thought you were happy here," I mindspeak.

"I was happy in Coconut Grove. You bloody well fixed that."

I glare at him. *"Get over it, Derek. You were wrong. You were beaten. No one said you couldn't go on and have a life somewhere else."*

"Just Pa."

"My God, you're older than me. You could have just gone."

"Just tell him to piss off? That would work. Sure. And you think the bugger wouldn't tear me from limb to limb?"

"No one says if we get out of here that you have to go back to live with them in Morgan's Hole. You could go look for an Undrae mate."

"Look, old man, I could get killed doing that. You know how many males they attract when they're in heat. Here I get plenty of food and plenty of quiff. . . ."

He pauses, looks at me with both eyes. *"Come to think of it, I'm surprised you're already up. I heard the circle last night—and the rest. You've had some of your own, haven't you?"* He makes a show of smelling the air. *"Righto! Quiff for sure."*

I frown at him. *"Give me a break, Derek. You know how I feel about Chloe. I'm sick over what happened."*

"Give yourself a break, old man. Do you think you could have resisted? No one can withstand the force of their songs. Sybyli told me in the old days dozens of them would form large groups called Syrees. They'd gather near rocks or cliffs and wait for ships to sail near them. Not one of those ships ever resisted the lure of their bloody songs, not a single, bloody sailor ever escaped."

"But they were humans. I am of the Blood."

"So am I. So was your bloody father."

I sigh. *"I just need to get out of here,"* I mindspeak.

Derek looks around. *"So? There's not a soul here to stop you. Mowdar and the men are all out on a dolphin hunt. My wives and the other females are above gardening or tending to other chores."*

"Aren't there any guards?"

"What for? As long as they have the antidote, we might as well be chained here."

"Have any of your women mentioned anything about a way to neutralize the poison?" I mindspeak.

He shakes his head twice. *"I only know I live in fear of not getting the antidote before the poison starts to burn."*

Derek stands, picks up the gourd, drinks from it again and mindspeaks as he puts it down, *"Come on. Now that you've woke me, I'm hungry. We might as well go above and see what the women have found for us."*

We walk toward the light streaming into the cave, stopping when we come upon a large pile of clothes. They look well worn and I wrinkle my nose at the musty smell they give off.

"Don't look down on them, old man. We need them to go above," Derek mindspeaks, shrinking, his scales smoothing, his wings compressing, sinking into his back. I shift shape too, smile as I feel the familiar form of my human body.

Even in his human form, Derek measures inches taller than I, his body broader, his muscles larger and better defined. Still, with our emerald-green eyes, our mutual choice of blond hair and our square-jawed good looks—Derek lacking only my cleft chin—I wouldn't be surprised if a stranger took us for brothers.

We rummage through the pile like two women at a weekend department store sale, Derek holding out shirts and pants for my consideration, I doing the same for him. In the end we both choose shorts and tank tops—a red one for Derek, and a black one for me.

"Don't bother searching for shoes or sneakers. The Pelk don't like to cover their feet," Derek says and smiles. "God, it feels bloody good to talk out loud to someone again. Even in their human form these people only mindspeak. You'd think they'd want to learn English—so they can go into town sometimes—but Sybyli says Mowdar forbids them from having much to do with human ways. It's too bloody Undrae, she said."

Narrow steps have been carved into the cavern wall, and I follow Derek as he makes his way up them. I squint at the glare of the daylight that comes through the hole in the cavern wall at the top of the steps. Derek squints too, ducking when he reaches the hole and squeezing through it. I follow, blinking when I come out from under a large rock into a bright, small clearing surrounded by mangrove trees—each one clustered just inches from the next.

Looking up, I see that the sun has yet to reach its apex. "It's early still," I say.

Derek nods, stretches, inhales a long breath, "Good go that, waking me up. I always feel best up here."

I look around the small clearing and see only the knee-high arched roots and the rough, reddish brown branches and dark green leaves of red mangrove trees clustered so close that it looks like an impenetrable wall of green, thirty feet high, encircling us. "So where did everyone go?"

Stepping onto the gnarled reddish gray arch of a nearby mangrove root, Derek grabs a branch and pulls himself into a tree. "There are no paths on the ground. They travel through the branches." He points forward. "The lagoon is this way. By now they should have some fish for us." Then he gestures to the right. "The gardens are that way. None of them are very large. They trim away branches so sunlight can hit the ground. Pretty smart of them, huh? Everything they do above, they do to avoid discovery. That's why they come above in their human forms, wearing clothes. It makes problems less likely in case some bloody human wanders by or flies overhead."

After going only a few yards I begin to recognize why Derek steps on certain roots, grabs particular branches and knows when and where to turn. The bark on the top of the roots and branches we walk on has become smooth and glossy from the constant traffic of Pelk feet. Likewise, smaller branches, higher up, used for gripping have lost most of the leaves and the brown berries and long green seed pods that dangle from their undisturbed neighbors.

Traveling through the trees reminds me of the jungle gym I played in at school as a child—only springier. I have little trouble keeping up with Derek's pace, and within minutes we find ourselves in the branches of a large mangrove, overlooking the lagoon that Lorrel and I swam through the day before.

Pelk women in their human forms busy themselves on the lagoon's beach, some carrying baskets full of lobsters, crabs and flopping fish, others simply sitting in the sun and weaving seaweed nets. They wear a dizzying array of mismatched shorts and pants, T-shirts and blouses, a few even decked out in long skirts. Other Pelks swim nude in the lagoon, diving and surfacing with even more crustaceans and fish. After searching through them a few times now, I realize that Lorrel isn't among them.

"Look at that, old man," Derek says, tapping me on my shoulder and pointing to a large rock jutting over the water a dozen yards from us. I stare at the pale green iguana basking in the sun and think how much I'd like to do the same thing after spending so much time in the dark chill of the underground.

My brother-in-law stares with me. "My God, I'm tired of fish," he says, leaning out from the branches so he can be seen from below. *"Sybyli! Tantra! Delsi!"* he mindspeaks.

One female on the beach and two of the swimmers stop what they're doing and look up toward him. He points to the iguana.

The Pelk on the beach shakes her head and returns to her work. The two in the water look at each other. One dives, the other swims toward the rock. "That's my third wife, Tantra," Derek says.

I nod, examine her. She is the smallest of the three but thicker, her wet black hair hanging only as far as her shoulders, her breasts larger than Lorrel's, almost pendulous. The girl slows as she approaches the rock, her eyes only on the iguana. The beast stares at her too, his leg muscles bunching as he prepares for flight.

Tantra stops, treads water and begins to sing. Derek chuckles and says, "You're in for a treat, old man. I bet you've never seen anything like this."

The notes of her song waft up to us. To my relief they don't affect me. But the iguana tilts his head and relaxes his muscles, his eyes transfixed on her. She approaches slowly, returning the iguana's stare, singing the entire time, climbing the rock and finally sitting next to the beast, water dripping from her naked body, spreading over the stone, darkening it everywhere that turns wet.

Through it all, the iguana remains immobile. I want it to break free of her spell, to pull back, to turn and run. I know how it feels to have music penetrate both mind and soul.

The Pelk girl puts a hand on its head, strokes its neck with her other hand, the iguana's flesh quivering at her touch.

Drawing a breath, I consider shouting a warning. But for what? In the end, the iguana is just another beast to be preyed upon. Who am I to say this one should live, when I've killed so many myself?

Tantra's song turns deep and soft. She shifts one finger into a claw and draws it across the iguana's neck, a red line appearing as the beast's flesh parts open, blood welling up, flowing across the rock and dripping into the lagoon. The iguana shudders once and collapses.

The Pelk girl stops her song and looks up to Derek. *"That's my girl!"* he mindspeaks. "Wasn't that magnificent?" he says to me.

Shaking my head I mutter, "I was that iguana last night," but Derek either doesn't hear or chooses to ignore me. He clambers down from the tree and I follow him.

By the time we reach the rock, Tantra has cut off the iguana's tail and sliced it into two halves. She stands and holds them up to Derek. He takes one and motions for her to hand me the other. "What about her and the other two?" I say.

Derek laughs, takes a bite from his section. "She's given us the best part. It's their tradition. Why would I complain? They'll eat the rest of the body and be glad for it."

Tantra's stomach, certainly not as flat as Lorrel's, protrudes slightly and Derek rubs it with his free hand. The Pelk girl smiles at him. *"My child grows inside here, doesn't it girl?"* he mindspeaks.

Tantra puts her hand over his. She trills out a laugh. *"Your*

child grows here. . . ." She points to Derek's other wife on
shore and to the other in the water. *"And there, and there!"*

Then she looks at me and points toward the mangrove forest.
"And your child grows in Lorrel's stomach over there!"

My child. I look toward the forest and frown. I've been so
busy damning myself for my betrayal of Chloe that I haven't
thought at all about my new son and how he can possibly fit in
my world.

Derek looks at my face and nods. "Bloody inconvenient
that—how quickly our women conceive. Let one of them decide it's time, and the next casual romp you have with them
ends up in fatherhood. At least when humans do it, they have a
sporting chance of remaining unencumbered."

"I like being a parent," I growl. "I just would prefer to share
that experience with my own mate."

"Well, you don't owe this one anything." Derek takes a bite
from his share of the iguana's tail. "The way I look at it," he
says, chewing as he speaks, "is we were forced into this. So
whatever has to be done about our children is the damned
Pelks' problem, not ours."

I nod and Derek takes another bite from his meat. My stomach growls and I eat some of mine too. Closing my eyes at the
sweetness of the meat, savoring its firm texture after the soft
meat of fish and lobster, I think about the boy and the name,
Dela, that Lorrel has already chosen for him.

She has already begun to act as if I have no part in any decisions about the child. So why should I care? I can think of no
reason why Derek's words aren't true. Yet, no matter what, my
blood will run in the child's veins. "I don't know," I say, as
much to Derek as to myself. "The child hasn't done anything to
me."

25

After I finish enough to fill my stomach, I ask Derek for instructions on how to find Lorrel. He grins at the half chunk of meat still left in my hand and says, "Bringing your woman a meal?"

"I need to talk to her. Being nice won't hurt anything."

He shrugs and gives me directions, pointing me on the way. I leave him at the lagoon and climb into the mangroves by myself. The directions seem simple enough, just a matter of following the path of smoothed roots and branches until I come to a new, small clearing, where I'm to cross the ground and find the trail on the other side.

But as I circle the clearing, to make sure I don't mistake any natural markings for the shiny, worn signs of a trail, I find two trees to choose from. I go back and forth from one to another, examining their roots and branches and, in the end, I take the right one just to see if it leads me anywhere.

Almost as soon as I've traveled long enough for the clearing to be out of sight, the path begins to fade. Peering at the roots below me, I slow and take only a few more steps before I stop. "At least I know what tree I should have taken," I mutter and turn.

Something rustles the branches to my right. I stare through the leaves and see the rust-red body of some sort of creature moving past me. Placing the chunk of iguana meat on the Y of a branch near me, I grab the branches to my right, yank them apart and see the animal.

I gasp and it freezes, its green eyes wide, its mouth open as if it's shrieking, though it makes no sound. *"Away go!"* it mind-speaks, and I almost fall from the branches.

The beast's scaled body, similar to my natural form, except much thinner and reddish colored, can't measure more than a yard. Its skinny tail, curled at its end and within my reach, looks to be about as long.

Its mouth still open, sharp white fangs showing, it begins to move away. *"Wait,"* I mindspeak, reaching out with one hand and seizing the curled tip of its tail. *"Please."*

The creature hisses and freezes again, its tail twitching in my hand, trying to pull free. *"Undrae, hold not me!"* it mindspeaks.

"Will you stay?"

"Hold not and again ask."

I open my hand and the creature yanks its tail out of reach and backs up a few more feet. *"Now stay I,"* it mindspeaks. *"Not many time.*

"What—who—are you?" I mindspeak, staring at it.

The animal spreads its wings as best it can within the confines of the branches. Far more delicate than mine, they appear almost translucent, glowing deep pink where the sunlight strikes them. *"Teacher not had you? Guess not castryll mine?"*

From its size alone, it can only be a member of one castryll. *"I assume you're a Thryll. But what makes you so sure I'm Undrae?"*

"Much hear and see we Thryll, I Clieee. Too big for Pelk and too small for Zal be you." The Thryll stares at the chunk of iguana meat on the bough next to me. *"Not fish that be. Fish Pelk eat. Undrae be you."*

I pause before I answer. Because of the way it speaks, I have to concentrate on each word and rearrange them in my mind. *"Do the Pelk know you're here?"* I mindspeak.

The creature spits toward the ground and hisses again. *"Fish eaters. Nothing here know them of Thryll or Clieee. Kill us if they do. Now go I."*

"Wait, Clieee," I mindspeak, but the Thryll begins to wend his way through the branches. I look at the iguana meat and shrug. Lorrel has no reason to expect me to bring it to her. Picking the meat up, I hold it out to the creature. "Are you hungry?"

He stops and turns, eyeing the meat.

"*It's fresh. It was killed within the hour,*" I mindspeak.

Returning, Clieee takes the chunk from me with both hands and smells it. "Iguana," he mindspeaks. "*Like it I.*" He bites into it and tears off a piece.

I wait for him to gulp it down before I mindspeak, "*You live here too, right?*"

"*Why tell you I? Tell you not them?*"

Shaking my head, I mindspeak. "*Why would I put you at risk? The Pelk are no more my friends than they are yours. One of their females poisoned me. They use that to hold me prisoner, giving me a temporary antidote every few days. Without it I will die in agony. I am in need of allies. I must find a way to go home.*"

Clieee considers my words, tearing off another piece of meat, gulping it down before he mindspeaks, "*Need not allies we. Here live Thryll since before Great War. Live us places many, trees many. No need to shapechange us like Undrae or Pelk or Zal. Have us trees many, have us wings.*"

"*But do you know much about the Pelk? Anything about their potions and their antidotes? If you do I can bring you much more meat.*"

"*For my whole flight enough?*" The creature busies himself gulping down the last of the iguana meat before he continues. "*Not many years have I. Rear fly I. Point flies Zalman. Question can I him.*"

I sigh. "*But I have no idea when or where we can meet again.*"

"*Not worry you. Find you I. Meat bring you.*"

"*I'll bring it back to you after I get home. I can't promise more than that.*"

"*Decide will Zalman. But meat only, fish no.*"

Smiling, I nod and mindspeak, "*Fish no.*"

"*Zalman's words bring you I,*" Clieee mindspeaks and slips away into the mangroves.

It takes me only minutes to return to the clearing and set forth on the correct path, and only minutes more to reach the clearing where Lorrel gardens in the company of a white-haired, much wrinkled Pelk female. Weeding with her hands around the base of a Dragon's Tear plant, Lorrel looks up as I walk out of the mangroves and mindspeaks, *"Hi."*

She stands and motions for me to come to her. Dressed in a small pink polka-dot sundress that fits her petite frame almost perfectly, she twirls around modeling it. *"It looks good, does it not?"* She mindspeaks, *"Malka picked it out for me."* She tilts her head toward the older woman, who, clad in a baggy T-shirt and too-tight electric blue shorts, is busy picking seeds and berries from the nearby mangroves and putting each in separate bowls.

I nod toward Malka and smile, but she scowls at me in return, her wrinkles compacting as she does so, making her skin look like a series of white furrows.

"Never mind her. She is just jealous she has no one to love her in her nest," Lorrel says, putting her arms around me, trying to press her body against mine.

Pulling away, I mindspeak, *"We have to talk."*

She turns her back on me, goes back to the Dragon's Tear bush and begins to yank weeds out as quickly and violently as she can. *"Is that all you Undrae do? Talk and talk and talk? All I want are strong arms around me and something equally strong thrust between my legs. If you want to have a conversation, go find Derek. His wives tell me he never stops talking—even when they have sex! You are my lover. Act like it!"*

Malka grins at Lorrel's outburst. Clenching my fists, I glare at her and then turn my attention back to Lorrel. I want to lash out at both of them but see little possible gain. Even if I killed them both I would still be a prisoner of Pelk poison. Taking long breaths, I concentrate on reducing the adrenaline coursing through my blood.

When my heartbeat returns to normal, I mindspeak, *"I am not your lover. What we had last night was a virtual rape—not lovemaking. You have made me your prisoner and your victim. You hold out your temporary antidote in the hope I will be your willing slave. I will never be willing."*

"Yes, you will, Undrae," Malka says. *"You have already felt our power. What makes you think you can resist it again?"*

Whirling in her direction, I shapeshift my right hand and point one sharp talon at her. *"Old woman, is this your way of telling me you're tired of living?"*

"You must not speak to her like that. Malka leads our li-srrynn," Lorrel mindspeaks, standing up, moving between me and the elder Pelk. *"She is our maker of potions, our mother of mothers. The antidote you take comes from her hands. She has yet to pass that knowledge to any of us in this srrynn."*

"Silence, child!" The old woman walks over to me, takes my right claw and places my talon against her throat. *"I have lived as long as I have only because I swore I wouldn't die until our srrynn returned to Atalan. Mowdar asked me to train this one before I choose my last sleep. I promised him I would. I am tired and would welcome your releasing me from that promise."* She grins. *"Slice my neck, please. The knowledge that you would soon die in great pain from my poison would give me one last pleasure before I passed."*

Shifting my claw back into its human form, I sigh, turn my back on both females and walk toward the mangrove path. Lorrel catches up to me as I put my foot on the first root. *"Wait, Peter,"* she mindspeaks. *"Go where you want to now, but please return to our nest tonight."*

"Why should I?"

"Mowdar knows about our son. He is most pleased with the success of his plan. I have told him it is too soon for you to be used elsewhere, that he owes us the pleasure of our company for the next few months. He has given us that gift. If you choose to be away from me, I will be shamed and he will own my shame too."

I snort. *"I don't see what difference that would make to me."*

"He will place you with another female and you will be forced again," Lorrel mindspeaks. She looks at the ground. *"Have you not enjoyed any of the time we spent together? I have. I do not want to make a slave of you. I will not use our songs on you ever again. I want you to come to me of your own will."*

Shaking my head, I mindspeak, *"But I can't, I'm . . ."*

"Mated for life, I know. But even now your child grows inside me. For now I promise to be satisfied with only your company. Spend time with me, sleep beside me, warm my nest, and I will not complain to Mowdar. Perhaps one day you will change your mind."

26

In the evening, the Pelk bring back the prey they've caught during the day and we all feast on it together. Afterwards small groups gather for conversations and share jars of Dragon's Tear wine. Derek and his wives and Lorrel and I sit and talk and drink with Mowdar, his lieutenants and their females and Malka. Few other Pelk show any inclination to seek out either Derek's or my company.

Mowdar's youngest lieutenant, a Pelk named Jessai, who seems not to have any female, explains it after a little too much Dragon's Tear wine, *"Why would any of us want to share time with any Undrae? You have nothing we want. You have brought our people only death. Now that our women have taken your seed, I asked Mowdar for permission to use my trident against you both. But he sees fit to protect you. It is my hope that one day he won't."*

Later, in our nest, after Lorrel gives me my antidote, I ask about him. She sighs and mindspeaks, *"Jessai only has two more years than me. We grew up together. Before we learned we could return to Atalan, Mowdar smiled on the thought that Jessai would share my nest and father my children. When he changed his mind and decided to send me for you instead, Jessai became so enraged that he left the srrynn for weeks."*

"Aré you sad he doesn't share your nest?"

She nestles against me. *"I like Jessai, but I have no regrets. I am only sad that you have been inside me just once."*

After her breathing slows and her body grows warm against mine, I stay awake and count the days since my first encounter with Lorrel. I shake my head when I realize a week has already passed. Chloe will be home the next day. As soon as she hears my message she'll be on the phone with Claudia. Within a few days at most she should be back on Caya DelaSangre.

I sigh into the dark. Surely she'll come looking for me soon after that. Finding me will be easy as soon as she comes within mindspeaking range. I should hear from her within a week. But what then? As long as the Pelk poison courses through my veins, the Pelk rule my body.

The week passes, and then the next day and the next, without any word from Chloe. I begin to worry about her and to have difficulty remembering how long my stay with the srrynn has been. Except for every third night, when Lorrel gives me my antidote, each evening passes much the same way as the last. Each new day seems no different from the old one.

The men refuse to let either Derek or me accompany them on their forays into the ocean. We have little to do but spend most of our time wandering above. While I would love to hunt again, even if the prey is dolphin, Derek seems not to mind being left behind.

I think if I didn't prod him, he'd sleep through most of his days. In the mornings, after the males have gone to sea and the females climbed the steps to the above, I take the opportunity to explore the cavern, looking for anything I can put to use before I wake my brother-in-law. While I find the creature a better companion than I would have expected, I still have no more trust in him than I ever did.

Malka's nest, in another alcove on the opposite side of Mowbar's from mine, interests me most. I go through it each morning using a glass jar full of glow-water for illumination as I sort through the containers on her shelves and floor. She maintains a dizzying array of herbs, powders, roots, branches, seeds, leaves, berries, dried creatures and flowers, but without the knowledge of how to use them, they are worthless to me.

On my second visit to her alcove I discover a small wood chest hidden behind two larger ones. When I open it I find dozens of antidote bottles. My heart races as I sort through them. But I find only four full ones. Pulling their stoppers, I sniff their contents and taste a drop from each and groan. All smell and taste no different from the temporary antidote I'm given every other night.

I bring my father's journal above with me each day and spend hours going through its brittle pages looking for any words I might recognize that might point to a permanent antidote for the poison. But no amount of staring can make up for my sparse knowledge of the Spanish language.

Derek scowls and walks away from me any time I open the book. Likewise, he refuses to follow me into the mangroves when I wander off—always with extra food in hand—in search for any sign of the Thryll. "You're getting almost as bloody boring as the Pelk," he growls. But still, he wakes when I shake his body each morning, and he stays by my side when I'm not reading or exploring.

Things change late in the afternoon, the day after Lorrel gives me my fourth dose of antidote. Derek and I are lazing near the lagoon, sitting on the rock where his Tantra killed the iguana and watching the Pelk females work.

Derek sees it first. "Bloody hell! Look at that old man!" he says, pointing to the center of the lagoon where a light pink cloud has just started to blossom in the water. The women swimming in the lagoon back away from it as it darkens to crimson and spreads.

Two Pelk males in their natural forms erupt from the water far enough to show their upper bodies and the third Pelk they hold, bleeding from his mouth, his side and neck. *"We were attacked by Notch Fin's pod! Three are dead. We have six wounded. Mowdar wants a healing circle now!"* one of the males mindspeaks, and they sink out of sight.

All the women in the water dive after them. The others on the beach gather up their things and rush toward the mangrove tree path. Derek and I wait for them to pass and then follow. At the hole to the cave under the rock, the women working in the gardens stream in too.

By the time Derek and I squeeze through the hole and start down the stairs the entire srrynn has assembled, some women mixing phosphorescence into all the dark glowpools, others bringing fish and lobsters to the wounded Pelk lying on the sand near the water, and others wrapping the three dead Pelk in blankets of seaweed.

Malka and fourteen other females, including Lorrel and Sybyli have already formed a li-srrynn and gathered in a circle around the wounded. The cavern vibrates with their slow, deep tune. The song grows louder after all the glowpools have been made as bright as possible and every available woman joins the li-srrynn.

Mowdar, his lieutenants and all the other males stand back a few paces from the circle. When Derek and I, the only ones still in their natural forms, join them, Jessai turns to the Pelk leader and mindspeaks, *"We do not need them."*

"Look around you. Three of your comrades are dead. Six will be of no use for days. We need whatever help we can get!" Mowdar mindspeaks, slamming the bottom of his trident onto the floor for emphasis.

Jessai hisses and turns his back on the Pelk leader. *"I will not allow us to go into battle to lose again,"* Mowdar mindspeaks.

He turns to Derek and me. *"I know you may think this not your fight, but what the dolphins did today cannot go unanswered. If we allow you tridents of your own, do you think you can be of help?"*

Derek scowls. "Why should I risk getting bleeding hurt?" he says out loud.

I ignore him and mindspeak. *"One of your men said it was Notch Fin's pod. How many were they?"*

"More than twice as many as us. They were waiting for us near the blue hole when we returned from hunting. . . ."

"Why would we have expected to find them there? They've never dared to come so far into our hunting grounds before," one of the other lieutenants mindspeaks. Mowdar's glare silences him.

"We never took one of his young from his own pod before," Mowdar turns his gaze on me. *"Thanks to my daughter, your nest mate, it seems that things have changed. Can I count on you?"*

"You can count on both of us," I mindspeak. The Pelk nods and turns his attention to his recalcitrant lieutenant.

"What?" Derek says, tugging me a few yards away from the gathering, whispering in my ear. "You're not really thinking of us helping that bugger, are you?"

"Look," I say, "if I had to pick sides, I would probably tend toward the dolphins right now. But that would do nothing to help me. The more Mowdar and the rest trust us, the easier our lives will be. Don't you want to get out of here, go do something else once in a while?"

"Sure," Derek says. "But not by risking injury or death."

"Well, I want to get out of here. Even if we're in the water, even if we have to fight dolphins, it's better than sitting in this dark hole doing nothing."

Derek shakes his head. "I was pretty content doing nothing until you came along. I'll come, but it's on your head. Something regrettable happens to me, it will be on your head."

Jessai wakes me with a curt, *"Undrae! Get up!"*

I sit up, look past him and see no light streaming into the cave. *"It's still night. Are we going to leave in the dark?"* I mindspeak.

He turns his back on me. *"You will not leave at all if you do not follow now."*

"Jessai, stop being such a dolt," Lorrel says, stretching and yawning. She runs her tail over mine as I slip out of the nest and follow Jessai down to the water.

All the other grown and healthy males gather there, Derek coming last, pushing in next to me. In our natural forms we tower over the rest. *"I'm impressed. How'd they wake you?"* I mindspeak.

The creature rubs his rump with one of his front claws. *"Carrying bloody spears like bloody savages,"* he mindspeaks. *"How would you like it—being impaled during your bleeding dreams?"*

Mowdar arrives shortly after that. *"No need for many words,"* he mindspeaks. *"I want Notch Fin dead and his pod dead. If you fight well we will have a great feast on our return. If not . . ."* He shrugs.

He turns his attention to Derek and me. *"Where are your tridents?"*

"We don't need any bloody toys to fight with," Derek mindspeaks.

I slap his tail, hard, with mine, mindspeaking, *"Yes, we do. We just haven't been given any."*

The Pelk leader points to Jessai, mindspeaks, *"Take care of it."*

He nods and motions for us to follow, and we wend our way through the cave, to a crevice in the wall on the side away from the stairs. The Pelk squeezes through the crevice, and Derek and I squeeze after him, coming out into a small, dark cave.

Jessai mixes phosphorescence into a glowpool, and our eyes go wide at the profusion of tridents stacked against every wall. *"Choose whichever you want,"* he mindspeaks.

We leave the srrynn through the underwater passageway that leads to the ocean blue hole, the rest of the males in front of us, Derek and I struggling to keep up. Night still rules when we surface in the open ocean, the water rough and churning, wind gusting overhead. Even underwater, the currents tug and bully us.

I've shown Derek how to broaden his tail, and we scull through the water together, keeping our heads near the surface, taking breaths as we wish. *"If they are still near, they will be sleeping in more protected waters,"* Mowdar says. He leads us toward the lee side of a nearby island.

By the time we near it, the sun has broken free of the horizon, throwing a murky light through a sky crowded with gray clouds. Rain begins lashing the ocean's surface and I smile momentarily, glad that we're protected by the water's warm embrace.

A Pelk surfacing to take a breath bellows out in pain and another mindspeaks, *"They are here!"* and the water churns all around us as Notch Fin and his pod's males attack. Mowdar speeds toward the nearest dolphin, ignoring a glancing blow from another and slashing out with his trident. He offers no plan of battle, does nothing to organize the Pelk.

Notch Fin, on the other hand, always has a portion of his dolphins, circling around the fight. They seem to shoot in and fall back on the orders he clicks and whistles. *"This is ridiculous,"* I tell Derek. *"Put your back to mine."*

Jessai swims by in pursuit of another dolphin, and I mindspeak to him, *"Jessai, join us! Together we can kill more."* He pauses and stares at me, just as I see a large, almost pure white dolphin racing toward my side. I twist my body and drop, glad at least that Derek has prevented it from ramming me from the rear.

The dolphin only manages to strike my head a glancing blow as it passes. Still, as large as the beast is, the blow stuns me. I float, not reacting, as another, larger dolphin shoots toward me and takes my throat in its jaws. The pain of its teeth digging through my scales brings me back to awareness. I jab at it with my trident, slicing its side, drawing blood, and the beast releases me and darts off.

"That was Notch Fin," Jessai mindspeaks. *"The other one— the albino one that first attacked you—we call Ghost. We think he's one of Notch Fin's lieutenants."* The Pelk joins me at my side, calling others over to fill in defensive positions on the sides and to our top and bottom. We take turns, swimming up in pairs to take breaths.

Dolphins swarm around us, ramming and biting. We slash and stab back at them. *"Got the bugger!"* Derek mindspeaks, driving his trident deep into the midsection of one of his attackers, making the first kill. Jessai kills the next. When he blurts out, *"Got the bugger!"* too, Derek and I both lose air laughing into the water.

Mowdar finally recognizes our success and forms a defensive ring of his own. The water turns a pale red all around us as one dolphin after another dies.

Notch Fin races by me, Ghost just behind him, both clicking and whistling, the rest of the dolphins breaking away and following them. *"No!"* I mindspeak, shooting after them, Jessai, Derek and the rest following me.

I swim faster than I ever have. I want Notch Fin. I've yet to have my first kill today. My neck stings from the beast's bites. I grin as we close on him and his pod.

Notch Fin realizes they can't outrun us and wheels his pod around, the dolphins racing toward us, Notch Fin in the lead, as we speed toward them. This time there is no time for strategy, no way to plan defense—just the pending impact of large creatures racing toward an underwater collision.

I drive my trident into Notch Fin's underbelly with my right arm just before he rams me in my right shoulder. My arm going numb, I keep forcing all three prongs into him even as he tries to turn away. The beast batters me with his flippers, twists us around with strokes of his powerful flukes, but still I dig my trident into him.

Notch Fin cracks his head against mine. I almost fall away, but somehow I manage to continue my attack. He cracks his head into mine again and I look around for help. I see Jessai approaching out of the corner of my eye and I hope he'll arrive before Notch Fin batters me to death.

"Peter! Peter, are you all right?" someone mindspeaks. I assume it has to be Jessai and I glance toward him, wondering why he would ask such a thing. But the Pelk has stopped his approach and stares at me with wide eyes.

"Peter! Answer me. Are you all right?"

Notch Fin twists again and I feel the trident begin to pull loose. I realize who's called out to me. {*Later!*} I mindspeak, masked, {*Later! But masked!*} I drive the trident into the large dolphin with all my force.

{*Yes, Peter, later.*}

Jessai finally joins my attack, plunging his trident into Notch Fin's throat. Together we hold the shafts of our tridents, pushing, shoving them in further as Notch Fin tries every move he can to escape us and together we feel him grow weaker until he finally falls still. *"We got the bugger!"* Jessai mindspeaks. *"We killed Notch Fin!"*

But I say nothing. My mind is too full of the sound of Chloe's words.

27

Long after Lorrel stills beside me and her breaths turn slow and regular, I lie staring into the dark, listening to her and to the faint rustle of our drapes. As gorged with dolphin meat and as flooded with Dragon's Tear wine as I am, I yearn to sleep too.

Instead, I shake my head and sit up. Somewhere, Chloe sits awake too, waiting to hear from me. I have put her off too many times already today. She'd tried to contact me three more times during the day. But I'd been too surrounded by celebrating Pelk—all demanding I retell the story how Jessai and I had finally killed Notch Fin. I couldn't risk their suspicion over any silence or detachment on my part.

Finally, when she contacted me in the evening during Mowdar's toast to me and I curtly put her off again, she mindspoke, {*You contact me when you can. I'll wait up.*}

I sigh. We've been married long enough for me to picture the annoyed look she surely had on her face when she mindspoke those words—not that I blame her.

Listening for any signs of activity outside our alcove, I nod when I hear none. After hours and hours of feasting and celebration, I'd begun to worry that the last of the Pelk revelers would never retreat to their nests. Careful not to disturb Lorrel, I sidle away from her and slip out of our nest. I have no desire to communicate with my wife while lying with the warmth of another female pressed against me.

It takes only a few moments for me to feel my way in the dark to the alcove's drapes. I part them and sit on a nearby seaweed seat. Here and there a few glowpools still give off some dim glimmers of light, barely enough to let me see through the dark that now blankets the cavern. A dozen yards away from me a Pelk couple, either too tired or too drunk on Dragon's Tear wine to put up their tent, lie in their nest, entwined in the throes of sex, oblivious to my stare.

I smile and watch them couple, my mind more on Chloe than on their rutting. As glad as I am to hear from her, I worry about her reaction to my infidelity. I know I had no choice. Still, I wonder if I can make her understand.

The Pelks have a final spasm of movement and then grow still, lying with limbs and tails interwoven as they fall off to sleep. I shake my head and sigh, wishing Chloe and I were that couple. Taking a deep breath I mindspeak, masked, {*Chloe. It's Peter. Can you hear me?*}

No answer comes and I try again. {*Chloe, please answer me.*}

{*Are you sure you have time? Or would it be more convenient for you if we spoke tomorrow or the day after?*} Chloe mindspeaks.

I frown into the dark. {*Please, Chloe, this is difficult enough.*}

{*Difficult? Claudia tells me I have to rush home because you're gone and it has something to do with the Pelk and the Bahamas. So I arrange for my parents to take care of the kids— believe me there was nothing easy about that—and I come home to find your boat gone and someone else's scent in our house and on my sweatshirt and my sweatpants. And then when I finally can contact you, you're too busy to bother with me— five times! You think that's not difficult?*}

{*You have to understand. . . .*}

{*Understand what? You missed your deposition. Ian's in the stratosphere, he's so pissed at you. That rag,* The Weekly Dish, *has been screaming for your arrest. Pepe Santos's attorney finally got the district attorney to get a court order for it. So many patrol boats have our island under around-the-clock surveillance that I couldn't even fly here from home.*}

{*Where are you now?*}

{*Bimini. Claudia brought me over in her boat. I tried to contact you as soon as we checked into the Blue Water Marina but you were too busy for me. . . .*}

Gnashing my fangs, I resist the urge to slap my tail on the

cavern's stone floor. {*Damn it, Chloe, I was fighting for my life! Will you calm down a minute and listen to me?*}

She says nothing and I pour out the story of Lorrel's attack, the poison she injected into me, our trip to Andros, Derek's presence there, my father's involvement and Mowdar's desire to keep me with his srrynn—leaving out only Lorrel's attempts to bed me and our eventual coupling.

{*When you tried to contact me I was in the middle of a fight with the largest dolphin I've ever seen. It was part of a battle the Pelk were having with the dolphins. After one of the Pelk and I killed the dolphin and we won the fight, everyone was so busy celebrating that they wouldn't leave me alone for a minute. You know how strange people seem when they're mind-speaking masked—like their minds are off somewhere else entirely. I didn't want any of the Pelk to think I was communicating with anyone.*}

{*And all this started because of something Derek said and something Don Henri did?*} Chloe mindspeaks.

{*Yes.*}

{*I don't understand. If they're angry with you, why didn't they just kill you? Why do they want you or Derek there so much? Why did they want to keep Don Henri prisoner in the first place?*}

I take in a deep breath and explain about the Pelk's problem with inbreeding and their need for outside blood. {*Don Henri's wife had died. He bedded a Pelk woman willingly, but they wouldn't let him leave after that. Same thing with Derek . . .*}

Chloe mindspeaks, {*But you're mated. What use would they have with you?*}

Stretching my body, I search for the words, for any way to make this less painful. Chloe speaks before I get out the first word. {*Peter, you didn't, did you?*}

I sigh. {*I didn't want to. But I couldn't help it.*}

{*Oh, Peter, we were supposed to be better than those stupid humans on Jerry Springer. We mated for life. How could you?*}

{*I tried not to. I refused her every time, but they have this strange way of singing that penetrates your mind. After we came to Andros they had this gathering called a li-srrynn, and*} fifteen of their females all sang to me. They took over my mind. . . .}

{It's what your body did that bothers me!}

If we were together and speaking, I'm sure those words would have been snarled. {That's unfair, Chloe. It would be like my being mad at you for being raped. There's a poison in my body that will kill me if I don't drink a temporary antidote every three days. I'm held prisoner here. Had I had any control over it, I never would have bedded that female.}

{So take control. Kill her! That way you won't have to fuck her again.}

I let out a breath. {Chloe, you don't mean that.}

{Don't I?}

{She's carrying a child of mine—a son.}

{And I carried your daughter, and my sister carried your son. How many other Pelk do you plan to screw? How many other babies do you want to be responsible for?}

Lorrel mindspeaks, "Peter, where are you? It's cold beside me." I wince at the strength of her mindthought. Hoping she'll go back to sleep, I say nothing. Even as loud as Lorrel is, with any luck Chloe is too far away to pick up on her mindthoughts.

{Is that her?} Chloe mindspeaks. {Did I hear that right? You sleep with her each night?}

"Peter?"

Looking back to the drapes, I groan. {Only sleep, nothing more,} I mindspeak.

{If that's all you've done, how did you make a son?} Chloe mindspeaks.

The drapes rustle and Lorrel mindspeaks, "Peter?" and steps through them.

I groan again and then mindspeak, masked, to Chloe, {I am mated to you for life. I want no one else.}

Lorrel walks up to me. "Peter, why are you ignoring me? Why will you not answer?"

Glaring at her, I mindspeak, "In a minute Lorrel!" and turn my face from her.

{Chloe, please!} I mindspeak. {I love you.}

{I love you too, Peter. But I'm glad I don't have to see you just now.}

{*Chloe!*}

Lorrel sits besides me. "*Something is wrong, Peter. What is it?*"

I shake my head and mindspeak, "*Just go away please.*"

The Pelk girl moves closer and strokes my tail with hers.

Ignoring her, I mindspeak to Chloe. {*You're being unfair. I was forced. I don't deserve this.*}

{*I don't deserve it either. I don't want to talk to you anymore now, Peter. Contact me tomorrow—sometime when your girlfriend isn't around.*}

{*Lorrel isn't my girlfriend!*}

{*Lorrel . . . what a pretty name,*} Chloe mindspeaks. {*Now leave me be, Peter, please.*}

Yanking my tail away from Lorrel's, I slam it down hard on the stone floor. Lorrel winces. I stare at her and think of Chloe's words. I could kill this Pelk female in seconds. Just a few slashes or a well placed bite and no healing circle on earth could put her back together again.

"*I do not like the way you are looking at me,*" Lorrel says, getting up. "*You have been mindspeaking masked with someone, have you not? Has it been with your wife?*"

I shake my head. "*Not with her, not with anyone, not with anything,*" I mindspeak. "*You know I'm unhappy here. You know I'm lonely.*"

Lorrel studies my face, staring as if she can distill the truth from my expression. Finally, she mindspeaks, "*I can soothe you, you know. Come lie with me again and let me help you.*"

"*No!*" I mindspeak, slamming my tail down again. "*You are not who I want!*"

The Pelk girl hisses and steps back. "*Undrae! Watch your words with me,*" she mindspeaks. "*I am the daughter of Mowdar and the mother of your son. Take care you do not reject me one time too many. I can also use my words to hurt.*"

I stay seated as she walks away. My body aches for sleep, but I have no intention of returning to the nest until the creature has gone back to sleep. I long to call out to Chloe again. But I can no more do that this evening than I can leave this vile place.

28

A muted boom of thunder wakes me. I sit up to find Lorrel still asleep. She has her back turned to me and lies as far from me as she can without leaving the nest. I smile and shake my head. Those few times in our relationship when Chloe and I have had problems, I'd agonized over any distance we had between us. But Lorrel's rejection causes no pain. I miss the warmth of a body pressed against me, nothing more.

Getting up, taking care not to wake the Pelk girl, I make my way out of the alcove. Outside the drapes I stop and stare at the dull gray light coming from the hole in the cavern wall at the top of the stone stairs. It barely illuminates the cavern much better than the glowpools do at night. I shake my head. I've become used to the bright glow that usually streams through the hole each day, and I regret its absence. Thunder rumbles again and I wonder what type of storm now darkens the sky and lashes at the ground above me.

Either the rain or the celebration the evening before has kept most of the Pelk sleeping in their nests. Here and there only a few of them have woken and stirred phosphorescence into their glowpools, the pools' green glow positively bright compared to the dim light coming this morning from above.

My stomach growls when I notice three males sitting outside Mowdar's drapes and feeding on the remnants of a dolphin carcass left over from the evening's feast. I can't put names to two of them, but the third I recognize as Jessai. I walk over to them and sit on a seaweed seat next to him.

"Undrae, you are up early today," Jessai mindspeaks.

Another clap of thunder vibrates through the cavern and I tilt my head upward. *"The storm woke me,"* I mindspeak.

Jessai shakes his head. *"If I had Lorrel lying beside me, I do not think I would leave my warm nest on a day like this to feed alongside the three of us."*

I smile. *"She's still asleep and I'm hungry. Nothing says I can't return to her after I fill my stomach."*

He laughs, leans over, slices a chunk of meat from the carcass' tail—where it's sweetest—with one of his talons and offers it to me. The other two Pelk stop eating and stare at him. I do too. Among the Pelk, males hardly ever serve other males.

Jessai mindspeaks, *"If anyone in the srrynn has a right to this meat it is him."*

The other two Pelk nod and I accept the meat from Jessai. I eat it slowly to show my appreciation,

While we eat we talk mostly of the last day's battle with the dolphins and of the weather. After we've all eaten our fill, the other two leave to return to their nests. Jessai stays, waits till they're gone and turns to me. *"I was not pleased to have you join our srrynn. Lorrel should have been mine. . . ."*

I shake my head. *"I didn't ask for her. . . ."*

"Undrae, we both know she must do as Mowdar directs. I want you to know I no longer have any quarrel with you. You shared a great victory with me yesterday. I thank you for it. I want you to know I think you welcome here. From now on I will be proud to hunt and fight at your side."

"Thank you," I mindspeak.

He dismisses my gratitude with a wave of his claw. *"You need not thank me. But I do have a matter I think we should discuss. It is something I have not spoken about with Mowdar yet."*

I nod.

"During the fight with Notch Fin someone called out to you, did they not?"

"I think so . . ." I mindspeak, cocking my head as if I'm trying to remember. *"I'm not exactly sure when or what it was about. I was in the middle of the fight. Remember—the damned beast was battering my head—but I think Derek said something."*

Jessai cocks his head. *"Derek?"* he mindspeaks. *"It did not sound like Derek to me. And you never answered him."*

"Come on. You were there. You know I was too busy for any conversation."

"True," Jessai says, nodding his head. *"But I also know you and Derek are not the only Undrae on this earth. We are all aware of the damage your father did to our people. Mowdar has cautioned us to report any strangeness to him. He has pledged to kill you if you threaten to draw us into danger. I would not want to see that."*

"Ask Derek if you care to," I mindspeak, hoping that either Jessai will not take me up on my invitation or that Derek won't botch backing up my story.

"I may," Jessai mindspeaks. *"Later, after he wakes."*

A particularly loud thunderclap booms out above us and the Pelk looks up and smiles. *"I doubt he or any us will leave the srrynn today."*

"How do you know the storm is so bad?" I mindspeak.

Jessai points to a place on the cavern wall between Mowdar's alcove and mine where a three-foot swath of stone running from the cavern's roof to the floor has turned dark and slick with moisture. He points to similar flows of water on the walls around the cavern and to a few thin streams of water that fall from cracks in the roof's stone, one drizzle striking the floor and forming a puddle a dozen or so yards from us, the rest fortunately cascading into the cavern's lagoon.

"This only happens during the worst of storms," he mindspeaks. *"On days like this, the wind beats at you above and the ocean tumbles you along below. Especially after yesterday, it will be a pleasure to rest inside."*

No matter the weather, I've little desire to spend the day lazing with Lorrel. I want to be alone, to have time enough to talk again with Chloe. I shake my head and mindspeak, *"You Pelk like living in your caves. I need to go above, at least for a little while, just so I can breathe the air in the open and look at more than stone walls and a stone ceiling."*

"What is the difference between this and the stone house that Lorrel has told me you lived in?" Jessai mindspeaks.

I think about my coral stone house, how warm and comfortable it is when it storms outside like this, how much I miss it and I mindspeak only, *"Windows."*

As I expected, Derek refuses to venture from his warm, dry nest when I wake him. He nods when I tell him about my conversation with Jessai, nods again when I ask him to back up my story and immediately falls back to sleep. I consider waking him again, just to see if he truly understood what I said, but shake my head. Better to hope he understood. My brother-in-law never takes kindly to having his sleep disturbed.

The grumble of thunder resonates through the cavern and I wonder whether to venture above. It will be too wet to bring Don Henri's journal to ponder over and too blustery to sit anywhere in comfort. But I need to go somewhere where I can communicate with Chloe without any interruption, and—with the exception of the day before—I haven't missed a day searching for the Thryll and leaving him food.

I vaguely remember seeing a flash of yellow at the bottom of the clothing pile the Pelk keep. Going to the pile, putting down the two chunks of dolphin meat I've brought from the carcass, I change to my human shape and dig through the clothes. I smile when I finally see the yellow material and touch the rubberized surface of a foul-weather jacket and grin even more when I find its matching pants.

Both give off the rank smell of mildew. Still, I put them on over my bare flesh and pull up the hood. If the weather above is as bad as it sounds, I'll be glad to be protected from it no matter what the odor. My body immediately turns too hot, overprotected as it is from the calm air of the cavern. I pick up the dolphin meat and walk toward the stairs.

Rain lashes the ground. Lightning crackles through the sky, followed by loud claps of thunder. Gusts of wind bend the mangroves, their branches jerking and bowing with each sudden change. I stand in the middle of the clearing next to the entrance to the Pelks' cavern—my body warm and dry inside the foul-weather gear, only my bare face, hands and feet wet and cold from the storm—and try to decide whether to talk to Chloe or search for Clieee first.

In the end, my reluctance to talk just yet with my angry wife makes it easy for me to choose looking for the Thryll. I take a bite from one of the cold, wet chunks of meat I'm carrying and climb up, into the mangroves.

By now I usually make my way to the end of this path within minutes, but in the storm's gloom and rain it takes much longer. I have to study each branch and root to determine whether it's part of the path. I have to place my hands and feet so I don't slip—tasks made even more difficult by the wind, which makes walking through the trees like stepping from one writhing beast to the next.

I finally reach what I think is the end of the path. Balancing the dolphin meat on the Y of the bough of a tree near me, I use one hand to hold onto tree branches for balance and the other to push branches out of the way—to see if the Thryll hides anywhere nearby.

But I spot no sign of his reddish scales. I shake my head. *"Clieee?"* I mindspeak. *"Where the hell are you?"*

He doesn't answer and I sigh, though after all the days he hasn't shown, I'm not really surprised by his absence. Chances are, I think, he may have promised what he did only to leave my presence unharmed. I sigh again and pick up a chunk of dolphin meat and take a bite.

"No! Eat mine not!" Clieee mindspeaks from somewhere in the wet greenery.

I stare at the leaves in front of me, not sure just where to look for him, and mindspeak, *"This meat is mine. I can eat what I want of it, you worthless creature. I have left food for you every day. . . ."*

"Yesterday not. For Clieee no food. For Clieee empty stomach."

"Why should I give you anything more? You promised me help," I mindspeak. *"And you've brought me nothing."* I take another, larger bite from the meat and make a show of chewing it.

The leaves rustle behind me and I turn just as Clieee comes close enough to be seen. *"Promise not help. Only Zalman's words promise I."*

I scowl at the creature. *"Why haven't you told me his words before?"*

"Bring you meat for 1 day by day." Clieee stares at the meat in my hand. *"Not like answer my—no more meat bring you."*

"Tell me Zalman's words now or I'll eat every bit of this meat right now." I mindspeak. *"Let me be the judge of whether I like them or not."*

The Thryll comes closer, though he still makes sure to stay out of my reach. *"Says Zalman, Pelk poison knows he. Says Zalman, poison antidote knows he. Says Zalman, around you look in the trees. In the trees, says Zalman, find answer you."*

I stare at the trees around us. *"Look in the trees for what?"*

"Know not I. Zalman knows and says Zalman, know will you."

"Take me to him! Let him explain his answer to me," I mindspeak, stepping toward the Thryll.

Clieee shakes his head and backs up. *"Explain not Zalman. Never. Are true his words. Always. Meet you not he. Ever. Food want I. Now."*

In the trees. I shake my head. Tree snails, birds, lizards, crabs, spiders and myriad other insects, plus God knows what types of fungus and algae, all live on the mangroves above the water. I assume an equally diverse group of creatures live on or among its roots underwater. *"I need more than word games,"* I mindspeak.

"Told you all say Zalman to me," Clieee mindspeaks. *"Think his words you and well will be all. Now meat give please you."*

Anger flushes through me. Glaring at the Thryll, I take the dolphin meat in my hand, wind up and throw it at his chest as hard as I can. It strikes him and Clieee shrieks as it bounces from his chest, falling into the roots below. The Thryll drops from his branch, working his way to the roots to find it before some fish takes it away.

"Undrae wrong you. Go now I," Clieee mindspeaks. *"Says Zalman, owe us you much meat."*

"Not a chance," I growl out loud, not caring whether the Thryll understands me.

29

Left alone with only the storm for company, I sit shaking my head. How foolish of me to set my hopes on another. How naive to think that a simple creature living in the trees could solve any problem of mine.

I welcome the rain pounding down on me. I pray that the wind buffets me even more. I smile at the wet cold numbing my bare feet and hands. Let it all overtake me. Let me drown in the storm's misery. I deserve every bit of it as punishment for my stupidity.

A sudden gust of wind batters the mangrove where I'm perched and the bough I've been holding jerks out of my grip. I gasp, reach for another branch, but it breaks when I pull on it. My right foot slips and I fall, my upper body crashing through branches, my legs slipping between the tree's roots.

I land in shallow water, my bare feet sinking into cold muck, cold water immediately soaking my legs inside my pants, up to my knees. I bark out a laugh, mutter, "So much for self pity," and climb back up onto the slippery roots.

It takes a good half hour for me to work my way back to the clearing and from there to the large rock overlooking the lagoon where Derek and I often sit. I sit on the edge of the rock, dangle my legs and stare at the lagoon, watching as wind gusts rush over it, ruffling and swirling the water, shifting the ever changing pattern of pockmarks the raindrops leave on its surface.

Somehow moisture finds its way through my jacket's collar. A thin, cold trickle of it starts making its way down my neck and then down my back. I sigh and ignore it. More important things need to be attended to than my comfort.

{*Chloe,*} I mindspeak, masked. {*Chloe, will you talk with me?*}

{*Are you alone now?*}

{*I'm up on land, out of the cavern, away from all the Pelk.*}

{*Even her?*}

{*Especially her,*} I mindspeak.

{*Isn't it storming there? It's horrid here. Claudia and I haven't even thought about leaving the hotel. On the TV they're calling it a tropical disturbance.*}

{*I don't doubt it,*} I mindspeak. {*But I found some foul-weather gear, so it's not too bad. At least no one will venture above to bother me.*}

{*Peter, you know I'm still mad at you.*}

I know Chloe too well to think anything else. {*I do,*} I mindspeak.

{*But that doesn't mean I don't want to help you.*}

{*I didn't think it did.*}

{*What are we going to do?*}

I shake my head. There's so much I've been thinking about—some of which I have no idea whether we can do or not. I mindspeak, {*First of all, we can't have everyone back home thinking that the killings of boaters have stopped just because I'm missing. . . .*}

{*I've been worrying about the same thing here, Peter,*} Chloe mindspeaks. {*I'm so tired of seeing all of Jordan David-son's stupid headlines. I don't think it will be very hard for me to start making boaters disappear again. I've been watching the patrol boats around the island. If I swim out like we did the night we attacked the patrol boat, I'm sure I can come and go without being noticed.*}

{*You have to be very careful. It's not worth doing if it puts you in too much risk.*}

{*Don't be silly. You know I can handle it.*}

I nod, even though she can't see me.

{*What else can I do to help?*} Chloe mindspeaks.

{*If you can, I'd like you and Claudia to get my boat and bring it back.*} I look up at the gray, angry clouds scudding overhead and frown.{*If the damn thing's still floating.*}

{Are you sure that's a good idea? Won't there be questions if I suddenly cruise up to the island on your Grady White?}

{LaMar Assosciates owns a marina in Key Largo. Just bring the boat back to Bimini. Claudia can arrange for someone to bring it over.} I describe the island where I left the boat and the small cove where she can find it anchored.

Chloe mindspeaks, *{The storm's supposed to pass later today. We can get the boat tomorrow, drop it off in Bimini and still be home by dark. But those are easy things. What can we do to get you home?}*

I take a deep breath and tell her about my meeting with the Thryll and about Zalman's words.

Chloe doesn't reply for a few moments, finally mindspeaking, *{In the trees?}*

{Yes. Red mangroves—that's what's all around here.}

{We have them too, all over the island. What should I look for?}

{Did you read or study anything about red mangroves when your mother taught you how to make potions?}

{No, I don't think so. When I get back I can see what I can find in my books.}

{Good,} I mindspeak, though I doubt she'll find anything.

{What about your father? Shouldn't we be trying to find out how he found the antidote?}

I laugh. If only it were that easy. *{They gave me a journal he wrote when he was here. . . .}*

{Didn't it say anything you could use?}

{It's in Spanish, like his log books at home. I keep going over it hoping I'll find some words that I can figure out. But even if we could read it, we don't know if he wrote anything about the antidote.}

{Claudia could translate it for us. You could read it to me and have me repeat it to her.}

Shaking my head, I mindspeak, *{I thought about it, but it's over a hundred pages. Can you imagine how cumbersome that would be? I've been trying to figure out where I could hide the journal up here so you could come and get it during the night.}*

{Whenever you say,} Chloe mindspeaks. *{What about his*

log books? Claudia could read through them when we get home. He may have mentioned the antidote in one of them.}

I think about all the old log books stored with Father's ancient maps in the great room. {*Chloe, there are dozens of them. It will take Claudia forever to read them all. . . .}*

{*She doesn't have to read them all. They're log books, so they're dated.`. . .}*

Seeing where she's going, nodding, I mindspeak, {*His pirate fleet was disbanded around 1700. I think his first wife died in the early 1600s. He would have found his Pelk female after that. So if Claudia reads backwards from the most recent date she'll have the best chance of finding something quickly.}*

{*Exactly. Then we can get you out of there, deal with your whole mess with Jordan Davidson and get back to living our lives.}*

Getting back to living our lives. I can think of nothing I want more—if only we can. A new blast of wind rushes over the lagoon, almost knocking me over, blowing the hood off my head. Raindrops sting my skin, instantly soak my hair. I ignore it all. {*Davidson is the least of our problems. I think I have a solution figured out. All we need to do is get me home. My concern is how you and I can get back to living our life like we used to. As soon as we can.}*

{*Not yet, Peter. I'm not ready to have that conversation with you now.}*

30

Jessai meets me at the bottom of the stairs when I return to the cavern. *"Mowdar wants you to come to him immediately,"* he mindspeaks.

I cock an eyebrow. *"About what?"*

"He told me only to bring you, nothing else."

After the cool of the storm, the foul-weather gear threatens to roast me in the cavern's calm protection. I rip off the jacket, step out of the pants and walk toward the clothes pile.

Jessai follows me, mindspeaking, *"Mowdar said immediately."*

After all the grief Mowdar has brought me, just after my wife refused to discuss how we can repair our relationship, the last thing I want to hear is any demand from the Pelk leader. I stop and whirl around, glaring at the Pelk. *"Or what?"*

He glares back. *"Undrae, I offered you my friendship. Do not force me to take it back. I must do as I am bid."*

Shaking my head, I look at Jessai, at the cavern now lit by all of its glowpools, at the other Pelk all going about enjoying their holiday, lolling in their nests, gathering in groups to share food and drink and conversation. I want no part of any of it. I want to be gone. Still, I know can't leave yet, and I know I would rather have Jessai as a friend than an enemy. I take a breath, calm myself and mindspeak, *"We Undrae have no leaders. I'm not used to being ordered about."*

Jessai nods. *"I am too used to it myself,"* he mindspeaks, and we both laugh. To my relief, he offers no further resistance when I still insist on returning the foul-weather gear to the clothes pile and shifting into my natural form before we go to Mowdar.

*   *   *

We arrive to find the Pelk leader sitting alone on one of the seaweed seats outside his alcove, sharpening the points of his trident with a small stone. He waves me to a seat beside him and motions for Jessai to leave, busying himself with the trident until the Pelk lieutenant's out of sight. Then he stops sharpening the trident and turns his gaze on me, saying nothing, shaking his head.

I stare back, hold my eyes on his until he turns his attention back to his trident, the stone rasping as he runs it up and down one prong and then the next.

"Undrae," he finally mindspeaks. *"What problem are you brewing up for me now?"*

"None," I mindspeak. *"What problem could I pose? Your poison runs in my veins. You have dozens who would kill me on your command."*

Mowdar stops sharpening, tests the point of one prong with his claw and shakes his head. He changes the angle of the stone and runs it up and down the prong again. *"I wish I felt as secure as you seem to think I am,"* he mindspeaks. *"Your actions trouble me."*

"I've done nothing to cause you concern."

"Nothing?" Mowdar drops the stone and turns toward me, swinging the trident in an arc that ends with the newly sharpened tips of all three prongs pressed against my neck. *"Why have you spent most of the morning above—in a storm? Why does my daughter come to me to complain that you have chosen to reject her?"*

I pull back to stop the trident's prongs from boring into my neck's scales, but Mowdar follows my move, keeps them in place. *"Don't bother,"* he mindspeaks. *"I can skewer you with one motion and behead you with the next before you can do anything to stop me."* He pushes the trident against me just a little more. *"Tell me why I should not, Undrae."*

Gnashing my fangs, clenching my claws, it takes all my will to resist grabbing the trident and turning it on the creature. I have been taught never to act from anger alone. But I have also been taught never to give in to intimidation.

Forcing a breath, relaxing my tense muscles, I lean into the trident's prongs, ignore the pain as they break through my scales into the soft tissue below. I stop just before one pierces my main artery. The scent of my blood fills the air around us and I smile at Mowdar. He may have chosen this game, but I have chosen to raise its stakes. The slightest wrong move by me or him can bring my death. He has no choice now except to kill me or pull back.

"Pelk, do whatever you want," I mindspeak. *"I know I'm your prisoner, but does that mean I have to suffer the stink of this cavern every moment of the day? Unlike your kind, I am no cave dweller. Is it your rule that I can no longer go above to smell clean air?"*

"And you want me to believe you went above to sit in the rain and just breathe?"

"I don't care what you think."

Mowdar growls and mindspeaks, *"Take care, Undrae,"* but he moves no more than a statue, his frozen muscles keeping the trident perfectly still.

Just as frozen in place, I mindspeak, *"As far as your daughter, I am mated for life already."*

"That can be changed in a moment. Do you think we cannot reach your wife whenever we want? You have already seen that we have no problem visiting your island. Thanks to Derek, we now know just as much about Morgan's Hole," Mowdar mindspeaks.

A chill runs through me. Suppressing a shudder, I shrug to show the Pelk leader my indifference to his words. The motion drives the trident's prongs another centimeter deeper into me, allowing more blood to run from my wounds.

Mowdar watches the blood flow down my body and shakes his head. *"You are a stubborn creature,"* he mindspeaks, pulling the trident back, all three of its prongs' tips red with my blood. *"I still don't know if you're lying or not. I just know you're willing to die if necessary."*

"Or to kill, if I must, to protect my wife," I mindspeak.

Dipping his trident in a glowpool, to rinse the blood off, Mowdar studies my face. *"Undrae, you need not worry about your wife's safety—for now. But I can't let you shame either my daughter or me any further. I talked to Malka. If you don't go to my daughter's bed willingly tonight, she will call a li-srrynn by your nest tomorrow night and every other night my daughter cares to have you."*

"I did not go to him to make you come to me," Lorrel mind-speaks as soon as I approach the nest.

I say nothing, pull the seaweed drapes closed so only our glowpool keeps us from darkness. *"Funny thing. He told me you did,"* I mindspeak, walking past where she sits on the edge of the nest, lying down behind her on the soft seaweed inside.

Lorrel keeps her back to me. *"When I woke up and you were gone, I was furious. I went to tell Mowdar that I caught you mindspeaking with your wife."*

Sitting up, I mindspeak, *"You don't know if you caught me speaking with anyone."*

She turns and flashes her angry green eyes at me. *"I am not a fool!"*

"Did you tell Mowdar?"

Lorrel shakes her head. *"When my father asked why I was so upset, I could not tell him. It would mean your wife's death. Possibly yours too. Either way, there would be no chance of you ever coming to me of your own will. I deserve that, Peter."*

"But you did tell him I refused to bed you."

"You are not the only one whose mind Malka and her li-srrynn can dominate. When my father said, 'Is Peter not pay-ing proper attention to you?' I was glad to tell him that lesser truth rather than have him ask Malka to search my mind and find out about your wife's mindspeaking."

I sigh and lie back down. Once, I thought my first wife, Eliz-abeth, the most spoiled and willful female alive. Next to Lorrel she now looks positively sweet. Still, in her own selfish way, the Pelk girl has managed to protect both me and my wife from Mowdar's anger.

Somehow, knowing that helps me accept what I must do. I reach for Lorrel's tail with mine and stroke it lightly. She shakes her head. *"My father has made you do this,"* she mind-speaks. *"I do not want to be serviced. I want you to want me."*

Stifling a groan, thinking how little I want to have my mind taken over by the li-srrynn again, I go to her and nuzzle my jowl against hers. *"Now I can tell Chloe I had no choice,"* I mindspeak. *"And I can finally confess that I want you."*

"Do you mean that, Peter?" she mindspeaks, her body relaxing, leaning into me.

I nod. I know it's a lie. She knows it's a lie. But as we proceed, our bodies don't seem to care one damned bit.

31

I wake and lie still, staring at the dark drapes, listening to the sounds of the Pelk waking and going about their morning business. Lorrel sleeps on, her body nestled against me, her tail overlapping mine, her head tucked just below my jaw, her sleepy breaths blowing hot against my throat.

At home I love waking intertwined with Chloe like this. Some mornings I let her sleep another fifteen minutes or half hour just so I can savor the quiet pleasure of her sleep-warm body heating mine. I feel no such joy waking with this female.

Shifting my body a few inches away from Lorrel's, I smile as the air cools those parts of my body that had just been warmed by hers. If, for my survival and Chloe's, I must have sex with this creature, I will. But I will not allow her the intimacy I would give my wife.

Lorrel's breathing changes rhythm. She moves a little and then turns, stretching and yawning, her eyes still closed. *"You moved,"* she mindspeaks. *"Is it morning already?"*

"Yes, it is."

She stretches again, extending her tail, her arms and legs, flexing her claws. *"Maybe it is still storming outside. Maybe we will not have to get up."*

"Sounds to me like everyone else is already going about their business," I mindspeak, sitting up and stretching too, wishing Lorrel gone. I want time to myself so I can search Malka's alcove again, and so I can mindspeak with Chloe without worry of discovery.

Lorrel opens her eyes and mindspeaks, looking at me, *"I feel too good to rush above this morning."* She smiles. *"Thanks to you."*

I nod. If not for the guilt I feel, I'd be luxuriating in the sweet soreness and the after-sex congestion I feel in my loins too. Still I have no desire to sit and share any morning-after reverie. *"Malka will be upset if you're late,"* I mindspeak.

"That old bag of seaweed is always upset about something." Lorrel trills out a laugh. *"She will have to understand if I stay back a little while to breakfast with my man."*

"But it's okay. . . ."

Holding an open claw up in front of my face, Lorrel mindspeaks, *"No, Peter. I want to do this. I want to share time with you. I will go tell Malka that I will not go above until later. I will go to Derek too and let him know that he should not wait for you. And then I will bring us back something to fill our stomachs."*

"I can go with you."

The Pelk girl shakes her head. *"Stay and rest,"* she mindspeaks, getting up and stepping out of the nest. Lorrel fumbles in the dark with something nearby and phosphorescence starts to shine, illuminating her in her human form crouching over the glowpool, pouring more phosphorescent powder into it.

"You already shifted shape?" I mindspeak.

She shrugs. *"I would have to when I went above anyway."* Lorrel holds out her arms and twirls around. *"I like my human form. Don't you?"*

I have had enough experience with females, both human and my kind, to know better than to answer a question like that with anything sounding any less than affirmative. *"Of course I do,"* I mindspeak.

Climbing back into the nest, Lorrel grabs my head and crushes it against her small breasts, kissing me on the hard ridge just above my eyes. *"Good,"* she mindspeaks. *"Why do you not change to your human form too while I'm gone? It will be more comfortable if we are both the same."*

After she makes her way through the drapes, I shift to my human shape, sprinkle more phosphorescence in the glowpool and pick up my father's journal. Sitting near the light, I sigh and begin to leaf through the brittle pages, studying my father's ancient handwritten words.

Here and there I recognize words that I learned in high

school Spanish, but not enough to translate any full sentence. Flipping toward the back, choosing a page at random, I stare at each word and find nothing. I do the same on the next page, with the same result. On the next, at the bottom, I stop, my eyes frozen on the last word on the page, *antidoto*.

Shaking my head, my heart racing, I put my index finger on it, trace back to the beginning of the sentence and read the words, *No tengo el antidoto*. I flip to the next page and read the rest of the sentence, *pero creo tener una idea*.

{*Chloe!*} I mindspeak masked. {*I found something in the journal.*}

{*Peter! What is it?*}

{*I found where Father wrote the word 'antidoto'. I assume that's Spanish for antidote. He says, 'No tengo,' which means, 'I don't have,' but I'm not sure about the rest of the sentence. Would you repeat the whole thing to Claudia for me?*}

{*She's at the dock getting her boat ready. I'm supposed to meet her in a few minutes. We're going to go get your boat. Tell me the whole sentence and I'll write it down and bring it to her.*}

I mindspeak the words, {*No tengo el antidoto pero creo tener una idea,*} to Chloe, repeat it as she writes it and have her read it back to me.

{*Good,*} she mindspeaks. {*I'll bring this to Claudia. It shouldn't be more than a few minutes.*}

The drapes rustle and I mindspeak, {*Don't! I'll contact you later.*}

{*She's there, isn't she, Peter?*}

{*Later,*} I mindspeak, just as Lorrel works her way through the drapes, two chunks of dried fish in her hand.

Closing the journal, I look at the Pelk girl and smile, "Good," I mindspeak. "*I was starting to get hungry.*"

Lorrel sits next to me, her hip touching mine, as we eat. "*I am glad you changed shape,*" she mindspeaks. "*I like your human form.*" Holding a piece of fish in one hand, she strokes the top of my leg with her other, not far from my crotch.

"*If you keep that up we'll never go above,*" I mindspeak.

"*You forget. I have spoken to Malka. She does not require me this morning. She said it is good we are finally behaving like lovers—maybe that will convince Mowdar of your intentions. She does not want him to risk any of our males by sending them after your wife."*

"Wait." Putting down my fish, I swivel toward Lorrel so I face her. *"Mowdar indicated he had no plan to go after Chloe for now. I thought she'd be safe as long as we were together."*

Lorrel frowns, takes her hand off my thigh. *"Is that your only reason for being with me?"*

"No, but I want no harm to come to her."

"No more!" The Pelk girl turns her back toward me. *"I am tired of hearing about your wife."*

I stare at her thin, pale back, her long, thick black hair hanging almost to her buttocks. Obviously she knows things concerning my wife that I should hear. Just as clearly, asking her now would lead nowhere. I reach for her hair and stroke it. *"What if we concentrated on you instead?"* I mindspeak.

Lorrel shrugs and takes a bite from her fish. I move closer, cupping one breast from the back with my hand, putting my lips on the nape of her neck. *"Didn't you tell me you wanted to know how it felt to have sex as a human?"* I mindspeak, kissing her soft flesh.

She continues to eat, saying nothing, showing no reaction to my touch. I uncup her breast, take her nipple between my fingers and squeeze just enough to have it crinkle up and turn hard. Lorrel sighs and leans back into me, and I take my other hand and do the same to her other breast. The Pelk girl drops the remainder of her fish, turns toward me, and I put my lips on hers, kissing her, holding her as we tumble together into the nest.

Afterwards, we lie together, Lorrel on top of me, her head on my chest, her legs straddling me, her hands holding my shoulders. I stroke her back, her buttocks, her hair. *"I like this,"* she mindspeaks.

For her sake, I nod.

"Shall we again?" Lorrel mindspeaks.

"In a bit. Let me rest a little first," I mindspeak. But I begin to explore her body with my hands, stroking, probing, palpating until she begins to move with each touch of my fingers.

"Is this resting?" she mindspeaks, pressing her crotch against mine.

I press back, smile as I will myself to stiffen. *"Sort of,"* I mindspeak, maneuvering my body, sliding myself into her.

She starts to ride me, but I grip her hips and hold her still. *"Easy, there's no rush,"* I mindspeak. *"Please, I know you don't want to talk about this, but I need to ease my mind. Please help me."* Holding her, kissing her ear, I partially withdraw and slowly thrust back into her. *"Is Mowdar planning to harm my family?"*

Lorrel stiffens and tries to pull away, but I hold her and press myself against her. *"I enjoy doing this with you. I enjoy it so much that I'm ashamed,"* I mindspeak. *"But I could enjoy it more if I could be sure my family was safe."*

"No one cares to hurt your children," Lorrel mindspeaks, her body no longer reacting to my touch. *"Mowdar worries that your wife might do us harm."*

I say nothing, only touch and stroke and thrust until her body relaxes and begins to move in rhythm with mine again. Then I mindspeak, *"Why is he worried about one female?"*

The Pelk girl groans and pushes herself free of me, rolling onto her back. *"This is so unfair of you,"* she mindspeaks.

I sit up, wishing my erection would go away quicker. *"But I need to know. Would you expect any less if you were my mate? Please answer my questions now and I promise you, I won't bother you with them anymore. We can lie down and just concentrate on each other."*

Lorrel sighs and sits up too. *"No more after this?"* she mindspeaks.

"No more."

"You've seen what our li-srrynn can do to your mind," she mindspeaks. *"But just as only our females have the power to sing into other's minds, your females have the power to resist our songs. Because of this, during the Great War your females won all the battles, not your males. You Undrae are much larger than we, and much more powerful. Mowdar knows it would cost many of our deaths to defeat her."*

"But if she's in Jamaica or even on our island, she poses no threat to the Pelk."

Lorrel glares at me. *"You think us fools. If she comes close enough to mindspeak with you, masked, then she can pose a threat to us. I am not the only one to think you have been in contact with someone. Jessai has shared his concerns with my father."*

"I told him that was Derek!"

"He told Mowdar you said that, and Derek confirmed it. Still, Mowdar has to watch for the safety of his people. But you should know he has not decided to send anyone after your wife. I think, if you give him no further cause, she will be safe."

"But what else can I do?" I mindspeak.

"I do not know." Lorrel shrugs. *"I am tired of this conversation. You now have your answers."* She lies back down on her back, her legs spread. *"You promised to concentrate on me,"* she mindspeaks. *"So do it."*

By the time we finish and open our drapes, most of the males have left the cavern for a day of hunting, and most of the females have gone above to start their chores. Lorrel walks close to my side, choosing clothes for me from the clothes pile and insisting I try to choose clothes for her that she'd find pleasing—laughing at and rejecting my first three picks.

She leaves me once we get outside, taking the path to the gardens. I go to the lagoon, find Derek lounging on the rock, watching the women work, and join him there. "So, old man," he says. "Saw your drapes pulled this morning. Looks like you were a busy dodger. I'd hate to hear what my sister would say about that."

I frown at him and say, "So would I." Lying down on the rock on my stomach, I bury my face in my arms.

"Tired you out, did she?" Derek says.

"Just let me rest a little," I say, then mindspeak masked, {*Chloe?*}

{*You son of a bitch!*}

{*What?*} I mindspeak, stifling a gasp, wondering for a moment if she could know what Lorrel and I have just done.

{*Claudia and I are on the Grady White. Fortunately she can't smell what I can. Your Pelk girl's scent is everywhere. On the seat where I sit. On the back bench, mixed with yours. In the*

cabin, in the same berth as you. You had to give her my blue
bikini too?}

{*She's not my Pelk girl. I told you what happened,*} I mindspeak. {*I had no choice.*}

{*She forced you to sleep in the same berth with her?*}

{*Not exactly.*}

{*What exactly is she forcing you to do now?*}

I say nothing.

Chloe waits for a minute and then mindspeaks. {*Well, I guess
I have my answer. We're going to leave. I want to get the boat
back to Bimini in time for me to get home before dark.*}

{*Wait a minute. This isn't fair of you,*} I mindspeak.

{*Fuck fair,*} Chloe mindspeaks. {*I'm going home. I need to
let Claudia read through your father's log books for you, and I
need to make some humans disappear for you, and right now I
don't want to do a damned thing for you. So fuck fair, Peter, and
fuck you too!*}

I want to shout. I want to pound the rock with my fist. But I
can do nothing that might appear as if I were mindspeaking
masked with someone. {*Chloe, I love you,*} I mindspeak.

{*Obviously not enough,*} she mindspeaks. {*I'm going to go
now. Oh, by the way, Claudia translated that sentence for you.
It means, 'I don't have the antidote, but I think I have an idea.'
I'll be back in a week with her. God knows why. Try to have the
next few paragraphs ready so I can give them to her then.*}

{*Chloe . . .*}

{*Enough, Peter. I'll be back in a week. I promise I'll be
calmer then. Right now I've had enough. Let me go now.*}

I lie on my stomach until the rock begins to hurt my elbows
and knees. Rolling over, I sigh and stare at the blue sky above,
the white puffs of cloud barely moving in it.

"You look sad, old man," Derek says. "Anything wrong?"

"The question is—is anything right?" I say.

32

In the evening, Lorrel and I take dinner in the company of Mowdar, Jessai and Malka, just as we have each night since I arrived. Everything seems the same as before, as it does the next night and the evening after it.

On the fourth day after my talk with the Pelk leader, the hunting party returns early, carrying barely any catch with them. *"Bad day?"* I mindspeak to Jessai. He nods and averts his eyes.

When dinnertime comes and I get up to go join Mowdar, Lorrel shakes her head. *"Not tonight,"* she mindspeaks. *"We will feed here. Derek will feed at his nest. Mowdar has called for a hunting council. They will not want us about."*

"What's going on?" I mindspeak.

Lorrel shrugs. *"Whatever it is does not concern us."* She pulls the shades early and insists on coupling over and over again.

The clank of a trident striking stone wakes me. I lie in the nest, my eyes open, and listen to the shuffling of feet, the occasional splash of someone entering water too quickly. Standing, I make my way to the drapes, part them and stare through the gloom in the cavern toward the lagoon.

Hunters carrying their tridents slip one by one into the water. I look from them to the hole at the top of the stairs. No light shows from there at all. But even in the gloom, I can make out the dark shape of a Pelk male standing guard at the top of the steps, holding his trident at ready.

"Come back to bed," Lorrel mindspeaks, touching my back, stroking it.

I whirl around. *"What the hell is going on?"*

"They have gone for an early hunt." Lorrel grips my arm with her claw and tugs me back. *"Come back, lie down with me. It is too early to rise."*

Jerking my arm out of her grip, I growl and mindspeak, *"Don't lie to me. What are they doing?"*

"It's too late, Peter. You cannot do anything about it. The boat should not have been moved."

"What?"

"Mowdar and his men went to Waylach's Rock yesterday to salvage what they could from your boat. It wasn't there."

"So what? The storm could have taken it."

"Or someone else, your wife perhaps," Lorrel mindspeaks.

"And they're on their way to my island?"

Lorrel says nothing.

I look into her eyes. *"You know I'm going to have to go."*

"Why, if she is not there?"

"But we both know she is," I mindspeak.

"You are to take the antidote tomorrow night again. You will die without it."

"If I'm without it," I mindspeak. I peer out through the drapes again and nod when I see no one left on the beach. Behind me Lorrel begins to hum. I turn, rush to her, grab her throat with both of my claws and squeeze hard enough to choke off any sound.

She claws at me but I ignore each rip and gouge. *"Please don't fight me,"* I mindspeak. *"I don't want to harm you. Think of our son inside you."* But she continues to struggle, and I squeeze more. I hold her throat only as long as it takes for her to go limp, not a second more.

Releasing her, lying her body down, I check to see if she's still breathing and nod when her chest moves. Before she can wake and call for help, I rush out through the drapes and hurry to Malka's alcove.

The old creature sits up and stands as soon as I burst through her drapes. *"Get out, fool!"* she mindspeaks.

I have a claw at her throat, another pressed against her temple, before she can make a sound. *"If you mindspeak for help I will drive my claw into your brain. If any note comes from you, I will rip your throat out. Do you understand me?"*

"I have no fear of dying," she mindspeaks. *"And I will go with the satisfaction of knowing your death will be much more painful than mine."*

"Possibly," I mindspeak. *"It depends on whether I can find out how to make the antidote."*

"Lorrel has not learned how to make it yet. The knowledge will die with me." She begins to sing a low note that vibrates through my bones, and I slice through her throat, her blood spraying out, coating me.

"You forget," I mindspeak. *"My father Don Henri Dela-Sangre found a way to reverse your poison. He may yet show his son the way."*

"Undrae, you are a fool," Malka mindspeaks, wavering but still standing. *"What makes you so sure we have given you the same poison?"* She begins to blast a thought, *"HE . . ."*

I drive my claw through her temple, into her brain, before she can finish calling for help. Malka collapses, her body falling back into her nest. Still I slice at her, again and again, ripping her open to make sure she never rises again.

Going to the small chest holding the bottles of temporary antidote, I rummage through it, searching for full bottles. I find pitiful few, line them up on the floor and count them. Only five. I sigh.

By killing Malka I've taken away all of Derek's options. I can't keep the bottles just for myself and leave him to die a miserable death. If he insists on going his own way, I will give him three of the bottles. That will leave me with a week's worth of antidote. At best, if we can find no permanent antidote and share all five bottles, it will give me eight and a half days.

Time enough either way, I hope, to try to save my wife.

Taking a woven seaweed bag off of one of Malka's shelves, I upend it. Roots and herbs and bags full of powder spill to the floor. Putting the bottles in the bag, I rush from the alcove.

No more Pelk seem to be up. No more glowpools shine around the cavern. I smile into the gloom, glad that Malka's partial cry has gone unnoticed. Pushing through the drapes into my alcove, I find Lorrel just sitting up, rubbing her neck.

Her eyes widen and she gasps when she sees me. *"There is blood all over you!"*

"I had to kill Malka," I mindspeak, picking up my father's journal and putting it in the bag with the bottles. *"Please don't do anything to make me hurt you any more."*

"Now no one here knows how to make the antidote," she mindspeaks, shaking her head. *"You're going to die. For what?"*

"I can't sit by while they attack my wife," I mindspeak. *"I have to go to her."*

Lorrel sighs and I look into her eyes. I see no signs of rage or thirst for revenge on her face. She has yet to call out, to raise any alarm. I wonder if just maybe I can turn to her. *"You could help me,"* I mindspeak. *"What have you heard? Do you know anything that might help me?"*

She trills out a laugh. *"Why would I tell you?"*

"Because if my wife dies and I live, I'll come back here and do more damage to the Pelk than my father ever did. I won't rest until every one of you is dead, here and in Jamaica, in-cluding you and my child—as much as it may pain me."

"If my father and his men don't kill you, the poison will. Your threats mean nothing."

I hold up my father's journal. *"My father survived your poi-son. He wrote about it in this book. As soon as we translate it, your poison will mean nothing,"* I mindspeak, hoping my words prove true.

Lorrel shrugs.

"But if you help me, I'll allow your srrynn to live here in peace. Your son, our son, grows inside you. I would like to know him. I would like to be able to come and visit him as he grows. I would like him to know my other children. That won't happen if you don't help."

"And you expect me to betray my kind so my son can know his father?" Lorrel mindspeaks.

"Mowdar was wrong to order you to poison me and bed me. He should have allowed you to go to Jessai. He is wrong to lead his men against Chloe. Had you left us alone we would never have posed a threat to you. You know that and I know that."

Lorrel nods and says nothing. I stay by her and let her think. Finally she mindspeaks, *"They will not rush to attack her. They*

*will stop and rest at each safehold along the way. When they
reach Miami they will rest again in our safehold and scout before they attack."*

"There's a safehold in Miami?" I mindspeak.

Lorrel smiles and nods. *"Where did you think I rested?"* she
mindspeaks. I gasp when she tells me its location.

"Now," Lorrel mindspeaks, *"you must promise me something."*

I nod.

*"Mowdar has left Jessai behind. He has been instructed to
keep you here. You must promise not to kill him."*

"I promise to try."

The Pelk girl shakes her head. *"No. If I am not to have you,
I must have him. Promise he will live."*

"Done," I mindspeak, wondering if I can keep the promise,
picking up the bag and walking toward the drapes.

"Undrae," Lorrel mindspeaks. *"Did you not enjoy your time
with me at all? Did you not like bedding me?"*

Turning toward her, I smile. *"Yes, there were times I enjoyed
myself with you very much. As far as bedding you, I liked it
more than I care to admit."*

"Will you miss it?"

I think about it. Given a choice, I would always turn to
Chloe. Still, I see no reason not to give Lorrel what she wants.
I nod.

Lorrel grins and mindspeaks, *"Good."*

Derek growls when I kick him awake, growls even more
when I drag him away from his nest. *"Bloody hell, old man. It's
the middle of the night. What bug do you have up your ass?"*

I tell him about Mowdar's hunting party and about Malka's
death. The big creature groans. *"Well,"* he mindspeaks. *"I
guess that fixes me. Didn't it occur to you that I might prefer to
stay here? I don't much care for dying, you know."*

"Your sister is in danger, damn it! It may come as a shock to
you, but you weren't on my mind. Stay here if you want. I can't
waste any more time with you." I take three bottles of temporary antidote from the bag and hand them to him. Turning away,
I begin to walk toward the steps. *"I need to go while it's still*

dark outside. Just remember, the only hope of finding a permanent antidote is in Miami now."

At the bottom of the steps, I stop and look up. The sentry Mowdar posted at the top of the steps stares down at me and our eyes meet. *"So Undrae, do you plan to fight me alone?"* Jessai mindspeaks, pointing his trident at me.

Putting my bag down, I mindspeak, *"Why would we want others?"*

"Good." The Pelk warrior takes a practice swing with his trident. *"Will you come up to me or should I come down to you?"*

"Whichever you prefer," I mindspeak, looking around, hoping another sentry left his trident lying nearby, finding nothing.

"You are larger. You come up to me. It will take away that advantage."

Taking a deep breath, I study the Pelk warrior, the way he holds his trident, one claw almost to the back of the shaft, the other to the middle. It may be good for hunting, but I wonder whether another grip might work better for close combat. With any luck I can grab the upper shaft before he can cut into me.

"You are daft," Derek mindspeaks, coming up behind me. *"Do you really intend to fight him without a weapon? Do you think he can't hurt you with that bloody thing?"*

I turn and find him holding out a trident to me. *"Here. I took it from the storeroom. This should even things up. But don't expect any more help from me if things go badly. This is your bloody fight, not mine."*

Feeling the heft of the trident's ironwood shaft, I mimic Jessai's grip and take a few practice jabs and slices. I scowl at how clumsy it feels and move my hands upward so I grip the trident at the middle of its shaft and just below its head—the way a soldier grasps a rifle with bayonet. I take a few more practice moves, including a savage uppercut with the butt of the shaft, then nod, placing my foot on the bottom step.

"Ah, Undrae. You finally have found your nerve," Jessai mindspeaks.

"I would rather we not fight." My eyes on the Pelk, I take each step slowly, holding the trident out in front of me.

Jessai smiles and steps down one step with his left foot—I assume to make it easier to drive the weapon downward. *"But I would prefer we did,"* he mindspeaks.

I stop four steps below him, my trident in front of me but just out of his reach. *"Listen to me,"* I mindspeak. *"I'm leaving here tonight. Whatever happens, I won't be coming back. Lorrel knows that. She wants to be with you. I've promised not to kill you."*

"Fortunately, I have made no such promise." The Pelk darts down the stairs, thrusting his trident at my throat. I gasp and bat it to the side just before it reaches my scales.

Jessai withdraws to the top step and laughs. *"I am surprised you could do that. You hold your trident so badly. Should I stop now and teach you how to use it before we go any further?"*

I take another step up. Jessai puts his left foot on the next step down and holds his trident pointed at me. Each of us waits for the other to attack. Finally I see his eyes move from me for a moment, his muscles relax just a hair, and I spring forward, slicing out with the trident.

He blocks it, his trident's prongs locked against mine, his weight bearing down, threatening to push my trident to the step. I pull back, freeing my trident's head and swinging up its hilt in a vicious uppercut that slams into the Pelk's left leg.

It buckles and he gasps, almost falling, saving himself at the last moment by throwing his weight on his trident, using it as a staff. I shoot forward and bury my trident's prongs into his other thigh. Jessai crashes down on the step and swings his trident so it slices across my chest.

Hot pain traces its path and I stifle a yowl and pull back, the air thick with the smell of his blood and mine, the steps turning slick as it pours from our bodies. *"Undrae,"* Jessai mindspeaks. *"What kind of fight is this? Do you intend to attack only my legs?"*

I smile. I hadn't expected it to turn into an advantage. But my promise to Lorrel has relieved me of having to take the risk of attacking the Pelk's chest or head. While he has to concentrate on killing me, I need only attack his extremities.

"I intend to disable you," I mindspeak. *"But leave you alive."*

"*Either get it done or fight more quietly!*" Derek mindspeaks from the bottom of the steps. "*I can hear you two scuffling from here. Much more bloody ruckus and they'll all be on our necks.*"

Jessai pulls himself up to the top step and tries to stand. But his legs can no longer support him. "*Just let us by,*" I mindspeak. "*We don't have to do any more of this.*"

Shaking his head, sitting erect, holding his trident in a defensive position, the Pelk mindspeaks, "*Mowdar has given his instructions. I must do as he says.*"

I rush up and jab at his left shoulder. Jessai blocks the trident, deflects it, slicing my arm in the same move. Pain shoots through me, but my growing anger overwhelms it. This time, instead of withdrawing I stand my ground, hammering his head with the butt of the trident's hilt, ignoring the next slice from his trident and hammering him again and again. His guard drops and I plunge the trident into his left shoulder, blood everywhere, his and mine.

Jessai moans but somehow manages to turn his trident again with his right arm and bury its prongs into the thick meat of my left leg. The pain barely registers through my anger and I slam him with the trident's butt again, battering his head and upper body until he can no longer maintain his grip on his trident.

Grabbing it, yanking it clear of my leg, I throw the trident from the steps and nod when it splashes into the water. The Pelk moans again. He opens one eye. I raise my claw to slice him open, to finish him once and for all.

"*So, Undrae. What happened to your promise?*" Jessai mindspeaks.

I hold my claw in place. My leg, my chest, my arm all throb and burn. I bleed from nicks and cuts almost everywhere. Why should I let this creature live to possibly threaten me another day? But I have sworn to Lorrel that I would do so. I sigh and lower my claw.

Jessai coughs out a laugh. "*Malka will call for a healing circle and I'll be whole before the next day is done. Are you sure you want to leave your enemy the opportunity to attack you again?*"

"*Malka is dead,*" I mindspeak. "*And my hope is that you

won't always be my enemy. Lorrel will lead the healing circle now. You should go to her bed after you've been made well."

I groan as I step over the Pelk. I yearn to lie down and rest but know I can't. Still, I must give my body an opportunity to heal. Shifting into my human form so I can fit through the hole, my body trembling from the pain of my wounds, I mindspeak to Derek to find some dried fish, bring it and my bag and join me above.

Outside, bright stars crowd the dark sky, and the moon rides high enough to assure me we should have more than enough time to fly to Florida's waters before dawn comes. I drop to my knees and then fall back, staring upward, wishing I could take flight this instant.

"Soon enough," I mutter. "Soon enough."

33

"The whole thing's a bloody pain. Damned foolish of you. My sister's perfectly capable of defending herself, old man. Could you imagine the mincemeat my mother would make out of a little old creature like Mowdar? If she didn't eat him whole, she'd make him into a shish kebob! You didn't have to sign our death warrants to come flying back as some kind of hero."

I smile into the dark and make no attempt to answer. Derek has maintained a constant litany of complaints from the moment he and I took to the air over Andros. If he needs to grouse, I have no objection. I roar into the air and dive toward the ocean, reveling in the feel of the wind buffeting my body.

Leveling off just above the wave tips, I shoot forward, flapping my wings as quickly as I can, realizing how much I've missed the speed, the freedom of flight. Derek follows right behind me, mindspeaking, "This is all bloody foolishness. What's your rush? We're passing boats full of good prey. Damn it all, can't we at least eat something proper for once?"

If not for the scattered lights around Alicetown and the dozens of anchor lights dotting Bimini's harbor, the small island could be easily missed in the dark. I smile as we pass over it and mindspeak to Derek, "Almost home."

"Bloody lot of good that does me," Derek mindspeaks. "You've made it clear there will be no hunting after we get there. That bit of fish we had when we left the srrynn barely dulled my hunger. My stomach's completely empty, old man. I don't want to fill it with your frozen cow meat when we have the chance to take some human prey right now. Look below. There are boats everywhere."

I nod. My stomach aches too. Shifting the seaweed bag I've been carrying in my right front claw to my left, I think about its contents. Because of the patrols, we'll have to swim the last few miles to my island. The five bottles of temporary antidote can survive such an immersion without any problem, but my father's journal could disintegrate.

Shaking my head, staring at the water's calm surface, I go over in my mind the arrangements that have to be made. As much as I want to ignore my hunger and my problems and rush home, it will take some time to put everything into motion. Mindspeaking to Derek, I say, *"Okay, but not this close to Bimini. Hopefully we'll see a good opportunity before we finish crossing the Gulf Stream."*

Then I turn my attention toward home. *"Chloe,"* I mindspeak. *"Chloe, we're on the way to you."*

I wait for an answer. When none comes, I call out again, *"Chloe! Derek and I are close to home. Wake up, baby. Answer me."*

"Peter? What? Where are you?"

"Not far from Bimini."

"My God, you're almost here! I don't understand. What about the poison? Why are you saying we? Is that Pelk female with you?"

"No, she isn't," I mindspeak, explaining about Mowdar's plans and Derek's and my departure from the srrynn.

"Oh, Peter, the poison," Chloe says. *"We still have no idea how to make an antidote for it. Claudia's been struggling through your father's log books, but she hasn't found a thing yet."*

"I have his journal with me, and we have enough temporary antidote to take the both of us through another week."

"You'll have to be careful coming in. I did what we discussed. I killed a boater and made him disappear the night I got back. The media and police were crazed the next day. I killed another two the next night and they went ballistic. Jordan Davidson's paper had a headline that said, HAS PETER DELASAN-GRE RETURNED?*"*

I growl into the air and mindspeak, *"Now that I am returning maybe we'll be able to make that little asshole regret all his headlines."*

"*Peter, we have more important problems than that.*"

"*He is another problem we have to resolve,*" I mindspeak.

Derek flies a little too close, almost bumping me. "*Sorry, old man,*" he mindspeaks.

Shaking my head at the irritating creature, I flex my wings and readjust my position. But then I take a long look at my brother-in-law, realize how I might be able to use him, and smile. "*And, Chloe,*" I mindspeak, "*I may have just thought of a way to take care of our Mr. Davidson.*"

"*Good for you, Peter. First you have to find a way home. There are patrol boats all over the bay and up and down the coast, and helicopter patrols constantly.*"

"*Any of them as far out as Fowey Rocks?*" I mindspeak.

"*I don't think so. All the ones on the outside are mostly hugging the shore. Remember, all the disappearances have been in the bay.*"

"*Good, then I want you to call Claudia right now.*" I tell Chloe what I need her to do so we can bring the journal safely to the island.

"*And then what?*" she mindspeaks. "*Couldn't you have found a way to warn me and still stay on Andros until we figured out how to make the antidote?*"

"*No. Mowdar and his men will be near our island in three days at the latest. They'll probably attack a day or two after that. I couldn't wait for you to come back into mindspeaking range to warn you, and I had no way to sneak out. Mowdar posted guards. Even if Lorrel kept her silence, someone would have noticed. If I did get out, they'd never have allowed me to live if I returned. Not that they could have anyway—remember, Malka's dead.*"

"*I wish you hadn't killed her,*" Chloe mindspeaks. "*I know you wanted to come and help me fight Mowdar. But without any antidote, I'll lose you no matter how well we do against them.*"

Frowning into the dark, I mindspeak, "*You would never sit still if you knew I was in danger. In my place I doubt you would have done any differently. If we survive the Pelks' attack and if we don't figure out an antidote sometime in the next week, at least I'll die knowing you and the kids are okay.*"

"*Somehow that doesn't comfort me,*" Chloe mindspeaks.

"How do you think I feel?" Derek mindspeaks. *"Nothing about this whole bloody affair comforts me one whit!"*

Derek thinks every ship we pass makes for a good opportunity. I reject more than a dozen boats before we see a oil tanker riding low in the water, its cargo most probably destined for the oil tanks at Fort Lauderdale's Port Everglades. The dark form of a solitary crew member making his way toward the rear of the ship catches my attention.

I wonder whether he's out for a late-night inspection or just taking a restless walk around the deck. No matter. He looks tall and thick-framed—a perfect meal for two beings as hungry as we. I point him out to Derek.

We circle over the ship, watching the big man until he stops at the stern and stares out at the sea, his hands on the ship's rail. *"I'll take him,"* Derek mindspeaks.

Staring at the rear windows of the ship's bridge, I see no sign of anyone else. Typically ships like this travel on autopilot when they're at sea. I'm relatively sure if the helmsman hasn't dozed off, he's most likely busying himself with instruments or staring forward into the night. I shrug. It's an acceptable risk.

As much as I'd like to take the kill, I mindspeak, *"Go ahead."*

Derek folds his wings and plummets away from me. He spreads them open again at a hundred feet and shoots toward the tanker, adjusting his position so he crosses the boat from the starboard side, just a few feet over the stern rail. The man seems to sense nothing until Derek seizes his shoulders with his rear claws and jerks him into the air, carrying him away in an instant.

Derek has already killed the man and gorged on his entire right thigh by the time he rejoins me. He passes the carcass to me as soon as he arrives. After weeks of Pelk food, just the smell of fresh human blood is enough to send me into a feeding frenzy. I bite a huge hunk from the body, swallowing and taking another bite before I pass it back to Derek.

He does the same, and we share the carcass, passing it back and forth, gorging as we fly until little more than the man's skeleton remains. Derek drops that into the sea, and we turn toward the Gulf Stream and the glow of Miami's lights beyond the dark horizon.

By the time I see the Fowey Rocks lighthouse beacon, the sky behind us has started to show the first gray tinges of dawn. Derek and I both drop down, skimming just above the ocean's surface to minimize the risk of being seen.

"You heard Chloe's warning. There are patrol boats everywhere closer to shore. They're pretty intent on catching someone," I mindspeak. *"We're going to have to swim the rest of the way—as soon as we get closer to the lighthouse."*

"Terrific. You and your wife certainly know how to welcome a guest, don't you?"

I ignore my brother-in-law and concentrate on watching for boat lights. When I spot running lights approaching the lighthouse, I mindspeak, *"Here,"* and pass the woven seaweed bag to Derek. *"It's going to be tricky, but I need you to give the bag back to me after I get into the water. You have to be careful. We can't get it wet."*

Derek shrugs. *"Whatever you say, old man."*

Dropping into the water and sinking below the surface, I immediately concentrate on what Lorrel taught me, changing shape, my body streamlining, growing fins and fluke until I'm ready to surface as a full-sized dolphin male. Flying close by, Derek pays no attention to me until I whistle, rise halfway out of the water and mindspeak, *"Here, Derek. Bring it to me here."*

He flies by too high and too fast on his first approach. *"Damn it. It's your fault. For a second I thought you were a Pelk. You should have told me you were going to shift to being a dolphin. And you accused me of going native with them. I never changed into any damned fish."*

"Dolphins aren't fish," I mindspeak, then talk him through the next approach, grabbing the bag's loop handles with my mouth and flipping the bag back so it rests on my head, out of the water. Balancing the bag there, I swim toward the Fowey Rocks lighthouse and the boat drifting near it, waiting for me to arrive.

Derek splashes into the water five yards behind me and follows underwater, mindspeaking, *"If she brought a boat, she could have brought clothes and she could damned well have brought us in. I don't see why we have to swim in the bloody water all the way to your island like we're the Pelk, when we just risked everything by leaving the loathsome creatures and their fishy ways."*

The sun has risen above the horizon and turned the sky bright by the time I near Fowey Rocks. Claudia puts down her fishing rod and throws her boat's motors into neutral as soon as she sees me approaching from her port side. Shaking her head, muttering, "A dolphin. I have to have the most peculiar job on earth," she leans over the side and takes the bag from my mouth. I tolerate a few pats on my head from her before I sink into the water and dive away.

The water erupts with the growls of her engines revving up and speeding away, and I turn toward shore and begin swimming as fast as I can. Behind me Derek mindspeaks, *"Damn it. Slow down, old man. You know I can't swim as fast as you can in that form."*

Tempted as I am to leave him behind, I don't trust that he'll hug the bottom on his approach to the island. I slow down, wait for him to catch up, and then speed up as much as he can tolerate.

Once we near the island, knowing no patrol boat will see anything suspicious in a dolphin, I surface and continue forward, watching for patrol boats and helicopters. Derek complains when I make him dodge from reefs to kelp beds, avoiding stretches of sand wherever possible, but I want to take no chances that his dark mass might be spotted from above.

We encounter no helicopters along the way, slip by the two patrol boats guarding the entrance to Wayward Channel and pass by yet another patrol twenty yards outside the entrance to the channel into my island's channel. Speeding ahead, leaving Derek to follow, I mindspeak, *"Chloe! I'm home! Come down to the dock!"*

I hit the harbor at full speed. Wheeling around, kicking toward the dock, shooting upward between Chloe's and Claudia's boats, I change into my human form as soon as I break the water. I slam down on the dock, landing on my stomach—wet, naked and embarrassed to find Chloe's feet and Claudia's just inches from my nose.

"This has to be the strangest job ever," Claudia says to Chloe as I scramble to my feet. I ignore her, ignore the woven seaweed bag in her hand, ignore the nakedness of my damp body and stare at my wife, her brown face and full brown lips, her startling green eyes. I take her into my arms and hug her close to me.

She holds me tight too, both of us oblivious to Claudia's stare, neither of us caring that how the dampness of my body soaks her clothes. I press my lips against hers and we kiss, our mouths open, our tongues as together as the rest of us, the morning sun warming our bodies.

A loud bark warns us just moments before Max runs up and launches his body at us. As massive as he is, he almost knocks us over. Both Chloe and I pet him as he woofs, repeatedly jumping up on one or the other of us, wagging his short stump of a tail furiously.

Derek surfaces alongside the dock in his human form and pulls himself out of the water. "Damn," he says, standing up, his body as wet and naked as mine, his blond hair plastered to his scalp, dripping water down his forehead. He looks around. "Bloody, bloody damn. Doesn't anyone have any towels?"

His eyes stop on Claudia and he nods, suddenly standing as if he were dressed in his finest. With his best bar-pickup expression he says, "Well, hello. How are you today?"

In his human form he has the look and stance of a natural athlete. Claudia eyes him over, up and down, and guffaws. "I love it!" she shrieks. "This has to be the best job ever!"

In my arms, Chloe begins to giggle too.

34

After Derek and I have dried off and dressed, we all gather together in the great room. I can't keep my eyes—or my hands—off Chloe. I try to stay as close as possible, following her into the kitchen, helping as she prepares steaks to warm up in the microwave for breakfast, brushing against her as we pass each other. Finally, she gently pushes me away, saying, "Go sit. I'll do the rest."

I join Derek and Claudia at the large oak table and look around the room from window to window, taking in the views of the ocean, the bay and the islands to the north and south of us. Nothing could appear more beautiful to me. No place could feel more comfortable. The aroma of meat warming fills the room, and I sigh and sink back into my seat. No doubt attracted by the smell, Max pads into the room and lies down near my feet. "It's so good to be home," I say.

Derek frowns at me. "I'm sure it is, old man—for you. But you're forgetting about that damned Pelk poison in both of us. I'm not sure I would have chosen to die in terrible pain, in a week, for the pleasure of being here."

"We have a good chance of figuring out the antidote," I say, sitting straight, pointing at the woven seaweed bag that Claudia's left at the far end of the table. "My father's journal is in there. I'm sure Claudia will find something there."

Claudia shakes her head just a little as she says, "Wait a minute, you guys. *Maybe* I'll find something. I've already been going through the logs. It's tough reading that stuff. The handwriting alone could make you cry. It's all in old-fashioned Spanish too. How would you like to read page after page of old English?"

"Not very much," Chloe says, bringing four plates with warm, almost-raw steaks to the table. She serves Derek and me, puts a plate on the floor for Max and sits down next to me with her steak. "But Peter already found that sentence about the antidote. He can show you where he found it."

Both Max and Derek dive into their food immediately, Derek cutting and eating pieces as fast as he can, Max biting and chewing chunks of his. Claudia, who'd rather go hungry than eat bloody meat, stares from one to the other as they wolf down their food and shakes her head.

"Just because I can speak and read the language," she says, "you both think of me as Spanish. I am, but you forget that my family came here hundreds of years ago with Don Henri. I only really learned to read Spanish after I took it in college. Maybe we should get someone else to read through the stuff, someone who knows the language better than I do."

Chloe looks at me. I shake my head. "We can't have an outsider reading my father's words."

Claudia nods. "I can understand that. I read about some pretty strange things in the log books. Don't worry—none of it bothered me. In the Gomez family we're sort of raised to ignore anything weird about you DelaSangres. But it sure could shock anyone out of the family . . . maybe not the Tindalls, but anyone else," she says.

I cut a large piece of meat, put it in my mouth, chew and swallow it before I say, "I'm sure you'll find the answer somewhere in my father's writings."

"I certainly hope so," Claudia says.

"Of course, old man," Derek says, pushing his now empty plate away from him. "An antidote won't be worth spit if we're killed by those damned Pelks."

"You're a ray of sunshine today, aren't you?" Chloe says to her brother.

He waves his hand as if to dispel her words. "Your husband got me into all of this. I had a perfectly nice nest, with three perfectly good females. Not the best food, mind you, but more than enough to eat, and nothing but sex expected from me." Derek points at me. "He had to come, bonking the srrynn leader's daughter, riling Mowdar up with his resistance, killing the only person who knew how to make our antidote and dragging me over here with him—where I may either die of poison or be killed fighting. And you expect me to be happy about that?"

I frown at Derek. "You would have lived that way the rest of your life?"

He nods. "I would have given it a try. It certainly beats dying."

"No one here's going to die!" I growl, wishing I felt as sure as my words sounded.

Once we finish breakfast, Derek leaves the table, sits in my reclining chair and falls instantly asleep. While Chloe carries the plates back to the kitchen and busies herself there, I go to the seaweed bag. Opening it, I take out my father's journal and feel it for dampness. I let out a sigh when I find it dry.

Searching through the pages until I find the one with the word *antidoto*, I think about all that Derek said. I can't fault the man for worrying. When I think about all that must happen and how little time we have to pull it off, I despair too.

I find the page and hand the book, open, to Claudia. "Read from there," I say, pointing to the sentence at the bottom of the page. Standing next to her, I watch as she reads the paragraph and the next page.

She looks up at me and says, "Nothing yet, Peter. Please stop staring. Go away."

Chloe looks up from the sink when I come into the kitchen area. I walk over and try to hug her, but she blocks me with her hand and shakes her head. "You're going to have to understand this is hard for me," she says. "I am glad you're back. I was thrilled to see you. But I'm furious too . . . and hurt."

"But I already told you it was against my will."

"Apparently my brother doesn't think so. Didn't he just say you were bonking her?"

"Chloe, I didn't want her. . . ."

"When was the last time you had sex?"

I sigh. If I could lie to my wife, I would at this moment. But I have never wanted to have a relationship based on untruths. "Last night," I say. "But I had to. . . ."

Chloe turns back to the sink, opens the spigot and begins washing the dishes. "You had to," she says, her voice acid. "I'll tell you something else you have to do. Get away from me—right now!"

Max follows me downstairs and out onto the veranda. He stays at my side as I pace from the ocean side to the stairs leading down to the dock. One minute, rage makes me want to rush back to the great room and shout to my wife how unfair she is. The next minute, sorrow overtakes me. I chose nothing that brought me to this point. I wanted nothing but the life I had with my wife and children.

Finally, I walk over to the gumbo limbo tree overlooking the harbor where I buried Elizabeth and sit down in its shade, my back to its trunk. Max lies down next to me, dropping his massive head in my lap. Studying the harbor, scratching behind the dog's ears, Max making a sound halfway between a sigh and a growl as I do, I wonder just where the Pelk attack will come from and how I can defend my wife and myself.

Just the process of thinking it out seems to diminish my sorrow. I remember my father's saying, *"Action always trumps despair,"* and I smile.

Thanks to Lorrel, I know where their safehold lies. But I can't be sure that they'll attack directly from there. I look back to the veranda and the large oak door that opens to the nearest of my father's arms rooms. I can make good use of his ancient cannons, rifles and deck guns, and the barrels of gunpowder, canisters of shot and stacks of lead cannonballs stored with them.

But I also think it might be good to have Claudia arrange some modern firepower. I check my watch and nod when I see it reads only ten forty-five. Plenty of time left for other things. I turn my mind to Jordan Davidson and what I need to do to finish with him.

"Chloe," I mindspeak.

"No, Peter. I told you I don't want to deal with you right now."

"I love you and you love me, right?" I mindspeak.

"Of course. This isn't about that."

"Good. Then let's not deal with me or what I did right now. Let's table the whole thing until after we take care of everything else. I need your help. We have to prepare for the Pelks' attack. I think we have a couple of days' leeway, but it could come any time after that. I'd like to settle this whole mess with The Weekly Dish *and Pepe Santos's lawsuit before it happens."*

Chloe mindspeaks, *"Why bother with that now?"*

Max's ears pick up when I sigh. *"Because, if the Pelk win, our children will have troubles enough without having to contend with the legal system and the media over my problems. I think I have it all pretty much worked out. I'm going to wake Derek. After that I'm coming back upstairs to go over what I need with you and Claudia."*

I'd been prepared to offer my brother-in-law money or to threaten him if necessary, but to my surprise, after I spell out everything I need, Derek says. "Why not, old man? It doesn't sound very difficult to me."

"And you're sure you remember how to do it?" I say.

"Bloody sure," he says. "You know our kind doesn't forget things like that."

It pains me to stop Claudia from reading through the journal, but I say, "I need you to put the journal down for now. I'd like you to go to shore for me and arrange some things."

"No problem, boss," she says, closing the book. "I haven't found anything useful in there yet anyway."

I nod. "I need you to get in touch with Toba. Didn't you say that she and Pepe like to go fishing a lot?"

Claudia looks at me. "Yeah, I did, I think."

"Can she get him to go fishing at night, when and where I want?"

"Probably."

"'Probably' won't work," I say. "I want to know exactly when they can be available. Also, I want to know what type of gun she uses. Your father did say she's a great shot, didn't he?"

Claudia nods. "She's won a lot of marksmanship awards. I think she can shoot most anything, but she carries a small automatic."

"I need you to find out the make and model."

"Okay, boss," Claudia says.

"And Jordan Davidson still has his own boat?"

"A Robalo 28. He keeps it behind his house."

"Can you get one of your operatives to do something so he can't use it in the next few days? Something that could be easily reversed?"

"Sure."

"You said he likes to play with guns. I need to know whether he has any registered."

Claudia nods and I tell her the rest of what I want from her and Toba. She stares at me a moment and then says, "You sure all this will make whatever you're planning work?"

"I think so," I say.

After Claudia leaves, Chloe says, "Okay, now tell me what's going on."

I explain all of it to her—my plans for Derek, how I intend to use Toba and Pepe, how all of it should come together.

"And Derek went along with it?" she says.

"Without even one question."

Chloe shakes her head. "It sounds as if it could work. Do you really think we can pull this off?"

"With luck, maybe," I say.

She smiles. "So now what?"

"I have to call Ian. I thought maybe you'd take a swim with me after that."

"You want to go swimming now?"

I grin. "I want to show you something."

Ian Tindall picks up his phone as soon as his secretary tells him who's on the line. "Damn you, Peter," he says. "Where the hell have you been?"

I smile, say into the receiver, "Hi, Ian. Good to hear from you too."

"Look, don't expect sweetness and light from me. Your disappearance has made it unbelievably difficult for me to do my job for you. Missing the deposition is probably the stupidest thing you've ever done. Gil Martinez is sick to his stomach over it. When he ran for district attorney we were his biggest contributors. And because of you, he had to ask for a warrant for your arrest."

"Believe me, Ian, it wasn't my choice to go. But I'm back now and I want to get things worked out."

"Are you out on Caya DelaSangre? No, don't tell me that. Just tell me what your plans are."

"That's why I'm calling. I want to come in and surrender, get the whole thing over with."

"Good. I can arrange it with Gil. We can probably have you in and bailed out within minutes, before the media even gets wind of it."

"No," I say, picturing Ian's expression, the red flush that will soon start spreading across his pale face. "I want the media there. I want Martinez to do the whole show, the perp walk, the fingerprints, everything. And I want to refuse bail. . . ."

"What? Are you crazy? There's no need for that."

"I want you to tell Martinez and the press that I'm refusing bail to show how unfair this accusation is. I want as many people as possible to know I'm in jail."

"It makes no sense, Peter."

"It doesn't have to make sense to you. It makes sense to me. Can you negotiate my surrender without it leaking?"

"Of course."

"Good, then start the conversation. I'll come in sometime in the next few days. It will be at night. You'll get an advance warning."

"Could you be any more melodramatic?"

"I don't need you to be a drama critic. Just get it arranged," I say.

35

"Peter, what's the big deal? Why did you rush away?" Chloe says, catching up to me just as I reach the stone jutting out into Wayward Channel.

I turn to her, look at the tiny blue bikini—so tight on her that the elastic digs into her flesh. "You and I both know you didn't choose that suit by accident," I say.

She looks down at her suit, her face all innocence. "That's no reason for you to walk away from me as soon as I walked out onto the veranda. It's my bikini. There's no reason I shouldn't wear it."

"I don't need to be shamed. I feel bad enough already."

Chloe's eyes narrow. "Not bad enough," she says.

Words well up in my mind, but I shake my head. I put my hands up, chest high, palms out. "No more. I didn't come back to fight with you. I thought we agreed to let all this alone until everything else is settled."

"We are going to have to deal with it sometime."

"Just later, okay?" I turn away from Chloe. I ache for her to touch me the way she always did before. I want to hold her again. But for now I have to accept that it's not a possibility.

I say nothing more, just stand still and stare at the dark blue water in the channel. The afternoon sun bakes me, the heat of it barely cooled by the light, steady ocean breeze. After all the time I've had to spend in caves and underwater, I have little desire to go below again. I take a breath and wonder just how deep I'll have to swim, how long it will take.

A Styrofoam cup floats by on its way to the ocean and I exhale. "The tide's going out," I say, studying the cup's rapid movement. "The current's going to be strong. Take a deep breath. We may be underwater for a long time."

I dive into the cool water. A moment later, Chloe splashes after me. *"Are you going to explain where we're going? What we're looking for?"* she mindspeaks.

"A safehold," I mindspeak, explaining what they are and how the Pelk use them, as I swim under the rock and run my hand over the island's sheer side, feeling for any indentation, any protruding piece of metal that might signify the existence of a trap door like Lorrel found near Bimini. But I encounter only stone.

"Lorrel said this one has two entrances. I need to know where they are so I can plan our defense. We're looking for a hole or a crevice—anything that might lead to a tunnel."

"Under our island?"

"I'm afraid so," I mindspeak, swimming further down, staring, feeling. *"Lorrel says she stayed in it."*

"That gives me the creeps," Chloe mindspeaks, swimming a few yards away, searching the island's wall too. About twenty feet down, she stops and points in front of her. *"Here, look at this."*

The hole is more angular than round—almost an irregular zig-zag cut through the stone—wide enough at its center for us to squeeze through. At my insistence, we surface for fresh air before we try to see what we can find.

Since it's too tight for both of us to swim through together, I go in first. Chloe follows, close enough that she occasionally brushes against my feet. The tunnel narrows and turns after fifteen feet, and we lose light shortly after that.

"We should have brought a light," Chloe mindspeaks.

"It's not necessary," I mindspeak, feeling my way forward. *"We'll have light once we reach the safehold."*

"What if your Pelk girlfriend lied and we're just lost in a tunnel to nowhere?"

"She isn't my girlfriend and we're not lost," I mindspeak. But I smile in the dark water a few minutes later when the tunnel ends and I feel a square stone shaft rising up from it.

I surface in a small underground pond, take a breath and feel my way around its edges until I find a stone ledge. Chloe surfaces behind me and gasps in air. I take her hand and tug her to the ledge. "Pull yourself up here," I say, hauling myself out of the water. "I'm going to get us some light."

Walking forward, I step into a glowpool with my right foot and almost fall over. A few yards later, I feel a wall and stone shelves. I run my hands along the shelf until I touch a small seaweed bag. I bring it back to the glowpool and dump the contents of the bag into it.

A green glow spreads across the water and illuminates the cavern. Sitting by the ledge, Chloe looks at me with wide eyes. She stares up at the cavern's stone ceiling. "What are we under?" she says.

I shrug.

"She really stayed down here?"

Pointing to a crumpled seaweed blanket by the far wall and a dozen or so discarded seaweed bags near it, I say, "For a while, I think."

"Isn't this too small for Mowdar and all of his men?" Chloe says.

Shaking my head, I walk to the shelves, opening chests, showing Chloe the stores of dried fish, the blankets, ropes and phosphorescent powder stored along the wall. At the end of the shelf I find a crevice in the wall.

I go back to the shelf, take a bag of phosphorescence and say, "Wait here a minute." I have to squeeze my way for only a few feet before I find myself in another underground chamber. I locate another glowpool, pour powder into it and call for Chloe to come. As I swirl the glowpool's water, the light grows, showing us a large room with even more supplies and another pool toward its far end.

Chloe comes through the crevice and puts her hands on her hips, looking around, studying everything. "Pretty sophisticated when you think of it," she says.

"Lorrel said in the old days they had safeholds all over the Carribean."

"Well, good for her," Chloe says.

I sigh and point toward the pond. "I have to take that—to see where it comes out. You can go back the other way if you want."

*   *   *

This time the tunnel leads to a crevice, a vertical slash in the stone really, so narrow that I scrape my back and chest squeezing through it. Chloe follows right behind me, both of us surprised to find ourselves at the far end of our harbor, close to a stand of red mangrove trees.

Chloe looks around, treading water, "We could blow up the entrances to their cave," she says.

I shake my head. "That would just make them set up camp elsewhere. This way, at least we'll know where they're going to come from."

"You hope," Chloe says. She walks away from me as soon as we get on the dock.

By the time I get to our bedroom, Chloe has already stepped out of her bikini. I stare at her naked human form, the brown swell of her breasts, the tight black curls of her pubic hair. She picks up a towel and covers herself. "I've been thinking about it. I'd be a lot more comfortable if you'd move to Henri's room for a while."

My mouth drops open and I say and do nothing.

"I'd appreciate it if you'd grab some clothes and go there now, Peter. I don't want you here right now."

I want to scream out, to refuse to go. Instead I say, "If not now, then when?"

Chloe shakes her head. "Go. You asked me not to fight with you until everything's over. I'll have this conversation with you then."

A small spot starts burning in my midriff. I wince and rub over the spot with my hand for a moment, though the motion brings absolutely no relief. The burning reminds me all too well that almost three days have gone by since I last drained a bottle of temporary antidote. It will grow from now until I take my next dose.

Fortunately, the bag holding the bottles lies on the dining table in the great room, only a matter of a minute or two to reach. I gather up an armload of clothes and rush from the room, muttering, "If either of us is still alive by then."

36

Sleep should have been elusive. I should have tossed and turned all night, consumed by worries, racked with anguish. I should have jumped out of bed at the first light of dawn, glad to be done with a night full of bad dreams and restless moments. But instead, I wake from a dreamless night to find light streaming into the room and Henri's alarm clock showing nine forty-five.

I jump from bed, wash, throw on cutoffs and a T-shirt and rush up the steps. In the great room, Claudia looks up from the table, a bowl of cereal and a bottle of milk by her right hand, my father's journal by her left.

"Haven't found anything in the journal yet," she says, taking a spoonful of cereal. She smiles at my stare, motions to a grocery bag on the kitchen counter. "Brought my own today."

Looking around the kitchen and the great room, I see no sign of my wife. "Where's Chloe?" I say.

Claudia eats another spoonful of cereal. "She's out working on her garden. I wouldn't go down to see her if I were you. I don't think she's in the mood. She said that when and if you ever get up, you should warm up your own breakfast."

I shrug. After my rejection yesterday, I have no desire to offer her another opportunity to hurt me. "And where's Derek?" I say.

"Still sleeping, I suppose." Claudia leans over, brings up a large leather purse, digs through it and pulls out a silver-cased Palm Pilot. Turning it on, she says, "I have some answers for you, boss."

"Go ahead." I walk to the refrigerator, take a steak out of the freezer while she searches through her Palm Pilot for her notes.

"Okay. You want the good or the bad first?"

"Is there a bad?" I say, putting the steak in the microwave, punching buttons.

"Not too bad," Claudia says. "Toba says Pepe went to Tampa. He won't be back until late tomorrow. They can go fishing the next night."

I grimace, thinking how few bottles of antidote remain. I'll have to take another one early on that evening. After that, only a half bottle will remain for me.

Claudia looks at my face. "It's not that bad, is it boss?"

"No. It's workable," I say.

She flashes me a wide-mouthed smile and looks at her Palm Pilot. "Good. Now let me give you the rest."

I nod. The microwave buzzer goes off and I take out my steak and carry it to the table.

"Toba carries a .25-caliber, Berretta Bobcat semiauto, model 21. Its magazine holds eight rounds, and she claims she can hit a fly with it at thirty feet."

"I want you to buy one of those." I cut a piece of meat and put it in my mouth.

Claudia grins and rummages in her purse again. She produces a small automatic, the gun dull-gray except for its black plastic grips, and puts it on the table. "Already did. I got it when I was arranging the other weapons you asked for. Cute, huh? I'll bring the others out tomorrow."

She turns her attention back to her Palm Pilot. "I recruited a team to take care of Davidson's boat. Two good guys. We can use them for the main operation too. That way you don't have to hassle with any wires or anything."

"Do we need to worry about any neighbors?"

"No. He lives on a point lot. No one behind him or in front."

"And next door?"

"Only to one side, and they've already gone back to their summer home in the Hamptons. We have Mr. Davidson all to ourselves. You don't have to worry about anything except for his guns."

I look up from my food.

Claudia shrugs. "You asked me to check. He has six registered, all nine millimeters—a SigSauer, two Lugers, a Walther

PPK and an HP and a Mauser. He must like German stuff. The boys will have to be careful when they go in."

"And my father's journal?" I say, returning to my food.

"I don't know. He writes that he has an idea, but the rest of it is about leaving. I don't think he had any grand design. He just planned to fly away one night. That's the last thing he wrote. I've gone back and started at the front of the journal to see if I can find anything else," she says.

I groan and she stares at me, her forehead furrowed. "Sorry," I say. "I was sure that we'd find the answer in the journal. Now I feel like a fool for making you come out to pick it up offshore in the dark."

"Hey. You know me. I like it on the water in the dark. I didn't mind at all."

"I mind," I say, thinking how little time remains before the antidote runs out. "Forget the journal. Try going back to his log books. Maybe he mentioned something in them."

After I finish eating I make another steak and bring it downstairs to Lizzie's room. As I expected, I find Derek still asleep in my daughter's bed. The warm aroma of the blood puddled on the plate wakes him, saving me from a few frustrating minutes of prodding. As he gulps down his food, I remind him of his promise to help.

"No problem, old man, I told you I would," he says.

We spend the day together, going from one arms room to the next, hauling the cannons out, loading them with powder and grapeshot and rolling them into the cannon ports spaced out along the veranda's wall. Aiming each as low as possible, so each cannon shot can rake just above the ground, I frown when I find that no matter how we try, we can't depress any cannon low enough to fire into the harbor.

"We can use some of the rail guns," Derek says.

I nod and go along with cleaning and then loading six of the huge flintlock blunderbusses with as much as they can handle and putting them in place along the wall facing the harbor. But while their barrels are large enough to handle a lead ball the size of a golf ball, I fear the shot they throw will do far too little harm to the Pelk.

With as much accomplished as we can do for the day and the sun starting to settle in the west, Derek goes inside. I stay outside and study the harbor. Wandering from the veranda, down the steps, out to the dock and then back, my eyes always on the far end of the harbor, I rack my brain for new ideas.

Claudia has promised to bring out a few machine guns and two twelve-gauge semiautomatic shotguns the next day, but even with that firepower I still don't feel secure.

Something splashes in the harbor and I flinch. I stare at the water until I see the fluke of a manatee, and I let out a sigh. I wonder where the Pelk are now, wish they would attack and be done with it already. If a mere seacow can make my heart race, the wait has already gone on too long.

I stay outside until the sun settles out of sight and the dark takes over the sky. Then I go in through Henri's door and walk up the spiral staircase to the great room. I find Derek, Chloe and Claudia all sitting at the table, staring at one of my father's log books.

Claudia looks up. "Hi boss. Good news—I think. I found something at the beginning of one of the log books. Here. . . ."

She points to the second paragraph on the first page of the leatherbound book.

I walk over and stand behind her as she moves her finger from one Spanish word to the next, translating, halting to construct sentences. *"Yo no creo* . . . I don't think . . . I've ever dealt with a more . . . irritating race of creatures than the Thryll. I spent . . . months flattering and threatening one after another until they finally . . . brought me to their leader, an old . . . discolored thing who swore the—*unica razon*—only reason he offered help was because of his hatred for the Pelk. He made me swear . . . I would come back . . . to destroy them. After I made my oath he told me—*el antidoto*—the antidote to the Pelk poison was a simple tea. All I had to do was boil a broth from *un arbol rojo.*"

Claudia pauses and looks up. "I think he means a red mangrove tree."

Turning her gaze back to the log book she reads, *"Yo le pregunte* . . . I asked him . . . what part of the tree to use and he said *todo*—all of it. I asked him, how do I boil a whole tree? He laughed at me and said, 'It doesn't have to be a big one.' I left that night, and by the time I came home I realized what he probably meant was *un arbolillo*."

Claudia stops. She looks at me. "On the next page he says it worked and then he doesn't mention it again. I'm not sure about the word *arbolillo*. I can ask Pops about it—but I think Don Henri meant a very small tree. We're going to need a really big pot, a hundred quart or so. Do you have one?"

"Nothing that large," Chloe says.

"No problem, I can come back with one tomorrow. We can yank up one of the smaller mangroves and boil it until it makes a tea. . . . It's worth a try."

Derek nods in agreement. "As long as Peter's the one to try it."

I smile at my brother-in-law. At least with Derek, when things are bad, I can count on knowing I can't count on him. I turn to Chloe. "You're the one whose mother taught her how to make potions. What do you think?"

Chloe stares at the log book for what feels like minutes, slowly shaking her head as she does so. Finally she says, "I don't like the idea at all. I was taught to be very careful when I mixed any potion. Mum made me memorize all the properties and uses of every plant in our garden. Some work differently depending on how long they've grown. Some have to be dried. Mum warned me to be very careful with anything new.

"I don't know." She shrugs. "We don't even know what dose you should take. I don't think it will harm you. If it was poisonous Mum would have taught me about it. But I bet it will taste terrible."

She looks at me, her eyes troubled. "But it could work. Peter, I don't think we have any choice. Your father's words are all we have to go on."

I take the journal from Claudia and study my father's handwriting. I want to believe that the tea will work. But I wish I could be more confident of Claudia's translation. I hand the log book back to her. "Bring this to your father," I say. "If he agrees with your translation, bring the pot back with you."

"Sure," she says, checking her watch. "It's early enough for me to take it to him tonight. I wanted to leave soon anyway. Just—I was going to gas up at my marina, and Pop's house is the other way. If I'm going to go directly to him, I need to bother you for some gas, if you can spare it."

"Don't worry, we have plenty," Chloe says. "Peter always keeps an extra drum filled. Don't you, Peter?"

I nod, picturing the spare drum full of fifty-five gallons of gasoline and beginning to smile. "Claudia, tell your dad I want him to send someone to Amazon Hose first thing in the morning. I need him to pick up three lengths of two-inch fuel hose— each one hundred feet long, with couplings and connectors," I say, my smile now stretching across my face. "I want you to have them load it all on your boat so you can bring it out when you come."

Eyes wide, both women look at me. "That's a lot to expect Claudia to carry on her boat," Chloe says.

"I'm sure she can handle it," I say. "Oh, I need twelve Zippo lighters too, and lighter fuel."

My wife frowns at me. "And you want all this for?" she says.

I try to stop grinning but can't. "You'll see tomorrow," I say.

37

I wake shortly before dawn, dress and go out on the veranda to wait for the sun come up. Max pads along beside me. I pat him, grateful for his company. With Chloe still refusing to let me sleep beside her, he's become my companion in bed too. I look out at the ocean, the band of light starting to spread at the horizon, and think through the plans I've set in motion.

For the first time, I smile as I do so. If everything comes together as I hope, things just may work out. I know if Father were here he'd shake his head. *"The best plans are simple ones,"* he'd say. *"Grand thinkers most often end up with grand failures."* Still, now that the last piece has fallen into place, I think he'd approve.

Beyond the surf line, a dorsal fin breaks the water and my heart speeds up. Another fin shows and then a third, the dolphins humping their backs as they swim north, parallel to the shore. Too soon, I think, for a Pelk attack. But my heart continues to race until they pass out of sight.

I shake my head. I know it's most likely just a few dolphin out looking for their morning meal of fish. But if the Pelk attack before I put everything in place, all of my plans will have been for nothing. And worse, if the red mangrove tea doesn't work and they attack after my antidote runs out, all of my planning won't help Chloe one bit.

She'll have to flee to Jamaica, I think, rubbing my midriff, picturing my painful death. I sigh and walk toward the nearest cannon. I inspect it, check that we've aimed it correctly, check that the cover over the powder in the touchhole has worked and that the powder's remained dry. As the sun continues its ascent, I check each of the other cannons and then each of the deck guns.

Going down the steps from the veranda, I walk the length of the dock, studying the harbor. Then, starting at the fuel drums, I walk along the harbor shore, pacing off steps, nodding when I come to a good point.

I scuff out a line in the sand with my heel to mark it and continue on to the clump of red mangroves at the far end of the harbor. Wading in the water next to them, I examine the younger trees—some small bushes no higher than my waist, and others just twigs with leaves barely reaching my knees. Green seedlings, really just the torpedo-shaped seeds of the tree freshly rooted into the sand, sprouting only a single green stem and a few green leaves, grow interspersed around their arched roots.

Grabbing the trunk of a waist-high specimen, I tug on it. When it doesn't give, I pull as hard as I can. It still doesn't move.

"Hi, you."

I release the tree, turn, look at the shore and smile at Chloe. Dressed in an oversize red tank top that hangs down, covering almost all of her short white shorts, she looks more like a teen than a twenty-one-year-old mother of two. "Hi," I say. "What brings you out here so early?"

She shrugs and the left tank strap falls from her left shoulder, leaving it bare. I yearn to kiss her there, to put my lips to her smooth brown skin. If only she'd let me. Chloe tugs the strap back in place. "My guess is, same thing as you. I couldn't sleep. There's too much going on." She looks down at her feet and frowns. "It's strange being in our bed without you. It screws up my sleep too."

"We can fix that."

"No." Chloe shakes her head. "Not yet." She points at the mangrove. "Any reason you decided on that one?"

"I don't know. I really didn't decide. I just wanted to see how hard it would be to yank out." I smile. "Maybe a smaller one will be easier."

"Maybe you should wait for Claudia to come out and tell us what *arbolillo* means," Chloe says. "Come on in for now. I'm making breakfast. No reason I can't cook for both of us."

*　　*　　*

Once again, Derek sleeps until I come down to wake him. But I really can't fault him. He has proven to be far more help than I expected. Together we open up all the arms rooms and take out wood torches, which we place in torch brackets on the coral stone walls of the house—one near each cannon emplacement, two by the rail guns and four down by the docks.

He does prove almost useless, though, when it comes to installing the spare fuel pump on the second fifty-five gallon drum of gasoline. "Sorry, old man," he says when I tell him to splice two red wires together. "You know we didn't dither with anything electric back at Morgan's Hole."

Chloe joins us toward the end of our preparations. She shakes her head.

"Aren't you worried about the attention all this could bring, if you use it?"

"I'm more worried about the Pelk." I point across the bay. Nothing on the mainland shows above the horizon. "Anyway, we're too far from the mainland to be seen. We've fired cannon here before. No one's ever reacted."

I look at the lines leading from the fuel drums. "True. If we have to use these, they will see the glow from the fire." I shrug. "We can always claim it was an accident."

It's almost noon before Claudia's boat cruises into the harbor, three large rolls of hose crowding her cockpit. As I help her tie the boat off, Claudia begins to offload the rest of her cargo, handing me two shotguns first, then three Uzi machine guns—each weapon wrapped in towels. Passing them to Derek and Chloe, who lay them down on the dock, I say, "And ammo?"

Claudia rolls her eyes. "Of course, boss." She hands me a wood case marked ARMY SURPLUS. "Nine millimeter, steel-jacketed, for the Uzis," she says, picking up a large cardboard carton next. "And solid slugs for the shotguns. Each one has over an ounce of lead in it. Neil, the guy I got them from, says they can take down a charging rhino."

"Good," I say, still unsure just what it will take to stop a Pelk. I know it would take more than a few bullets to slow one of my own kind.

At the end, Claudia passes up a small box of Zippo lighters and then holds up a very large stainless steel cooking pot and says, "For the tea."

"It's huge," Chloe says.

"I know. It holds a bunch. I asked my parents about that word, *arbolillo*, like you asked me to. Mom said I should ask her cousin Raoul—he teaches advanced Spanish at the U of M. He wasn't home so I left a message. But Pops insisted it means sapling. So I figured, if we chopped one up, it would fit in this."

"Fine," Chloe says. "But how will it fit on the stove?"

Claudia flashes a smile. "You're talking to a former Girl Scout here. We'll heat it in the fireplace."

"That will take a while to get ready," Chloe says. She looks at me. "Do you mind if we pick out which mangrove sapling to use?"

I shrug. "Go ahead. Your guess is as good as mine."

Derek and I offload the hose. Attaching a hundred-foot length to the first fuel drum pump, we run it to the far end of the dock and leave its end hanging off over the water, facing the harbor's entrance. We attach the other two hundred feet to the second drum and run it down the harbor's shore to the line I scuffed in the sand.

Returning to the dock, we fill all the Zippo lighters and place each one on the deck near a torch. I point to the weapons and the ammo next, and Derek nods and says, "Okay, old man, I understand these and the cannons and the rail guns. But do you really think Mowdar and his men are just going to sit in the water while you pump petrol around them?"

Smiling, I shake my head. "They have a safehold under the island. One exit is over there." I point to the water by the mangroves. "It's the only one the guns don't really cover. Fortunately, if they do attack from there, they can only come out one or two at a time. A fire could slow them down."

"If you light it on time. Seems a bit dodgy, old man."

I pick up the three Uzis and nod. "It's all a bit dodgy," I say.

It takes us two trips to bring all the Uzis, shotguns and ammunition to Henri's room. Though I ache to go up to the great room to see how the mangrove tea is coming along, I stay and we load all the weapons first. When we finally do go upstairs, I carry one of the loaded Uzis with me.

A hot, swampy smell hits my nostrils as soon as I reach the third-floor landing. Derek wrinkles his nose and says, "Bloody hell, if it tastes as bad as it smells you'll be upchucking all night!"

The smell gets worse the closer we get to the great room— as does the heat. Inside we find the pot sitting on a metal grate over a pile of burning logs in the fireplace. Flames dance all around the pot, clouds of smoke and water vapor swirling above it and streaming up into the chimney.

Chloe and Claudia give us wan smiles from the kitchen, the coolest spot in the room. Their clothes stick to their bodies with sweat. A wet sheen of perspiration coats their skin wherever it's exposed.

"It's been boiling for over a half hour," Chloe says. "We chopped the whole tree up, branches, roots, bark and leaves."

Claudia nods. "It was such a cute little tree. I feel like a murderer."

I nod and look out the window. During the worst of winters, we rarely use the fireplace more than a few times, and even then the grand room usually gets too hot. The air conditioning certainly can't handle a large fire now, with the sun bright outside and the temperature in the high eighties. The whole room feels like the inside of a blast furnace.

The heat and the smell and the worry that it may all be in vain make me want to bolt from the room. I sigh, wish it were all done with already. "When can I try it?" I say.

Chloe shrugs, takes a long ladle and walks over to the pot. She stirs it a few times, beads of sweat forming on her forehead, running down her cheeks. Lifting a ladleful of the brew to her nose, she smells it and grimaces. "I guess now would be as good a time as any," she says.

Picking up an empty coffee mug, Claudia joins her and holds it out. Chloe empties one ladleful into it and then another. She looks toward me. "We don't really know what the dosage should be. My guess is, this should be fine."

Claudia brings the cup back and puts it on the countertop in front of me. "Let it cool a little before you try it," she says.

I nod and stare at the cup. Thick, dark brown liquid fills it to the top, giving off a rank, sulfuric aroma, as if a hundred cups of tea had been brewed too long and then intermixed with rotting vegetation. Stifling a gag, I back away.

Chloe, who's come back from the fireplace, puts her hand on my forearm. "Not very pleasant, is it?" she says.

"Not at all. But if it works, it will be worth it."

Frowning at the cup, rubbing my forearm, Chloe says, "Peter, if it doesn't work, we still have time. We'll figure something out."

"Sure," I say, not sure at all. Wrinkling my nose, I pick up the cup and blow at the vile liquid a few times, to cool it a little more. Steam still rises from it, but I'm tired of waiting. I take a sip, almost gag as the hot, noxious liquid burns its way down my throat.

"Does it taste as bad as your expression, old man?" Derek says.

I nod. "Like drinking hot, liquid garbage," I say, forcing myself to take another sip. A shudder runs through me and I close my eyes and gulp the rest of the drink down as quickly as I can.

Heat burns through me. My stomach rumbles and churns. My mind fogs and my balance seems to escape me for a moment. The now empty cup drops from my hand and shatters on the floor. I give it no thought. Just staying erect concerns me more. I waver on my feet and strong hands clamp on my arms.

"Peter! Are you alright?" Chloe says.

Opening my eyes, I find her in front of me, staring into my face, and Derek and Claudia flanking me, holding me up by my arms. My stomach convulses again. My entire midsection cramps. I groan and shake my head.

I start to heave and Chloe puts her hand over my mouth. "No! Don't, Peter," she says. "If you throw it up, you'll just have to drink another cup. You have to give it time."

Somehow I control the reflex, the taste of bile now competing with the bitter aftertaste of the tea. "Outside," I manage to say, "under the gumbo limbo."

The three of them walk me down the spiral staircase and out

onto the veranda. After the stifling heat of the great room, the warm, mid-afternoon breeze cools me. I take a breath of fresh air and sigh. As soon as we get to the shade of the gumbo limbo tree, I let my legs collapse and I sit with my back against the tree.

"Are you better now?" Chloe says.

I look up at all three of their concerned faces. "Better, but not good," I say.

Frowning, Chloe says, "What can we do?"

My stomach cramps again. I resist doubling over. If I must wait for my body's reaction to the tea to pass, I don't want to do it while others stare at me and worry. "Just leave me alone for a while. Let me sit here."

The cramps come irregularly. Sweats follow them, soaking me so that I shiver in the slightest breeze. My body burns after that—until the next cramp comes. I sit and endure it all, waiting for the cramps to lessen, for the sweat dampening my body to dry.

Time means little to me. I stare at the harbor or out to the bay, my mind on only my discomfort. Sometime during the day, a pod of dolphin passes by the end of my channel, swimming north. Another cramp hits me, and when I look again they're gone.

A particularly long pause occurs between cramps and I close my eyes and concentrate on the rustling of the tree leaves above me and the lapping of the water in the harbor. Something splashes. I ignore it until a second splash, a louder one follows. Opening my eyes, I find only two concentric rings of ripples expanding across the water, nothing else. Probably a manatee visit, I think. Yet another cramp strikes me and I give the splashes no more thought.

By the time the sun threatens to descend behind the mainland, the cramps have finally diminished. No sweats follow them, no chills. Only a general queasiness remains, along with a new sensation—a mild burning in my midriff where Lorrel had stabbed me.

I rub my hand over the spot and stand, using the tree for

support, my legs trembling so much that I don't trust them. The burning intensifies enough to make me grimace. *"Chloe!"* I mindspeak.

"Yes, Peter?"

"I don't think the tea worked. I think I need to drink my antidote."

"Now? But you're not due to drink it until tomorrow evening." Chloe mindspeaks.

"Is it possible the mangrove tea did something with the poison? Could it have counteracted the antidote?"

"It's possible, I guess. I don't think it's very likely."

"Well, you should tell that to my body. It feels like I have a red-hot piece of metal inside me."

Chloe rushes down with the bottle of antidote, Claudia and Derek right behind her. As soon as she puts the bottle to my lips, I drain it. The burning disappears within seconds. I suck in a deep breath of air and smile.

"It's good to see you smile again, boss," Claudia says.

I nod, leaning on the tree, swaying a little. "It's good to be able to," I say. "But if I'm going to be up for tomorrow night, I think I'm going to need to rest now."

Chloe insists on helping me back to the house by herself. She holds my right arm, supporting me whenever I waver. "Peter, that was your last full bottle of antidote. We have only a half of a bottle left for you—unless Derek offers to give up part of his share."

"I don't think that's likely." I smile.

"At least we have four and a half more days to figure out what we can do," she says.

"I'm not so sure about that."

Chloe stops and pulls me to a halt. "Wait. What are you saying?"

I blow out a breath, suck another in. "I think something changed when I drank that tea. It's like the poison morphed. I needed to drink that antidote a full day early. There's no telling how soon I'll need to drink more of it again."

"Oh, this is so unfair for both of us!" Chloe stomps her right foot down. She shakes her head and says, "Unfair," again.

"It is,' I say, and she hugs me. I wrap my arms around her too.

We stand pressed together, saying nothing more until the day turns dark around us. Chloe sighs and helps me the rest of the way to the house. I sigh too when she chooses to lead me to Henri's room, not to ours.

38

Sleep comes easy and stays long. Chloe wakes me after ten, bringing me a near-raw, twenty-ounce porterhouse to eat in bed. The aroma of blood and meat fills my nostrils and brings saliva to my mouth. I wolf the steak down, but it does little to diminish my hunger. "Could I have another one?" I say.

Chloe laughs. "Derek will be jealous. I told him one is all he gets." But she leaves to get me another.

I consider lying down again, but shake my head. I still have things to do, to prepare for the evening. Picking up the phone on Henri's nightstand, I dial LaMar Associates. Sarah answers in her official voice. I grin when she stammers a little after hearing mine.

"I hope you're calling to tell me you've changed your mind about this whole jail thing," Ian says when he picks up the phone.

"Not at all," I say. "That's why I'm calling. I want to surrender tonight. I'll be at your office at seven. I want you to make arrangements for my surrender at the jail at eight thirty. I want you to make sure I get the whole treatment, the handcuffs and fingerprinting and the perp walk. And I want you to make sure that our friends in the media cover it. I want them to give it live coverage."

"For God's sake, why?"

"I told you. I want to look persecuted. You can arrange to bail me out in the morning."

"Trust me, Peter. You won't like jail one bit."

Grinning, I say, "Don't worry, Ian. I think I'll handle it fine."

I have him transfer my call back to Sarah and ask for Arturo. "Hi, Peter," he says. "Are you okay? Claudia told me that whole *arbolillo* thing didn't work out."

"It didn't, but I'm fine right now."

"My wife's cousin's the one we should talk to. Raoul's the Spanish scholar in the family. He's been out of town, but he's due in tonight."

"Good," I say. "We'll see how he translates the word. Maybe he'll give us something new to work on—but that's not why I called."

Chloe walks back into the room while I'm in the midst of giving him instructions on what media coverage I expect to see given if an incident happens during the evening concerning Jordan Davidson. "No problem, Peter. They'll do what I ask," he says, and I hang up and turn my attention to consuming another, larger steak.

After I get up and dress, I go over the Uzis and the shotguns with Chloe, teaching her how to load, cock and shoot them. I take her outside and walk with her to each cannon and rail gun, pointing out the torches and the Zippo lighters. Then I take her down to the dock and show her the switches to the two fuel pumps.

"Do you think all of this is necessary? You said we're much larger than they are. Can't we just fight them? There *are* three of us you know."

"Only if your brother stays and fights," I say. "Derek hasn't always shown any great willingness to risk death. Even if he does stay, we still have the problem of facing too many Pelk. If we could just fight one-on-one or even two of them to one of us, I'd agree with you. But there will be more of them than that—and they use weapons. Tridents. I told you about them. They can slice right through our scales."

"Don't worry, Peter. I'll fight them any way you want. We'll win. I'm sure. Even if Derek wimps out on us."

I smile at her, wish I felt as confident as she sounds.

Claudia comes out at noon, docking her blue speedboat by herself, joining Chloe and me on the veranda. "Ready for tonight?" I say.

"Sure, boss."

"And Toba understands exactly what I want?"

"Yeah. She and Pepe will leave Black Point at nine thirty. They'll be through the Featherbed Channel and heading east by ten at the latest. I've gone over everything with her. "She's not too happy that Pepe has to be hurt. . . .""

"She does understand that I'm not out to hurt him? We just have to make things look right."

"Don't worry boss, she's great. She just hopes nothing screws up. She'll do everything just like she's told."

Leaving Claudia with Chloe, I go searching for Derek. When I can't find him anywhere outdoors or up in the great room, I walk down to the second floor, open Lizzie's door and grin at Derek's sleeping form on my daughter's bed. I shake him awake.

"Why? What? Is it time already?"

"No. It's early. We're not leaving until after six," I say. "I just wanted to go over everything with you again."

"For Christ's sake, Peter. How stupid do you think I am? It's nothing. Really."

"Are you sure you can still do it?"

"You should know you don't forget that sort of thing, old man," Derek says.

"Show me."

"Bloody hell," he says, but he stands and shifts shape while I watch.

I walk around him, examining his new form, nodding. "Good," I say. "You can change back now. It should work fine."

"Don't know any reason why you doubted it. It worked damned well the last time I used it in Miami," he grumbles.

Derek stays in his room after I leave. Chloe and Claudia go up to the great room, Claudia to read through my father's log books again and Chloe to review her mother's book of potions. "Maybe between the two of us, we'll come up with a way to handle the poison," Chloe says.

I find I can't sit and watch them. Nor can I read or watch TV. My mind keeps going to seven o'clock and the events that should unfold after that. I go downstairs and out on the veranda,

Max tagging along with me, glad to pace and wander aimlessly along with me.

Together, we wander out on the sand dunes on the ocean side of the island. The rest of the dog pack rushes up to us, surrounds us, their tails wagging furiously, their bodies bumping into us as they vie for our attention. But when I pet them only a few times, and when they realize I've brought no food, they drift away into the underbrush.

Going down to the beach, I pick up a piece of driftwood and fling it into the water. Some days the waves will rush it right back to the shore. But today, the few waves that lap up to the sand have hardly enough size or speed to carry anything along. I grin at the calm water and the weak breeze and hope little changes after dark. Rough water will only make everything more difficult.

Dorsal fins show again, far offshore this time, many more than the last time I spotted them. Holding my breath, I count each dolphin as it passes, before they all disappear from sight. Twelve in the pod, not too abnormal a size for the local waters. I let my breath out. When the Pelk come, it should be far more than that.

The pain returns shortly after three. As soon as I feel the first mild pangs of its heat, I go back inside and rush to the great room. I find both women reading at the table. They look up as soon as I enter the room. "It started again," I say.

"Shit!" Claudia says, slamming her log book closed.

"So soon?" Chloe says. "Is it as bad as yesterday?"

I shake my head. "Not yet . . . but it will be. I need to drink my share of the antidote."

Chloe stares at the bottles standing on the counter. "There are two bottles left. There's no reason you shouldn't drink one of them. . . ."

"No," I say. "Half of that bottle belongs to Derek."

"Peter, yesterday you took three days' worth and that lasted only one day. Half of a bottle might not take you until morning."

I shrug. "If it takes me through the night, at least we'll see part of my plan finished." I look at Claudia. "You'll have to help Chloe go tomorrow. If I'm not here, she'll have to leave for Jamaica."

Confused, Claudia looks from me to Chloe.

Chloe shakes her head. "I'm not going anywhere yet!"

She walks to the counter and picks up a bottle of antidote. *"Derek!"* she mindspeaks. *"Wake up, you lazy bugger! Peter needs to drink more antidote, and I'm going to give him your half bottle's worth!"*

Derek bellows loud enough for us to hear him from the second floor. *"Are you daft, woman? That's mine. Didn't your mate tell you that?"* he mindspeaks.

"Yes, he did. He told me he wouldn't drink your half. But if you don't give it to him and he dies before you because of that, I promise I'll turn my back on you. You will die in pain without any help or any comfort coming from me."

"Look at what your bloody help has done for him."

"There's still a chance we might find the antidote. But if you let my husband die, there will be no help for you, you fool!"

"You were always a strange child. Strange ways. Strange moods. I should have smothered you in your bed then. Give him the whole bloody damned bottle! Just bugger off now and leave me be."

Chloe turns, grinning, holding the bottle up as if she had won it as an award. She walks over to me, pulling the cork with her teeth, and hands it to me. I take it and gulp down its contents, my wife watching, her hands on her hips, until I finish the last drop.

Claudia, who's stared at us the whole time, says, "Okay, per usual, I have no idea what just happened."

"Nor will you ever," I say, smiling as the antidote quenches the heat inside me, erasing every vestige of pain.

"You know," I say, looking at Chloe. "We probably didn't gain that much more time. You still may have to go to Jamaica."

She returns my gaze, and I sigh at the sadness I see in her eyes. "Stop talking about Jamaica. For now, I prefer to concentrate on finding a way for you to survive."

39

Derek comes upstairs and joins us for an early meal before we leave for the mainland. But before he sits at the table he goes to the kitchen counter, picks up the last remaining bottle of antidote and pulls the cork.

"What are you doing?" I say. "You don't need to take that until tomorrow night."

"True enough, old man," he says. "But the way things are going, I don't know that I can count on it being here. Mind you, I trust you." He tilts his head toward Chloe. "It's my loving sister I worry about."

Putting the bottle to his lips, Derek drains it with two gulps. "Now," he says, "at least I can count on having three more days."

Dinner goes too quickly. I help clear the table, wash the dishes and put everything away. By six I can't find anything else to do. I consider going downstairs and walking around the island again, but I shake my head. I've spent too many days, too many hours waiting to take action. I need to do something, anything that feels as if it has purpose. "Let's get ready to go," I say.

Claudia checks her watch. "It's early. Are you sure you don't want to wait?"

I nod. "Let's at least get on the water," I say. "No one says we have to rush."

Ordinarily Claudia races across the bay as quickly as her boat can go. Even in bad weather, the trip takes less than half an hour. Today, the bay offers no more resistance than a light chop and a few small swells, and the wind barely blows at all. We cruise toward the mainland at half speed, the sun riding low in the west, throwing its heat at us and making us squint with its glare.

Chloe sits on the front bench next to Claudia, the two women talking. Derek lounges at the stern. I wander from one side of the cockpit to the other, staring back toward Caya DelaSangre for a few moments, turning toward the mainland, staring at the water to the south, looking north toward the Rickenbacker Causeway and the wall of high-rise condos lining Bayshore Drive just past it.

"Why don't you sit and relax, Peter?" Chloe says.

I shake my head. If anything, I'd prefer to take the throttle and wheel and tear across the water. I want it to be dark already. I want to be at Jordan Davidson's house. I sigh, concentrate instead on spotting what patrol boats are out.

Locating the first two just south of my island, I count another one north of Soldier Key and two more cruising south toward Boca Chita. Five altogether. Smiling, I nod. As I suspected, all the boats are positioned on the ocean side of the bay—where all the attacks took place.

Even taking our time, we arrive at the marina at Monty's fifteen minutes before seven. Claudia pulls her boat into our slip, and Derek jumps off without a word to any of us. We back out of the slip and turn back toward the bay.

"Anybody care to tell me what he's up to?" Claudia says.

"Later," Chloe says.

Glancing toward the front, I see that both women have their eyes on the water in front of them. I turn my attention back to land, to Derek walking from the dock. He pauses near some high shrubs and looks around to see if anyone is watching him. Suddenly he seems to shrink, just a little, become a hair leaner.

He looks out to the water and waves. I wave back and he turns and walks toward the Monroe building.

With time to kill before it turns dark, we take a tourist's tour south, cruising slow, close to shore, gawking at all the mansions. We motor up the Gables Waterway as far as Ingraham

Highway, return to the bay and continue south, taking detours into Gables Estates and Old Cutler. By the time we reach the channel to Gables on the Bay, the million-dollar homes we see in the dying light of the day look small and tawdry compared to the palatial retreats we've passed.

Claudia's cellphone rings. Taking it from her bag, she flips it open and says, "Yup." She listens, nods a few times and says, "Soon," and then closes her phone and returns it to her purse.

Turning toward me she says, "My boys are in. They're ready for us."

I smile, check my watch—8:10. I glance up at the sky. A few last gleams of the sun's rays still fight the dark, but gloom is quickly overwhelming them. I look around. On the water, I see boat lights cruising south toward the Featherbed Channel. House lights glow everywhere on the mainland, making windows warm with light. "Let's go," I say.

Jordan Davidson's cherry-red Robalo takes up most of his dock space. A large, gray inflatable raft—Claudia's men's no doubt—floats nearby, tied up to a cleat on the seawall. Claudia points her boat between the two and ties off the bow on one of the remaining dock cleats. Picking up a shopping bag she's stored beneath her seat, she walks across the bow and onto the dock and motions for us to follow.

When we reach the lawn, a man dressed in black, his face covered by a nylon stocking, steps out of an open screen door leading into the screened pool area of the house. He waves us toward him.

"We have him in the bedroom," he says, pointing to another open door, this time leading into the house.

I put my hand out to Claudia and say, "The gun."

She shakes her head and reaches into the shopping bag, rummaging for a few moments and producing two pairs of clear latex gloves. She hands me one pair and slips the other on herself. "Put yours on," she says.

As I squeeze my hands into the gloves, she reaches into her purse and pulls out a small automatic. I put my hand out again and she hands it to me. It looks like a toy, but its weight surprises me. Holding it by its grip, my finger on the trigger, I pull back on the slide and chamber a round. "This is Toba's Berretta, right?" I say, clicking the safety on, handing it back.

Claudia nods. "Just like you told me, boss."

Jordan Davidson sits on the edge of his king-size bed, his hands tied behind him, his mouth gagged, his eyes blindfolded. The large bed, its massive leather headboard, the oversize room, all conspire to make him look even smaller than he is. I study his small frame, his light brown linen pants and tropical-printed silk Tommy Bahama shirt and shake my head. I wish he were a little larger. It would make it easier for me.

Another man, also dressed in black, his face also concealed by a stocking, stands next to him, a large black semiautomatic in his hand. "Everything's under control," he says. He points to a gun on the bed's maroon bedspread. "He had that in his nightstand. A SigSauer. At least the little guy has good taste in guns."

I nod. "Did you have him fire it?"

The man points to a pillow with a singed hole in its middle. "Through that, into the water, like we were told."

"Good," I say. "Take off the blindfold and gag."

Davidson stares at me, moving his mouth around to relieve the stiffness from the gag before he speaks. "DelaSangre," he says. "I thought you might be a murderer, my dear man. I didn't think you were a fool."

"Nothing foolish going on here," I say.

The small man turns his gaze to Chloe. "And your pretty wife—isn't she adorable?" He smiles. "So this is a family outing for you two. Shame on you for not bringing the boy. He is such a darling thing."

A hot flush of rage runs through me. I want to strike this creature, to rip him apart. But I control the impulse. I have better plans for him. I check my watch and look at the nearest man. "Put the TV on, on Channel Seven."

"Oh, you came to watch TV with me. How special!" Davidson coos.

"Just watch," I say. "I want you to remember this later tonight when you're talking to the police."

As I expected, exactly at eight thirty programming is interrupted for a live special report. Davidson gasps as the camera shows me being led in handcuffs into the Miami jail and the reporter relates how I turned myself in and refused bail. "You must have taped this earlier," the man says.

I shrug, say, "Believe what you want." Turning toward Claudia I find her eyes focused on the TV, the girl smiling, shaking her head. I clear my throat to get her attention.

She looks at me, gives me a wide grin. "So that's what . . ."

"Not now," I say. I tilt my head toward Davidson. "It's time for us to pay attention to Mr. Davidson."

She nods, turns to her men and says, "Stand him up. Untie him. Strip his clothes off."

Once he's naked, Chloe and I both study him, motioning when we want the men to turn him. Davidson squirms in their grasp, glaring at them, at Claudia and at both of us. "Are you insane?" he says. "What do you think you're going to accomplish with this?"

Ignoring him, I take his pants and shoes and walk toward the bathroom. Chloe picks up the shopping bag that Claudia brought and follows me. As soon as she closes the door I take off my clothes and start to change shape.

"So compact," Chloe says as I shrink my body to Jordan Davidson's height. "I could just pick you up and keep you as a pet."

I frown at her teasing and concentrate on thinning my hair, rounding my face and compressing my lips to match the man's constantly puckered expression. Chloe watches, says, "Don't forget the ears. They're smaller. And the butt needs to be flatter."

"My dear girl." I smirk. "Whatever would you know about forming a man's body?"

She giggles. "At least you have the voice dead on," she says.

After a few more minor adjustments, I put on Davidson's linen pants and his boat shoes. Chloe takes a white silk Tommy Bahama shirt from the bag and I put that on too. She stuffs my clothes in the bag and we walk back into the bedroom.

Claudia's two men show no reaction, but Jordan Davidson's eyes go wide when he sees me. Chloe digs in the bag and pulls out a matching Tommy Bahama shirt. Handing it to Claudia, she says, "Have him put it on."

Once the two men release their grip on him, Davidson steps back and shakes his head. "I don't know how you could get someone to impersonate me like that, but I can't think of any reason I should cooperate in this," he says.

Claudia says, "The man wants a reason," and the larger of her two men grabs the naked man's shoulder, spins him around and punches him in the stomach.

Davidson doubles over, his lungs emptying in an explosive "Oof!" Gasping, wheezing, trying to regain his air, he remains bent over until Claudia's man turns his back to face me and straightens him up.

I look at Davidson and shake my head. "I thought you were smarter than that," I say in my own voice. "Why give us any opportunity to hurt you any more than we need to?"

The man stares at me, his eyes wide.

"Yes, it's me, Peter," I say.

Claudia holds out the shirt again. This time he takes it, his hands trembling, and pulls it on, adjusting it a few times so it hangs correctly. Claudia's men grab him again, by the elbows, and hold him still as he stands naked from the waist down, legs shaking, facing me, saying nothing.

"You shouldn't have published a picture of my son," I say. "At the least, you should have backed off when we told you to." I hold my hand out to Claudia. She places Toba's Berretta in it.

Davidson draws in a breath. His trembling increases. Staring at the gun, he says, "I will. I will now. I promise."

Backing up a few feet, I unclick the safety and take aim. "Too late," I say, aiming at his right biceps, slowly squeezing the trigger.

"Please!" Davidson screams, going limp just as the gun goes off, his body sagging a few inches before Claudia's men catch him, enough for the bullet to miss his biceps and smash into the small man's right shoulder joint, tearing flesh, splintering bone. Davidson howls in pain.

"Shit!" I say. "God damned shit."

Blood immediately stains Davidson's shirt red and begins to run down his arm. Claudia takes a compress out of the bag and presses it over the wound from the outside of the shirt. "Take him out to my boat. Keep him in the cabin," she says to her men.

When we're alone, Claudia says, "That was Derek on TV, wasn't it? Impersonating you again like he did the last time he was in Miami?"

I nod.

"You could have told me you were going to have him do it. And Ian doesn't know?"

"No."

She grins. "Way cool. Looks like things have gone pretty good so far."

"Good?" Chloe says, "Peter was supposed to shoot Davidson in the biceps, not the shoulder. Now what are we going to do?"

"Toba has her cellphone. I can call her," Claudia says.

"Make sure you tell her exactly where he was shot," I say, picking up Jordan Davidson's SigSauer. Chloe takes the shopping bag and the pillow, and together we walk out to Davidson's boat.

I far prefer my Grady White to Davidson's Robalo. Still, I can't help but smile as we speed through the night, our running lights off. I like having a boat's wheel in my hands again, feeling the sway of the boat cutting through the water, the wind blowing in my face, the growl of racing motors filling my ears.

For the first time since Chloe hugged me when I returned, she stands close beside me, her hand resting on my shoulder, sometimes or stroking my arm, but always in contact with me. "Davidson thought you were going to kill him," she says.

I smile, remembering his expression. "If we didn't need him, I would have loved to."

When we reach a point in the bay offshore of where no lights show from the mainland, I kill the engines and let us coast to a stop. The wind that was so feeble during the day barely blows at all now. The water lies flat all around us. After a few minutes we barely move.

Turning on our anchor light, I take a battery-powered lantern out of Claudia's shopping bag and place it on the floor near me. I move over in my seat and motion for Chloe to sit next to me. "Now we wait," I say.

40

I see the running lights far before I can hear any sound of boat engines. They race up from the south, through the center of the bay, where Featherbed Channel runs, and then go north of us—to bypass some shallows. When they loop back in our direction, I get up, tuck the SigSauer into my waistband, pat my left pocket to make sure the Berretta's in place and grab the lantern.

After another few minutes, the howl of a single motor running at top speed starts to reach us. Smiling, I turn to Chloe and say, "It's time for you to go below, out of sight. It's all my show now." I walk to the stern, turn on the blinker in my lantern and begin to wave the lantern over my head.

The lights turn and head directly toward me and I mutter, "Good."

The boat slows and coasts toward me, its white hull looking ghost-like in the dark. The man at the wheel, Pepe Santos, his square face lit by the glow of the instrument panel in front of him, stares toward me. I back up a little so the dark obscures my features, moving my lantern so it shines at his face—like a novice boater might do.

Holding his hand up to shield his eyes, he shouts over his motor. "Having problems?"

"Just need some help," I say in a gruff voice. "Had an accident. Can you tie up and help me?"

"Sure!" the blond girl sitting next to him says. She says something to him and then walks back into the cockpit as he guides his boat alongside the Robalo.

I wait until she takes hold of the Robalo's coaming. Stepping forward, I pull out the SigSauer, cock it and point it at her.

"You're such a pretty little thing," I say in Jordan Davidson's voice. "Wouldn't it be a pity if I had to shoot you between those pretty blue eyes? Why don't you tell your friend up there to cut his engine so we can have a pretty little chat?"

Toba turns her head toward Pepe. "Cut the engine, honey! Please!" she shouts.

The motor goes dead and silence engulfs us. Pepe turns in his seat and his eyes grow large. "Don't move!" Toba shouts. "He has a gun."

I look at Pepe, drop my mouth open and say, "Oh my."

"Jordan? What the hell?" Pepe says, starting to get up.

Shifting the gun so it points at Pepe, I say, "I'm so sorry, dear boy. I didn't realize it was your boat. But as unfortunate as it is, I have to ask you to stay in your seat for now while this darling little girl of yours secures a line to my cleat." I glance at Toba. "Won't you do that now, dear girl? You know I'll have to shoot him if you try something silly."

Toba nods, reaches for a line and begins tying it to a cleat.

"Now what?" Pepe says.

Letting out a loud sigh, I say, "This is a dilemma. I rather liked you, you know. Why don't you be a dear and lie on the deck, on your stomach, facing away from me with your hands behind your back?"

Pepe glares at me and doesn't move. I fire a bullet to his right, shattering part of his instrument panel. *"Now!"* I say.

"Please, honey, do it!" Toba says.

The man gets up slowly, gives me a last glare and moves as if he's about to lie down on the deck. I glance over to Toba, to see if I can pass her Berretta to her, and Pepe launches himself at me.

I swivel toward him, firing twice into his thigh, but the Cuban's momentum carries him to me. Crashing into me, he knocks me into my cockpit, landing on top of me, pinning both of my arms with his body, grabbing my throat with both of his hands, trying to choke off my air.

"Don't hurt him!" Toba shouts to me. She jumps on top of me too, pummeling me and pushing at me, her hands feeling each of my pockets, finding the Berretta in my left pocket and managing to tug it out.

"*Peter, is he attacking you? He isn't supposed to, is he?*" Chloe mindspeaks from below.

"*No, he isn't supposed to be attacking me,*" I mindspeak, trying to push the larger man off of me, trying to break his grip. "*But he is.*"

"*Do you need my help?*" Chloe mindspeaks.

"*Maybe, but not yet,*" I mindspeak.

In my own human form I'm sure I could overpower Pepe, but in Davidson's form I find I have neither the bulk nor the strength. If I make myself larger or shift shape or let Chloe help me, then Pepe Santos will know something's wrong. I shove against the man one more time. In return he lifts my head and smashes it into the deck once and then again.

The movement shifts his body a little bit—just enough for me to wiggle my right hand a little, the one holding Jordan Davidson's SigSauer. I yank hard on it, but manage to move it only a few inches. Pepe slams my head against the deck again. I ignore the jarring pain and concentrate on moving that arm, flexing my shoulders and tugging, gaining a few inches each time.

Pepe shifts his weight again, tightening his grip on my neck, cutting off almost all of my air. I tug again and again, trying to free my arm up before I lose the ability to resist. It budges an inch, then an inch more and another inch, and finally I rip it free. I dig the gun's muzzle into his side, just below his armpit.

I try to yell, but with Pepe's fingers squeezing my throat, I can only croak out the words, "*Let go and back off, both of you!*"

Toba scrambles back, tucking the Berretta behind her. "Listen to him, Pepe," she says. "Please, he'll kill you."

The Cuban sighs, releases his grip on my throat and rolls off of me.

"That's better, dear boy," I say, getting to my feet, keeping my gun trained on him. "Now, why don't you and your sweet little thing get back on your own boat?"

I wait while Toba helps Pepe to his feet, the man grimacing as the pain from his wounds hit him, putting all of his weight on his good leg, half hopping, half hobbling to the side of the Robalo. Motioning with the SigSauer for both of them to keep going, I watch Toba struggle to help him across to his boat.

As soon as they're back in their cockpit I say, "Thank you both." I point the SigSauer first at Toba and then aim it at Pepe. "And now we'll have to end this. Please excuse this little indulgence of mine—it's just something exciting I like to do now and then. I like you, dear boy. I'll try to make this quick for both of you."

"No! Get away, Pepe!" Toba yells, backing away from me, her hand coming from behind her, pointing her Berretta at me.

But Pepe lunges toward me again, slowed by his wounded leg this time—slow enough to give me time to aim at his other leg and fire into his thigh. As he collapses, Toba aims her gun and fires.

The bullet slams into my right shoulder, shattering bone, digging into the joint. I scream the same high-pitched scream as I heard Jordan Davidson yell and let the gun drop from my hand so it falls into Pepe's boat. My shoulder throbbing with pain, my right arm hanging and useless, I run back to my boat's wheel.

Toba fires again as she unties her boat from mine, and shoots twice more as I turn the ignition with my left hand, each bullet whizzing by me and slamming into the Robalo's fiberglass. I throw the throttles forward as soon as the engines fire, and race off into the dark, Toba firing one last time, the bullet buzzing past my right ear.

Gritting my teeth at the pain in my shoulder, I cut off my lights and steer a course toward the channel to Gables on the Bay.

"Good show," Chloe says as she comes up from the cabin.

Frowning, shaking my head, I say, "Hardly. It was supposed to go a lot smoother. I just hope Pepe buys it."

"Can't think of why he wouldn't," Chloe says.

I go over it in my mind and nod. "Anyway, if he has any confusion, Toba will straighten him out. The girl's a trooper. Everything changed and she still went along with it."

The boat slaps across a small wave, sending a new jolt of pain through my damaged shoulder. "Oh, man," I groan. "Who would think that a .25-caliber bullet would hurt this bad? Take the wheel, please. I need to heal this up."

As arranged, we find Claudia's speedboat and her men's inflatable bobbing in the water near Gables on the Bay's last channel marker—both boats dark, showing neither running lights nor anchor lights.

My body healed, back in my own human form, dressed in my own clothes, I say, "Quick," as Chloe brings us alongside Claudia's boat. "Get Davidson up here."

He moans, but offers no resistance as Claudia's men manhandle him onto the Robalo and force him into his pants and shoes. I have them put him in the boat's helm seat. "Listen to me," I say.

Davidson looks at my face, his skin drained of all color, his shirt soaked with his blood. "The police will be coming for you soon," I say. "You've tried to kill two people—Pepe Santos and his girlfriend."

"Pepe? Why would I do that?" Davidson says.

"Because you're a sick fuck. You shot Pepe three times—twice in one leg and once in the other—with your SigSauer. You would have killed them both if the girl hadn't shot you. Her bullet is still in your shoulder. . . ."

"But that's not what happened," he mutters. "You shot me."

I smile. "They'll testify that you attacked them. Your gun, with your fingerprints, was dropped in their boat. Ballistics and fingerprints will support their testimony. When they test your hand they'll find you recently fired your gun."

"No." Shaking his head, Davidson says, "Pepe won't lie against me . . . especially for you. He hates you."

"Pepe won't be lying. As far as he knows you attacked him."

"But you did it! With them!" He points toward Chloe and Claudia.

"Tell the police that. They won't believe you. They'll tell you I was in jail all night. The women will swear that they spent the evening together at my house. Pepe and his girlfriend will testify that you tried to kill them. You tell the police whatever you want. But later, when the district attorney comes to you and offers you a very soft plea arrangement if you admit you're the Nautical Killer, I suggest you forget your story and accept it."

"My mother won't let this happen. My paper will fight this!"

"Your mother will be heartbroken," I say. "But my bet is, without you there, she'll sell the paper for the first good offer. I think one will be made within the next few days."

Davidson stares at me. "What type of monster are you?"

Grinning, I shrug. "Just being human," I say.

We leave him on his boat. Claudia's two men head north toward Dinner Key in their inflatable. The three of us speed toward my island in Claudia's boat, our lights off. "Look!" Chloe says, pointing to the boat lights racing south and the others rushing north—all the patrol boats on the bay headed for the area where we left Toba and Pepe.

"It won't be long before they come after Mr. Davidson," Claudia says.

"Good riddance," Chloe says.

Knowing even Claudia would struggle navigating it without lights, I take the wheel when we get to my channel. It takes me only a few minutes to negotiate its hidden twists and turns. Entering the harbor I find the dog pack nowhere in view, but smile when their barks, yips and growls sound in the distance as we pull up to the dock.

Chloe and I step off the boat. "Thanks," I say to Claudia. "You can use your lights now. If anyone stops you, you're just heading home after spending the evening with Chloe."

"Sure you don't want me to stay for a while?"

"Just come out in the morning. All we want now is something to eat, and then sleep," Chloe says, putting her hand on my shoulder.

We stand, our bodies touching, and watch her motor away.

"So?" Chloe says, bumping her hip against mine. "You think this ends it?"

Something splashes in the harbor and I stare out at the dark water. "Some of it," I say, wondering why no dogs have come to the dock yet, why even Max hasn't padded up to greet us.

I whistle for him. He answers with a short bark, followed by a low, rumbling growl. Looking toward the sound, I finally make out his black form lying crouched in the dark shadows near the far end of the dock, staring at the bushes, ready to attack.

The bushes rustle. I grin, turning toward Chloe, and say, "He must smell a raccoon or a possum in there."

She stares at the bushes, her eyes growing wide, and points. "No, Peter, look!"

I spin around, gasp as a Pelk warrior, his trident held in front of him, crashes through the greenery and rushes toward me. A second Pelk follows and Chloe yells, "They're everywhere!"

41

"Run for the door to the treasure room!" I shout, and Chloe dashes for the door hidden in the bushes behind us. My eyes on the lead Pelk, I shift my position to block any possibility that he might follow her. Bracing for his attack, I try to shift into my natural form before he reaches me, my clothes ripping from my body as it grows and changes.

But he's on me before my change finishes, his trident arcing toward me, slicing a deep gash across my cheek. Half screaming and half roaring at the pain and at the shock of smelling my own blood, I back up, trying to concentrate on speeding my change. The Pelk warrior follows me, repositioning his trident so he can thrust forward, waiting for the right moment to come in for the kill.

His muscles tense and I suck in a breath, expecting his attack. But just as he lunges forward, a black form flies through the air between us. Teeth bared, hackles raised, Max crashes into the warrior, knocking him down.

Hissing, rolling away from the dog's attack, the Pelk scrambles to his feet and thrusts his trident toward me. Max catches him in mid-thrust, the dog chomping his massive jaws down on the Pelk's forearm, biting through it. The Pelk warrior yowls and drops his trident.

Max drops back and darts forward, biting him again. Two other dogs charge onto the dock and rush at the second Pelk, and suddenly the night erupts with the barks and growls of the whole pack. Dog after dog, they stream onto the dock, their clawed feet skittering on the wood as they rush to engage each Pelk who reaches the dock.

I finish changing shape, grab the trident and join Max's

attack on the lead Pelk warrior, plunging the trident into the creature's chest. As soon as he falls, I yank the trident out and whirl around, attacking the nearest Pelk. Max stays close, fighting beside me, biting limbs and tails, jumping and tearing at throats.

Around us, Pelk roar and howl. Dogs yelp as they're speared or gouged. The air thickens with the sweet smell of fresh blood. But even with Max's and the other dogs' help, I know I'm too exposed. I block lunging tridents with mine, slash and kick and bite my way toward the wall, so at least my back will be protected. When I get there, I glance toward the water, see more Pelk swimming toward us, their tridents ready, and groan.

{*Chloe?*} I mindspeak, masked.

{*I'm inside, almost at Henri's room.*}

{*I need your help. Quick!*} I mindspeak. {*Use the Uzis first!*}

Three Pelk rush me at once. I bury my trident into one, pull his trident from his hands and use it to ward off the second Pelk. The third one attacks from my side, slicing my left thigh open. Max chomps down on his tail, shaking his head as he digs his teeth deep into the creature's flesh.

Hissing, the Pelk swivels, swinging his trident around, ripping through the dog's coat just above his right front leg. Max whimpers, but continues to bite down, blood pouring from his wound, soaking his dark fur.

I refuse to see my dog killed for defending me. Growling, holding my trident as I had with Jessai, I batter the second Pelk with a flurry of blows, driving him back, knocking his trident from his claws.

Wheeling around, I swing my trident in an arc, slicing the throat of Max's attacker. My return swing severs his neck and he collapses. Pivoting back, I find the second Pelk rearmed. Before I can react, he darts forward and plunges his trident into my chest, just above my heart.

Pain shoots through me. I stare at the Pelk. He stares back, waiting for me to fall. I recognize him as one of Mowdar's more junior warriors and slowly shake my head. Maybe Mowdar or one of his lieutenants can best me, but I will not be beaten by this insignificant creature.

My anger brings on a new surge of adrenaline. It rushes

through me, temporarily overwhelming my pain and erasing my exhaustion. A growl rumbles up from deep inside me. If I am to die soon, I want no more of distant combat. I want to feel my claws rip through Pelk flesh. I want to taste Pelk blood.

Dropping my trident, I grab the shaft of his with my right foreclaw. The Pelk's eyes grow wide. He tries to yank the trident out of me. It resists and he pulls harder, tearing the flesh inside me as the trident starts to pull free. Howling from the pain, I tug along with him, helping him tear the trident from my chest with my right foreclaw—slashing out at the same time with my left, ripping a gouge from the Pelk's stomach to under his jaw.

Blood pouring from his massive wound, he sways in place. I lunge at him, catch his throat in my jaws and rip a huge chunk from it as he falls. Ordinarily I would spit it out. Except to honor a valiant foe, my kind does not feed upon itself. But pain racks my body and exhaustion threatens to overwhelm it. I need food. My empty stomach convulses at the taste and smell of the Pelk's fresh meat and blood.

Swallowing it, I let out a roar. I attack his body again, howling as I tear chunk after chunk from the Pelk's carcass, gulping each down for my body to use.

"Since when does our kind feed on each other?" Mowdar mindspeaks.

I look up and find the remaining Pelk have stopped advancing. I see no sign of their leader among them and mindspeak, *"Since when does Mowdar hide from sight?"*

"I have no need to show myself—not yet."

The Pelk warriors begin to back away, leaving six of their own and four dogs lying dead on the deck behind them. My remaining dogs slink after them, crouched and prepared to spring, rumbling low growls.

"Undrae, enough! I've called my men back for a moment. Call your beasts off."

I whistle and the dogs stop. One by one, they slip back, settling on the dock in front of me, licking their wounds. "So?" I mindspeak.

"I had not expected to meet you here. . . ."

"I didn't expect you to go after my wife."

"Undrae," Mowdar mindspeaks. *"I do what I must to protect my people."*

"As do I—to protect my family."

"I admire your bravery, but not your intelligence. It would have been better for you to stay in my daughter's bed."

"But it would not have been better for my wife," I mindspeak.

"Undrae, you are a difficult creature. Your wife is going to die. There is time yet for you to choose to live. Stop opposing us. Go back to the srrynn. Let Lorrel comfort you. Let Malka's antidote tend to your poison. Be a father to my unborn grandson."

"Malka is dead. I killed her," I mindspeak. *"Now, why don't you go home? I'm willing to promise I won't attack you."*

"Withdraw on your promise? I am afraid not," Mowdar mindspeaks. *"I cannot chance it. I fear we will have to kill you both."*

Responding no doubt to Mowdar's masked mindthoughts, the Pelk warriors mass at the end of the dock, ready their tridents and prepare to rush at me again. I face them, trying to will my body to heal, Max and the remainder of the dogs getting up, gathering around me, teeth bared, snarling. *"Try it,"* I mindspeak. *"But please show yourself and give this Undrae the pleasure of killing you."*

{*Peter,*} Chloe mindspeaks, masked. {*The switches. Now. Behind you.*}

I wonder how she knows, but glance back and see the two fuel pump switches and flick them on. Grinning at the twin drone that follows and the smell of gasoline that begins to rise into the air, I look down and try to locate one of the lighters Derek and I left on the deck.

Max growls and I glance up. On the dock, the Pelk have already begun to advance, moving slowly, their tridents held out in front of them. I sigh. I may have enough strength left to defeat two or three of them, but I doubt whether I can handle any more.

{*Peter!*} Chloe mindspeaks. {*Up here!*}

I look up at the veranda, behind the Pelk, and smile. Chloe, now in her natural form, stands at the top of the steps, watching the Pelk too, an Uzi held in each foreclaw.

She mindspeaks, {*Now?*}

{*Please.*}

Both barrels spit fire at once, the noise shattering the night, nine-millimeter bullets thudding into the Pelk, tearing through them. A third of the warriors fall. The rest scatter, some running up onto the island, dogs in pursuit, and the others diving into the water.

Looking down again, I finally spot a lighter. Scooping it up, I hobble toward the steps, each movement sending jolts of agony through my body. Whining, Max limps after me. Chloe throws down the Uzis when I reach the veranda. {*They're empty,*} she mindspeaks. {*You're bleeding!*}

{*I know. I haven't had enough time to heal,*} I mindspeak. {*Get the shotguns.*}

She nods and rushes toward the house, mindspeaking, {*I did good, right?*}

{*You did good.*}

Yanking a torch from the wall, I light it with the Zippo, staring at it as it begins to burn bright.

"*Undrae! There are too many of us for you to resist, even with your guns,*" Mowdar mindspeaks.

I stare at the harbor, the water rippling as Pelk warriors swim through it. "*Perhaps,*" I mindspeak. "*And then again, maybe not.*" I grunt as I throw the torch as hard as I can.

What a pretty sight it makes, arcing through the air, its light sparkling on the dark water as it falls. It splashes down, and for a moment I worry that it's gone out. Then everything turns bright with a sudden *woosh.*

Fire engulfs the harbor. Its light exposes other Pelk making their way toward the veranda by land. Chloe rejoins me with both loaded shotguns and I point to the Pelk. {*Shoot as many as you can,*} I mindspeak, masked.

She lays one shotgun down on the deck and aims at the Pelk with the other. Her shotgun booms, one round after another, until it clicks empty. Discarding it, she picks up the other shotgun and begins to fire again.

Ignoring my pain, I light another torch and limp from cannon to cannon, setting each one off, fire and lead belching from their barrels, each blast shaking the deck. I turn to the rail guns next, ignoring the incredible heat of the fire, firing into the water at anything that moves.

Max barks and I whirl around to see four Pelk climbing over the veranda wall. They rush me. Grabbing the shaft of the leading one's trident, I yank it from his grasp and turn it on him, ripping him open. But the other three get behind me, each one plunging his trident deep into my back.

Pain overwhelms me. I howl into the night and collapse.

{*Peter!*} Chloe mindspeaks. {*What have they done to you?*} She rushes toward me, her shotgun at ready.

The Pelk yank their tridents from my body and turn toward her. She aims her shotgun, pulls the trigger and the hammer clicks on an empty chamber. Dropping the shotgun, baring her teeth, unfolding her claws, Chloe braces for their assault.

An enormous explosion roars up from the dock, a fireball shooting into the sky as the two fuel tanks finally overheat and explode. The shock wave blasts across the veranda, knocking down Chloe and all the Pelk.

By the time the warriors regain their feet, Chloe has disappeared from sight. She emerges from Henri's room a moment later, the last loaded Uzi in her foreclaws. Roaring, she fires into them, emptying the clip, replacing it with another and firing again until the last Pelk falls. She reloads again and fires until her gun clicks on its empty chamber.

None of them yet dead, all three Pelk writhe on the deck, moaning. {*I was afraid of that,*} I mindspeak. {*If you shoot enough nine-millimeter bullets, you can stop them—but the bullets aren't always powerful enough to kill them the way the shotgun slugs can.*}

Chloe shrugs. {*Then I'll do it the old-fashioned way.*} She walks over to the closest Pelk and rips his throat open with her claws.

{*No! We don't have time!*} Groaning, I try to stand, but as soon as I put weight on my legs, they buckle. {*You need to reload the shotguns now. The Pelk may attack again any moment.*} I sigh and begin pulling myself toward the Pelk I killed.

{*Right now you can't count on me. Until I take some time to eat and heal, I won't be able to help at all.*}

A small explosion rocks the air. Everything brightens for a moment. Chloe turns toward the dock. {*That was my Donzi's gas tank. All the boats are on fire, the dock too. Peter, I don't think we have to worry about any of the Pelk left on the dock or in the water.*}

She bends down by the next Pelk and rips him open too. {*I don't know if there's going to be another attack, Peter. They may all be dead.*}

The smell of Pelk blood, even intermixed as it is with the foul aromas of burnt fuel and singed vegetation, makes my stomach tighten with hunger. {*And they may not be,*} I mindspeak. {*I didn't see Mowdar and his lieutenants anywhere.*}

"Mowdar!" I mindspeak. "You've been beaten. Come show yourself! Call out to me!"

When no answer comes, Chloe smiles. {*They could have been part of the group attacking the veranda from the land. I killed eight of them with the shotguns.*} She goes to the remaining Pelk and rakes him open with her claws. {*That makes twelve we've killed up here. Between you, me and the fire, at least another dozen have been killed down by the harbor. How many do you think there were?*}

{*Probably not much more than two dozen,*} I mindspeak. {*But we should still mask our thoughts, and you should still reload the shotguns.*}

{*You are a stubborn man, Peter,*} Chloe mindspeaks, ripping a chunk of meat from the Pelk she just killed. She brings it to me, bending beside me, putting it to my lips and holding it until I take it into my mouth and begin to chew.

I close my eyes as I eat, wish I could just rest and sleep. But I know I must heal and regain my strength. Even with Chloe pulling me along, it takes almost all my energy to drag myself the last few feet to the dead Pelk.

{*Now I'll go reload,*} Chloe says, ripping a large opening in the Pelk's side to make it easier for me to feed. I nod, tear out a chunk of meat with my teeth and swallow, my mind for the moment only on the food and my injuries.

* * *

By the time I feel strong enough to sit up, only the dock and the boats and a few trees on the far side of the harbor still burn. Though dimmer than the initial conflagration, their flames still throw off enough light for me to inspect the damage done to my island.

Wincing at the stiffness still left from my wounds, I get to my feet and make my way to the veranda wall, where Chloe stands peering across the island toward the Wayward Channel, both shotguns and all three Uzis at her side. I rub my jowl against hers.

{*About time,*} she mindspeaks, laying her tail over mine. {*I was starting to worry that you were going to eat yourself to death.*} She points to the dead Pelk scattered on the ground. {*We're going to have to do something about them . . . and about the harbor.*}

{*No sign of any more Pelk?*}

Chloe shakes her head. {*Just a few dolphins out in the channel,*} she mindspeaks, masked.

I sigh and mindspeak,{*Pelk change shape into dolphins all the time—just like we do into humans.*}

{*Peter, the best time for them to have attacked would have been while you were healing. They never did. I think they're all dead. Look out there! Nothing's moving.*}

Staring across the island, I search for any signs of life. Except for a few of our dogs limping from one hiding place to another, nothing moves. Finally I nod and mindspeak, without masking, *"Okay, maybe you're right."*

Before we do anything else, we carry Max into the house, lay him on a bed of hay in Henri's room and bandage his wounds as best we can. Then we turn our attention to the outside, digging holes near Pelk bodies with our foreclaws, burying three or four at a time.

We do the same with the burnt carcasses we find in the harbor. Hardly anything remains of the ones who died on the dock, but we bury what we find of that too. Within an hour, no trace of the Pelk remains. We turn to the cannons next, rolling them back into my father's arms rooms and stowing away the rail guns with them.

We've just closed the last of the arms rooms' doors when Chloe points toward the bay. *"Look,"* she mindspeaks, pointing to boat lights approaching the island. *"I think it's a patrol boat."*

I grin. *"We still have some time,"* I mindspeak, picking up our shotguns. *"They have no idea how to negotiate our channel. They'll have to come up on our ocean side."* I nod to Chloe to take the Uzis, and we carry them to Henri's room. We then shift to our human shapes and dress.

A few minutes later, a loudspeaker blares, "Is anybody there? Are you alright?"

Chloe looks at me. "You have to go out by yourself," I say. "I'm not supposed to be here."

She walks out on the veranda, leaving the door open behind her. *"It's a marine patrol boat,"* she mindspeaks. *"They're on the ocean side now, by the beach."*

"Ma'am, are you all right?" the loudspeaker calls. "If your channel were marked we could have come in sooner to check on you."

"No need for that! I'm fine!" Chloe shouts.

"Someone reported seeing a large flash and a fire out here."

"My fault really, I guess! I wasn't careful fueling one of the boats . . . Somehow I set off the fuel tanks!"

"You're lucky you weren't hurt, ma'am. Is there anything we can do for you now?"

"No!" Chloe shouts. "One of our friends knows her way through our channel. I'll ask her to come out in the morning." She waves as they cruise away.

After a few minutes, I join her on the veranda, a loaded shotgun cradled in my arms.

Chloe stares at me, at the gun. "Now what? Can't we just go to bed now?"

"You can if you want to. I want to take a last walk around the island. Make sure everything's okay," I say.

Together we circle the island twice. Other than the destruction from our battle with the Pelk and the wounded dogs we find skulking in the bushes, we find nothing unusual.

"Satisfied?" Chloe says when we return to the veranda.

I gently bump my hip against hers. "I guess I will be if I get to sleep in my own bed tonight," I say.

Chloe smiles and thinks for a moment. "I would like your company," she says, bumping me back, a little harder. "But not yet. Not tonight. Later, when everything's settled."

"*If* everything ever gets settled," I say, rubbing my midriff where Lorrel had stabbed me.

42

Pain. I open my eyes and stare into the dark, not sure where I am at first, then finally remembering, Henri's room. I look for his clock, sigh when I read the time, 4:50.

Another jolt of pain shoots through me and I shudder. Rubbing my midriff with my palm, becoming aware of the dull, hot ache building inside me, I get up and throw on a pair of cutoffs. I consider waking Chloe, but know that without the correct formula or ingredients, there's little she can do for me.

Picking up my cellphone, I dial Claudia's number. After the fifth ring, she picks up. "What? What time is it?" she says.

Yet another pain rockets up my insides. I gnash my teeth and say, "A little before five. Have you talked to your cousin Raoul yet?"

"Come on, boss. Who's had the time? I was going to call him this morning. . . ."

"Call him now," I say.

"The sun's not even out. He's going to think I'm nuts."

"Let him think whatever he wants. Listen to me, Claudia, I'm hurting."

"Already?" Claudia says.

"Already."

"Oh. Sorry, Peter. I'll call him right now. I'll call you back as soon as we get off. Don't worry, boss. We'll work it out."

After I disconnect, I clip the phone to my shorts and go to the door. Throwing it open, I inhale the cool, early-morning air. I smile. Warmth seems to be overtaking my body, like a fever out of control, and I welcome anything that cools it the least bit.

Max snorts and whines in his sleep and I turn and look at him. He remains asleep, his sides heaving but his body still. I notice a shotgun propped against the wall near him and return to the room to take it. Though all is supposed to be over, it brings me a little peace.

I walk up and down the veranda, waiting for Claudia's call. After fifteen minutes, I move down to the beach, pacing across the sand, letting each wave that rushes to shore cool my feet.

The cellphone rings and I pick it up. "Yes?"

"Bingo," Claudia says.

"Bingo what?"

"I found out that cousin Raoul doesn't like to be woken up before dawn. He told me so, many times, in many different ways."

"What about the word? What did he say about the word?"

"Oh, that?" Claudia says. "He said Pop was right about it meaning sapling."

I groan. Claudia continues to talk, but I pay no attention to her words. After everything, after my long journey to Andros and back, after all my plans and battles, I will never be able to lie with my wife again, never be able to see my children. How ridiculous. For what purpose?

"Peter? Peter? Aren't you listening? Raoul said *arbolillo* also can mean seedling. Couldn't that make a difference for the antidote—if we boiled a seedling instead?"

I nod. "Of course, that has to be what my father meant—you can't get a smaller tree than that," I say. "It could have a different chemical composition at that stage. It makes sense."

"Let Chloe know I'm coming. I'll get dressed right now. I should be out there in an hour or so," Claudia says and hangs up.

The pain blossoms inside me again, but this time I merely tense my body, grit my teeth and wait for it to pass. I decide I'll wake Chloe after I go to the harbor and pull up one of the red mangrove seedlings.

Then I remember the fire, the burning trees at the far end of the harbor, and I shudder. I begin to run across the island, hoping at least some of the mangroves have survived.

It takes almost no time for me to arrive at the grassy area under the gumbo limbo tree, looking down on the harbor. I shake my head at the burnt remnants of my boats and dock and the blackened coral wall on the side of my house facing the harbor. Turning toward the stand of red mangroves that grew at the far end of the harbor, I gasp.

Not a single tree still stands. Only a few blackened branches and an occasional scorched root remain to show where they grew. I look for any sign of green growth, any possibility of life, but see only dark ashes. I shake my head again, refusing to believe that nothing has survived. The pain burns inside me and I moan, stumbling toward the far end of the harbor, holding my shotgun by its barrel, dragging its butt through the sand.

Scorched branches, twigs and roots snap and crunch as I walk though them. I kneel by the water's edge, laying my shotgun down on the dry land behind me, and sift through the ashes with my hands. Though I can see fairly well in the dark, I wish that the sun would rise and aid me in my search.

My fingers touch something soft and pliable. Drawing in a breath, I brush ashes away from it. Water bubbles near me, but I pay no attention, running my fingers up a small slender stalk, touching and flexing two tiny, supple leaves.

"Undrae," Mowdar mindspeaks. I look up and find him and two of his warriors standing near me, all three dripping, their tridents pointed at me.

"You need not say anything, Undrae. Before we kill you, I want you to know that I think you've defended yourself and your island well." Mowdar pauses and looks at me. *"I want you to know we will try to make your wife's death as painless as possible."*

"If she doesn't kill you first," I mindspeak.

Mowdar laughs. *"I admire bravado,"* he says. *"But dawn will soon come, and we want to be gone before that. Do you want to receive your death kneeling in the dirt or standing?"*

"Standing," I mindspeak, wondering what, if anything, I can do. In my human form I have no chance of overpowering any one of them, let alone all three. And I have no time to shift to my natural form. I see my shotgun in my peripheral vision. Even that lies too far from my reach.

Getting up, I stand straight and stare into Mowdar's hard green eyes. If he's going to kill me, at least I will watch him do it. Heat rises in my midriff again and an immense jolt of pain slams me. I gasp, doubling over, shutting my eyes.

"*Ahh, Undrae, you've run out of antidote,*" Mowdar says. "*You should thank us for saving you from a terrible death.*"

Still doubled over, I nod and another jolt of pain strikes me. I gasp again and stagger a few feet to the side. Taking deep breaths I wait for the pain to abate, opening my eyes only then, finding my right foot now near the shotgun.

"*Enough! Stand straight and let us finish this,*" Mowdar mindspeaks.

I make my body spasm, as if another attack has hit me, and I fall to the ground next to the shotgun. Grabbing it, I roll to my side and fire. The slug rips through the fleshy part of Mowdar's chest, just below his right shoulder.

The Pelk howls and drops his trident. Backing away he mindspeaks to his lieutenants, "*What are you waiting for? Kill him!*"

Rising on one knee, I alternate shots, dropping one warrior with a slug to his chest and shooting the other in his midsection. Standing, I finish each with a shot to the head. Then I look for Mowdar.

I see no sign of him anywhere along the harbor. Nor do I find any ripples on the water's surface. I turn and stare across the island, finally spotting the Pelk leader crashing through the underbrush, running toward the Wayward Channel.

Still holding the shotgun, I sprint after him, gaining on him with each wide stride. But he has too great a lead. By the time he reaches the water's edge, forty yards remain between us.

Mowdar stops on top of the rock jutting into the water, turns and grins at me. I stop too, take aim and fire. The slug misses him and he laughs. "*I'll be back, Undrae,*" he mindspeaks. "*And when I return I'll have more than enough warriors with me.*"

I fire and miss again and he slips into the water. Running the rest of the way, I stop when I reach the rock. Gasping air, my chest heaving, I stare at the channel. But the sun has finally broken through the horizon. Its light glares off the water surface and makes it difficult for me to see what lies beneath it.

Dorsal fins appear. Two, then four, then a dozen and a dozen more until the surface of the channel convulses with the movements of more than a half hundred dolphins. I gasp, wondering if this is the first wave of Pelk warriors that Mowdar threatened to bring.

A large dolphin sounds just a few yards away from me, blasting air as it clears its blowhole. I aim the shotgun at it, prepared to at least use my last few rounds in my own defense. The dolphin seems to sense my intent. It whistles at me, as if to reassure me it means no harm, and raises partially out of the water, balancing on its tail.

I suck in a breath at the sight of its almost pure-white body. I've seen only one albino dolphin in my life—the one that the Pelk called Ghost. Smiling, I nod at the beast and lower my gun. Ghost dives from sight. Staring at the water, I wait to see just what he and the rest of Notch Fin's pod plan to do.

The water in the middle of the channel begins to churn and boil, and moments later Ghost and nine other large dolphins push Mowdar's dark, bleeding body out of the water and hold it up by their beaks. *"Undrae!"* Mowdar mindspeaks, blood oozing from his mouth and pouring from at least a dozen wounds scattered across his body. *"Help me!"*

The dolphins pull away and Mowdar crashes into the water and sinks from sight. The water churns again and I stay, watching as it boils—first turning pink, then turning deep red with the Pelk's blood. I sigh and mindspeak, *"Mowdar?"*

No answer comes.

Fins disappear as the dolphins begin to swim away, the water calming, the channel's swift current diffusing and carrying off the crimson tint of the Pelk's blood. Within minutes no sign remains of either the Pelk or the dolphins, and the channel's blue water runs clear, just as it had before.

Pain strikes me again. When it abates, I turn and walk back to the harbor.

I shake my head at the two dead Pelk warriors lying near the burnt mangrove stand. Though I hate spending the time, I move blackened branches and twigs over them so they won't be seen before Chloe and I have a chance to bury them.

At first I can't find the seedling. I run my eyes over the

scorched trees, the piles of ashes around them. Finally I spot a tiny flash of green near a pile of ash. Walking over, peering at it, I see it's the edge of a small leaf. I kneel next to the seedling and brush the ashes off of it as best I can. Then I dig my hands in the dirt and loosen the soil around its roots.

Pulling as carefully as if it were a child I was delivering from the womb, I tug on it. It rewards my care by coming free from the ground without one tendril of its roots breaking.

Such a small thing. Holding it in my hands, shaking my head, I marvel that something so tiny and fragile could promise to bring so much good fortune into my world. Because of it, I will soon be able to hold my son and my daughter in my arms again. Because of it, I will have time to mend my relationship with my wife. Because of it, my family will grow to be whole again.

I sigh and brush some ash from its leaves. It will benefit Derek too, free him from the threat of the Pelk poison coursing through his veins. I wonder if my brother-in-law will want to return to his life in Jamaica. I hope not. My struggle would have been more difficult without his companionship and help. If he cares to travel in search of a mate of his own kind, I'll be glad to sponsor him with enough money to allow him to do so in comfort.

Some smudge still remains on the seedling no matter how carefully I brush it. I rinse it in the water, shake it off and hold it up. Its green surface glistens in the early-morning sunlight. No trace of ashes mars any part of it. I smile, turning the plant in my hands, admiring it.

A new shock of pain courses through me. I grit my teeth and wait until it passes, leaving only a hot, continuous ache in my midriff.

Standing up, I grin. I have no doubt Chloe will know how to prepare this seedling, no doubt that all of my pain will soon end. Holding the seedling in one hand, my shotgun in the other, I walk toward my house. My wife is still asleep and I can't wait to wake her.

Read on for a preview of Alan F. Troop's
next DelaSangre novel

A HOST OF DRAGONS

Coming from Roc Books in Winter 2005

Miami, Florida

I notice the stranger as soon as I finish pulling our Grady-White into our slip at Monty's. Slouched against the white concrete wall of the dockmaster's office, he stares in our direction, his eyes shielded against the bright Miami sun by dark sunglasses, his muscular arms crossed over a broad chest. I think little of it. People at marinas watch boats come and go all the time.

But the man continues to watch as Chloe and I and our son and daughter get off of our boat. When he still stares as we make our way down the dock, I glare back at his long, oval face. He surprises me by not looking away. Instead, he smiles as if he were watching a buddy approach.

Chloe notices him too and says, "Who is that?"

"I have no idea," I say, wondering what the man has in mind, whether he's a salesman waiting to pitch a product or a con man hoping to score off a mark. Dressed as he is, in a tan silk shirt, brown linen pants, and pointed leather loafers, he might belong up at Monty's Restaurant, but he certainly isn't waiting to go boating for the day.

I sigh. Months have passed since the last time Chloe wanted to go anywhere on a family outing. Last night, after all that time, after all the days that she's spent silent and withdrawn from me, she suggested we go to Calle Ocho—

all of us. I smiled and agreed, even though I had little desire
to spend a day surrounded by thousands of people.

This morning when Chloe woke and grinned at me, I
knew my choice was the right one. She joked and laughed
with the children and me as we were all getting ready,
even hugging me twice. I want nothing to happen today
that might dim her mood.

Though the stranger has given no offense and made no
threatening move, something about him makes my muscles
tense. I know the man probably can't pose any threat that either I or Chloe or even our nine-year-old son or four-year-
old daughter can't overcome. Still, when we near him, I
move slightly in front of my family, my pulse quickening,
my senses alert. "Always trust your instincts," my father
taught me. "It's better to be wrong than sorry."

I stop in front of the man. "Is there something you want
from me?" I say, looking at him.

He uncrosses his arms and stands straight, the change in
posture emphasizing his height advantage—a few inches
over my own six feet, two inches. His long, dark, slicked-
back hair barely moves as he shakes his head. *"Nein,"* he
says, "I was just admiring your family. They're very hand-
some, especially the little girl. She's *liebenswert* . . . how
you say . . . adorable?"

The man speaks with a fairly thick but understandable
German accent. I look back at my daughter and nod. "Yes,
she is. Thank you," I say, and we walk on to the parking lot.

I take no great pride from the man's compliment. People
often stop to admire the children. Just as I often catch men
staring at my wife and women glancing at me. We are no ordinary family. For creatures like us, beauty and youth are
simple things to achieve. We can change anything about our

appearances that we wish, whenever we wish—except for our emerald green eyes.

When I was younger, I modeled my own features, including my white skin, blond hair, and cleft chin, after popular movie stars. My wife, Chloe, who grew up in inland Jamaica without exposure to either movies or television, chose to look like an islander, her chocolate brown skin offering a striking contrast to her brilliant eyes.

The children have made divergent choices. Henri has so far copied my looks while Lizzie has taken what she prefers from both of our features, giving herself Chloe's more rounded face, but with my cleft chin, and adopting my blond hair, but making it wiry like her mother's. Even her mocha skin color is a blend, darker than mine and many shades lighter than Chloe's.

We stop by our two cars, Chloe's new red Porsche Boxster and my new dark green Porsche Cayenne SUV. I smile just looking at the two cars, remembering the good time we had shopping for a new car for Papa. By the time Chloe and I finished test driving every model the dealer had, we were laughing and hugging like we had in the old days.

So when she couldn't make her mind up between the Boxster and the Cayenne I couldn't resist saying, "We're rich. We can afford it. Let's get both." I'm not sure who was more delighted, the salesman or Chloe, but I know, for an evening, it was like I had my wife back. She didn't turn distant again until the next morning.

I hope today will be at least as good for us. We haven't had many good days since I returned from Andros Island almost two years ago.

"Pops, he's still looking," my son Henri says.

I resist the urge to tell him to call me Papa—like he used

to. The boy has only a few months to go before his tenth birthday. As much as I'd like him not to act older, I know it's inevitable. Turning, I glance back at the marina. The German has a cellphone to his ear but just as Henri said, he has his eyes on us.

"There's no law against staring," I say shrugging and opening the door to the Cayenne. "Come on, get in. We're going to a street festival. Your mom says it's going to be fun."

We leave the car at the Coconut Grove station and ride Metrorail uptown to Brickell. The smells and sounds of Calle Ocho reach us as soon as we walk north two blocks from the station and turn onto Southwest Eighth Street. Even though we're still three blocks from the beginning of the festival, too many people already crowd the sidewalks and spill over onto the street.

I wrinkle my nose at the odors filling the air—the scents of countless humans intermixed with the aromas of grilled meat, chicken, pork, sausage, onions, and all types of Latin delicacies—and wish my kind had never been blessed with such an acute sense of smell.

Lizzie, seated on my shoulders, her hands on my head for balance, says, "It smells funny here."

"Supposed to. We're around a bunch of humans," Henri, walking to my right, says with all the authority of an older brother.

I take in another breath, frown at the smell and the growing crowd, and turn to Chloe on my left. "Are you sure we want to do this?"

She looks at me, studies my expression and laughs. "It's Carnaval, Peter. Of course I'm sure. They say this is the largest Hispanic festival in the country."

"They also say more than a million people are going to cram themselves into just twenty-three blocks," I say and glance up at the clear, blue March sky. "It's beautiful today. We could go to Fairchild Gardens or Metrozoo."

Chloe's smile fades and her voice turns brittle. "I want to go to Calle Ocho. I think it will be fun for the kids."

I ignore her harsh tone and resist the urge to snap back at her. We've argued too much, for too long.

The crowd on the sidewalk picks up speed as we walk under I-95 and cross into Little Havana. People begin to stream onto the street. It's as if we've left Miami and traveled to another country. Most buildings look as if they were built in the fifties or before. None top over two stories. Storefront signs are in Spanish, and loudspeakers blare Latin music everywhere, filling the air with the pulsing rhythms of salsa, meringue, mambo. Cubans, Puerto Ricans, South and Central Americans chatter in Spanish, laughing and dancing as they push their way through the crowd.

A large Latina woman lurches toward me and I sidestep just before she dances into me. *"Excusa,"* she says and dances on. Lizzie laughs, points to a magician on a nearby stage and says, "Over there, Papa, please!"

I look at Chloe. "Don't you think she should have something to eat before she does anything else? I know she's good at controlling herself but she's never been in the middle of so much temptation."

"Lizzie, honey, are you hungry?" Chloe says.

Lizzie shakes her head and points at the stage. "I want to get down and go watch," she says.

Chloe smiles at her and turns to me. "Why don't I take the kids to the stage and you go get burgers for everybody?"

I nod and lift Lizzie off my shoulders. I marvel at how

well she behaves. At this age, Henri had just begun to be able to control his hunger. It takes only a moment for the crowd to swallow my wife and children and I walk off to find a food concession where I can get four very rare hamburgers.

Food concessions line both sides of the street and it only takes me a few minutes of pushing through the crowd to find one cooking hamburgers. Ordinarily just being in the middle of so many people, enduring their jostles and bumps, would make me want to lash out. But all their smiles and laughter soon have me smiling with them.

Though it's not even noon yet, the line at the hamburger stand already juts a quarter of the way into the street.

A young woman, not more than twenty, pauses near me, undulating her hips to the rhythm. I study her as she dances, examine the lines and shape of her body, and she flashes me a grin and thrusts her hips suggestively.

I smile back and look away before I grow too hungry. The woman misunderstands my interest. True, at another time in my life, I might have been willing to take her as a bedmate, but she stirs another hunger in me today.

My stomach growls and I smile even wider. How shocked she'd be if she knew my interest was in how she'd taste, how horrified she'd be if I showed her my true form.

A drunken man dances into me and I stop smiling. He begins to dance with the young woman, loses his balance and slams into me again. I stifle a growl and shove him away, suddenly tired of all of them, of their music and food, and their dancing and their laughter. At best my family and I can come and watch them but we can never truly be part of them.

If only these humans prancing around me, feeding so happily on meat from cows and pigs and sheep, could know that they are not the lords of the planet they think themselves to be, that another species sits atop the food chain. I wish I could tell them that there are others who feed on them, others who can speak with thoughts alone and change shapes at will—that dragons do exist.

"Peter!" Chloe mindspeaks to me. *"I don't know where Lizzie is!"*

About the Author

Alan F. Troop's poems, essays, short stories, and articles have appeared in Miami's *Tropic* magazine, Fort Lauderdale's *Sunshine* magazine, and a number of national publications. A lifelong resident of South Florida, Troop lives near Fort Lauderdale with his wife, Susan, and manages a hardware-wholesale business in Miami. He often spends his leisure time sailing his catamaran around the islands off the coast of South Miami. You can visit him on the Web at www.DragonNovels.com.

Alan F. Troop

THE DRAGON DELASANGRE
0-451-45871-0

A breathtaking adventure begins with the
confessions of one Peter DelaSangre, who tells
of his life on an island off the coast of
Miami...of his lonely balancing act between the
worlds of humans and dragons...and of the
overwhelming need that gives his life purpose:
To find a woman of his own kind...

Four years after the murder of his
beloved wife, the confessions of
Peter DelaSangre continue...

DRAGON MOON
0-451-45920-2

Available wherever books are sold or at
www.penguin.com

National Bestselling Authors
Barb & J.C. Hendee
The Noble Dead Saga

Dhampir
A conartist who poses as a vampire slayer learns that she is, in fact, a true slayer—and half-vampire herslef—whose actions have attracted the unwanted attention of a trio of powerful vampires seeking her blood.

0-451-45906-7

Thief of Lives
Magiere the dhampir and Leesil, her half-elf partner, are called out of their self-imposed retirement when vampires besiege the capitol city of Bela.

0-451-45953-9

Coming in Janaury 2005
Sister of the Dead

"A mix of *Lord of the Rings* and *Buffy the Vampire Slayer*."
—Kevin J. Anderson

Available wherever books are sold or at
www.penguin.com

THE
DRESDEN FILES
By
Jim Butcher

"Fans of Laurell K. Hamilton and Tanya Huff will love
this new fantasy series."
—*Midwest Book Review*

STORM FRONT: Book One of the Dresden Files

0-451-45781-1

FOOL MOON: Book Two of the Dresden Files

0-451-45812-5

GRAVE PERIL: Book Three of the Dresden Files

0-451-45844-3

SUMMER KNIGHT: Book Four of the Dresden Files

0-451-45892-3

DEATH MASKS: Book Five of the Dresden Files

0-451-45940-7

BLOOD RITES: Book Six of the Dresden Files

0-451-45987-3

**Available wherever books are sold or at
www.penguin.com**

S602